SEIZE
THE
NIGHT

SEIZE THE NIGHT

New Tales of Vampiric Terror

EDITED BY
CHRISTOPHER GOLDEN

G

GALLERY BOOKS

New York London Toronto Sydney New Delhi

G

Gallery Books
An Imprint of Simon & Schuster, Inc.
1230 Avenue of the Americas
New York, NY 10020

First Gallery Books trade paperback edition October 2015

GALLERY BOOKS and colophon are registered trademarks
of Simon & Schuster, Inc.

For information about special discounts for bulk purchases,
please contact Simon & Schuster Special Sales at 1-866-506-1949
or business@simonandschuster.com.

The Simon & Schuster Speakers Bureau can bring authors
to your live event. For more information or to book an event,
contact the Simon & Schuster Speakers Bureau at 1-866-248-3049
or visit our website at www.simonspeakers.com.

Interior design by Jaime Putorti

Manufactured in the United States of America

10 9 8 7 6 5 4 3 2 1

Library of Congress Cataloging-in-Publication Data

Seize the night : new tales of vampiric terror / edited by Christopher Golden.—First Gallery
Books trade paperback edition.
    pages ; cm
    1. Vampires—Fiction. 2. Horror tales, American. I. Golden, Christopher, editor.
 PS648.V35S45 2015
 813'.0873808375—dc23   2015024193

ISBN 978-1-4767-8309-3
ISBN 978-1-4767-8313-0 (ebook)

CONTENTS

RECLAIMING THE SHADOWS

AN INTRODUCTION

Once upon a time, vampires were figures of terror . . .

If you're reading these words, chances are you don't require a lesson on the history of the vampire in legend, fiction, and pop culture. I don't have to discuss my love of *Dracula* in its many iterations, of *'Salem's Lot* and *I Am Legend*, of divergent tales like Tim Lucas's *Throat Sprockets* and Tim Powers's *The Stress of Her Regard*. Instead, let me begin by saying that *Seize the Night* is not an indictment of variations on the vampire story. Urban fantasy and paranormal romance and supernatural thrillers have not watered down the legend of the vampire so much as expanded it. I've written a fair number of variations on the theme myself, but my favorite vampire stories are the ones full of darkness and evil, and those seem to have been few and far between in recent years. While I'm happy that all of those variations exist, we run the risk of forgetting just how terrifying vampires can be.

I'm not just talking about Dracula's heirs. Vampire legends can be found throughout history in nearly every corner of the world. Hebrew myth presented Lilith and her offspring drinking the blood of babies. Lamashtu had the head of a lion and the body of a donkey.

The ancient Greek goddess Empusa had feet made of bronze. This is to say nothing of the lamia or strigoi, or the fantastic and terrifying vampiric creatures of African and Asian legend, dangling from trees or turning into fireflies. There have been infinite variations in folklore and fiction—and even more await us in the shadows of human imagination.

Yes, once upon a time, vampires were figures of terror . . .

And they can be again.

Say the word *vampire* to a reader, or someone who loves movies or television, and each person is likely to have a different image in her or his mind. Most of us will have a variety of such images, indelible marks made by the creations of Bram Stoker, Richard Matheson, Stephen King, Anne Rice, Charlaine Harris, and more. The beauty of the vampire story as a vehicle for fiction is that although beauty and sexuality and mortality/immortality frequently come into play, these tales can be used to explore infinite themes.

In *Seize the Night*, however . . . what matters is the *terror*.

When I began to make overtures to the exceptional writers whose works fill the following pages, I invited them to strike back against the notion that the vampire has lost its ability to inspire fear. I can't begin to tell you how thrilled I am with the responses I received and the twisted tales that resulted. Up ahead, you'll find new takes on ancient folklore and variations on tradition, stories full of sorrow and desperation and childhood fear, and true invention.

Some say that vampire fiction has run its course, that nothing new can be done with these monsters.

On behalf of the twenty-one writers in this volume . . .

Challenge accepted.

—*Christopher Golden*
Bradford, Massachusetts
September 2014

None of the old fears had been staked—
only tucked away in their tiny,
child-sized coffins with a wild rose on top.

—*'SALEM'S LOT*, STEPHEN KING

SEIZE
THE
NIGHT

UP IN OLD VERMONT

SCOTT SMITH

The first time he asked, Ally had been there only a few months, and the idea seemed sweet but absurd—so much the latter, in fact, that she wondered if the old man might not be just as befuddled as his wife; it was easy for Ally to say no. She was happy for a change, still newly arrived in Huntington (new town, new job, new boyfriend), and feeling cocky with all the high hopes attendant to such beginnings. It was early autumn in the Berkshires—the first slaps of color appearing in the trees alongside the road, the morning light so clear it hit her eyes like cold water from a pump. Ally had dyed her long hair blond the previous summer; she'd taken up running and had grown ropy with the exercise, the veins standing out on her arms, dark blue beneath the skin. She felt good about herself after a long period where quite the opposite had been true; she was even beginning to think that maybe, if she could just keep her head straight here, her years of wandering—all those false starts and wrong turns—might at last be behind her. She wanted to believe this: that she'd finally found herself a home.

Even after she learned their names, Ally thought of the couple as "the Hobbits." They were short and stout and friendly, essential qualities that their advanced age seemed only to have heightened. The woman's name was Eleanor. She had Alzheimer's, and her condition had deteriorated to the point where she could no longer remember her husband's name. Eleanor called him Edward, or Ed, or even Big Ed—someone from her distant past, Stan explained to Ally, though he didn't know who. It didn't seem to bother him. "If she liked the man, that's good enough for me," he said, and he happily responded to the name. They both had thick white hair and oddly large hands, and their skin was noticeably ruddy, as if they spent a great deal of their time outdoors. When they dressed in matching sweaters—which they often did—they could look so much alike that Ally would find herself thinking of them as brother and sister rather than husband and wife.

The second time Stan asked, it was deep winter. If Ally had said no the first time out of an excess of optimism, she did so on this subsequent occasion from an utter deficit. She was fairly certain that her boyfriend was sleeping with her roommate, though she hadn't caught them yet—this wouldn't happen for another month or so. She was cold all the time; business was slack at the diner; she had a yeast infection that kept reasserting itself each time she imagined it finally cured. She felt bored and poor and unhappy enough that she would've liked to crawl out of her own skin, if such a thing were possible. She couldn't see how anyone would want anything to do with her—even this sad, lonely couple. So when Stan repeated his invitation, she just smiled and said no again. It was more difficult to decline this time around, however: after the Hobbits departed, Ally went into the diner's restroom and wept, sobbing as vigorously as she had since childhood, running both faucets and the electric hand dryer in an attempt to mask the sound of her distress. It was the sight of Stan helping Eleanor to their car that had prompted this outburst, his hand under her elbow as he guided her across the icy lot—it was the years of love implicit in the gesture, along with Ally's sudden, self-pitying certainty that she herself would never feel a touch so tender.

The Hobbits ate a late lunch in the diner toward the end of every month, stopping on their way down from Vermont before they turned east for Boston, where Eleanor had appointments with various specialists—"Hopes raised and hopes dashed," was how Stan described the expeditions. He'd order a grilled cheese sandwich for Eleanor—American cheese, white bread, the purest sort of comfort food—and New England clam chowder for himself. He'd drink a cup of coffee; Eleanor would quickly drain a vanilla shake through its long straw, rocking back and forth with childlike pleasure. If it was quiet, as it often was in those late afternoon hours, Ally would pull up a chair beside their booth and chat with them while they ate. Eleanor called Ally Reba, which Stan assured her was the highest sort of compliment: Reba had been Eleanor's college roommate. A beautiful girl, Stan said, smart and funny and more than a little impish, dead now for forty years, one of the first friends they'd lost, so sad, breast cancer, with three young children left behind, but what a pleasure now to find her resurrected so unexpectedly in Ally. Eleanor continued to suck contentedly at her milkshake, swaying to her internal music, while Stan spoke in this manner. She rarely ate more than a bite or two of her sandwich, and sometimes, after they departed, Ally would stand in the kitchen and quickly devour the rest. All that winter, with each successive day seeming darker and colder than the last, she felt an incessant hunger. By March, she'd gained twenty pounds. Her waitressing uniform had grown snug around her midsection and rear, making her feel like an overstuffed sausage.

It was late April when Stan asked the third time, and as soon as Ally heard the words, she realized she'd been waiting for them, hoping he might try again. By this point, Ally's boyfriend had moved to Springfield with her roommate. Ally was behind on her rent and lonely enough that she'd begun to drift into the diner on her evenings off—a new low. She knew she couldn't stay in Huntington much longer, but she had no idea where to go instead. She'd just turned thirty-three, and she sensed this was far too old to be living in such a rootless, aimless manner. She wasn't so desperate that she imagined the Hobbits might save her, but why shouldn't they be able to offer a brief reprieve, a little space in which she might lick her wounds?

She and Stan quickly agreed upon an arrangement: room and board, plus what Stan called "a small weekly stipend," which was nonetheless nearly equal to what Ally had been taking home from the diner. And in exchange? Some cooking and cleaning, a little light weeding in the garden, the occasional trip into town to pick up groceries or Eleanor's medications, but mostly just the pleasure of Ally's company—"Eleanor likes you," Stan said. "You calm her. Merely having you in the house will make her days so much easier."

The Hobbits picked her up outside the diner three days later, on their way back from Boston. Ally had two suitcases and a large cardboard box, which they loaded into the Volvo's deep trunk.

Then they started north.

It was the sort of early April afternoon that can throw a line into summer, with pockets of dirty snow still melting in the hollows but the day suddenly hot and thick, the world seeming to hold its breath as dark gray clouds mass in the west, an errant July thunderstorm, arriving three months too early. The air inside the Volvo was stuffy; it smelled of cherry cough drops. Before they'd even made it out of town, Ally began to feel carsick. Her stomach gave a queasy swing with every turn. She started to count upward by sevens, a calming exercise a stranger had taught her once, during a cross-country bus trip, when Ally was heading back east from Reno. She'd been working as a barmaid in a second-tier casino: another lost job, another failed relationship, another aborted attempt to make a life. This had been almost a decade ago, and Ally remembered how ancient the stranger on the bus had seemed, so ill used and depleted, though the woman couldn't have been much older than Ally was now. Seven, fourteen, twenty-one, twenty-eight . . . Ally was at eighty-four when Stan glanced back from the front seat, asking if she minded music. Ally shook her head, shut her eyes, feeling abruptly tired, almost drugged. A moment later, a Beatles song began to play: "Hey Jude." She was asleep before the first chorus, dropping into a tropical dream, to match the oddly tropical weather. Ally was on a sailboat in the Caribbean, where she'd never been, and Mrs. Henderson, her high school gym teacher, was trying to teach her how to tie nautical knots, with mounting impatience—mounting urgency, too—because a storm was rising, seemingly out of nowhere; one moment the sky was clear, the sea calm and sun-splashed, and the next, rain was sweeping across the deck, the boat pitching, the wind seeming to rage through the rigging, sounding tormented, howling, shriek-ing, a pure cry of animal pain, so loud that Mrs. Henderson had to shout to be heard, and Ally couldn't follow her instructions, which meant they were doomed—Ally somehow understood this, that if she couldn't learn the necessary knots, the boat would surely founder. She awakened as the first wave broke over the deck, open-ing her eyes to a changed world, her dream panic still gripping her. Rain was running down the car's windows, blurring the view beyond the glass, the trees seeming too close to the road (murky, animate, swaying in the storm's onslaught), the car swaying, too, rocking and thumping over the deep ruts of a narrow lane—no, not a lane, a driveway—and now the trees were parting before them and the Volvo was splashing through one final pothole, deeper and wider than the others, moatlike, the car almost bottoming out before emerging into a clearing, a large irregularly shaped circle of muddy grass, on the far side of which stood a tall, narrow house. The house looked gray in the rain and fading light, though somehow Ally could tell it was really white. The movement of the surrounding trees lent the house a sense of motion, too; the structure seemed to rock in counterpoint to the plunging branches. Beyond the house, Ally could just make out a small barn. Beyond the barn, a steep—almost sheer—pine-covered hill rose abruptly skyward. Stan put the car in park and turned off the engine, and for a long moment the three of them just sat there, waiting for the rain to slacken enough so that they might dash across the lawn and enter the house. Ally could hear "Hey Jude" still playing, though there was something odd about it now—the speed was off, the pitch, too. It took her a handful of seconds to realize that it wasn't the CD; it was Eleanor softly singing in the front seat, her voice as high as a child's and so out of tune that it sounded intentional, as if the old woman might have been mocking the Beatles' lyrics.

Remember to let her under your skin . . .

This was Ally's nadir, what would be the lowest dip of her spirits for a long time to come. She realized she didn't know these people, not really—not at all—and that no one she actually did know had any idea where she was; even *she* didn't know where she was, just Vermont, northern Vermont, somewhere east of Burlington, in the rain, at the base of a hill that looked too steep to climb . . . yes, she'd made a terrible mistake. She thought briefly of fleeing, pushing open the Volvo's door and darting off into the storm, beneath the swaying trees, through the mud and wind. She could make her way back down the drive to whatever road might lay at its end; she could put her hope in the prospect of a passing car, a stranger's kindness. She'd hitch a ride to the nearest town, where she'd make a collect call to . . . whom, exactly? Ally was picturing her ex-roommate and her ex-boyfriend, the two lovers just sitting down to an early dinner in Springfield, the phone starting to ring, one of them rising, reaching to pick up the receiver—Ally felt her face flush at the thought, the shame she'd feel as she announced herself, as she extended her hand for their assistance, their pity—and at that precise moment the rain stopped. It didn't slacken or abate; it just ceased—the wind did, too. The world seemed so silent in the storm's wake that Ally experienced the sudden quiet as its own sort of noise, loud and unsettling. Stan shifted in his seat, turned to look at Eleanor. "Well, love," he said. "Shall we?"

"Is Reba staying for supper?"

Stan glanced at Ally in the rearview mirror, gave her a smile of playful complicity; it was growing familiar now, this smile—a cherub peeking out from behind a rose-tinted cloud. "What do you think, Reba? Would you like to stay for supper?"

And as easily as that, everything was okay again. The idea of fleeing through the trees seemed suddenly absurd; it was already being forgotten. Ally smiled back at the old man, smiled and nodded: "Yes, Stan," she said. "That would be lovely."

When Eleanor's condition first began to reveal itself, Stan had moved their bedroom to the house's first floor. They rarely ventured upstairs anymore. This meant that Ally would have free run of the entire second story. The evening of her arrival, after a dinner of hot dogs and potato salad, Ally climbed a steep flight of stairs to discover three bedrooms and a large bathroom awaiting her. She hesitated at the first doorway she came to . . . *This one?* Beyond the threshold was a canopied bed, a mahogany bureau and matching night table, a red-and-white rag rug to complement the red-and-white-striped curtains. Ally heard a creaking sound behind her, and when she turned, she saw her footprints in the dust on the floor—not just her footprints, but paw prints, too, a complicated skein of them trailing up and down the hallway. And then, in the shadows at the far end of the corridor, peering toward her—so big that Ally initially mistook it for a bear—she glimpsed an immense black dog. Ally felt a surge of heat pass through her body: an adrenaline dump. For an instant, she was so frightened that it was difficult to breathe. She could hear the dog audibly sniffing, taking in her scent. Without making a conscious decision to do so, Ally began to retreat, first one slow step, then another. When she reached the head of the stairs, she turned and scampered quickly back down to the first floor.

Stan was still in the kitchen, wiping the counter with a sponge. He turned at her approach, greeted her with one of his cherub's smiles.

"There's a dog upstairs," Ally said.

Stan nodded. "That would be Bo. I hope you're not allergic?"

"No. I was just . . . I didn't realize there was a dog in the house."

"Ah, of course not—I should've introduced you. So sorry, my dear. Did he startle you?"

Before Ally could answer, she sensed movement behind her, very close. Bo had followed her downstairs. He pressed his big head against Ally's right buttock, sniffing again. Ally jumped, let out a yelp, and the dog scrambled backward, nearly losing his footing on the slippery kitchen tiles. Once more, Ally felt herself go hot—this time from embarrassment rather than terror. Up close, there was nothing at all frightening about the animal. Like his aged master and mistress, he was clearly tottering through his final stretch here on earth. His eyes had a gray sheen to them, and his joints seemed so stiff that even his massive size came across as a handicap. There was Great Dane in him, maybe some St. Bernard, too, but Ally's original perception remained dominant: what Bo resembled most was an ailing, elderly black bear.

"Blind and deaf," Stan said. "If I had any mercy, I'd put him out to pasture. But he has such a good effect on Eleanor. It will be hard to lose him."

"He was here by himself? While you were in Boston?"

Stan dismissed Ally's concern with a flick of his hand. "The doctor comes twice a day when we're gone. Lets him out. Makes sure he has food and water. Bo doesn't require much more than that."

"The doctor?"

"Eleanor's physician. Dr. Thornton. You'll meet him soon enough."

Eleanor's voice came warbling toward them from the rear of the house, as if by speaking her name, Stan had summoned her: "Ed . . . ?"

Stan reached out, patted Ally's arm. "Duty calls." He tossed the sponge into the sink, then turned and started from the room.

"Eddie . . . ?"

"Coming, love!"

Ally clicked off the kitchen light, made her way back upstairs, the dog trailing closely behind her, panting from the effort of the climb. A quick tour of the three available bedrooms convinced Ally that there was nothing to distinguish one above the others, and so, after a trip to the bathroom (she peed, and when she flushed the toilet, it sounded like a malfunctioning jet engine, a high-pitched hydraulic shriek that seemed to shake the entire house), she returned to the first room she'd glimpsed, with its red-and-white curtains: it felt marginally more fa-miliar. Bo had followed her up and down the corridor, standing just beyond each successive threshold as Ally examined the bedrooms, and now, when she tried to shut the door to what she was already thinking of as *her* room, the dog shuffled forward and pushed it back open with his nose. His head was the size and shape of a basketball; his thick black fur had traces of silver in it. His eyes were as large as a cow's and slightly protuberant. Ally had to remind herself that he couldn't see with them, because there was something so alert about the animal—alert and observant. He stood there, front paws inside the room, back paws in the corridor, not watching, not listening, but somehow obviously appraising her.

Ally realized with a lurch that her suitcases and her cardboard box were still in the Volvo's trunk. She was feeling far too worn out to contemplate unraveling the tangled knot of their retrieval—the trip back downstairs, the hunt for a flashlight to guide her across the dark expanse of muddy lawn, the possibility of finding the Volvo locked, of needing to rouse Stan to ask for his assistance—so she took the path of least resistance. She removed her clothes and climbed beneath the musty-smelling sheets. *In the morning,* she told herself: *everything will be resolved in the morning.* Then she turned out the light.

For such a large and enfeebled animal, Bo could move with surprising stealth. Ally didn't hear him approach from the doorway; she just felt the bed shudder as he bumped against it. At first she assumed this was an accident, that he'd simply stumbled against the bed as he blindly crossed the room, but then the mattress kept swaying, the frame making a soft creaking sound, and gradually Ally had to concede that something intentional was happening in the darkness, though she couldn't guess what it might be. The bed's persistent rocking began to assume an oddly sexual overtone. It roused a memory for Ally, of her one attempt at hitchhiking: what had appeared to be a perfectly harmless old man had picked her up outside of Los Angeles as she was heading north toward her ill-fated interlude in Reno. She'd fallen asleep a few miles beyond Bakersfield, then awakened sometime later, in the dark of a highway rest stop, slumped against the car's passenger-side door with the old man pressed against her, thrusting rhythmically. He was still fully clothed, but she could feel his erection, the eager, animal-like insistence of it, prodding at her hip. The old man's face was only inches away from hers, his eyes clenched shut, his mouth gaping; his breath smelled sharply of bacon. Ally fumbled for the door handle, spilled out of the car, ran off across the parking lot—it all came back to her now, even the smell of bacon—and she pictured Bo attempting a similar assault, clambering on top of her, his thick paws pressing her shoulders to the mattress, pinning her in place, his penis emerging in its bright red sheath . . . she rolled to her right, turned on the bed-side lamp, leapt from beneath the sheets.

Poor Bo. He just wanted to climb onto the bed, but he was apparently too ponderous, too aged to manage the feat. He'd lift his left front paw, rest it on the edge of the mattress, then give a feeble sort of jump and try to place the right one beside it, but each time he did this, the left paw would lose its hold and he'd thump back to the floor. He kept repeating the maneuver, without either progress or apparent discouragement: this was what had caused the bed to rock in such a suggestive manner. Ally edged toward him, bent to help haul his heavy body up onto the mattress. Her inclination was to shift rooms—if the dog wanted to sleep on this bed, she'd happily surrender it to him—but then it occurred to her that it might be her company Bo desired. If she changed rooms, it seemed possible that the dog might follow her. She watched him settle onto the mattress, his head coming to rest with an audible sigh on one of the pillows. It was a double bed; there was more than enough room for Ally on the opposite side. So that was where she went: she slid under the sheet and comforter, then reached again to turn out the light.

Darkness.

The mattress tilted in the dog's direction, weighed down by his bulk. Ally could sense herself sliding toward him. She felt the heat of his body against her bare shoulder, and then, a moment later, his fur: coarse as a man's beard. His breathing had a strange rhythm, a sequence that started with a small intake of air, followed by a slightly larger one, then an even larger one still, and finally a deep inhalation that seemed to double the size of the dog's already prodigious body. A dramatic, wheezing exhalation would come at the end of this, filling the entire room for an instant with the meaty stench of Bo's breath. Then the dog would start all over again, right back at the beginning.

Ally thought of the stale hot dog buns they'd eaten with dinner, the slightly brownish tint to the water emerging from the bathroom's faucet, the layer of dust that covered everything on the house's second story—thick as peach fuzz. She thought of the disquieting sensation that the hill beyond the barn had given her when they first pulled into the yard, its looming quality, like a wave about to break. She thought of Eleanor's voice, so high-pitched and out of tune, with its undertone of mockery, as the old woman sang "Hey Jude." And while Ally's mind moved in such a manner, Bo kept inhaling, inhaling, inhaling, and then, with that long, raspy sigh, immersing her in his smell.

It's okay, Ally said to herself. *I'm okay.*

And it was true: she'd been in far worse places in her life. She'd slept with a friend in the friend's van for a week, parked in the East Village, August in New York, the temperature hitting ninety each afternoon, but the windows of the van kept shut because Ally's friend was certain they'd be robbed, raped, and murdered in their sleep if they so much as cracked one open. She'd squatted with a boyfriend in an abandoned house in Bucks County one spring—no electricity, no heat—the basement ankle-deep with sewage from the overflowing septic system, their own waste rising implacably toward them with each flush of the toilet, a perfect metaphor for their relationship, as the boyfriend had told Ally on the morning he left for good. Nothing here could compare to any of that.

Everything's going to be okay.

It was with this final thought—a reassuring pat to her own head—that Ally at long last slipped into sleep.

And, for a while, everything was indeed okay.

Ally settled into an easy routine with the Hobbits. On most days, the entire household rose early, shortly after dawn. Ally would help Stan with the breakfast—cold cereal and milk, slices of jam-smeared toast, glasses of orange juice and mugs of coffee. Afterward, she'd wash the dishes, sweep the kitchen floor, tidy up the Hobbits' already tidy bedroom. Then she'd drive the Volvo down into town and fetch whatever needed picking up that day: Eleanor's pills from the pharmacy, a bag of groceries from the local Stop & Shop. It was a beautiful little town, with houses arrayed around a central green. The houses were old and postcard pretty: white clapboard with black shutters. There was a Civil War memorial in one corner of the green, a marble soldier standing at attention with a rifle slung over his shoulder. A century and a half's worth of Vermont winters had worn the young man's face almost blank, reducing his expression to a ghostly version of Munch's famous *Scream*. It was the one unsettling note in an otherwise uniformly serene setting, and often Ally would find herself taking the long way around the green as she ran her errands, simply to avoid glimpsing the statue's frozen expression of anguish.

Stan had converted the old barn on the Hobbits' property into an aviary. There were a dozen parakeets inside, and an African gray parrot. Only the parrot could speak, and even he possessed just a limited vocabulary. Mostly, he simply shrieked: "Ed!" Or: "Big Ed!" Or: "Eddie!" Sometimes he'd cry out, quite clearly: "It's raining, it's pouring!" But this had nothing to do with the actual weather. One afternoon Ally heard him shouting, in a disconcertingly deep voice: "You liar . . . ! You liar . . . ! You fucking liar . . . !" Eleanor spent most of her mornings in the barn, sitting on a folding lawn chair. There was netting over the building's entrance, so if the weather was warm enough, Stan could roll back the big wooden door. All of the birds seemed to enjoy this event; they'd swoop and hop and glide from perch to perch, filling the barn with their cries of pleasure. Eleanor would sit in their midst, watching their antics with a serene expression. Stan and Ally could leave her there unattended for hours. Often, Stan would set her up in her chair, then go and work in the garden. Sometimes the parrot would scream "Ed!" And Stan would call back "Yes, dear?" Then the bird would make an eerie cackling sound, something almost like laughter, but also not like laughter at all.

The house was really two houses: a relatively modern structure built around the shell of a much older one. The original house had two low-ceilinged rooms and a deep root cellar. At some point, the Hobbits' present bedroom, the kitchen, a sunroom, and a mudroom had been added onto the first floor, along with the entire second story. Ally disliked the two older rooms; they felt claustrophobic and depressing, with their flagstone floors—cold and slightly damp to the touch, even on the warmest of days—and their tiny porthole-like windows. But it was the root cellar that truly unsettled her. Stan stored jars of preserves and pickles in its darkness, and Ally dreaded her trips down the ladder-like flight of stairs to retrieve them. For some reason, the space had never been wired with electricity, so you had to bring a flashlight with you. There was an earthen floor, walls of raw stone. It was a tiny space, but large enough so that the flashlight never managed to illuminate all of it at once; there was always one corner or another left in shadow. You entered through a heavy trapdoor in the mudroom's floor, and once, while Ally was crouched in front of the shelves of preserves, searching for a jar of blackberry jam, Eleanor swung this door shut. Ally scraped her shin in her scramble back up the stairs—she'd been half-certain she wouldn't be able to force the trapdoor open again, that she'd find herself entombed in the cellar forever. But the trapdoor had lifted free easily enough, and it was Eleanor who ended up screaming, startled by the sight of Ally emerging into the daylight: "Ed!" she cried. "There's a woman under the floor!"

Dr. Thornton came twice a week to check on Eleanor. He was tall and dark haired and extremely lean—gaunt, even—with deep shadows under his eyes, which made him look much older than he actually was. Ally was astonished to learn that he was only forty-two; she would've guessed he was in his midfifties, at least. It wasn't just his eyes, either, or his slight stoop, or the tentative way he'd approach across the lawn, as if he were testing the solidity of each foothold before committing his full weight to it: he had the personality of an older man, too. Or perhaps a better way to put it would be to say that he had the personality of a man from an older era, an aura of politeness and formality that Ally associated with movies in which men wore frock coats and top hats. It took him weeks to stop calling her "ma'am." As Stan had promised, though, the doctor was a kind man—consistently good-natured, and full of concern for not only the Hobbits but Ally, too.

When summer arrived with enough vigor to ensure that the roads were consistently mud-free, the doctor began to make his visits on horseback, riding a large bay mare named Molly. He'd tie the horse to an old hitching post in the Hobbits' yard. Sometimes Ally would walk out and feed Molly carrots straight from the garden, combing the horse's mane with her fingers while Dr. Thornton chatted to Eleanor and Stan on the far side of the lawn. Everyone enjoyed the doctor's visits. Eleanor always appeared less anxious on the evenings after he'd come, and Stan tended to be chattier, almost buoyant. Bo liked Dr. Thornton, too: sometimes, when the doctor departed, the dog would follow his horse out of the yard, and Ally would have to jog down the road to fetch him back. Even the birds seemed livelier on the afternoons when the doctor was in attendance. So perhaps it was inevitable that Ally began to feel a similar charge. Sometimes, standing out by the hitching post with Molly, she'd sense the doctor's eyes upon her—it was a familiar feeling from all her years of waitressing, the weight of a man's appraising gaze— and she'd think to herself: *Why not?* He wasn't married; he lived alone in one of the big white houses facing the village green, seeing patients in an examination room at the building's rear. *A doctor's wife*, Ally thought. It wasn't a fate she ever would've aspired to, but she could see how it might come to feel like a happy ending of sorts, especially in comparison to some of the other paths she'd tried to follow over the preceding years.

Almost from her first day in the house, Ally had resumed her running. She'd head out in the late afternoon, when Eleanor was napping. The roads around the house were hilly, winding, tree lined. It was rare to encounter traffic of any sort. There were only a handful of other residences within running distance. Like the Hobbits' place, all of these houses had retained their old-fashioned hitching posts. The only horse Ally ever glimpsed was Dr. Thornton's mare, but sometimes she'd see other animals tied up in the day's fading light: a weary-looking cow who lifted her head to watch Ally jog past, a spavined donkey, and even an immense goose once, secured to the post with a collar and leash. The bird lifted its wings and honked, frightening Ally, and then kept scolding her till she was out of sight. Perhaps it was simply the company Ally was keeping, but the animals she saw always had an elderly air to them, as if they were shuffling painfully forward through their final days of life. Glimpsing them, Ally would feel her thoughts turn in a melancholy direction. She was happy living with the Hobbits—exceptionally so—perhaps as happy as she'd ever been. But she knew it couldn't last. Sooner or later, a hard wind would begin to blow through her life, ruining everything. One of these days, Eleanor's health would take a turn for the worse. And then what? Ally would be left to her own devices once again, which had never served her well. She'd pack up her two suitcases and her cardboard box; she'd step back into the larger world.

And she was right, too. Even as summer reached its height, that wind was approaching. But when it finally arrived, it didn't come from the direction Ally had anticipated, so it caught her completely by surprise—as hard winds often do.

Because it wasn't Eleanor who took a turn for the worse.

It was Stan.

All through July, the weather had remained bright and cool, with afternoon breezes rolling down the hillside beyond the barn to sweep across the property. The air smelled of honeysuckle. The scent seemed to energize the parakeets in the aviary—they swooped and sang, darting toward the barn's open doorway, their tiny, brightly colored bodies ricocheting off the netting. The parrot was affected, too: he roused another phrase from his slumbering vocabulary. "Come back!" he began to yell. "Come back . . . !" Then August arrived, and the breezes vanished. The world turned hot and humid, a moist haze blurring the horizon. There was no more scent of honeysuckle, and in its absence, another, more pungent aroma asserted itself: the yard began to smell tartly of Bo's urine.

It happened on a Saturday.

Ally was planning to do a load of laundry. She stripped the sheets off her bed, carried them down to the mudroom, where Stan had installed a washing machine years before. Bo shadowed her, as always, then stood at the mudroom's door, waiting for her to unlatch it. It was shortly after dawn. When Ally followed Bo out into the yard, she could hear the morning chatter of the parakeets. The parrot was awake, too. "Liar!" he called. "Come back . . . !" The barn's door was still shut. Usually, Stan would've already rolled it open for the birds, but Ally hardly registered this uncharacteristic lapse, only recognizing its significance in hindsight. She stood on the grass in her bare feet, watching as Bo's urine spread into a vast puddle around him. When he turned to come back inside, his paws made a slapping sound through the mud he'd created.

Eleanor was sitting at the kitchen table, waiting for breakfast. She was completely naked. As soon as Ally saw her, she knew. "Eleanor?" she said. "Where's Stan?"

"Stan?"

"Ed. Where's Ed?"

"Big Ed won't get up."

Ally started for the Hobbits' bedroom. She was thinking, *CPR*, trying to remember the proper sequence, the pushes and the breaths—there were more of the one than the other, but how many more? She was thinking, *911*, wondering how long an ambulance would take, and where it would even come from, and would she need to give directions, and did she know them. She was thinking: *Come back!*

But none of this mattered. Ally knew it on the threshold of the room, when she saw Stan lying half in, half out of the bed, his head and shoulder hanging off the edge of the mattress, the fingertips of his right hand touching the floor. She knew it more deeply when she smelled the shit—at first, she assumed this was coming from Bo, who'd followed her in from the kitchen, but then she saw the dark stain on the sheet tangled around Stan's waist (*like a shroud*: she actually thought the words). And she knew it for certain when she got close enough to touch the old man, to press her palm against his pale back, his stubbled cheek, his hand—so cold and heavy and strangely plump when she lifted it from the floor.

Ally didn't cry. She didn't feel the slightest pull in that direction. It was too shocking for tears.

She did her best to shift Stan back onto the bed. She drew the comforter over him—all the way at first, as she'd seen people do in movies—but then this felt immediately wrong, and she pulled it back down, tucking it under his chin instead. Bo had begun to whimper; Ally herded him from the room. When he kept trying to push his way back in, she grabbed him by his collar and dragged him to the mudroom. She opened the screen door and nudged the dog out into the yard. In the kitchen, Eleanor was still sitting patiently at the table, without any clothes on, waiting for her breakfast to appear before her. Ally fetched a robe for the old woman. It felt good to be in motion, to be accomplishing things that needed doing; it made it easier not to think. She filled a bowl with Cheerios, added a splash of milk, dug a spoon out of the utensil drawer, and set everything on the placemat in front of Eleanor. And then, finally, once Eleanor had started to eat, swaying back and forth, her eyes drifting shut with pleasure, Ally picked up the cordless phone, stepped into the mudroom, and called Dr. Thornton.

After the doctor arrived, after Ally helped Eleanor dress and guided her to her chair in the aviary, after the coroner came, and the men from the funeral home in their black van, after they'd taken the body away, after Ally made peanut butter and jelly sandwiches for herself and Eleanor and Dr. Thornton, after Eleanor lay down in the sunroom for her afternoon nap, the doctor and Ally sat together in the kitchen and tried to decide what ought to be done. Could it really be possible that Stan, who'd gone to such lengths to cradle Eleanor while he was alive, had done nothing to ensure her continued care in the event of his death? Dr. Thornton seemed disappointed to discover that Ally had no answer to this question. Was there a place in the house where Stan might've kept a will? Ally couldn't say. Did he ever mention a lawyer? Not as far as Ally could remember. Had he discussed with her, even casually, what his wishes might be, should he predecease Eleanor? Never. The doctor sagged back in his chair. He said that he supposed he should contact the Vermont Agency of Human Services. The idea seemed to depress him. "The problem," he said, "is that once we do that, we can't undo it."

Bo was lying on the floor beneath the kitchen table. He struggled to his feet now, shook himself awake. Then he shuffled toward the mudroom. He wanted to go out, Ally knew; he wanted to piss another puddle onto the lawn. Ally rose and opened the door for him, then stood there, waiting for Bo to find the right spot. He crouched like a female dog to empty his bladder; he no longer had the balance to lift his leg. He peed and peed and peed. Ally wondered if there might be something wrong with his kidneys. But this wasn't her problem now, was it? She was finding it difficult, in her present circumstances, to decide how far her sense of obligation ought to stretch. She opened the drawer that contained this question, then immediately slammed it shut again, flinching from the prospect of delving too deeply, worried that if she tried to draw a line at one particular point, she might discover it was impossible to draw it anywhere. Maybe everything was her problem now.

Back in the kitchen, the doctor was still slumped in his chair. It made Ally feel sad, seeing him like this: so defeated. She wanted to cheer him up, to reassure him that things were going to be okay, even though this obviously wasn't the case. Stan was the keystone; without him, the arch collapsed, and without the arch, the roof must fall. Ally could see no point in pretending otherwise.

"Can you handle her for a few days?" Dr. Thornton asked. "On your own?"

"Of course," Ally said, trying to sound more upbeat about this prospect than she actually felt. She didn't know what the doctor imagined might change in the coming days. Whether it was today or tomorrow or next week or the one after that, someone was going to come and take Eleanor away.

"I'll stop by in the morning to check on things," the doctor said. "And you can call me anytime."

Ally thanked him. There was an awkward moment at the door, when it seemed like he thought she might expect a consoling hug. Maybe she did, too—she felt herself leaning toward him and only managed to regain her center of gravity an instant before the point of no return. The doctor touched her shoulder, gave her something between a pat and a squeeze. Then he was gone.

If Ally had been at any risk of imagining she might be able to fill the vacancy Stan had left behind—that she might find a way to keep

watch in the house until death came to claim Eleanor in her turn—
the remainder of that first day alone there would've cured her of all
such illusions. Ally couldn't understand how Stan had managed on
his own for so many years. Eleanor had a habit of wandering. She
was always shifting from one room to the other, searching for something, though if you asked her what it was, she was never able to remember. Sometimes she'd drift outside: she'd head to the aviary and
try to drag open the barn's door, or start to shuffle down the drive
toward the road, or just stand on the lawn, staring at the steep hill
beyond the barn with an air of concentrated attention—a deep sort
of listening—that Ally always found slightly spooky. With Stan
around, it had seemed easy enough to keep track of her. But now, as
soon as Ally glanced away, Eleanor would vanish. For some reason,
she kept taking Bo out and tying him by a length of rope to the
hitching post at the far edge of the lawn. Ally would have to go out
and free the poor dog, and while she was doing this, Eleanor would
turn on the stove, or take off her clothes again, or remove all the
food from the refrigerator and stack it neatly on the kitchen floor.

"Where's Ed?" she kept asking. "Have you seen Ed?"

It didn't matter how Ally answered; whatever she said was immediately forgotten. So there seemed no point in struggling to communicate some version of the truth. Instead, Ally told Eleanor that Ed
had gone to the store, that he was resting, or showering, or out for a
long walk. And no matter where she said he was, the same questions
would be asked a moment later.

"Where's Ed? Have you seen Ed?"

It was a relief when the sun finally began to set. They had soup
for dinner (*Where's Ed?*), and then Ally helped Eleanor take a bath
(*Have you seen Ed?*), and brush her teeth (*Where's Ed?*), and pull on
her nightgown (*Have you seen Ed?*), and climb into bed. It was then
that things got tricky again. Every time Ally turned out the light and
tried to leave the room, Eleanor would get up and follow her

(*Where's Ed? Have you seen Ed?*). Ally assumed the old woman would eventually grow tired of this dance—that if Ally could just persuade her to lie motionless in the darkness for a handful of minutes, sleep would come and lay hold of the old woman. But it wasn't working that way: it was Ally who was growing tired. Finally, in desperation, when Eleanor yet again asked if she'd seen Ed, Ally answered: "I'm Ed."

"You're not Ed."

"Of course I am. Why shouldn't I be Ed?" This little experiment might have ended here, had Ally not detected the slightest flicker of uncertainty in Eleanor's expression. Ally seized on it, stepping to the big bureau against the wall. She dragged open the top drawer, then the drawer beneath it, searching till she found a clean pair of Stan's pajamas. She took off her shorts and T-shirt and pulled on the pajamas while Eleanor watched from across the room. "Come on, love," Ally said, imitating Stan's voice as closely as she could. "Time for bed."

Absurdly, it worked. When Ally climbed beneath the sheets, Eleanor did, too. Ally reached to turn out the light, and, as she settled back onto the pillow, Eleanor shifted toward her, resting her head heavily on Ally's shoulder. Ally's plan was to wait for Eleanor to drift into sleep and then quietly slip out of the room. But each time she attempted this—with Eleanor softly snoring only inches from her face—Eleanor would startle back awake, clinging to Ally's arm with surprising strength. "Ed?" she'd cry out.

"Yes?" Ally would say.

"Where are you going?"

"Nowhere, love. Go back to sleep."

At some point, Bo entered the room. He stood beside the bed, sniffing loudly. Then he turned and shuffled back out. It was hot, especially with Eleanor's plump body pressed so tightly against her side, and Ally was beginning to sweat through Stan's pajamas. She'd never be able to sleep here—she was certain of this. For one thing, it was impossible not to remember that this was where the old man had died, in this very bed. Ally thought she could still detect the smell of shit in the room. Or was it the stench of death itself?

Bo returned. He stood in the darkness beside the bed. Ally reached out a hand to pat him, aiming for the sound of his sniffing, but all she touched was air. It gave her a shivery feeling, as if the dog weren't actually there. To calm herself, she thought about leaving, planning her escape as if it were something she might actually attempt. She could get up in the morning, feed Eleanor, install her on her chair in the aviary, then climb into the Volvo and go. She knew where Stan had kept the ATM card; she even knew the code—sometimes she'd made withdrawals for the Hobbits as she ran her errands down in town. The car, whatever cash she could get from the bank: that was all she'd need in order to vanish. By nightfall, she could be in Philadelphia, or Buffalo, or Wilmington, cities she'd never visited before, blank slates, new starts. Ally lay on her back in the hot room, wondering if there were people who would do such a thing—no, that's not true, because of course there were such people: what she wondered was if she herself could ever be that type of person. She was thinking about the *Titanic*, the listing deck, the band playing, the icy sea. There were men who'd donned dresses, she knew, pretending to be women so that they could claim a spot for themselves in the meager allotment of lifeboats. Ally didn't want to be like that, but she didn't want to be left on the deck, either; she didn't want to stand there in the North Atlantic night, while the ship sank beneath her feet . . . *and Mrs. Henderson was making her retie the knots, raising her voice above the wind, telling her to go over and around and then under again, and Ally (always so clumsy with her hands, but all the more so now, her fingers cramping in the cold rain) kept losing hold of the rope.* Part of her realized she was dreaming, and it was this part that roused her back into waking, into the Hobbits' stuffy bedroom, with its faint smell of shit. It was still dark, but later now, and empty—the bed, the room.

Ally pushed herself into a sitting position. She listened. Softly, in the distance, she could hear someone whimpering. It was faint enough for Ally to think that she might be imagining it—but no, there it was again, louder now, irrefutable. She climbed out of bed, stood in the dark room, trying to find her bearings, to shake off the last vestiges of sleep; she wanted to be certain she wasn't dreaming. The pajamas clung to her body, heavy with perspiration, smelling of both her and Stan all at once.

"Eleanor?" she called.

The whimpering continued. It wasn't Eleanor, Ally realized: it was Bo. She started out of the room, moved quickly down the hall into the kitchen. The dog was outside, Ally could tell. His whimpering had roused the birds; they'd begun to caw and shriek and whistle in the shuttered barn. Ally was hurrying—across the kitchen, into the mudroom—she didn't pause to turn on a light, so it was a shock to come across Eleanor, standing there in the darkness, naked again, staring out the screen door toward the lawn.

"Eleanor?"

Eleanor held up a hand: "Shh."

Outside, Bo's whimpering climbed a notch, becoming a sustained sort of yelp. There was pain in the sound, and fear, and helplessness. Ally pushed past Eleanor, out the door. The old woman grabbed at her arm—again with that surprising strength of hers—but Ally wrenched herself free. The dew on the grass felt cold against her bare feet, almost like frost. It was a pleasant sensation, sobering and clarifying: now, at last, she was fully awake. There was a half-moon, hanging just above the barn, but a cloud was moving slowly across its face, which meant the yard was dark enough for Ally to need half a dozen steps to realize that there wasn't, as she first thought, a child lying in a white dress halfway across the lawn: it was

Eleanor's nightgown, cast aside on the grass. Bo would be tied to the hitching post, Ally knew, and as she approached, she began to hear not only his continued keening, but also a wet slapping, a heavy panting, and what sounded like the flapping of a flag in a light breeze. She could see him then, struggling to rise, falling, struggling up again—this was the slapping sound, his paws churning at the muddy puddle he'd peed into the dirt around the hitching post—he fell, he whimpered, he fell again. "It's okay," Ally said. "I'm here. It's okay, sweetie." She was reaching to untie the rope from his collar when the moon broke free from its masking cloud, and she saw the thing hanging from his neck. She flinched back with a stifled scream.

Her first, startled impression was that it was some sort of immense insect, oval shaped, at least a foot long and half again as wide, with something frighteningly spider-like about it, the sense of multiple legs emerging from its central torso. Then Bo fell again, and a pair of wings spread open from the creature's back; they gave a single flap to stabilize the beast. The wings were shockingly long, with a leathery appearance; Ally could make out the bones beneath the skin, even in the moonlight. There was fur, too: on the creature's back and legs—brown or black, Ally couldn't tell which. And the legs (there were six of them, she saw, with a tug of nausea) were prehensile; each of them ended in a monkey-like hand, all six of which were gripping tightly at Bo's fur. Its head was the size of a grapefruit, its face buried in the dog's neck: burrowing, feeding.

Bo made no effort to rise again. He seemed to sense Ally's presence, and it was as if her arrival had prompted him to relinquish his fight: she would either free him from his tormentor, or he'd succumb.

The birds continued to cry out in the barn. The parrot was calling: "Ed . . . ! Ed . . . ! Ed . . . !" Another cloud obscured the moon, and Ally felt her panic ratchet upward—the creature was just a shadow now, a deeper darkness against Bo's black body, its wings going *flap*, *flap*. Ally backed away. One step. Then another. Stan had been digging a hole the day before—a rhododendron beneath the kitchen window had died, poisoned, Ally suspected, by Bo's urine, and Stan had been working all afternoon to excavate its withered remains. He'd left the job half-finished, intending to resume his digging in the morning: the shovel was still leaning against the side of the house. Ally turned, started for it at a run.

Behind her, Bo let out a long, warbling cry of pain.

The shovel was exactly where she'd pictured it, waiting for her. She headed back across the lawn, grasping the tool's handle in both hands, like a baseball bat. The moon emerged again, just as she arrived at the hitching post. Bo had rolled onto his side; she could see his chest rising and falling, could hear him panting. The creature had folded its wings back into its body. Ally watched it open one of its furry hands, then reach and claim a better grip.

She swung with all her strength.

Her fear of the creature, her revulsion, seemed to give her strength. The shovel's blade landed with a loud thump. Bo yelped, kicked his legs. The creature relinquished its hold on the dog. It fell to the ground, instantly righting itself, and turned to face its attacker. Ally had time to register the thing's face: round and pale and hairless, with a pair of large eyes and what she at first mistook for a flat, simian nose. But then this orifice opened, revealing a set of startling white teeth—sharp and double-tiered—and she realized the thing had two mouths, this smaller one where a nose would normally reside, a few inches above its much larger companion. Both were stretched wide now. Ally could see rows of teeth, a pair of thick pink tongues. The creature shrieked, enraged. Then it spread its wings and leapt into the air, flying straight at her.

Ally swung again. This time, it was nothing but reflex, straight from the spine, her animal core taking command; she managed a glancing blow that knocked the creature back onto the ground. It was in the air again so quickly that it seemed as if it had bounced off the dirt, like a ball. It was still shrieking. Ally swung, connected; the thing thudded against the earth, sprang into the air once more, and this time when Ally swung, she heard the crack of a bone snapping.

The creature fell to the lawn, scrambling with its legs in the dirt, one wing wildly flapping, the other dragging, its shrieking taking on a higher note, pain mixing into its fury: Ally lunged forward and swung again—and again—and again. She could hear more bones cracking, could feel them break through the shovel's wooden handle, and the sensation seemed to drive her onward, into a growing frenzy. She would've killed the thing, would've continued swinging until her strength gave out, pounding the creature into the sodden earth, but then, in the brief hesitation between blows, she glimpsed its face. There was something unavoidably human in those eyes—intelligence, terror, bewilderment—and it knocked Ally back into herself. She heard the creature's cries: the rage had vanished. Pain was triumphant now, with a childlike undertone suddenly emerging; the creature sounded like a frightened toddler. It was trying to crawl away. All of its limbs but one appeared to be broken, and it kept grabbing at the dirt with its single undamaged hand, struggling to pull the limp weight of its body out of the yard, into the trees, to what it must've imagined was safety—struggling, failing.

Ally heard herself start to sob. She dropped the shovel, stepped toward Bo. The dog was still lying on his side, eyes shut, panting. Ally untied the rope from his collar. "Come on, sweetie," she said, crying, wiping at her face, at the tears, the snot. "Can you get up?"

Bo lifted his head, peered blindly toward her. His tail thumped against the ground, a feeble wag . . . wag . . . wag. Ally didn't think he'd be able to rise, but she prodded at him anyway; she wanted to get him back into the house, away from his attacker. Bo groaned, rolled onto his stomach. She pulled at his collar, straining to lift him, and he surprised her by lurching upward; he swayed, almost fell, but then, when Ally gave another tug, started to stumble back across the lawn toward the house, whimpering with every step. Ally glanced back at the creature as they fled. It had fallen silent now—so had the birds; the only sounds were Ally's weeping and Bo's cries of pain as he staggered forward. Ally could see the creature continuing to move, that single limb reaching to claw impotently at the dirt.

Eleanor was still standing in the mudroom, just inside the screen door. She followed Ally and Bo into the kitchen, watching as Ally led the dog to his bed beside the stove. Bo collapsed onto the bed, immediately shut his eyes. Ally nudged his water bowl toward him, but he ignored it. There was blood on his fur, thickly caked—his neck, his shoulder, most of his flank—but when Ally tried to examine his wound, the dog gave a yelp and started to thrash his legs, scrambling backward. So Ally let him be. It took him a minute to stop whimpering; it took Ally even longer to stop crying.

"Oh, Ed," Eleanor said. "No, no, no. Oh, dear. Oh, no." She was standing in the doorway, still naked, wringing her hands, staring at the dog in obvious distress.

"It's okay," Ally said. "He'll be okay. Here—sit." She took Eleanor by her elbow, guided her to a chair at the head of the table. Once she got her seated, Ally turned and went out through the mudroom again. She peered at the lawn through the screen door. Dawn was just beginning to break; the first traces of red had appeared in the east, beyond the barn. There was already enough light so that, even from this distance, Ally could discern the creature, feebly shifting about in the dirt beside the hitching post.

She heard a noise behind her, in the kitchen, and when she turned, she saw that Eleanor had gotten up from her chair. She was standing over Bo, dragging at his collar, trying to pull him to his feet. Ally hurried toward them: "Leave him. He needs to rest."

"We have to," Eleanor said.

"Shh."

"The sun's coming up."

"I know. Stop it now. Let him go." Ally eased Eleanor's grip off Bo's collar, led the old woman back across the kitchen.

Eleanor was peering toward the window, the sky growing lighter with each passing second. She covered her mouth with her hand. "What do we do, Ed? What do we do?"

Ally sat the old woman down in the chair again.

Then she did the only thing she could think of: she picked up the phone and called Dr. Thornton.

She'd awakened him, she could tell. There was a burred quality to his voice, a sleepy lag before he recognized her name. But she'd hardly begun to tell her story when she felt him snap into clarity. The whimpering . . . Eleanor standing in the mudroom . . . Bo tied to the hitching post . . . the creature hanging from the dog's neck . . . the shovel—that was as far as the doctor allowed her to get. "Stay inside," he said. "I'll be right there." And then he hung up.

Ally got Eleanor into her robe. She placed a bowl of Cheerios on the table in front of her, a glass of orange juice. Then she quickly changed out of Stan's pajamas, back into the shorts and T-shirt she'd been wearing the night before. There was blood on the pajamas: spattered and smeared. Whether it was Bo's or the creature's, Ally couldn't tell. By the time she returned to the kitchen, the dog was asleep. Ally worried for an instant that he might've died, but then she heard that familiar rising sequence of inhalations and the long wheezy sigh that followed. Eleanor was eating her cereal. She'd grown quieter as soon as the sun broke free of the trees, filling the room with light: it was possible, Ally supposed, that she'd already forgotten the entire drama. Ally stepped into the mudroom, peered out the screen door. The creature was still there, lying in the dirt beside the hitching post. It had stopped moving now.

Ally went back into the kitchen, poured herself a glass of juice, quickly drank it. Then she got Eleanor onto her feet, led her through the mudroom, out onto the lawn. She knew the only way to keep Eleanor occupied was to put her in the barn with the birds. All the way across the yard, she worked to keep herself from turning to glance at the hitching post. Even in the daylight, even with the creature so grievously wounded, it felt frightening to be out in the open again. She pulled back the big wooden door, set up Eleanor's chair. Eleanor was still in her bathrobe—teeth unbrushed, body unbathed, hair uncombed—but she didn't seem to mind. She sat down, smiling toward the gray parrot, who was perched above her, on the edge of the hayloft. "It's raining," the bird said, muttering the words. He lifted his right foot and gnawed at it for a moment with his beak. Then he spoke again, with more vehemence: "It's pouring!" All of the birds were calmer now. It was almost as if nothing had happened in the night.

Ally could hear Dr. Thornton's car approaching down the drive. She stepped to the doorway and watched through the netting as the doctor parked, turned off the engine, climbed out. She assumed he'd come to the barn when he saw her standing there, but he just glanced in her direction and then walked to the hitching post instead. He stood for a long moment, staring down at the creature. Ally pushed aside the netting and started toward him.

Dr. Thornton didn't hear her coming, but the creature seemed to. It had gone still once the sun had risen—quiet, too—but now it roused itself with a screech of panic, making the doctor jump. The creature's hairy little leg started to thrash about, its head twisting to peer at Ally, its eyes looking huge in its tiny face, terrified. The doctor turned, following its gaze. He had an uncharacteristically disheveled look to him: it was a window into the urgency of his morning thus far—roused from sleep by her call, hurriedly dressing, skipping the shower, the razor, grabbing whatever clothes came to hand, pulling on his shoes, plucking up the car keys, rushing out the door. It seemed improper somehow for Ally to glimpse him in such a state, and she realized for the first time how much care he normally took with his appearance. He was a vain man—how could she have missed this?

The creature kept looking at her. Screaming. Thrashing.

"Do you know what it is?" Ally asked.

The doctor nodded.

"You've seen it before?"

He shook his head. "But I know what it is."

Ally hugged herself. She wished the thing would fall silent again, but if anything it only seemed to be growing louder. She glanced around them, at the trees bordering the yard, the hillside above the barn. "Are there others?"

The doctor didn't answer. He said: "I think it might be best if you went back inside."

"What are you going to do?"

"I have to make some calls."

"To who?"

"Please, Ally. Go back into the house."

So she went inside. She showered, put on fresh clothes, combed out her hair. She stood at the kitchen sink and ate a piece of toast, watching out the window as the doctor paced in the dirt beside the hitching post, on his cell phone, making his calls. As soon as Ally had left, the creature had fallen silent again. Eleanor remained in the barn with the birds. Every now and then, Ally heard the parrot call out: "Ed! Big Ed!" But otherwise, all was quiet.

The first car arrived thirty minutes later. Ron Hillman, the village pharmacist, was driving. He climbed out and stood with the doctor, both of them frowning down at the creature, their hands on their hips. Ally watched them as they talked. Whatever Ron was saying, the doctor didn't appear to like it; he kept shaking his head. It was odd to see Ron without his white coat, dressed in khaki shorts and a golf shirt, his legs looking so pale and thin in the early morning sun. Another car arrived: this one held Philip and Christina Larchmont. They joined Ron and the doctor by the hitching post, forming a little circle around the wounded creature. Philip was the village's mayor. He owned a small trucking company. In the winter, according to what Stan had once told Ally, he liked to head out in one of his trucks and help plow the local roads, charging nothing for this service. Christina worked part-time in the little library beside the village green. Ben Trevor, from the hardware store, was the next to arrive, then Mike and Jessica Stahl, then Mickey Wheelock. Ally thought she should make a pitcher of iced tea, bring it out to them on a platter, but there was something about the way everyone kept turning to glance toward the house that gave her pause. She couldn't say precisely how it made her feel, but it wasn't a pleasant sensation—wary, a bit uneasy. The doctor had told her to wait inside, so that was what she would do. She turned from the window, sat at the kitchen table, and tried not to think about the people on the lawn, tried not to think about the blood on Stan's pajamas, tried most of all not to think about the creature.

Ally heard the sound of water softly falling, and when she looked up, she saw urine soaking the dog's bed, running off it onto the floor in little rivulets: Bo had lost his bladder in his sleep. Ally tried to rouse him, but he just opened a single eye, stared blindly toward her, and then slipped back into unconsciousness. She was cleaning the mess up as best as she could, when there was a knocking at the screen door.

"Come in!" she called.

It was Christina and Jessica. Neither of them could've been more than a handful of years older than Ally, but there was something about both women—so stout and competent and matronly—that always made Ally feel very young. Whenever she encountered one or the other of them, she ended up wondering how she could've managed to live so many years without ever really growing up. The two women bustled into the kitchen with a friendly air of command, each talking over the other.

"Oh, dear," Christina said. "Did someone have an accident?"

"We'll take care of that," Jessica said. She was already by the sink, rummaging in the cabinet underneath, pulling out a bucket, filling it with hot water from the faucet.

Christina stepped to the little closet beside the refrigerator, opened its door, found a mop. "Why don't you try to get some rest?"

"Yes," Jessica agreed. "It sounds like you've had quite the night, haven't you?"

"Would you mind if we made some coffee for the men?"

"What's happening?" Ally asked.

Christina waved the question aside. "It's all right, honey."

Jessica nodded, hefting the bucket out of the sink. "Everything's going to be fine."

Christina came toward her, mop in hand. She took Ally by her elbow, guided her toward the doorway. "You go on upstairs. Try to lie down."

Ally allowed herself to be herded in this fashion; she was too worn out to resist. But she didn't believe she'd ever be able to sleep. She climbed the stairs to her room and stood at the window, watching the men in the yard. Ollie Seymour, the village barber, had arrived. And Chad Sample, who owned the house just up the road. Ally couldn't see the creature from this angle, just the men gathered around it, talking among themselves, turning now and then to glance at the house. She lay down on the bed. She didn't expect to sleep, or even to rest, but her head had begun to ache, and she thought it might help to shut her eyes. There was the Hobbits' Volvo, and the bank card . . . she could still just vanish . . . but all those cars were blocking the drive now . . . and the doctor had told her to stay in the house . . . and the women in the kitchen had sent her upstairs . . . she should remind them to bring Eleanor her lunch . . . there was roast beef in the fridge . . . Eleanor always enjoyed roast beef . . . they could fetch a jar of pickles from the root cellar—

"Ally?" It was Dr. Thornton's voice.

Ally glanced blearily around the room. She could tell from the way the light had shifted that it was much later now. She fumbled for the clock on the night table: it said 4:03. Somehow, she'd managed to sleep for almost six hours.

"Ally . . . ?" He was calling to her from downstairs.

"Coming!" Ally pushed herself off the bed, stepped out into the hallway.

The doctor was on the landing halfway down, peering up at her. "Would you mind joining me for a drive?" he asked. "There's something I'd like to show you."

Most of the cars had left. But Christina was still there, sitting in the kitchen with Eleanor. They were drinking tea and eating cookies. The kitchen had been cleaned; everything smelled sharply of bleach. Bo had been cleaned, too—his fur, his wound. He seemed to sense Ally's arrival downstairs. He lifted his head, gave a single slow wag to his tail. Ally had washed her face, changed her T-shirt. She asked Christina if she'd be okay here on her own, and Christina smiled, waved her toward the door.

The doctor was waiting in his car, its engine already running. When he saw Ally approaching, he climbed out, stepped around to the passenger side, and opened her door for her. It made Ally feel like this was a date, and—ridiculously—she felt herself begin to blush.

There was no sign of the creature. As they were pulling away from the house, Ally asked: "Did it die?"

The doctor shook his head.

"Where is it?"

Dr. Thornton made a vague gesture. "Ron Hillman took it into town."

Ally assumed that this must be where they were headed, too, but then the doctor turned north at the first crossroads they reached, and they began to climb higher into the hills. They passed the house where Ally had seen the goose, and then the doctor made another turn, onto a narrow gravel lane, and suddenly they were in a part of the country Ally had never glimpsed before. Pine trees grew close to the road on both sides, cutting off the view.

"You've seen the war memorial, I assume," the doctor said. "On the green?"

Ally nodded.

"Did you ever look closely at the names?"

There was a carved scroll at the base of the memorial, Ally knew; it listed the young men from the village who'd died fighting to keep the union whole. But she'd always been too unsettled by the statue's ghostly grimace to pause long enough to read the names. She shook her head.

"Seventeen names," the doctor said. "And two are Thorntons: Thaddeus and Michael. Which is all just to say that my family has lived in the village for a very long time. One of the first white men to establish a farm in this part of the state was a Thornton. And for all those many years, we've been living with the skad."

"The skad?"

The doctor nodded. "The Abenaki Indians used a longer word, which sounded something like 'skadegamutch.' When the first white settlers came, they shortened this to *skad*. If you go to Harvard's Houghton Library, they have a book with a drawing a French priest made in 1742. *Mythical Beasts of the New World*. It shows the creature that you encountered last night. Quite a fine rendering, really. Only much larger."

"Larger?"

Another nod from the doctor. "If you think of a bear? What you saw was a cub. A young cub. Recently weaned, would be my guess."

Ally shut her eyes. She imagined a creature like the one she'd fought, imagined it the size of a bear. Then she pictured more than one of them, an entire clan or pack or troop, lurking somewhere in these hills.

"The Abenaki were hunters. And at some point, they developed a tradition. When they wounded an animal—a deer, a moose, a beaver—they'd leave it outside their encampments at night, tied to a tree, as an offering for the skad. In this manner, the two groups found a way to live in peace with each other."

Ally thought of the animals she'd glimpse on her late afternoon runs. The old cow, the spavined donkey. "The hitching posts," she said.

Dr. Thornton nodded. "The white settlers adopted the practice when they began to establish themselves in the area. Horses, cattle . . . as they neared the end of their usefulness, they'd be tied to a hitching post. Left out in the night."

"And dogs."

"That's right—dogs, too."

The gravel road came to an end. A chain had been strung across its path, from one tree to another. Beyond the chain, a narrow trail wound up the hillside, climbing steeply. It led to a house, which was just visible through the pines. Dr. Thornton put the car in park, shut off the engine. He didn't undo his seat belt, didn't reach to push open his door, and Ally was happy for this. There was something about the house she didn't like.

"There were probably other times when the arrangement broke down," the doctor said. "But the only occasion I know of for certain happened in 1973. A man named Bert Rogers was elected mayor of the village. Bert had served in the marines, a career officer. He'd been a lieutenant in Korea. He'd commanded an entire battalion in Vietnam. He was a serious man. A hard man. He decided it was time to resolve the issue of the skad—that there was something cowardly about how we'd been accommodating their presence in our lives. They were nocturnal creatures, and Bert argued that it ought to be possible for us to hunt them during the day. That the men of the village could hike up into the hills and ferret the creatures out of their caves and burrows. That they could kill the skad off."

The doctor unhooked his seat belt, reached to push open his door. *No*, Ally thought. *Whatever this is, I don't want to see it.* But when the doctor climbed out of the car, she found she couldn't help herself. She climbed out, too. Then they started up the path through the trees, Dr. Thornton walking in front with Ally a few feet behind him.

"There were two problems with Bert's idea, as it turned out," the doctor said. "One is that it's not as easy as it might seem to kill a skad. The juvenile you encountered last night—you broke both of its wings and most of its legs. But you didn't kill it. And—given suffi- cient time—it will recover completely. Pretty much the only way to kill them, in fact, is to burn them. And even that isn't as simple as it sounds—you have to burn them completely. You have to reduce them practically to ash."

It was a large house, two stories, with a high, steeply slanting roof. And it was in ruins. It looked as if it had once been painted blue, but this was decades ago, and the weather had long ago stripped most of the color from the exterior. The windows were empty of glass; most of the shingles had blown free from the roof. Ally didn't want to get any closer, but Dr. Thornton kept walking. So she did, too.

"The other problem," the doctor continued, "is that while the skad are indeed more or less helpless during the day, at night, it's we who are the helpless ones. So Bert Rogers and his men went up into the hills and attacked the skad while the sun was in the sky. Then, once the sun had set, the skad came down out of the hills and did their own hunting. And it turned out that they were far better at this than we were."

The house's porch had collapsed. To reach the front door, which was hanging partway open, the doctor had to prop a fallen shutter against the foundation and scramble up it, using it as a ramp. Then he turned and held out his hand to Ally. One part of her mind tried to tell her head to shake—*no*—but a more powerful part submissively ordered her arm to rise. Dr. Thornton grasped her by the wrist, pulled her up. He pushed the house's front door all the way open, and they stepped into the building.

"This is where the Baggers lived," he said. "Steve and Katherine and their four children."

They were in a small foyer. Across from them, a flight of stairs climbed toward the second story. There was a long hallway to the left of the stairs, leading to the rear of the house. To the right, an archway opened into what Ally guessed had once been the Baggers' living room. The doctor had retained his hold on her wrist. When he stepped toward the archway, he gave her a tug, pulling her with him. The room still showed evidence of its former occupants. There were the ragged remains of a brown carpet on the floor, a sagging couch, two armchairs, a large coffee table lying on its side, several broken lamps—even a painting lying faceup on the floor. It didn't look abandoned, though. It looked vandalized, as if someone had come here one day long ago and worked to destroy the room, laboring at the task with a malevolent vigor.

Or no, Ally realized; that wasn't right. It wasn't *one day*. It was *one night*.

"After this—and two other similar incidents—the village turned against Bert. They went back to the old ways. They made peace with the skad."

"How?" Ally asked.

"Careful," the doctor said. She'd taken a hesitant step into the room, wanting, despite herself, to see what the painting depicted, and in the process her foot had come into contact with something lying among the tumbled debris littering the floor. The doctor pulled her back from it. Ally stared down at the object, struggling to decipher what it might be. It took her a moment, but then it came all at once: it was a hand, a child's hand, stripped of flesh, only the bones remaining, the bones and the leathery brown ligaments that held them in place. Seeing this—*really* seeing it—yanked other objects in the room into focus. Beyond the couch: a dirty-looking pair of jeans, with a shattered femur poking through a tear in the denim. And then, between the two armchairs: what Ally had at first mistaken for a stone, revealed now for what it actually was—the top half of a man's skull.

Inside, Ally could feel herself fleeing from this place. Fleeing and screaming. But she didn't make a move, didn't make a sound. She was conscious of the doctor's grip on her wrist, conscious of the slant of sunlight through the glassless windows across the room. It was getting late, but how late? How soon would it be dark?

"Why is it still like this?" she asked.

"Like what?"

She waved at the room, the broken furniture, the tumbled bones. "All these years. Why hasn't it been cleaned up?"

"It's a gesture of respect."

Respect? The word felt obscene to Ally; she couldn't imagine it ever having any connection to such a setting. "Toward who?"

The doctor shrugged, as if he believed the answer ought to be obvious. "The skad."

Ally felt exhausted suddenly: nauseated, and empty of any desire but the urgent need to leave. "I want to go," she said.

The doctor nodded. "Of course."

He seemed to think that by "go," she meant leave the house. And, as a start, this would suffice for Ally. Dr. Thornton guided her back through the foyer to the front door; he helped her down to the ground, then began to lead her back along the winding path to the road. The dirt here was thickly carpeted with pine needles; their footsteps didn't make a sound.

Go, go, go, go, go . . .

They climbed into the car, pulled on their seat belts. The road was too narrow for the doctor to turn around at first, so he had to drive in reverse, twisting sideways in his seat to see the way. Ally sat facing forward, watching the house slowly disappear into the trees.

Go, go, go, go, go . . .

They didn't speak. The road finally widened enough for the car to turn around, and then the doctor drove more quickly. Ally felt herself begin to breathe again. She must've been breathing all along, of course, but for a while there it had felt as if she hadn't.

Go, go, go, go, go . . .

By *go* what Ally meant was leave altogether. She didn't need to return to the Hobbits'; there was nothing there she could imagine as being worth the time it would take to retrieve it. So when the doctor reached the crossroads and continued south, toward the village, rather than turning back toward Stan and Eleanor's house, Ally remained silent. She'd find someone in the village to drive her west, toward Burlington. She didn't know how she'd accomplish this; she just knew that she would. She'd go door-to-door, if she needed to, pleading for help. There had to be someone in the village who would take pity on her. If she hurried, if she were lucky—and why shouldn't she be lucky for once in her life—she'd be miles away from here before it began to grow dark.

They entered the village. The doctor pulled to a stop alongside the green. Ally was surprised to see that a crowd had collected here. All of the people who'd been up at the Hobbits' house that morning were once again present, along with many others from the town, some of whom Ally only recognized by sight. They were gathered together now, she was certain, because of what had happened last night, but Ally had no desire to know anything beyond this. However they intended to deal with the wrath of the skad, it was their problem to solve, not hers. She would go from one to another of them, begging for her ride west. Somewhere within that crowd, there was bound to be a man or woman with a kind heart.

The doctor shut off the car. "I showed you all that because I wanted you to understand."

Ally wasn't really listening. She was watching the people on the green, most of whom had turned now to peer at the car. Ally wanted the doctor to stop talking. The sun was lower than she'd thought. She didn't have much time.

"You do understand, don't you?" the doctor asked.

Ally nodded. She had no idea what he was asking, but she didn't care. She just wanted to get out of the car.

"I'm so glad to hear that, ma'am. So glad. Thank you."

The word *ma'am* hung in the air between them, tugging at Ally's consciousness—*when had he stopped using her name? And why?* But then the doctor was pushing open his door, climbing out onto the green, and Ally was, too: they moved forward together, side by side. As they neared the crowd, it parted, and Ally stopped short, startled to glimpse Eleanor and Bo. Eleanor was sitting in a lawn chair, smiling first at one person, then another; she always seemed to enjoy large gatherings. Bo was lying in the dirt a few yards to her right; he appeared to be asleep. It took Ally a moment to realize that they were both tied to hitching posts. As soon as she saw this, she understood why, and she turned to the doctor, intending to protest, to insist that this couldn't possibly be the right solution, no matter how old the two of them might be, no matter how close to death. But then, before Ally could speak, she glimpsed the third hitching post.

This one was empty.

Empty, that is, except for a short length of chain attached to its base.

She tried to flee. And—to her credit—when flight proved impossible, she tried to fight. She kicked, she clawed, she screamed. Then Ollie Seymour, who was a big man, struck her on the side of her head, knocking her to the ground. Ally didn't lose consciousness, but the blow stunned her into immobility. Helpless, she felt herself being dragged across the grass by her feet—felt them chaining her ankle to the post. It was Dr. Thornton who locked the cuff. Still too dazed to resist, Ally saw him give the chain a tug, making sure it was secure.

After that, the crowd quickly dispersed. Ally heard car doors slamming, engines starting, the crunch of gravel as people drove away. Others were walking off across the green toward their houses. The doctor was among this latter group. Ally called out to him: "Dr. Thornton . . . !"

He didn't glance back.

The dusk had deepened enough now for Ally to realize that there were lights on in many of the houses that lined the green. She could see figures beyond the windows, watching.

Oh, those beautiful houses! The well-kept lawns, the rows of carefully trimmed shrubbery. The gliders on the porches, the flowerpots full of geraniums on the window ledges.

And the hitching posts.

Soon, only one man remained on the green, standing near its far corner. Ally called to him: "Help me . . . ! Please help . . . !" She managed to climb painfully to her feet, then staggered a few steps in his direction, until the chain yanked her to a stop with a clatter. That was when she realized her mistake. It wasn't a man; it was the war memorial, the statue of the young soldier, staring west toward the now vanished sun, his face immobilized in that silent howl of torment.

It was only now that Ally noticed the cardboard box, sitting in front of the three hitching posts, about fifteen feet away, its top folded open. There was bedding inside—a little nest of blankets. And nestled among the bedding was the creature. It had been silent all this time, but as the dusk continued to settle upon the village, it began to make a mewling sound. The only language Ally had ever known was English, yet there had been times in her life when she'd overheard people speaking in a foreign tongue and known immediately what they were saying, simply from the pitch of their voices. The same thing happened here, with the creature. Perhaps it was simply because the box looked so much like a cradle—the blankets so much like swaddling—but what Ally heard was a frightened child, calling for its mother.

Mommy . . . ? Mommy . . . ? Mommy . . . ?

The creature's voice seemed to gain strength with the advancing darkness: a wounded child, calling for someone to protect it.

Mama . . . Mama . . . Mama . . .

Ally could picture how the hills above the village must look at this time of day, the shadows already triumphant beneath the trees. The creature had started to shift about in the box, waving its broken limbs in the air: an angry child, calling for someone to avenge it.

Mother . . . ! Mother . . . ! Mother . . . !

Ally hugged herself, shivering. All around her, the light was fading fast.

Night was coming.

And with the night, an answer to the child's cries.

SOMETHING LOST, SOMETHING GAINED

SEANAN McGUIRE

Lightning lashed across the summer sky, coloring it with the purple-black of a fresh hematoma. It was followed by a roll of thunder some three seconds later. No rain, not yet, but the air was heavy with the taste of it, a heady, electric smell that promised downpours yet to come. Lou picked her way along the bank of the creek, mud squishing between her toes, keeping a wary eye on that sky. Summer storms were the best kind for watching and the worst kind for getting caught in. They were unpredictable, temperamental, like her stepdaddy when he had a couple of beers in him and his eyes started to wander along the curves of her sundress.

Lou stopped for a moment, clenching her fingers a little tighter around the jar in her hand as she shook off the memory of his eyes and breathed in the clean scent of yet-unfallen rain. Those were thoughts for another time and place, huddled under her blanket and listening to the shouts from downstairs. She was thirteen: old enough to understand that she was what her mother and her stepfather fought about half the time, and nowhere near old enough to understand why it had to be that way. She sometimes thought that she would never be old enough, that "old enough" was the sort of idea that came only to frightened thirteen-year-old girls, waiting for the doorknob to turn. It hadn't happened yet, but she saw the way he looked at her, and she listened to the way the other girls at school talked sometimes in the locker room, when the teachers weren't around. She knew what came after the sundresses and the shouting.

(There was a smell in the locker room sometimes, when the teachers were away and the girls started talking. It was a sharp, hot smell, and it made Lou think of storms on the way, even though there were no clouds in the locker room, never could be; even though they were safe, small, contained when they sat in that room. Maybe girls and storms weren't so different after all.)

She resumed her pacing along the creek bed, eyes flicking from the fresh-bruised sky to the black branches of the trees that grew beside the water. Lightning flashed again. This time, the thunder was only a second behind. It was time to go back, time to get home before the rain came down and she got another lecture about behaving like a child. She started to turn—

Lights appeared in the branches of the nearest tree, as unsteady as birthday candles, flickering luminescent green through the darkness. Lou's cheeks stretched into a grin as she uncapped the jam jar she'd been carrying all this while.

"Gotcha," she whispered.

Catching fireflies was an art form. Most of the girls her age had already lost whatever skill at it they'd once possessed, trading the steady hand on the collecting jar for a steady hand on a mascara wand. She didn't see anything wrong with that, exactly—everyone had to grow up to be who they were going to be—but she sometimes felt like there'd been a bell rung over the course of the past two years, one that all her classmates could hear, while she couldn't hear anything but the siren song of the creek and the woods and the promise of summer fireflies.

When she went back to school in the fall, she would be a high school student, expected to buckle down and fight for her future. What's worse, she would be a little deeper into her teens, and those sidelong glances from her stepfather would no longer have as much reason to be coy. She couldn't say exactly what she feared would happen; she didn't have the words for it, any more than she had the words for the smell that accompanied an impending storm. She just knew that she was afraid.

But that was a fear for later. Right now, it was just her, and the storm, and the fireflies that she swept, one by one, into her collecting jar, until it glowed with the will-o'-wisp light of dozens of circling insects. She held it up to her eye, looking critically at the fireflies as they flew. Lightning flashed again overhead. She barely noticed.

"You're big ones, aren't you," she said, tipping the jar a bit to give herself a better angle. "Must have been a good season for you guys. Never seen ones quite like you before . . ."

And the sky ripped open, and the rain came down.

All summers are unique to the places in which they happen. California summers are hot desert things, brutal in the daylight and cold at night. Florida summers are humid and wet, unforgiving in their unrelenting heat. Indiana summers are alight with storms and fireflies, the sky always the color of a bruise, from the angry green of the impending twister to the acid yellow tainting the edges of an otherwise perfect blue. Indiana summers never let anyone forget that they are wounds carved out of the flesh of the calendar, warm not because of the presence of the sun, but because they are still bleeding.

Lou ran through the rain, her feet squelching in the increasingly sodden grass, her jam jar full of fireflies clutched against her chest like some sort of talisman of safe passage through the storm. She ran, and the storm pursued, sending down torrents of water that threatened to sweep her legs out from underneath her and send her sprawling into the grass. The conditions weren't right for a flash flood, she knew, but she ran all the same, because the longer she stayed out here, the more her mother would worry. Her mother seemed to worry all the time these days, and maybe that was another sign of how dangerous the impending storm at home was growing. The time between the lightning and the thunder had worn away to almost nothing, one lingering look at a time.

The motion seemed to be agitating the fireflies. They lit up a little brighter every time her foot came down, until she was carrying a jar full of light across the field, as bright as a fallen star, beating back the darkness as fiercely as it could. She could see the back side of her neighborhood from the hill, the lights on and glowing a little more gently than her captives. All the windows would be closed against the rain, she knew, and the back door with its bad latch would be locked to keep the wind from blowing it open. She was going to have to go around the front of the house and knock like a guest, begging for entrance to her own place. What if they didn't let her in? The fear wasn't new, but it was shocking every time it showed its face. She tried to push it aside, and it came springing back, twice as big. What if they said "*You want to be a storm's child, go be a storm's child, don't bring any of your rain or wrongness here,*" and turned their faces away, and turned the porch light off?

No. No, and no, and no again. That was her home down there, nestled safe in its line of homes just like it, and it was always going to be hers, no matter how many bad looks she got from her drunken stepdaddy (and he was never going to be her father, no; her father had bled his life out on the Indiana highway, rushing home from work, and what was sacrificed could never be so easily replaced), no matter how many times her mother pretended not to see. That was her home. She was going home, and nothing was going to stop her.

Lou was so focused on where she was planning to wind up that she stopped paying attention to where she was. Her foot found a rabbit hole in the hillside, already half-flooded, the rabbits either fled or drowned, and the sound of her ankle snapping was like a bolt of lightning, followed a second later by the dull thunder rumble of pain so big and so unheard of that it seemed to fill her entire body, leaving no room for anything else. She fell, landing hard on the jar in her arms, which shattered and drove glass shards deep into the flesh of her chest and throat.

There wasn't time to scream, and it wouldn't have mattered if she had, for the storm took all such sounds as its own. Lou lay sprawled and shattered on the hillside, her own weight driving the glass deeper. She didn't move.

The storm raged on.

There was something dream-like about the storm. It beat its fists against the rooftops and hammered against the windows, but the works of man held fast; save for a little bit of a leak up in the attic, the house was a fortress. Mary twitched the curtain aside and looked out on the backyard. The slope of the hill beyond the fence was a black hump in the darkness, almost obscured by the pounding rain.

"Where *is* that girl?" she muttered, before glancing guiltily over her shoulder. Spenser was angry at the rain, said it was interfering with the television reception, and he was angry with Mary too, for trying to say that digital cable didn't work like that. The picture had looked perfectly clear to her, but what did she know? She was just the woman who put the beer in his hand and the remote on the arm of his chair before she backed away, keeping clear of his fists, which seemed to swing especially hard when the rain came down. He didn't like nights like this one. He wouldn't be happy when he realized that Lou was still out there, chasing fireflies like a little kid.

"*It's time for that girl to grow up and realize that she can't be a hellion forever,*" that was what he'd said to Mary not two months before, when Lou had come bursting in excited by the first summer fireflies. *"If I need to smack some sense into her, I will."*

Mary liked to think that she would throw him out the first time Spenser laid a hand on her baby girl, but she knew better than to believe it. This house was in her name, but his paychecks paid the bills, and she couldn't cover the mortgage without him. If her contribution had to be paid in bruises, there were worse things in the world. Crawling back to her mother with her hat in her hands, for example. Pulling Lou out of school and away from all her friends, and all because Mary didn't know how to pick a man.

It was all justification and she knew it, but that didn't change the necessity of it. *Why didn't you leave?* was a question asked by women who lived in safe, comfortable houses with money in their bank accounts, who had never fed their daughters flour dumplings in soy-sauce soup.

"Mary! Get your ass in here!" Spenser sounded furious.

Mary tore her eyes away from the black hills behind the house. "Coming," she called, and unlocked the back door with a quick, decisive flick of her wrist before walking quickly—not running, no, see? She still had her dignity; she didn't run when he called her name—out to the living room. The television was on, the picture clear as shallow water. Spenser was seated in his armchair, the special one that no one else was allowed to touch without his invitation. He looked like a poisonous toad, squatting there, stockpiling his venom.

"What's going on, sweetheart?" she asked, putting every ounce of love and affection she could find into her voice.

"Someone's on the damn porch," he said. He turned to look at her, narrow-eyed, and added, "It better not be that girl of yours. I told her to go up to her room after dinner and get started on her homework. I'm not going to be happy if she's not been minding me."

"I'm sure it's not Lou," said Mary, who knew full well that her daughter would have tried the back door before she came around front. "It's probably one of the neighbors, coming over to borrow a bucket." It would have to be some leak for anyone to be willing to brave the storm rather than use a pot or pan to catch the water. Still, it was the best excuse she had.

Spenser looked at her for a moment more, still narrow-eyed and suspicious, before he turned back to the television. Mary let out a breath she had barely been aware of holding and walked onward, toward the door. The storm wasn't even half-over yet: she could feel the electric pressure of it pushing her down, making her skin feel too tight and her hair tingle at the edges.

Please go around the back, baby girl, she thought, and turned the knob.

The blue-and-red flashing lights of the police cars parked outside filled the room even through the rain. Spenser choked on his beer before twisting to watch Mary talk to the police. The rain was pounding down; he couldn't hear what they were saying. But he saw her go pale, until the only color in her face came from those dancing lights. He saw her clutch her chest, eyes wide and childlike and filled with a painful confusion.

He saw her sink to her knees on the floor and start to sob as lightning split the sky in two and the world was reduced to the sound of thunder.

That was when he realized that something was truly wrong, and rose from his chair to find out what that little brat had done now.

It had been the rain. It had fallen so hard and so suddenly that the ground hadn't been prepared to absorb it all. There hadn't been enough to shift the body of a thirteen-year-old girl, but there had been enough to wash her blood down the hillside in a crimson ribbon, one that held together despite all odds, until it swirled into the gutter near a stopped police car. Even then, it might have been missed, had the junior of the two policemen not been returning to the vehicle after writing a speeding ticket for a woman who just wanted to get home, out of the storm.

He had stopped when he saw the blood, looking at it speculatively. Odds were that it belonged to some animal, a cat-killed bird or a rabbit with its leg in a snare. But the storm had been a vicious one, and odds weren't enough to justify potentially leaving someone out there when they were hurt and in need of assistance. He had knocked on the police car window. He had shown his partner the blood. Together, the two of them had gone up the hillside, flashlights in hand, hoping that they wouldn't find anything worth getting wet over.

They had found a little girl.

The world transforms when a child dies. As the officers attempted to comfort Lou's sobbing mother, the coroners were removing her body from the hillside, where the rain had already washed away any forensic evidence—not that they were really thinking of this as a murder. The story was too easy to see, written in broken bone and shattered glass. A terrible accident, a terrible fall, the sort of thing that could happen to anyone, if they ran down the wrong hillside in the rain. She was very small. She would never get any bigger.

As Spenser demanded proof that the little girl they had found was his stepdaughter, Lou was being bundled into the back of an ambulance, which drove through town with its flashers off, obeying all the traffic laws. There was no need to use the siren. There was nothing there in need of saving.

As the officers handcuffed Spenser for taking a swing at them, Lou was being transferred into the freezer at the county morgue. She would be shown to her mother later, after one of the medical examiners had removed the larger pieces of glass from her chest. Just enough so that the sheet would lie flat, and Mary wouldn't have to confront the story told by those planes and angles, that impossible geometry of loss.

As Mary and Spenser were being loaded into separate police cars for the ride across town—one as grieving mother, the other as drunken assailant—Lou was alone.

Lou opened her eyes, and they were filled with firefly lightning. Somewhere, thunder rolled.

"What do you mean, you lost the body?" The officer tried to keep his voice low as he spoke with the medical examiner. He couldn't keep himself from glancing back to where Mary sat on a hard plastic chair, folded nearly double in her grief. Spenser was elsewhere, being given a stern warning. They weren't going to book the man. Not when his stepdaughter had just died; not when his wife needed him so badly.

And besides, there were other things to worry about.

"I've called the crew that brought her in; I'm sure they just put her in the wrong drawer." The medical examiner held up her hands, expression baffled. "Don't shoot the messenger. We're looking for her now."

"I have her parents waiting to identify the body," snapped the officer. A little too loudly: Mary's head came up, eyes questing in his direction. He hunched his shoulders, turning partially away. "We need to be sure. The ID was made from a library card in her pocket, and that's not sufficient."

"Look, we're doing everything we can," said the medical examiner. "You have to give us time to figure out where she is."

"This is a little girl we're talking about here," he said. "Find her."

"I will," she said.

They didn't.

By the time they sent Mary home—wrung out and exhausted from her crying, with Spenser standing like a sullen shadow by her side—they had turned the entire building upside down repeatedly, only to find no trace of the thirteen-year-old girl who had been found on the hillside. Lou was, quite simply, gone.

The sky was bruised black and silent, unmoving. The rain had stopped somewhere between the cruiser's leaving the police station and pulling up in front of Mary and Spenser's home. The streets remained empty; no one wanted to risk being caught in another torrential downpour. Both of them had been silent for the entire drive, Mary sunk deep into confused grief that was beginning to mingle with denial, Spenser dwelling on the way he'd been treated. By the time the police dropped them off and drove away, he was a powder keg, ready to explode.

Mary dug for her keys as she stepped onto the porch. Spenser tried the doorknob. The door swung open. That was the spark that he'd been waiting for.

"Well, would you look at that," he said in a wondering tone. He prodded the door with his finger. It swung open wider. "Some dumb bitch didn't lock the door. Let's go in and see what's worth stealing, huh? I bet we can clean these dummies out before they get back. What do you think, Mary?"

"Please, Spenser, not right now," she said, voice little more than a moan. "I'm sorry I didn't lock it, but no one was out in this storm. No one except for . . . except for . . ." She began crying again. She stopped after shedding only a few tears. There just wasn't that much moisture left inside of her.

"We don't even know if those police were telling the truth," scoffed Spenser. "It could have been someone else's kid. It could have been a fucked-up prank. Who knows what these cops get up to when nobody's keeping an eye on them? Crooks, the whole lot of them. We should sue the bastards."

Mary stared at him, eyes wide and wet and uncomprehending.

"What are you saying?" she whispered. "Are you saying that they lied? They lied about my Louise?" Her daughter's full name fit oddly in her mouth. She used it so rarely, usually when the girl was in trouble. Lou had been her name since the day she was born, and it should have been her name now, on the night she'd . . . that she had . . .

"I'm saying the police twist the truth to suit themselves," said Spenser. He seemed oblivious to the fact that they were still standing on the porch, exposed to the night air: he had his teeth in something that would allow him to work off some of his aggression, and he wasn't letting go. "She's a pretty thing. Maybe they couldn't find her because they're the ones who snatched her, and she'll show up in the morgue when she's good and used—"

Her palm caught him across the cheek, rocking his head back more from surprise than from the actual pain of impact. Mary squealed and snatched her hand to her chest, cradling it there like an animal with an injured paw. Spenser's eyes went wide. Then, slowly, his eyes narrowed, the color flaring up in his cheeks like a flame.

"Did you lay a hand on me, you little bitch?" The question was calm. The swing that accompanied it was not. His fist hit Mary in the eye, sending her crashing to the floor, where she huddled, sobbing. She was halfway inside the house, her feet still on the porch, her torso on the hallway floor.

"Cow," he said, and kicked her casually as he stepped over her body and left her where she lay. Mary didn't try to move. She stayed where she was, and cried, and waited for the long, dark night to end.

The mud squished between Lou's toes as she walked, black and viscous and sticky. She looked down at it and frowned, trying to remember why it mattered. A piece of glass caught her eye, protruding from the left side of her chest. She grasped it firmly and yanked it out of her body with a wet sucking sound, very similar to what her feet made every time she took a step. The edges sliced her fingers, creating long, bloodless cuts. She looked at the glass for a moment, dispassionately, before she threw it aside and kept on walking.

She had been walking for miles now. Hours, even, across the city and down the rain-soaked sidewalks until she had reached the edge of the fields that extended behind her housing development. Then she had left the sidewalks behind, understanding on some level—even if it was a blurred, distorted one, still tangled with the sound of distant thunder—that she didn't want to answer any questions about where she was going, or why she wasn't wearing shoes, or why there was so much blood on the front of her dress.

(Why *was* there so much blood? Why didn't she bleed when she pulled the glass out of her body? Every time she'd cut herself before, there had been blood, but now there was only a faint tugging sensation and a momentary light, like one of the fireflies she'd lost in the storm was hiding somewhere in her skin.)

The clouds were starting to clear, and the stars were coming out. They looked like fireflies hanging up there in the black. Lou walked on. She was going home. She knew that much. No matter how confused she was, no matter what else was going on, she was going home. She just had to . . . she just had to make it home.

Fireflies began to drift up from the grass at her feet, swirling around her in a great, silent cloud. Lou stopped walking and held out her hands. The fireflies landed on her palms, covering them, until she could feel the weight of a thousand pinprick feet pushing down on her.

"Hello," said Lou.

The fireflies took flight. They swirled around her, and it was like standing in the middle of a special effect, like something from a Disney movie, the moment where the servant girl becomes a princess or learns that she's been a princess all along. Lou laughed out loud, and then gasped as the sound knocked something loose inside of her, some small, essential scab on her soul.

She remembered lightning splitting the sky.

She remembered the feeling of her ankle breaking.

She remembered—

"Who are you?" The man who appeared out of the cloud of fire-flies was tall and thin and oddly pale, seeming to shine with the same soft, internal light as the fireflies. Most of them seemed to have vanished when he came; the few that remained alighted on his hair and shoulders, glowing dimly. "What are you doing out here, all alone? Where are your parents?"

"I'm Lou," she said. Speaking made the glass in her chest tug oddly. She pulled out another shard. This one was longer than the others, and there was actual blood at the tip, gleaming when the light from the fireflies touched it. She threw it thoughtlessly aside. "I'm out here because out here is between me and where I live. My daddy's dead. My mom's at home. She's probably real worried by now. I'm going home to her."

The man leaned a little closer and sniffed at her. Lou blinked at him.

"I don't smell bad," she said.

"Child, you smell *dead*," he replied. "Do you remember what happened to you?"

"I was catching fireflies and I fell down."

The man sighed. It was a deep, hollow sound. "The adze choose who they will, and I have no recourse but to call you kin. You are my sister, child, and you are not going home, because home will no longer have you."

Lou frowned. "I *am* going home. I promised."

"And what will you do when you get there? Will you fly to your mother's arms and cover her with kisses? You, whose breath smells of the grave and whose body will not bleed?" He leaned closer to her. "You will not be welcome there. You will not be welcome any-where."

"I'll be welcome," said Lou. "I have to go home."

He sighed again. "Very well, then, sister. Let me show you the way." He offered her his hand. After a moment's hesitation, Lou took it.

The man exploded into fireflies.

So did she.

The flight across the fields was dizzyingly fast and filtered through a hundred pairs of eyes. It was like her entire body had learned to see and was looking at the world for the first time. Lou would have laughed with delight, but she no longer had lungs or a throat to laugh with; all the parts of her were strange, from her uncounted wings to her bristling legs. She flew, and the sky was hers, and no one was ever going to take it away from her again.

There were words in the sky, in the buzz of wings and the flash of glittering bodies. *The adze are older than this nation, if not older than this land; we came when the settlers came, nestled in the holds of their ships, hidden in the shapes of their slaves. You would not have known us, child, but you would have felt our touch all the same.*

Memories then, memories that were not hers, or had not been until this moment, for the swarm was a single organism, and what the man knew, she knew also: what he had seen, she saw, broken and reassembled through so many swarms just like this one, over so many hot summer nights.

Saw the children who were found dead by their mothers, bloodless and unmoving.

Saw the women who were burned as witches while the adze walked free, indistinguishable from anyone else.

Saw the *bukwus* of this new world meeting the vampires the Europeans had brought with them, and later, the *jiangshi* of the Chinese and the *patasola* of the South Americans. The night was a bloodbath, and only the fact that creatures who did not breathe moved slow and lived long kept the world from being washed red. Through all of this moved the adze, who reproduced only rarely and fed only when the summer sky was dark with storms and the trees were ripe with fireflies.

Saw herself running along the creek toward the place where the swarm had paused. Lou felt more than heard her new companion's understanding: he had not realized before that she and the girl who had chased his component fireflies all through the summer were one and the same.

But why? she asked. *My face is still my face.*

You were alive before, and now you are not, he replied. *That which is living can never truly resemble that which is dead. Something is lost.*

Lou was silent.

Ah, child. Something is gained; something is always gained. Only believe me, and let us go home.

The swarm spiraled downward, toward the backyard of the house where she had lived all the short years of her life.

Too short. The fireflies swirled a few feet above the ground, shaping themselves into two human figures. The holes in Lou's dress were gone, and the bloodstains were gone as well; she no longer needed them. The man—whose name she still did not know— watched impassively as she ran for the back door. She was going home. It was a thing that could happen only once, and so he waited, allowing her to have her moment.

He could wait until the screams began.

Lou tested the back door and, finding it unlocked, let herself inside. The thought that she might need permission to enter never crossed her mind. She wasn't a *vampire*, after all. She was just . . . she was just a dead girl, coming home to the place where she would always be welcome. If her flesh was bloodless and filled with light, what did that matter? This was her place. This would always be her place. Her father had promised her that, before he died and left her and her mother alone.

She walked through the kitchen to the front room. The door was closed, but she could taste violence in the air, a bitter sense-memory of the moment when her mother struck Spenser and Spenser struck her mother. There was something else there as well, a hot, stormy scent, like bright copper pennies. She walked forward, toward the shape of Spenser sitting motionless in his chair. It was time to tell him why he didn't belong here. Then he would go away, and it would just be her and her mother and the fireflies. Surely her mother would welcome the fireflies. Surely her mother wouldn't mind when they tangled themselves together and became a man. Surely.

Lou stopped when she reached Spenser's chair, blinking as she looked at him. He was red all over. He had always been a florid man, but this was something different, this was scarlet and carmine and the slow darkness of burgundy. This was blood, everywhere blood, so much blood, all of it spreading from the knife that was buried in the center of his chest. She reached out and touched the handle. It was stuck in so deep that she didn't think she could ever pull it loose.

It was disappointing, to realize that she wasn't going to kill him. To realize that someone else got there first and took the chance away from her.

"Mom?" She turned to look at the stairs. The hot storm smell continued up the stairs, up to the bedroom her mother had shared with her father, once, before the world changed. "Are you there?"

No one answered. Lou began to climb the stairs, slowly at first, and then faster, and faster, until she was taking them three at a time.

Silence.

Mary was not a religious person. If ever she had been, that urge had died the moment the state troopers came to her door and said, "*There's been an accident,*" and began the process of putting the best man she'd ever known into the ground. But she sat on the floor of her bedroom, looking at her bloody hands, and prayed for an angel to come and take this horrible night away. Her little girl was dead, and her body was lost. Her second husband—who hadn't been a good man, not for one moment, but he had never claimed to be, and for all his faults, had never lied to her—was dead, by her hand. She needed a miracle. She needed the world to be kind.

"Mom?"

Mary raised her head and beheld her miracle.

To anyone else, Lou might still have looked like a normal little girl. To her mother, who knew her better than anyone in the world, she was a stranger. Her flesh was too smooth, too pale, and glowed with a soft inner light that wasn't human in the least. When she spoke, her lips moved around a mouthful of teeth that were too long and too sharp, designed to pierce flesh.

"I came home, Mom," said Lou. She stepped into the room. "I came home."

Mary made a small keening noise.

"Did you kill Spenser? I would've done it for you. You made an awful mess."

Mary pressed herself back against the bed.

Lou looked at the blood on her mother's hands. "I can clean that up for you," she said. "I'm so hungry. I didn't know I would be this hungry."

Mary's scream was a bolt of lightning lashing through the summer night. In the bedroom, Lou's body exploded into fireflies. In the backyard, the man who no longer needed a name nodded to himself and dissolved into a sparkling cloud of insects that flew through the open door to join the feast that was beginning upstairs.

After the lightning, the thunder.

ON THE DARK SIDE OF SUNLIGHT BASIN

MICHAEL KORYTA

It was in the year before the great fire, the one that consumed half of Yellowstone and turned the nation's eyes toward Montana and Wyoming, when Joe took the man named Medoc from California out hunting. They were after bighorn sheep, and what Medoc had been told—that Joe was the best guide in the area and also the cheapest, because he didn't work for an outfitter—was true enough, and what Medoc promised—cash on the barrelhead—was good enough.

They'd been out for two days without any luck when the wind shifted and began to blow hard out of the north and Joe warned that snow was chasing it. That was no reason to call off the hunt, but by then he'd had plenty of time to learn that his Californian was softer than forgotten butter at a picnic and that the likelihood of their taking a bighorn in any conditions was slim. Joe had considered doing the shooting himself—he wasn't above that if it guaranteed the bonus that Medoc had promised—but the Californian was so slow and bumbling and so damn *loud* that he'd begun to think even his own odds were poor.

"Might get rough out here," he said, looking at Medoc in the flickering lantern light. "Shooting a white sheep in a curtain of driving snow? It's not easy."

Medoc was a tall, angular-faced man with a tendency toward nervous tremors—he'd spilled his water three times already on the trip while trying to free it from his pack—that wasn't inspiring any more confidence in his shooting ability. He seemed in pain, which made sense considering the shiny new boots he was wearing, probably fresh out of the box.

"We'll give it a try," he said. "I've got buddies at home who are going to have a field day with me if I show up empty-handed. I said I'd have a sheep above the fireplace, and I laid some bets on it."

Joe figured that his buddies were country club types and that they'd already taken plenty of money from Medoc in various bets over the years.

"Besides," Medoc said, "that's why I have you, right? To get me through the weather? You people, you're supposed to be the best."

You could add racism to the kindling pile that was burning within Joe as they wasted days out there without coming close to getting a kill. Medoc tossed offhand remarks about Indians around in a way that suggested he suspected Joe was either too greedy to care or too dumb to notice. The man seemed to think his money bought a lot more than guiding expertise.

"The best," Joe agreed, and then he unzipped the fly of his tent. "We'll keep at it, then."

Before he slept, Joe vowed that he'd walk the man into the ground the next day.

The snow blew in around dawn, and they drank coffee standing up. Joe ate oatmeal; Medoc declined, saying he wanted to get moving. Joe was happy to oblige.

They'd been hiking for five hours and the pace had slowed to a crawl as Medoc stopped to apply moleskin bandages to the various blisters he was gathering. The flesh on his feet was as white as the snow he sat in as he awkwardly applied the bandages and Joe stood and watched.

"You want to help me, or you just gonna stand there, Tonto?"

Joe didn't answer this immediately. He spat into the snow and looked north and saw the craggy face of mountains that he knew held no sheep. They'd have moved down and east by now, and the mountains to the north were lined with abandoned old mines and sheer rock faces. It was difficult climbing in good weather, and in the snow it would be hell. He pointed at them.

"We hurry, we find sheep up there," he said, trying his best to give Medoc the expressionless face he seemed to desire in his guide. For the first time on the hunt, Joe was enjoying himself.

"We damn well better," Medoc said, and then he pulled his long hunting sock on in such a fashion that it promptly peeled the moleskin off his foot and bunched it up near the toes.

Joe turned back into the wind to hide his smile.

They never should have seen a sheep. The point was to make Medoc suffer, and so not only was Joe leading him toward an area he never would have hunted on his own, but he was paying no real attention to the possibility of an encounter. There was a stream crossing to be done before they reached the base of the mountain and began to climb, and he was eyeing the water and trying to determine the deepest spot to cross, one that would guarantee Medoc would fall on his ass and get soaked from head to toe, when the black wolf appeared out of the snow.

It was big, bigger than most Joe had ever seen, in fact, big enough that he slung his rifle around and let his hand drift toward the trigger even though he did not fear wolves and knew well that they wished to avoid him if at all possible. Here, it was very possible.

The wolf lingered, though, watching them through the snow, and behind Joe, Medoc came stumbling up, out of breath and oblivious to the grand animal ahead of them. Joe was just about to call his attention to it when the wolf broke and ran, and Joe followed him with his eyes only, his body motionless, and then he saw the second wolf, this one more gray than black, and then he saw the kill.

The bighorn was down just on the other side of the stream, and the gray wolf was covered with blood, her fur stained ruby red from the muzzle all the way through the chest. A third wolf flitted away and vanished into the snow, more troubled by the human presence than the other two seemed to be.

"I need a break. These damned boots . . ." Medoc fell silent for a few seconds, staring ahead, and then said, "Holy *shit*!"

Joe was silent, watching the wolves in wonder. He'd always felt closer to them than to most of the animals he encountered in these mountains. The black wolf in particular was inspiring. He was standing there staring at them, his breath fogging the air, when Medoc lifted his rifle.

"Don't," Joe said, but Medoc fired anyhow.

The shot never had a chance. The wolves were no more than sixty yards ahead, and with the caliber and scope Medoc was using, they should have been easy enough targets, but he was a terrible shot, and the first miss only rattled him into taking the next in an even greater hurry, the bullet winging harmlessly into the rocks just before Joe slapped him in the chest. It wasn't hard, designed only to get his attention and get him to stop firing, but Medoc still stumbled backward and fell on his ass in the snow and the muzzle of the rifle tracked right across Joe's face. If the Californian had accidentally fired, Joe would have been dead where he fell. A surge of real anger took him then.

"What in the fuck is the matter with you?"

"The fuck is the matter with *you*? I had a chance to shoot a wolf, and you—"

"First of all, you don't have a wolf tag, you idiot. You'd be poaching. Second, you didn't have a chance to shoot them, and you just proved it. If we ever *did* see a sheep that wasn't smart enough to clear out from all the damn noise you make, you'd still never hit it."

Medoc scrambled back to his feet, his face hot with anger. Joe was ready for a fight but realized once the man was upright that he was closer to tears than he was to blows. He looked away from Joe, out to the place where the wolves had abandoned their kill during the gunfire, and said, "Okay, Tonto. We're going to get that sheep."

"Like hell. And you call me that one more time, you'll be extracting your rifle from your small intestine."

"I came for a bighorn," Medoc said. "It's clear you aren't going to be able to find one, so I'm taking that one."

Joe had little use for the spiritual teachings of his people, but the feeling that washed over him then was carried from someplace far in the past.

"You don't mess around with a sheep that was killed by a wolf, Medoc. You just don't."

"They're not coming back for it. Not while we're here. And that's a damn nice rack."

"The rack doesn't matter. The wolves coming back don't matter, either. What I'm saying is, is . . ." He stuttered to a stop, unable to give voice to the fear.

"*What?*" Medoc said. "For the love of Christ, just say what you mean."

Joe didn't want to say what he meant. He didn't believe in it himself, had no intention of repeating the words to anyone, let alone to this white man, this arrogant prick of a white man who believed he could just buy someone like Joe, truly buy him. But still . . .

"You don't tamper with a sheep that's been killed by a wolf," he said. "It's the way I was raised, understand? If you do . . ." He fought for the right words, and for an instant he thought he saw the gray wolf again, the one with the ruby-colored stains on her muzzle. "If you do, you run a risk. Those sheep, they've been marked. And not for us, okay? Not for mankind. You tamper with them, and you're . . . you're going to want blood."

"Want blood?" Medoc's face was incredulous.

"Yes. Not just *want* it, but *need* it. You'll fear the sun even though it gives life. You'll crave darkness and you'll crave blood and you'll fear the sun and you'll—"

When Medoc started laughing, it was the loudest sound he'd made on the entire hunt. Seemed louder than his gunshots even, which had scared the wolves away.

"Goddamn," he said. "I got myself the real deal, don't I? I wanted an Indian guide because it would tell well, back home. It would tell better than any other story. But this? This is beautiful. You're saying I'll turn into a vampire? That the idea?"

"That's a white man's term."

"My apologies," Medoc said, making a fake bow. "But is it the idea?"

"Yes," Joe said. "It's the idea. You'd do well to keep on this side of the stream. And one of those wolves, the one you *didn't* see, it was a black wolf, and I think that means worse things, I think that means—"

"Christ," Medoc said, and laughed again. "I don't have time for this, but once I get that sheep's head, I'll listen to whatever you want to tell me, provided there's a fire and some booze to go along with it."

"Don't," Joe said, grabbing his arm as the taller man started for the stream. "You don't understand. It's not just about the wolves. It's . . ."

"What?"

Joe searched for words. His own breath was coming faster now.

"Let's go," he said. "Leave that one be, and I'll get you another. I swear it."

"What's your problem? I'm claiming something I *found*. No game warden is going to give a shit if—"

"It's not the wardens, and it's not the wolves."

"Then *what* is the *problem*?"

Joe licked ice off his lips. "It's bad luck," he said. "Beyond bad luck."

"You've got to be shitting me. The vampire crap is funny, but bad luck? No." Medoc stepped away from him and into the stream, nearly losing his balance again. He recovered, though, and began to wade toward the carcass with the curling horns and the wash of blood in the snow. Joe watched him and recalled the way the wolf had looked, dressed in blood, then remembered a voice that may have belonged to his grandfather or maybe to someone else's grandfather, he couldn't specify, knew only that it was *there* echoing around in his brain and his heart, and he turned and walked away from the stream.

"Where in the hell are you going?"

Joe didn't answer. He just kept on walking. He still had his rifle in his hands. Medoc's next call to him was a scream of outrage.

"I will see you put in jail for this, you son of a bitch! You can't walk away from me. I *paid* you!"

Joe walked on in silence, and when he was a few hundred yards away and no more screams had come, he turned back to see if Medoc had given up and decided to follow.

The path behind him was empty; his tracks were filling swiftly with snow.

He dropped to one knee and lifted the rifle and looked through the scope. Medoc was kneeling in the snow beside the bighorn, and he had his skinning knife out and was awkwardly trying to sever the dead animal's head. He wasn't any more skilled with the knife than he was with the rifle, and he kept snagging it against the sheep's spinal cord. He gave one furious tug and then the knife skittered off the bone, slid upward, and razored through his gloved hand. Fresh, hot blood spilled into the snow, joining the bighorn's.

"Bad luck," Joe whispered, still watching through the scope as Medoc screamed in pain and writhed.

But it was more than bad luck, and he knew it. Joe straightened, turned his back on the scene, and hurried into the snow, well aware that darkness fell fast here and he wanted to be far from the kill scene when it did. The wind had died down and all he could hear in the stillness was his own breathing and the whispering voice of a grandfather that might have once been his.

They had a good time taking photographs of the new-growth forest where nearly thirty years earlier an incredible forest fire had roared through Yellowstone, but Kristen began to joke that their trip was cursed when they ran out of gas at an overlook above the Sunlight Basin called Dead Indian Pass. Jim was defensive, having insisted that they could make it through after leaving Cody without stopping for a refill, but he still had to smile at her incessant stream of snark as they waited hopefully for the return of a passerby in a Chevy pickup who had accepted fifty dollars in cash and promised to return with a gas can. There was no guarantee that he wouldn't pocket the fifty, laugh at the tourists, and continue on his way, but it was the best option Jim had found.

"He'll come back for us," he told Kristen.

"I *know* he will. He'll come back and tell us that there was no gas station ahead for miles, but he's happy to report that there's a hotel with, like, ten rooms in the whole place. And he'll take us down there so we can sleep for the night in comfort. When we check in, we'll notice that he seems to know the owner. It'll be subtle, you know, just a little bit of eye contact, but it will be enough. The game will be in play then. And you know what the game is?"

He sighed and shook his head, trying not to smile.

"Cutting our heads off with a chain saw," she said, nodding. "Exactly. That is exactly right, babe."

There was the trembling roar of exhaust down the highway, and Jim turned and looked out and saw the Chevy returning.

"Here he is."

"When he mentions the motel—"

"I'll tell him that we have a tent," Jim said. "Got it."

The driver was as good as his word, handing over a five-gallon can of gas from an Exxon thirty miles up the highway, complete with a Post-it note that read "ha, ha, ha" signed by the wiseass who ran the gas station. He did not mention any motel, and even stayed until Jim had poured in the gasoline and proved that the car would start.

"Where y'all headed, anyhow? Cooke City, Silver Gate, Red Lodge?"

"Somewhere in the middle," Jim said.

"Ain't much in the middle. What are you after?"

"Pictures. I'm a photographer. We've been driving for close to two months now. Working on a project called *American Ghosts.*"

"American ghosts? You think there's phantoms out here?"

Jim couldn't tell if the man's smile was good-natured or offended. He would have made a hell of a poker player.

"There are plenty of abandoned places, at least," Jim said. "Things that were once and are no more. From forests to towns. That's what I'm after."

That got a slow nod and no verbal response. For some reason— probably because the good old boy had provided him with gasoline on a lonely highway—Jim pressed on.

"There are supposed to be old copper and silver mines up in those mountains north of us. Abandoned equipment, gated entrances, and—"

"Adits," the stranger said.

"Pardon?"

"Those gate mine shafts? They're called adits. In mining, a tunnel goes straight through and comes out the other side. A shaft goes down, and a winze goes up. A horizontal entrance that goes no-where? That's an adit."

"Okay. Good to know. Anyhow, I was hoping to get some pic-tures of them in the right light. You know, right at dusk. When they look good and spooky."

Jim smiled, but it wasn't returned. The stranger looked out across the Sunlight Basin and when he spoke again, his eyes were some-place far away.

"They're spooky enough. Just be careful which ones you pick."

"Some held on private lands?" Jim asked, having run into that li-censing issue before.

The stranger swiveled his head back to Jim. "Maybe. But some are damned dangerous. There are gates up for a reason, you know."

"I don't intend to go inside of them. Just take some photos."

"All right," the stranger said. "Go have fun, kids. But next time, fill 'er up. Not everybody around here is as helpful as yours truly, and those mountains?" He waved a hand out over the basin. "They look mighty pretty in your pictures, I know, but they're not jokers, either. They're the real deal. You want to pay attention out here. I'm serious."

Jim felt a flush of embarrassment—he'd taken pictures in rugged areas all over the country, and to be talked to like a child was infuri-ating, but he couldn't argue, because the stranger was right. Jim had fucked up, and in different circumstances and different places, that could cost you. He settled for thanking him again and shaking his hand and then turned back to the car and Kristen's wide, mocking smile.

"How's that male ego feeling?" she said when he opened the door.

"Bruised and battered, but still kicking." He put the car into gear. Below them, the aptly named basin held all the light of the day, a tease that suggested there was no need to rush, but the surrounding mountains were already catching shadows. They needed to get a base camp up in a hurry, and then, if things went just right, they'd catch the abandoned mines at twilight.

Some part of Jim expected another delay—missing tent stakes, a broken bootlace, any further harbinger of bad luck—but they reached their intended campsite and had the tent up and the bear bag hung with daylight still lingering. Kristen laughed at him for placing the bear bag so far away, every bit of three hundred yards from the camp, dangling from a branch twenty feet in the air.

"Overkill?" she said.

"Say that now, but you'll thank me in the middle of the night when you hear something big rustling around here. I was talking to a wildlife photographer who saw *fifty-nine* grizzlies in one day in this mountain range."

"You're serious?" Some of the amusement was gone from her face.

"I can show you the pictures."

"No need." She held up a hand. "I'd rather not imagine them, thanks."

"Wolves, too. There are several wolf packs in this area. I watched a documentary before we came out. I think it was about the Druid pack, up closer to Yellowstone. But they're out here. It's not a fiction in this part of the world. You have to take precautions."

Jim looked up at the jagged peaks that guarded the western sky and saw that dark clouds were massing, the descending sunlight breaking through here and there in long, slim beams that caught the western-facing slope of the mountain at their backs perfectly. About halfway up, maybe five hundred feet, maybe a thousand, he could see the rusted remnants of an ancient ore catch basin. He removed his camera and lens cap and took a few test shots.

"It looks gorgeous," Kristen said.

It was more than gorgeous. The way those slim beams were illuminating the abandoned mine shafts created a sense of bridged worlds, a place where past and present lived with an odd, eerie connection. He could camp in this spot for a month and never see the same tricks of light and shadow.

"I'm going up," he said. "You want to stay here, maybe get the cookstove going, and—"

"Did you really just ask the woman to stay back and cook?" Kristen said, mock horror in her voice.

"My apologies. If you'd rather scramble up those rocks and break your ankle, you're more than welcome to join me."

"Chivalry at last."

It was hard climbing—he hadn't been wrong with the word choice of *scramble*. The slope was steep enough that you had to work sideways at points and keep good momentum, leaning against the mountain at all times to avoid sliding right back down it. By the time they reached the first of the abandoned sites, both of them were covered in dust and dirt and sweat, breathing heavily. Out over the western range, the first thunder rumbled, and the wind that had blown all day had gone flat, the basin beneath them still and silent.

"We're pushing it," Jim said, but those shafts of light were still dappling the mountainside, and he had the chance he'd come for. In the gathering dusk, the rusted remains of time gone by seemed all the more haunting.

He shot a fast series of pictures, working to capture those light bridges, knowing that they wouldn't last long, and then moved in for close-ups of the entrance. Sorry, the *adit*. He'd never heard the term before, but the old-timer had been sure enough about it.

"How long ago were these active?" Kristen asked. She had tied her shoulder-length blond hair back and he could see trails along her neck where sweat had wiped the dust clean. His own shirt was plastered to his back. It was going to be ripe inside the tent tonight.

"The thirties, I think. Late twenties, early thirties. A last-gasp effort. No gold, and whatever copper ore they found was costly and difficult to remove."

"So they just . . . left." She moved toward the gate while he paused to change lenses, and his head was down, turned from her, when she gave an abrupt, pained shout. "*Shit!*"

"What happened?" He looked up to see her holding her right hand under her armpit, fat red drops of blood falling into the dust.

"Those bars are *sharp*. I barely grazed it, but it cut me pretty well." She held up her hand, and the gash down the center of her palm was long and bright with blood. Kristen had a high pain threshold, didn't like to show when she was hurting, but at the sight of this cut, she winced and turned her face away.

"That's going to need stitches," Jim said, coming closer and eyeing the rusty bars. "And I sure as hell hope your tetanus shot is up to date."

"It is. But I'll need to clean this out and get some butterfly bandages on it. We've got those, right?"

"In the kit. Come on, let's head down."

"No, no. Finish your work. We didn't hike all the way up here to waste it on a little blood." Her palm was pooling with it, and she gave her hand a shake, flung the blood through the bars of the adit, dappling the dusty rocks beyond. "I'll be fine. Finish your work."

"We should stick together," he said, thinking of the stranger who'd helped them with the gas, of that warning that these mountains were the real deal.

"The tent is *right there*," Kristen said, gesturing with her uninjured hand. And it was. A long way down, but plainly visible.

"Okay," he said. "I'll finish up. But make sure you don't clean that cut out near the tent. Walk down at least as far as the stream."

"You want me to crawl inside the bear bag tonight?" she said, a faint smile rising.

"This one is no joke," he said. "Bears can smell blood at unbelievable distances. I'm serious, Kristen."

She lifted her bleeding hand, palm out, and gave a solemn nod. "I swear to uphold the bear-country accords, captain."

He watched as she began to descend and then thunder boomed again, closer now, and he knew that he was running out of daylight. He finished the lens swap and then turned back to the mine, thinking that her blood would add a nice, creepy touch to an already creepy spot.

The lens showed no blood inside the iron gate. Jim blinked and pulled his head away from the viewfinder. There was fresh blood, still damp, in the dust all around them, but he'd watched her shake her hand and send fat, wet drops of it flying inside the adit. He'd seen it happen. How had it dried so fast?

He walked closer to the gate, knelt, and stared.

The rocks just inside were dry and unstained.

"Losing my damned mind," he muttered, and then he turned and saw that the sun was descending. That meant going back down the slope in darkness. Kristen was nearing the base and approaching camp, surely leaving a trail of blood the whole way, and he cursed himself for not thinking to bring the first-aid kit up here with them.

You want to pay attention out here, the stranger had said, and still Jim had made a fundamental mistake. First with the gas, and now with the first-aid kit.

He hoped they were allowed a third strike.

Behind him, something rustled, and when he turned back, he lifted the camera as if it were a club, as if he'd have to defend himself. But there was nothing there except for silent rocks and wind-whipped dust, and he laughed uneasily at himself. Kristen had made one too many jokes about bad luck back at Dead Indian Pass, that was all. The bars of the adit were spaced far enough apart to allow a determined and thin man to slip through, maybe, but no bears were coming out of there.

Jim knelt beside a bloodstained rock and lifted the camera again. The last of the light bridges between worlds was fading fast, and he didn't want to miss it.

Her hand was throbbing by the time she reached the base of the slope, and Kristen had tears in her eyes and was glad that Jim wasn't there. The truth of the matter was that she was scared of the mountains, and she didn't want him to know that. In the six months they'd been dating, he'd made so many references to appreciating her willingness to join him in his outings that it had become a part of her identity, and she'd gone too far along with the ruse. Initially, she'd wanted to impress him; it was that simple. Spending time with Jim in bizarre locations sounded intriguing, and once she was out with him she didn't want to be a complainer, so she'd done her best to put up a brave front. Then they'd returned from a trip through the backwoods of Maine that had been absolutely terrible—she'd counted fifty-seven mosquito bites—and he'd spent an entire dinner party with friends bragging about how tough she was. Why she couldn't tell him the truth, she didn't know. It was childish, but there was something about spoiling the illusion he had that seemed like failure. She was a librarian, and while Kristen loved her job, she had to admit she grew tired of the jokes that came with the territory. Traveling with Jim had added something to her identity that she thought she enjoyed. Discovering the truth that it was merely a mask, a falsehood, had probably disappointed her more than it would him.

Then he'd proposed the Montana and Wyoming trip, showing her photographs of the old town and collapsed storefronts, and that had sounded okay, certainly no worse than Maine.

Until they arrived. The mountains unsettled her instantly. Kristen thought she had an understanding of them, but you couldn't truly appreciate the vastness and the isolation until you were out there in it. She'd turned unease into teasing, giving him a hard time and labeling the trip as jinxed, but she really *had* been scared by the idea of running out of gas on that lonely road, and she really *had* been scared of the strange man who'd accepted a fifty-dollar bill and promised to return with gasoline. All of her jokes about the horror-movie motel were actually born from a desperate desire to convince Jim that a hotel was the better option, at least tonight. The base camp that he found so beautiful, she found terrifying. There wasn't another soul in sight, and down there in the basin by the stream, the mountains quite literally surrounded them, looking imposing and hostile. You could scream your head off and there would be nobody to hear it. Now Kristen was bleeding, and all of his concern over the bears was lodged in her brain. She knew that he was right; bears *could* smell blood at a great distance, and she was leaving a trail of it all over the mountain, a trail that led directly back to the flimsy tent she was supposed to sleep in. Now, *that* was a joke; there'd be no sleep tonight, not for her at least.

The first-aid kit was strapped to the back of her pack, a bright red swatch against the dark green fabric. She pressed her aching palm against her stomach as she awkwardly freed the kit with her left hand, and then she set off toward the stream, trying to put as much distance between the blood and the tent as possible. She passed the bear bag and kept going, and now she could feel warm moisture on her belly as the blood soaked through her shirt and found her skin. She'd have to leave the shirt behind, too, and that was just perfect—the only way to give the Maine mosquitoes a run for their money was to wander around out here shirtless, at dusk, and by a stream.

She sat down on a wide, flat rock next to the water and wiped her eyes, cursing herself for both the tears and her irrational inability to just tell him how she felt and what she wanted.

When she got the iodine and butterfly bandages out, she allowed herself her first real look at the damage the bars had inflicted. The wound was bad, and it hurt worse because the metal had been corroded, making an unclean, jagged cut. Jim had been right; it was going to require stitches. It was also going to be damn hard to stop the bleeding because the cut ran down the center of her palm, so every time she moved her fingers the sheared skin would flex. She set to work cleaning the cut and applying the bandages. The blood darkened the center of the bandage instantly, no clotting being achieved yet. Kristen said, "Those pictures had better be fucking incredible, James."

She kept looking over her shoulder as she worked, expecting bears to descend one of the slopes at any moment. With the stream and all the towering boulders around it, the place looked exactly like the background of every photograph of a grizzly she'd ever seen. The whole valley looked like a grizzly condo village, easy real estate to sell to a ten-foot monster with razor-sharp claws. Perfect place to put a tent.

Once the bandages were on, she remained on the rock in the gathering dusk and kept her hand still and waited for the wound to clot as best as possible, not wanting to carry the scent of fresh blood into her sleeping bag later. Taking deep breaths and letting the tears dry, she tried to calm herself so that when Jim returned he wouldn't have any indication of the meltdown she'd had out here.

Take in the beauty, she instructed herself. *Not the danger, just the beauty.*

And it *was* a beautiful spot. The mountains rising on all sides were majestic, but the valley in the center was truly special, lush and green and painted with golden light that made the stream twinkle and glitter. She listened to the water and felt her breathing slow and some level of peace return. The stream was absolutely gorgeous. Sure, it seemed to be begging for a few bears in the evening light, but other than that it was . . .

She leaned forward on the rock and strained her eyes, trying to simultaneously see clearer and deny the image her eyes had found.

There was an elk carcass in the water, resting high, propped up on a submerged boulder. She'd spotted the antlers first, but now she could make out the side of its head and part of the gutted body. Whatever had killed the elk was sure to return for it, and when it did, filled with hunger and bloodlust and territorial aggression, it would discover the place where Jim and Kristen had helpfully pitched their tent not even fifty yards away, her wilderness-photographer boyfriend so focused on the damn mountain behind them that he'd missed the elk kill entirely.

"Jim!" she shouted, but her echo died swiftly and she knew there was no way he could hear her. She got to her feet, stumbling and swearing, and started back for him, her bloody hand now the least of her concerns. They needed to get the hell away from this campsite, and do it before dusk.

Far away and halfway up the slope, the mountain was turning itself over to blackness and she could see Jim working right on the shadow line, still visible but almost lost. She had to squint to find him. The fading light played tricks on her eyes; at times she could swear there were two silhouettes instead of one—Jim's and a much taller, thinner version.

There were four mine shafts on the slope, and Jim shot all of them in the fading light, moving as fast as possible, feeling the sort of electric thrill you got when you knew you were getting both quality photographs and special ones because the conditions might never be the same. That was the point, the whole goal—capture the world as it was once but would not be again tomorrow. The mines had stood here for decades, and the sun rose and set every day, but you could sit here for twenty years and not get the same unique play of the dwindling beams of light on those ancient doors.

He'd gone up the slope and circled back down as the light forced him lower, and by the time he got back to the original adit, it was three-quarters in darkness. He decided to take one last series and then head down the mountain. He lifted the camera to his eye, moved his hand toward the lens, and then dropped the camera into the rocks and shouted.

There was a man inside the mine.

"Sorry!" the stranger said. "My goodness, you startle easily."

"*Jesus Christ,*" Jim said, reaching down for the camera with trembling hands. "I startle easily? What in the hell are you doing in there?"

"I'd expect we have similar interests. Are you not here for the mines?"

"I'm here to take pictures of them, not stand in them in the dark."

The man smiled—maybe. It was damn hard to tell, because his face was obscured by darkness, the only remaining sunlight playing over his feet and lower legs. His boots were old and worn. He was a tall man, and a thin one, but even in the dark, Jim had a sense that he was strong. It was a strange feeling, a certainty without any evidence to back it up.

"How in the hell did you even get in there?" Jim said.

"Oh, these gates aren't as secure as they look."

"Well, they're damn dangerous, I can tell you that. My girlfriend cut her hand pretty bad right where you're standing."

He thought of the blood then, of the last series of photos he'd taken in this place. The blood that had been there and then gone. He took a few steps away, making a show of looking at the camera to inspect it for damage. Really, he just wanted to clear some space between him and the tall man. The camera looked to be fine, some nicks and dirt on the body, but the lens intact.

"You'd better have a good flashlight," Jim said. "It's not going to be easy walking down that slope in the dark."

"Oh, I'm familiar with the terrain."

The man hadn't moved, was still just standing there on the other side of the bars, but there was an odd quality of bridling energy to him, like a racehorse waiting for the gate to go up. Jim couldn't see how he'd possibly gotten in there to begin with—the bars had seemed solid to him, and the lock was still in place—but he didn't want to linger to find out, either. There was something off about the guy, and for the first time, Jim was thinking that a motel sounded pretty nice tonight. Hell, they could leave the tent where it was. The hike back to the car would be a dark one, but they had flashlights and headlamps and it was not a long stretch. The cut on Kristen's hand would require attention anyhow. He was certain she wouldn't object to the idea of a night in a bed instead of a sleeping bag.

"Well, take care," Jim said. "Don't spook too many more tourists— you're going to give someone a heart attack eventually."

The tall man laughed. It was a strange, keening sound and drove Jim farther away. He glanced back once, and all he could see now were the tops of the man's boots, those torn leather flaps, covered with dust. Other than the boots, his silhouette was framed in blackness behind the bars. The image froze Jim.

That's pretty damn good, he thought. *That is, in fact, some supremely spooky shit.*

He decided he'd take just a few more pictures.

Leaning against the slope, braced on one knee, he lifted the camera, adjusted the zoom, and began to shoot. If the tall man disliked having his picture taken, or wanted to know the reason for it, he didn't give voice to the concerns. He didn't speak at all. Behind them the sun dropped that last fraction, and the frayed leather of the boots fell to darkness.

The man moved then, and Jim straightened, prepared to apologize and explain why he'd paused to take the pictures, but by the time he looked up, the tall man was already halfway through the gate. He hadn't opened it from the inside somehow, as Jim had expected—he simply slammed his torso between the bars and, astonishingly, managed to get his upper body through. He was snagged at the waist; it looked like he was caught in a trap, and Jim had a momentary, if unsettled, thought that perhaps he should offer to help when the man turned his face back to Jim's and smiled in the darkness.

His mouth would have been the envy of any grizzly or wolf in the valley. Long canines and twin rows of razor-sharp incisors. He braced both hands on the bars, the same bars that had lacerated Kristen's flesh, and then slammed forward again, and this time he drove his hips through the impossibly narrow gap and then he was free and facing Jim on the dark mountainside with no more than ten feet between them.

Jim screamed then, a scream that he didn't know he was capable of making, but it ended fast. The man covered the distance in a single, staggeringly fast bound and then his hands were on Jim's shoulders, his fingers strong as steel bands, and then they were both down and rolling on the loose scree and it was maybe another fifteen feet of terrifying, chaotic slide, the dark world spinning around them, before his teeth found Jim's throat.

Kristen was halfway back to the tent when she heard the scream. The sound was so horrific that she matched it without even understanding its source, though she feared she did.

"Jim! Jim!"

She ran back along the streambed, the basin here still bathed in warm sunlight, but on the high slopes where he had been, there was nothing but darkness. She could hear noises up there, sounds of struggle, sounds of pain.

A bear, she thought with sickening certainty. He'd been caught by a grizzly, probably one returning for the elk in the stream.

She ran to the tent and fumbled out the bear-spray canister she'd purchased upon arrival in Wyoming, cursing herself for not carrying it this whole time, what good was it supposed to do her in the tent? There were no other weapons except for a small camp ax that Jim used for splitting firewood. She grabbed that, too, her bloody hand throbbing with pain, and then clicked one of the headlamps on and set off up the hill, screaming, trying to make enough noise to scare the grizzly away, hoping that it was not too late, that she would not be scaring it away from a corpse.

When the man skittered into view, she came to a stop so fast that her feet tangled and she fell to her knees in the rocks.

He was tall, maybe six-six, maybe more, and incredibly thin, wearing worn, tattered clothes. In the beam of the headlamp, his face appeared so pale that she thought she could see the outline of the bones beneath, like an X-ray. Except for the wet, dark splotches on his cheeks and chin. They looked black in the light, patches of fresh tar.

"Hello, dear," he said, and when he spoke she saw his teeth and the blood in his mouth, and the scream that came from her then was far beyond what she'd been able to offer before, far beyond any she knew could exist.

She stumbled backward and fell again, and this time the beam from the headlamp found Jim. He was sprawled in the rocks near the shadow line, his head resting at an odd angle, allowed to flop that far sideways only because most of the ligaments and muscle had been severed.

No scream came then. She stared at him in horror and when she spoke again her voice was soft, a child's whisper: "Jim." There was no question to it this time, no urgency, because his time of hearing her voice or responding to his own name was done forever.

Kristen didn't understand why the tall man hadn't come down after her. She was within killing range easily enough.

When she swiveled her head and found him again, he was pacing the rocks, his footwork effortless. Every now and then he'd make a bounding leap, covering ten feet as if it were as easy as hopping from stone to stone in a creek.

"You're still bleeding," he said, his back to her. "It hasn't dried yet. I can smell that. That's dangerous in these parts, darling. I'm unique, certainly, but there are animals who can smell it, too. Grizzlies, wolves. It was a foolish mistake to get a cut like that out here. Though I do appreciate the taste!"

He laughed, and the sound washed over her like a cold wind.

"Who are you?" she said. Her voice was trembling and choked with tears. He didn't seem to like the beam, shifting away from it and making a face of distaste, but he answered the question.

"Any matter of identity is really irrelevant in our current circumstance, don't you think?"

Again she could see the flashing teeth, and a word slid into her brain that didn't belong there: *vampire*. It should have been a foolish thought, laughable, and yet she accepted it with certainty in that moment. Out here the rules of the world had just changed; fiction had become fact with horrible speed.

"I'd be quite happy to speak with you," he continued. "More than you realize. Have you ever considered the prospect of living alone? Well, I suppose with the recent developments"—he waved dismissively at Jim's corpse—"you surely have to. But it is a lonesome part of the world at any rate, and in a lonesome lifestyle? The isolation is profound."

He paced as he spoke, making nervous, jittery movements with his head, glancing back over his shoulder as if expecting pursuit. He came no closer to her, though.

I'm still in the light, she thought. The low portion of the slope where she had fallen was still bright with sunlight, and the shadow line didn't begin for another ten feet.

This is real. He needs the darkness. That's not a myth, it's the truth.

The sunlight was why he was pacing with such impatience. He was bound to the slope.

But not for long. No, it won't be long now.

Kristen turned and looked at the angular cut in the mountains that filled the basin with light. She couldn't see the sun any longer, but the cut filtered through radiant, golden light, the odd trick of the basin that had given it its name. The legend, according to what Jim had told her, involved a pair of old prospectors lost in a dark fog when they'd ventured out into a valley where the angled cuts of the mountains made a perfect path for sunlight.

In the basin. Not up above.

She took another look at the tall man—*No, not a man, he is not a man and you know this*—and then began to descend the rocks and retreat farther into the light. If there had been any doubt at all left in her mind, it was erased with the howl of rage that came from above.

"It won't take long! Go on and run. But it's a little late in the day for that!"

When she glanced over her shoulder, she saw that he'd begun to run. His speed and balance were astonishing, allowing him to caper across the steep slope and loose rocks without pause, but all of his movements were lateral. He couldn't descend any farther or close the gap between them. It was like watching a furious dog on an electric fence, penned in by something invisible.

An electric fence stayed in place, though. The shadow line of deepening dusk would not.

She made it off the slope and retreated as far as the tent, then looked in all directions at the empty basin around her. There was no point in screaming for help; she was alone here, alone in a way she had never been before in her life. The valley was filled with golden light and the mountaintops were dark. She looked at her watch, saw that it was just past eight, and knew that sunset wasn't far off, maybe twenty minutes at best. Twenty minutes to figure out how to hold off the inevitable.

He hadn't been wrong about the impotence of running. The tent was three miles from the car, three miles over rugged terrain. Even at a dead sprint she wouldn't be able to cover that distance before darkness fell, and based upon the horrific display of agility and speed he was putting on up there on the rocks, it wouldn't take him long to overtake her.

What in the hell was left, then? The light was her protector, but the light was going to disappear. She thought numbly of every myth she remembered from movies and books and campfire stories. Wooden stakes, crosses, silver bullets. She could fashion a cross, but even in the movies that didn't seem to be reliable, and out here it seemed ludicrous. Didn't you need a priest, anyhow? She had no gun, no bullets of any sort, and she couldn't imagine there was anything made of silver in the tent. Even if there was, you had to *do* something with it. You couldn't just hold it in your hand and enjoy safety. As for stakes, the tent was pinned down with plenty of them, but they were made of aluminum. With the ax and a piece of firewood, she might be able to cut something, but she'd never be able to use it against him. That brief display of strength and agility he'd already offered was more than enough to remove any notion of contending with him physically.

What was left, then? Only the setting sun. She sat down beside the tent and began to cry softly, and up above her the vampire let out a high laugh that seemed to be more of an animal's sound than a human's. He could see her helplessness and her defeat and he was enjoying himself as the shadows lengthened and drew him closer. She had a vision of Jim's head again, that ungodly angle, and she began to shake as she cried. The laughter on the slope grew louder and more delighted.

It was that sound, the delight he was taking in her impotence, that brought her tears to a stop. If she was going to die, she didn't want to die helpless, sniveling with tears while waiting for the sun to set and for him to have his way with her. She tightened her hand around the handle of the ax and felt the pulse of warm blood in her palm. She could get him with the ax, at least. Make him hurt, if nothing else.

But don't they heal so fast? A little pain probably means nothing to him.

She thought again of the silver, and of the crosses and the wooden stakes. What about fire? She could build a fire. Was that of any use? She couldn't remember. She wasn't a fan of vampire stories, had always found them trite and silly, which was a terrible irony when you were about to be killed by one. She'd watched bad movies with teenage friends around Halloween, that was all. And she'd had to read *Dracula* for a college lit seminar, which she'd actually enjoyed. Stoker was talented, and there were some vivid scenes, certainly. The arrival of the ship, the *Demeter*, that one had stuck with her. She'd had nightmares of the captain lashed to the helm, in fact. At one point in her life, nightmares had seemed awful. Kristen had never really paused to appreciate the ability to wake from one before.

"I thought we were going to run!"

The gleeful shout came from the slope, and when she turned back to look at him again she saw that the lengthening shadows had allowed him to come almost all the way down into the basin and that he was in an odd crouch, like a catcher in a baseball game. No. Different from that. Like a wolf.

"Come on, dear!" he shouted. "Give me a run. These old legs could use the exercise!"

Kristen wondered what they would say about her and Jim when this was done. Would they take a look at the terrible wounds and announce a grizzly attack, go out looking to trap or poison or shoot a bear to settle the score for humanity? Would their bodies even be found, or would he take them away, up into those dark, ancient mines? The only thing she was sure of was that no one would know how it had happened.

She retreated from the tent as the sun faded, holding the camp ax and walking backward into a narrowing beam of light. Behind her the sound of the stream was soft and reassuring, the proverbial babbling brook, but the area just beyond it was already dark. The only portion of the basin remaining in full sunlight was the deep water in the center where the elk corpse rested.

No, no, no, she thought, but then behind her came a flapping and popping sound like a flag in a stiff breeze, and when she turned she saw that he'd crushed their tent, had leaped directly onto the center of the roof. He sat crouched amid the billowing orange fabric, laughing.

"Time is not your friend," he called to her, advancing with a casual, loping pace.

She stepped into the water, gasping at the temperature—it had been a warm day, but this stream was fed by snowmelt high on the mountains and could hold on to the cold even in the sun. On her second step, her foot found a slick rock and she nearly lost her balance and fell in the water. Behind her, the vampire howled with delighted laughter. She pushed forward, the water waist-deep now and the current strong. The sunlight had contracted to one final beam, allowing her a clear view of the elk's dead eye staring up at her. His throat was torn open, so much like Jim's, but the damage was even worse here. She could see that the chest cavity had been pulled apart, white bones protruding into the water, and that his insides had been devoured methodically, almost tidily. Maybe he hadn't fallen victim to a bear, after all. Maybe it had been wolves.

Another howl came from behind her, but this time the pleasure was gone, and the sound was pure rage. When she chanced a look back, she couldn't see the vampire where he belonged, at the farthest part of the shadow line. She located his silhouette some thirty feet behind the extended dark, saw that he was engaged in whirling, frantic pacing, the dog on the electric fence routine again. But this time the fence was down. He could come so much farther. Why wasn't he?

The water, she realized as she watched him. *He won't enter the water.*

He was streaking up and down the streambed with appalling speed, and here and there he would splash into the shallows and then retreat as if the water had nipped his heels. She thought again of *Dracula,* those scenes on the *Demeter,* the captain lashed to the wheel. *The Count, even if he takes the form of a bat, cannot cross the running water of his own volition, and so he cannot leave the ship,* Van Helsing had explained.

But that was a story. Nothing more.

Story or not, the rules seemed to hold. As full dark settled in the Sunlight Basin and all of Kristen's protection vanished, the tall man remained on the shore. He could cross from one side to the other, but only far upstream, in a place where high boulders met and whatever water there was flowed trapped beneath them. Out here in the middle of the depths, though, she was apparently safe. Eventually he stopped running along the streambed, either having given up on finding a way to cross or having burned off his frustration, and called to her again.

"Very good, dear. But you'll be cold soon. You'll be freezing soon enough if you don't get out of that water."

Soon enough was an understatement—she was already shivering, her skin covered in gooseflesh, her teeth chattering.

"Ask yourself if that's really better," he continued, his tone sympathetic now, almost soothing. "Is a slow, agonizing death really a victory for you? I wouldn't want that. Not if I could have a swift end."

He wasn't wrong—she would die here before sunrise. She'd suc-ceeded in keeping him at bay but only by trapping herself in the icy water. It was a warm-enough night by mountain standards, and if she got out now, she knew she would survive. Even if she stayed in longer, she knew where Jim had stowed emergency heat blankets and fire starters. She could endure the cold for a while and still sur-vive, but there was a time limit to that. Just as her nemesis had been forced to wait on the sunset, she would be forced to wait on the sun-rise, and that was far too long in the frigid water. Any attempt to move out of the stream would be an immediate sacrifice to him, though. With that unbelievable speed, he'd go upstream and cross the rocks and catch her on either side without difficulty. Her op-tions, then, were as he said: the slow death or the swift.

She didn't want to give herself up to him, though. Better to let the river take her, something natural and of this world. As the night drew on and he waited patiently and her shaking became more vio-lent, she remained in the water, trying to keep moving, trying to keep her blood circulating. It was becoming harder and harder to do, though. Simple motions seemed difficult. She stumbled on the slick rocks several times, and then finally she fell, but that was all right, because she landed in warmth. It took her a minute to realize its source—she was pressed against the dead elk.

She recoiled immediately, splashing back into the water and managing to grab hold of one of the boulders to avoid being pulled downstream. For a time she stayed there, letting the frigid water wash over her, and then she spoke aloud.

"There are no good options, Kristen."

It was the truest thing she had ever said. She let go of the rock then and splashed back to the elk and found its fur with her hands. When her fingers slid over a sheared bone, she felt a surge of bile in the back of her throat, but she choked it down and continued to ex-plore the carcass by touch.

The chest cavity had been ripped apart and spread wide. It was a massive bull elk, probably every bit of five feet tall at the shoulder and seven hundred pounds. Kristen was five feet nothing, although she claimed five-one for dignity, and one hundred and five pounds. Just one day ago, she'd been frustrated by her own diminutive size as she struggled to adjust backpack straps on her too-narrow shoulders. Now she felt her way around the jagged bones of the dead elk and was grateful for every midget joke she'd ever endured.

It would still be cold, but it would also be dry, and that was what mattered. The elk was so big and the boulders that had caught his carcass were so high that his body rested above the waterline. Much of his hide remained, too, and that would provide a windbreak. All that mattered was her core temperature, the thing that the water was robbing from her with every passing minute. The night air was warm, and if she could find her way into it and dry, she could live to see the sunrise.

"How are you faring, dear?" The voice came from the shore not far from her, maybe thirty feet away. "Chilly night, isn't it? And I'm here on dry land. I can't imagine it's very comfortable for you in that water. You do know that's fed from the snowmelt, correct? And last winter, goodness, so much snow. Down here in the basin, there was so much. Up on the peaks, where the river finds it source? Oh, there might have been twenty feet there. And glaciers, you know. There are still glaciers up on top. This is a very cold part of the world."

Kristen looked to the sky, which was a wash of clean, bright stars, more stars than she had ever seen anywhere else in the world. Unspoiled by light pollution and, tonight, unmarred even by clouds. It was going to get colder, on a clear, cloudless night like this. It was only going to get colder.

She pressed her tongue to the roof of her mouth to hold down the gag reflex as she extended her arms into the hollowed-out remains of the elk. Her hands slid over bone and slick flesh and other, softer things. Some of them seemed to move of their own accord. She nearly lost her nerve then, but she willed an image of Jim's throat back into her mind, and of the blood that had shone on the thin man's mouth, and then she ducked her head and pushed forward and now the smell caught her and she couldn't hold back on the gagging any longer. She kept going, though, wriggling forward, and eventually her feet were out and all of her was above the waterline.

She realized her mistake then; she should have gone feetfirst so that her head was closer to the opening and not trapped in this dark, dank horror. When she tried to turn, though, the elk's body started to slip, and she froze, terrified that it would slide free from the boulders and splash back into the water and take her downstream.

The carcass held in place, though. It rocked and tilted precariously but she kept her panic down and held her breath and did not move, and eventually the carcass settled in the boulders once more, still high and dry. Still stinking of death. There were maggots in the rotting flesh and she could feel them moving around her own, living flesh as if trying to ascertain a difference, perhaps wondering how something alive had merged with something dead. Around her the water rippled and burbled but she couldn't see much of it. There was a gash that had pierced the bull elk's hide just above where Kristen's left eye now rested, and the wound gave her a window to the stars.

The water dripped from her and she dried slowly, and the elk skin that remained stretched over the rib bones shielded her from the wind in a way that had no doubt been used by ancient people desperate for shelter in this very place before. She was still shivering, but she thought that was a good thing. It was when you stopped shivering that you had to worry. She wrapped herself as tightly together as possible and let the air dry her as she watched the stars.

When the sky began to lighten, she thought it was an illusion. Or madness. Over the course of the night, madness had begun to feel not just threatening but inevitable, and she knew that she would stay entombed in the remains of the elk forever. She actually shut her eyes against the graying sky so she could not be fooled, but after a time she had the sensation that things continued to brighten, and when she opened her eyes again the elk bones directly above her were glowing a pale pink.

It was morning.

She tried to slide out carefully, but she was stiff and numb and unable to move with any grace at all, and when the carcass began to slide she felt certain it would trap her and she would drown within it. The current kicked the dead elk sideways, though, and spilled her out into the stream, and she managed to catch a boulder with a hand so numb that the pain didn't register.

Above her, the sky was crimson.

She got her heels braced on the slick streambed and stumbled forward, only to be washed downstream several times and bounced between rocks before it was finally shallow enough for her to rise to her hands and knees. She crawled forward, out of the water and onto a gravel bar, and lay there for a long time, shivering and gasping, as the sun continued to rise over the mountains. When she lifted her head again, she saw him just in front of her.

He was sitting back on his heels on the rocks. The shadow line where the mountain blocked the rising sun and preserved the night into the day came up almost to his feet and those worn leather boots.

"How about that?" he said. His voice was low and sad. Kristen didn't respond. The daylight continued to encroach, and he shuffled backward, a thin silhouette in the shadows. Kristen got to her feet. It was a laborious and painful process, but she made it.

"I'll come back for you," she said.

"I wouldn't. Those old tunnels are deep and dark, my dear."

"Not deep enough. I'll find you."

"Perhaps. Until then? Well, if I wore a hat, I'd take it off to you. In all its millennia, I doubt this valley has ever seen anything quite like *that* before. What's your name, anyhow, dear? I'd like to remember you as more than a face."

"Kristen," she said. "And I meant what I said. I'll come back, and I'll kill you."

"Kristen. That's beautiful. I'll remember it. They just called me Medoc, usually. Do your homework, and I'm sure you'll find a few stories about me. Not the real ones, though. You'll read about what a rugged wilderness this is and how deadly the weather can turn. You'll read about the way I perished, probably explained by a guide who knew better but found it safer to tell lies so that he would not bear the burdens that come with telling the world a truth that it would like to forget. You'll read all of that, but unlike everyone else, you'll know the truth. After last night? You'll know a truth that is very difficult to live with."

"I'll live with it," she said.

He rose and cast a displeased glance at the peaks to the east, then bowed to her. In the gathering twilight not that many hours before, it would have been a mocking gesture before her impending execution. At dawn, it seemed to carry true respect. The thing who called himself Medoc began to make his way up the dark side of the mountain face and back toward the adit that led to the abandoned mine. There he sat on a high rock in the shadows as Kristen limped to the remnants of Jim's tent and pulled her wet clothes off and dry ones on and then fumbled out one of the emergency blankets and wrapped it around herself like a cape. By the time she was done, the crimson sun was fully visible over the peaks and the adit on the slope above her was, too, standing exposed and empty. She watched it for a few moments but nothing moved, and then she turned and began to limp through a mountain basin that glowed as if it held all the light of the world.

THE NEIGHBORS

SHERRILYN KENYON

"I think there's something wrong with the Thompsons." Jamie stepped back from the window to frown at his mom. "Have you seen them?"

"Not since they moved in a few months ago and Teresa gave me her number."

"But not since, right?"

With long blond hair and bright green eyes that matched his, his mom picked up his little sister's backpack and set it on the table near him. "Teresa said that her husband's an international antiques dealer. He travels a lot and keeps weird hours whenever he works from home."

Jamie moved to sit down at the table to do his homework. "I'm telling you, Ma, there's something really, really off about them."

"Stop reading all those horror novels, and watching those creepy movies and TV shows. No more *Dexter* on Netflix! It's all making you paranoid."

Maybe, but still . . .

Jamie had a bad feeling that wouldn't go away. Unsettled, he watched as his mom collected Matilda's toys and sighed from exhaustion.

It'd been hard for all of them over the last few months since his dad had been killed while off on a "business" trip.

As Jamie opened his chemistry book, a motion outside caught his attention. Frowning, he slid out of his chair to get a closer look.

He gaped at the sight of his neighbor carrying a strange-shaped baggie out of his detached garage and tossing it into the trunk of his car . . . which, now that he thought about it, was *never* parked *in* the garage.

Neither was Teresa's.

His neighbor struggled with the weight and odd shape of whatever was in the bag.

Was that a body?

C'mon, dude. Don't be stupid. It's not a body.

But Jamie had seen plenty of horror movies where they moved corpses, and that was what it looked like. It didn't even bend right.

"James? What are you doing?"

He pulled back to see his mom glaring at him. "Being my usual delusional self. You?"

"Wondering what I got into while pregnant that caused your brain damage. Must have been those lead paint chips I craved."

"Ha-ha." He returned to his homework, but as he tried to focus on chemistry, he couldn't get his mind off what he'd just seen. The way his neighbor had carried that bag . . .

It *had* to be a body.

Unable to concentrate, he got up to look outside again. The moment he did, he saw his neighbor's wife, Teresa, with a huge white bucket that held some kind of thick red liquid she was spreading around the driveway.

Red?

Water?

Nah, man. It was too thick for water. Looked like blood. Diluted maybe, but definitely a hemoglobin-like substance.

He started to call for his mom, but the moment he opened his mouth, Teresa looked up and caught sight of him in the window. Terrified and shaking, he quickly hit the deck on his belly.

Oh God, she saw me!

What was he going to do? *I know what blood looks like. Even diluted.* And that was blood she'd been dumping.

Maybe she's a taxidermist.

Yeah, right.

"Jamie?"

He flinched at his sister's call. Crawling across the floor, he didn't get up until he was in the hallway. "Whatcha need, Matty?"

With honey-blond curls and bright blue eyes, his little sister stared up at him from the couch. "Can you come help me? I can't get the TV on the right channel."

"Sure." He moved toward her to check it out. The battery on the remote was low.

After changing it for her, he returned to the living room to put it on the kids' channel she preferred, then froze as he heard the news.

"Another body was found near Miller's Pond. Mutilated. The headless remains were burned beyond recognition. At this time, the authorities are investigating every lead. So far, they're at a loss over this horrific crime that appears to be related to a set of six murders over the last four months."

Jamie was frozen to the spot as he heard those words.

"Give me that!" Matilda jerked the remote from his hand and changed channels.

Sick to his stomach, Jamie bit his lip. Now that he thought about it, those murders had started only after the Thompsons had moved in.

Six months ago. Just a few weeks after his father had been killed outside of Memphis.

Weird.

It's nothing, dumb ass. Get back to your chemistry.

Yeah, but what if . . .

"Jamie?"

He turned at his mother's irate tone, which usually denoted one particular bad habit he had. "I put the seat down!"

She growled at him. "It's not the toilet seat. I just got a call from Teresa. Are you spying on her?"

Well, yeah, but he wasn't dumb enough to give her the truth with that tone of voice. "No."

Hands on hips, she glared at him. "You better not be! She said she's going to call the cops and report you for stalking if you do it again."

"'Cause I was looking out the window of my house? Really? When did *that* become a crime?"

"Don't get smart with me, boy. Now do your homework."

Grousing under his breath, Jamie returned to his book, but not before he texted his best friend.

By the time he'd finished his assignment, Ed was at his back door with an evil grin on his nerdy little face. Barely five foot three, Ed wasn't the most intimidating person on the planet, but he was one hell of an opponent on any science or math bowl team.

"So you think your neighbors are weird."

"Shh." Jamie looked over his shoulder to make sure his mom wasn't there before he pushed Ed out onto the back stoop. "Yeah. There's something not right. You feel up to some snooping?"

"Always. It's what I do best . . . Only time my compact body mass comes in handy."

Ignoring his mini-tirade, Jamie turned the back light off and crouched low as he made his way from the porch to the grass. Like a military assault squad, they headed across his backyard, toward the Thompsons'.

Halfway to the Thompson garage, Ed pulled back with a frown.

"What?" Jamie whispered.

Blanching, Ed held his hand up for him to see. "It's blood." He looked around. "The ground's saturated with it."

Sick to his stomach, Jamie lifted his hands to see them stained red. Just like Ed's. "Is it human?"

"How would I know? Blood's blood. And this is definitely blood." Ed's eyes widened. "You think they're the serial killers the cops are looking for?"

"I don't know."

Biting his lip, Jamie moved toward the detached two-car garage to look for clues. It took several minutes to jimmy the lock.

As silent as the grave, he and Ed moved into the small building, which was covered in plastic.

Like one of Dexter's kill zones.

Ed stepped closer to him. "We need to get out of here and call the cops."

"Not without some evidence."

"Yeah, no, I've seen this movie. Nerdy white boy dies first. I'm out of here."

He grabbed Ed's arm as his eyes adjusted to the darkness. "Hold on a minute."

Jamie went to the workbench, where someone had left a map of their small Mississippi town and a card case.

A card case that held driver's licenses.

What the hell? Opening it, Jamie saw men and women from all over the country. *What kind of* . . .

His thoughts scattered as he saw his dad's license there.

Why would they have his dad's license?

Confused and terrified, Jamie looked back at the map, which had his house and those of every family in town marked with a red high-lighter.

"Jamie," Ed snarled between clenched teeth. "I hear something."

As they started back for the window, Jamie froze at the sight of a mirrored wall.

Footsteps moved closer.

Ed ran for the window with Jamie one step behind him. They were both sweating and shaking by the time they were outside the garage. But as soon as their feet were on the ground, headlights lit up the entire yard.

They were trapped.

If they tried to get back to Jamie's house, they'd be seen for sure.

With no other course of action, Jamie crouched under the open window and listened as the driver turned the car off and got out. Footsteps echoed as the driver walked into the garage.

"Hey, hon?" Mr. Thompson called out. "Have you been messing in the garage again?"

Lights came on in the house an instant before Teresa walked the short distance to the garage. "What?"

Ed ran for Jamie's house while Jamie stayed behind. Rising slowly, he peeked in through the mirror to see the Thompsons standing in the center of their obvious kill zone.

"Someone's been flipping through my journal. Was that you?"

"No. I haven't been in here." She walked over to the mirror.

Jamie gasped at what he saw there.

Oh shit! I knew it!

He lifted his phone and quickly snapped a photo of her, then he did what Ed had done. He scampered across the lawn as fast as he could. Running into his house, he slammed the door and closed all the blinds.

"Mom!"

Ed met him in the living room, where he was holding on to Matilda for everything he was worth. "I thought those things were myths made up by teachers and parents to scare us."

"What?" his mom asked.

Jamie swallowed as his mother stared at them as if they were crazy. His breathing ragged, he held his phone out to his mom. "We've got to call the cops!"

"For what?"

"Our neighbors, Ma!" He showed her the picture. "They're humans . . . slayers. And they're here to destroy our colony!"

PAPER CUTS

GARY A. BRAUNBECK

*Mutato nomine de te
Fabula narratur.*

Change the name and it's about you, that story.
—HORACE, 65–8 BC

They came for us, as they always did, when the sun shone high in the safe daytime sky. They pulled us from our coffins, from our beds, from our corners and alleys and pits, and they hurt us; oh, how they hurt us. Driving stakes through our chests as their legends told them they should, and then cutting off our heads—ah, but not before tearing our limbs from our bodies one by one; not before burning out our eyes with acid; not before tearing our intestines out in their dripping fists, not before wrenching out our tongues with their fingers, or pliers, or cutting them out with dull scissors; not before shredding our members from between our legs or burning them closed with hot irons, laughing in God-fearing righteousness as the stink of our ruined flesh filled the air.

We did not scream, even though the pain of our dying was great.

Even when, once they were done, they built the massive fires upon which our physical remains were tossed. No indignity, no torture, no final humiliation was too terrible for the likes of us, not in their eyes.

Nowhere in the world did they show us mercy; at no time in the history of their laughable, pathetic talking-monkey race did they ever attempt to show understanding. It was always their fury, and then the pain, the degradation, the torture, agony, and dismemberment, and always, always, the flames to be fed after.

Annette Klein would be the first to admit that she wasn't the most graceful or coordinated person, even on her best days—she'd once twisted her ankle attempting to just *stand up* in a pair of high-heeled shoes that one of her friends had goaded her into trying on in a trendy shop—but even she wouldn't have thought it possible for her to cause herself to shed blood in, of all places, a second-hand bookstore, yet bleed there she did. To make matters worse, it wasn't just a little—no, that would have been a blessing; she had to get a series of not one, not two, but *three* paper cuts on the tips of the center fingers of her right hand, as well as a decent gash across the palm of that hand. Until that moment in the bookstore, she'd forgotten just how much blood flowed through the hand and its fingers, but as soon as she felt the sharp slices and saw the drops of blood spattering down on the pages of the book she'd been skimming, it came back to her. She'd always been something of a bleeder, even as a child, and for a few years her parents worried that her difficulty in clotting might be due to hemophilia, but luckily that turned out not to be the case. Her veins were just a slight bit closer to the surface than in most people, and as a result her bleeding was quick and her clotting slow, but it was never a genuine danger to her well-being.

That evening in the bookstore, however, she wondered just for a minute if things were about to—as many mystery and suspense writers might phrase it in the pulp novels she so loved to read—take a turn for the worse. Flash of lightning, roll of thunder, cue ominous background music.

A few minutes before wandering into the store, she had left her office, much later than usual, at the downtown branch of the community college where she worked as the school's website designer. She was heading to the parking garage when she got the sudden urge for a cruller from Riley's Bakery, so, despite the lateness of the hour, she turned abruptly and headed toward the fulfillment of her bliss. Riley's was unfortunately out of crullers by this time (*Well, duh!* she thought to herself, *it's after 7,* of course *they're out*), so she decided to mend her broken heart with a box of chocolate-coated sugar-dusted doughnut holes. Walking out the door, popping the first one whole into her mouth, she bit down and closed her eyes as the rich, heavy flavors and textures spread out over her tongue. Then she nearly tripped over her own feet because she was walking and eating with her eyes closed. Despite her skill and dexterity at the computer, multitasking in the real world was not her forte—okay, she wasn't quite *that* bad, she could walk and eat at the same time, even talk on her cell simultaneously without leaving a path of destruction in her wake, but that required that she not, well, have her eyes closed. It's the little things that keep us aboveground and breathing, so this one was on her.

She caught her balance just in time by shoving out her arm and catching her weight on the brick doorway of the adjacent second-hand bookstore. Her doughnuts, however, failed to survive the mishap, because the hand she used to brace herself against the doorway also happened to be the one that was holding the box of treats.

Cursing under her breath, she fished a small bottle of hand sanitizer out of her purse and applied it to her hands, and then—because she didn't have any tissues—surreptitiously dried them on the sides of her jacket. She might very well have walked back to her car right there and then, but she caught a glimpse of something in the bookstore's display window that caused her to remain: what appeared to be a near-pristine first edition of Carson McCullers's *Reflections in a*

Golden Eye, one of her all-time favorite novels. She had two other editions—a trade paperback and a cheap discarded hardcover found at a library book sale—and while each was in at least readable condition, she'd always wanted to have a really nice copy of the novel . . . and here it was, it seemed. She looked up at the streetlights that were just beginning to buzz and sputter to life and reminded herself that, despite the quaint appearance of the building fronts in this area, there was still enough serious crime taking place after dark that she really ought to be heading back to the garage—but just as quickly as these thoughts presented themselves, the book junkie in her laughed it off, its metaphorical gaze fixed unblinkingly on the McCullers novel.

Smiling to herself and feeling a bit like Helene Hanff finally walking into 84 Charing Cross Road, Annette opened the door and entered, wondering for a moment if she was about to meet the man who would play Frank P. Doel to her Helene. She couldn't quite figure out if the small hanging sign was supposed to be turned to OPEN or CLOSED, because one part of it had come loose from the string, leaving the rest hanging there like a desperate spelunker who'd lost his grip on the way down and now dangled, waiting for someone above to give the rope a tug and pull him to safety. Oh, well—if the place was closed, the proprietor would say so soon enough.

Those fires that consumed the degraded remains of our physical bodies burned well into the nights throughout history and the world over; a few flames could still be seen licking upward from the embers in the days following our deaths, when the men of the villages set about the final stage of their so-called holy tasks.

The pits were dug, our agonized ashes poured in, soil and dung spread atop the smoldering remains, and in the following mornings, saplings were planted in the spots. And there they thought it would end.

But eternal life means eternal; *it mattered not that we no longer had our meat puppets to transport us from place to place. Even in the core of a single agonized ash, eternal life remains eternal, as does the consciousness amassed during that life; and as such, we slowly felt ourselves absorbed into the young roots of the infant saplings, and then, slowly, into the rest of the trees that grew from the pits where our remains were buried.*

The Earth spun. The moon waxed and waned. Vegetation began to grow around the trees, snaking up through the ashes. The scarred spots where we had met our degrading deaths gave way to blankets of green. The trees grew straight and tall, branches reaching toward the sunlight.

A season passed, and then a year, and then ten more.

Many came to these trees to admire their beauty and to enjoy their shade. Many a young man proposed to his true love beneath these canopies. Weddings were performed beneath them. Children were christened there.

The stars shifted their courses. Constellations appeared and then vanished. The sky changed. The villagers who had watched our deaths, who participated in our brutalization, themselves died, as did their children, and their children's children, and the next three generations who followed.

But the trees remained, tall and imposing. Within their cores, we waited patiently, spreading our eternal strength throughout the trees until every leaf, every twig, every branch and piece of bark became one with us.

The Earth spun, the moon waxed and waned, townships replaced villages, and engineers and architects covered the land with roads and bridges and train tracks.

We waited, growing stronger in our new forms, our new homes. Through the vibrations above, below, and within the planet itself we found one another, and we shared our stories and our memories, and sang our bloodsongs to the night.

The Earth spun. The seasons changed. Telegraph wires were re-
placed by telephone poles.

The Earth spun. Townships were sacrificed in favor of cities; com-
munity was traded for commerce, cobblestone for asphalt and con-
crete, horse-drawn wagons for automobiles and airplanes. Telephones
were antiquated by cellular and satellite communications.

And we waited.

People moved on. Families grew larger. Cities sprang up, demand-
ing the death of trees to make room for them.

And we waited, knowing that it would begin again soon.

The first thing that threatened to seduce Annette's senses once she
was fully inside was the so-very-right *smell* of the place, something
only a true lover of books could understand; the comforting, intoxi-
cating, friendly scent of bindings and old paper was almost joyous;
decades' worth of floor wax and the almost pungent aroma of real
wooden in-wall bookcases were nectar.

The walls were lined from floor to ceiling with sagging shelves
full of books, and she could see at a glance that, though the stock in
this section immediately inside the entrance contained everything
from academic texts to the usual classics, its primary focus was on
matters philosophical and occult. Everywhere she turned, there
were books such as Agrippa's *De Occulta Philosophia*, the ancient
notes of Anaxagoras of Clazomenae detailing his conclusion that
the Earth was spherical, *The Gospel of Sri Ramakrishna*, the Hindu
Rig Veda, the poems of Ovid, the plays of Aeschylus, Lucan's *De
Bello Civili*; there were numerous sections that contained long-out-
of-print works by Robert Nathan, Booth Tarkington, even Jessamyn
West and Katherine Anne Porter. Annette's heart beat with surprising excitement. Aside from the rare edition of the McCullers novel
in the display window, who knew what other treasures she might
find in here?

Approaching the counter, she saw that the proprietor didn't use anything electronic when tallying up sales; no, he or she had an antique National Cash Register two-deep-drawer, three-key bank machine in polished cherrywood with flawless persimmon inlay, the kind of register that hadn't been in use for at least a hundred years, and this machine was in superb condition.

She was admiring a copy of *The Complete Short Stories of F. Scott Fitzgerald* that sat by itself on a wooden display square in a delicate, exquisite bell jar. The jar was on a small table by the counter; this book, too, seemed to be a first edition. Touching her fingertips against her thumbs to be certain no detritus from the late and much-lamented doughnut holes remained, she looked around the store for any sign of the proprietor. *Okay*, she said to herself, *you know damned well that this thing has to be set apart like this for a reason, right? They've put it inside a bell jar, for pity's sake. You shouldn't even be* thinking *about this*.

But even at thirty-six—just as she'd been at six, and twelve, and twenty-six—Annette Klein was never one to let common sense override curiosity, especially when it came to old books. She reached out, hesitated for only a moment, and then carefully, even delicately (for her), lifted the glass covering and set it to the side, making sure that it was balanced and in no danger of falling.

She picked up the book and began flipping through the pages until she came across "Bernice Bobs Her Hair," always her favorite of Fitzgerald's stories, and had just turned the page when she felt the unmistakable, fiery-sharp slice of paper cuts on her fingertips. Pulling back her hand, she watched in disgust as blood from her index, middle, and fourth finger spattered onto the page she'd been reading. *Shit*, she thought. *Oh, well—you bleed on it, you bought it*. She unconsciously stuck the tips of the three fingers into her mouth and sucked at them, tasting the faint coppery flavor and almost gagging. She fumbled the book, still opened to the pages she'd bled on, down onto the counter and was searching her jacket pockets for some tissues, or a handkerchief, or anything at all she could use to wrap around her bleeding digits, when she saw why she'd managed to get paper cuts on all three of her fingers; each upper corner of the two opened pages facing her had for some incomprehensible reason been dog-eared so that two surprisingly sharp-tipped triangles jutted up, and the paper stock itself was of a sufficiently strong quality that these dog-eared corners felt almost solid. Why on earth would anyone do that to a rare edition of a book, let alone a Fitzgerald? Squeezing the fingers of her left hand tightly in her right fist, she leaned forward and stared at the book.

Was she imagining things, or did it look somehow thicker than before she'd picked it up? She squinted, feeling the blood running down her wrist. Her unwounded hand unconsciously went to the silver crucifix hanging around her neck, an heirloom from her grandmother. As her fingers absentmindedly traced the shape of the cross (something she always did when nervous), she stared at the book. What else was it about this that seemed . . . off? She reached out to close the book and felt the edges of the page almost snap out. She knew she felt the sliver of fierce, quick pain slice across her palm. This time she cursed out loud at the pain and turned away from the book before she soaked it with any more of her blood.

Now there was another book on the wooden display block where the Fitzgerald had been a minute before. How the hell had it gotten there?

"Oh, dear me," someone said. "Oh, damn it, damn it, damn it. My fault, my fault, so very sorry."

A short, stocky man dressed in clothes easily twenty years out of date came up to her and took her bleeding hand in his. "Oh, Jesus Christ in a secondhand Chrysler," he said in a voice that sounded as if he gargled with Wild Turkey four times a day, "you really hurt yourself, didn't you?"

"They're just paper cuts."

The man shook his head, in obvious pain. "No cut is *just* any-thing. Not to me, anyway. Come back here with me, I'll fix you up. Lots of doctors in my family. I'm not one of them but I've picked up a few tricks here and there." He started to say something else but then noticed the Fitzgerald lying on the counter and the new book that had taken its place on the display block. "Excuse me one moment," he said. He grabbed the bell jar and covered the new book, and then glanced for a moment at the Fitzgerald. His face blanched, but he quickly gathered himself and smiled at Annette. "Sorry. I'm a bit fussy about certain things. People say it makes me colorful. That's what happens when you get to be as old as me. You become colorful. A local character, even." He led her to an area near the back of the store that was separated from the sales floor by a large wall of frosted glass.

"I was trying to close early. I guess I didn't check the sign." He wore a pressed white shirt open slightly at the collar so that the thin gray-and-black-striped tie wasn't completely strangling him. He sported not one but two pairs of glasses: a regular black-rimmed pair with a second, wire-framed pair just an inch farther down his nose; judging from the thickness of the lenses, this second set had either bi- or more likely trifocal lenses. His vest, like his tailored, cuffed pants, was pin-striped. A chain led from one vest pocket to another, where Annette could see the outline of a gold pocket watch.

Definitely old-school, she thought. She liked that.

He pulled out an ancient-looking wooden rolling stool and helped her to sit, then opened the tambour of a rolltop desk and removed what appeared to be a well-stocked medical kit from beneath stacks of receipts and order forms. The entire room was stuffed with books, stacked from the floor to almost shoulder height, and in some places the stacks were three deep. Annette couldn't help but marvel.

"I'll bet you know where every last book in this store is, even if it's buried in a stack like one of these and in the basement or something."

"You'd win that bet," said the bookseller. He opened the lid of the medical kit and began assembling everything he needed to tend to Annette's cuts. As he reached over to take hold of her hand his sleeve rode up slightly, and Annette saw the row of fading-but-not-faded numerals tattooed near his wrist. The bookseller caught sight of what she was looking at and so pulled his sleeve a bit farther up, turning his wrist to give her a better look.

"I'm sorry," said Annette. "I didn't mean to stare. It's just that I . . . I've never met anyone who was . . . was . . ."

"Yes, I was in a concentration camp," said the bookseller. "I was taken there as a child. My family and I were marched from our home in Hungary, along with thousands of others, to a camp called Gunskirchen Lager in the Austrian forest. Most of my family died on the way. My sister lasted until two days after we arrived. She'd hurt her feet on the march and gangrene set in. Her death was slow and agonizing—I still cry when I think about it too much. I haven't been one for long walks ever since. If it hadn't been for a boy named Uri who befriended me in those early days, I think I would have just willed myself to die."

His tone was so matter-of-fact that Annette felt momentarily anxious. Was this man a little on the crazy side? Who could talk about something so horrible in such an almost nonchalant manner, and to a total stranger?

"I don't mean to sound unfeeling," said the bookseller as he set about cleaning her cuts with some kind of ointment that immediately killed the pain, "but I find that if I talk about it any other way, I just . . . implode. Please, don't be offended. Sometimes I talk too much and go into stories by rote. I don't get a lot of company these days."

A dozen questions that she wanted to ask him flooded across

Annette's mind: Was he a widower? Didn't he have any children? Was he always alone here? But the question that won out was: "What happened out there with the books?"

He hesitated a moment, a fresh cotton ball hovering over the cut on her palm, and then released the breath he'd been holding and continued ministering to her. "That, I'm afraid, will take a bit of explaining, and I'd rather that you not think I'm loony-tunes and go screaming off the premises. Also it would be nice if you didn't sue me because of these cuts."

"Like I said, they're just paper cuts."

"And like I said, no cut is *just* anything, not to me." He finished cleaning the cuts and began rummaging around in the kit for a small tube of superglue. "Cyanoacrylate," he said, showing her the tube. "Believe it or not, it wasn't invented so guys could suspend themselves with their hard hats from steel beams—it was developed for medics to use in the field during Vietnam. Best way in the world to quickly and safely close a bleeding wound."

"Believe it or not," said Annette, "I already knew that."

"Of course you did. Anyone curious enough to take a Fitzgerald out from under glass *would* know something like that."

Annette cleared her throat. The bookseller paused and looked up at her.

"Speaking of the Fitzgerald . . . ," she said.

"You'll think I'm crazy."

"Will I? Let's review: I took a book out from under a bell jar. That book had pages with dog-eared corners that I swear *bit* my fingers. The pages absorbed my blood and the book grew thicker. And when I turned around, another book had taken the Fitzgerald's place, even though you were back here and I was alone in the store. Does that about cover it?"

"A worthy highlight reel if ever there was one."

"Do you think *I'm* crazy?"

"You don't strike me as being particularly unbalanced, no."

Annette smiled. "So tell me what happened out there. It wasn't normal."

The bookseller shrugged. "That depends on your definition of the word *normal.*"

"Please?"

He stared at her for a moment, then rubbed the back of his neck. "You want a drink? I'm going to have one. Pick your poison; I got a little bit of everything stashed around here."

"Got any wine?"

"White or red?"

"Red?"

He went behind the rolltop desk and emerged a few moments later with a bottle of red wine and a pair of tulip-shaped wineglasses. After pouring each of them a glass, the bookseller held up his wine and said, *"Doamne apara-me rău."*

"What's that mean?"

"It's a kind of Romanian blessing. It's a good thing, trust me."

"Okee-day," she replied, and took a drink of the wine. It was incredible. "This is the best red wine I've ever tasted."

"Really? I made it myself. I have another bottle in the back if you'd like one to take home."

"Oh, I'd *love* that."

The bookseller smiled widely; this genuinely pleased him. "What do you know? Someone thinks something I made with my own hands is the best they've ever encountered. And here I thought there wasn't going to be anything special happening today."

He put his glass aside and returned to Annette's hand. "Have you ever heard those rumors about Hitler seeking occult or supernatural assistance during the war?"

Annette shrugged. "I just thought it was the stuff of legend, or pulp fiction."

The bookseller snorted a laugh and shook his head. "Not all of it was as far-fetched as you might think. The Longinus spear, for instance, the spear that supposedly pierced Christ's side while he was on the cross—I know, I know, what a very Catholic way to describe it, it's late, I'm tired, so sue me. Anyway, that spear was purported to possess great power. It was said that whoever possessed the spear would have the power to conquer the world. Hitler very much believed that, and until the moment he blew his brains out down in the bunker, he had hundreds of people searching for it.

"One of the things that made Gunskirchen an oddball among the concentration camps is that the majority of people sent there were professionals—physicians, lawyers, professors, artists, musicians. During the first weeks there, Uri and I could almost get *drunk* on the conversations that were whispered at night in the barracks. Philosophy, music, law, mathematics, and myth . . . it seemed early enough on that maybe it wasn't going to be as horrible as we'd been told. That notion was quickly put out of its misery.

"The conditions were subhuman. There was a series of twenty toilet pits that had been dug out at the far edge of the camp, and if you went to the bathroom anywhere but in one of those pits, the Germans shot you dead on the spot. These pits were never covered and so the stench of it was always in the air. But the thing is, disease spreads quickly, and many people became afflicted with diarrhea. It didn't matter if a person was standing in line for one of the pits; if they lost control of their bowels—and many did—and soiled themselves in line, they were dragged out of line, made to kneel down, and shot in the head. We weren't allowed to move their bodies. The Germans liked to laugh at the dead Jews lying in a puddle of their own liquid filth. Of all the images I can't rid myself of, it's the image of all those people, those *skeletons*, standing in the pit lines, shuddering with all the strength they had, trying not to shit themselves."

He blinked his eyes and shivered. "Yeah, I'm a cheerful guy with many happy stories . . ."

"But what about—"

"—the bell jar and books, I know. Hang on, I need a refill."

"I think I do, too." Annette held out her glass. The bookseller refilled both, and they drank in an awkward, sad, sudden silence.

They came for us, as they always did, when the sun shone high in the safe daytime sky.

We waited in our majestic trees as the bulldozers and other heavy equipment came toward us. We listened as they broke through the heavy woods and overpowered the shale beneath the hillsides. We readied ourselves as they neared us. We heard the grinding of their gears, the snarl of their gas-powered saws. We stood tall and proud, so we could see them clearly as they arrived. The stench of their smoke and diesel fuel reached us before they and their machines did.

Workmen walked up to us wherever we stood across the surface of the planet, craning their necks to see our glory.

"Damn shame this has to come down," said one.

"Don't matter what we think," replied the second. "We got our orders."

The first one picked up his ax. "Trees're supposed to feel things just like a person does, y'know? My grandma told me that. Let's try to make it quick and clean, huh?"

"I've heard enough of that griping from you," said the second workman, powering up his chain saw. "Bad enough we got to cut down all these trees without you bellyachin' over every one of 'em. Least they'll be put to good use. That's something, anyway."

They set to work.

Our waiting was over.

Within half an hour, we came crashing down.

This was not death; it was the first stage of our rebirth.

And this time we did scream, but in ecstasy—sweet, all-consuming ecstasy.

The sound of rebirth.

"There was a group of occultists," said the bookseller, "called the Studiengruppe für Germanisches Altertum—'Study Group for Germanic Antiquity'—but most people know them by the name the Thule Society. The Thules had members like Hans Frank, Rudolf Hess, Heinrich Himmler . . . it was even rumored that Eichmann and Mengele were members. One of the commandants at Gunskirchen Lager, Gruppenführer Joseph Karl Steiner, was a member. I remember as a child huddling down at night in the mud and filth and cold—God, I hope you *never* experience that kind of cold, it almost made you wish for the warmth of a grave. At least then there would have been something above you to hold in the heat and gases as your body disintegrated and putrefied.

"Anyway, there were those nights when Steiner would have other Thule members in his expansive quarters, and the lights would burn, the glow mocking us, and I remember the sounds of their cackling laughter, their murmuring voices; sometimes they would sing drunken, obscene songs . . . there was so much . . . *haughtiness* in their tones. But always—*always*—there came a time during the night when they would send two SS officers out into the camp to select one of the healthier prisoners, a worker, to bring back into the building. I remember that I used to feel envious of those selected to be taken inside—and they were always taken by fellow prisoners. There were Jews in the camps who became . . . well, *collaborators* with the Germans. They were called 'kapos.' Many did whatever was commanded of them in order to secure more bread, or an extra blanket, or cigarettes. Sometimes the *kapos* did it in order to ensure the safety of a friend or family member. To this day, I cannot find it in my heart to condemn these poor souls for their actions, even though some of those actions led to the deaths of fellow Jews. But the *kapos* almost always took men. Rumor had it that these men—mostly it was men, sometimes a stronger woman or a younger boy, I never saw them take a young girl . . . but the rumors persisted that those who were selected were fed meat and cheese, given wine, a warm, clean blanket, and treated well. But we never saw them again. They would enter that building, there would be more celebratory noise for a while, and then things would quiet down. There was never silence . . . only an ebbing of sound. I swear to you I could hear the sounds of someone . . . not exactly groaning, there wasn't enough strength for it to be a groan, but a noise somewhere between a whimper and a grunt. And it would continue for a minute or two at a constant but low level, just low enough that I was never certain if I was actually hearing it or if it was just the cold and sores and hunger making me imagine some unseen depravity going on there. I was six years old, and the images those sounds created in my mind should never have existed in the mind of any truly decent human being.

"Uri would hold me close to him on these nights and hum soft songs in my ear. One of his favorites was 'Over There.' He always hummed it off-key. It made me laugh. He was taken away one morning for a burial detail, and he never came back. I prayed that he had gotten away somehow.

"The last time our dear *Gruppenführer* held a Thule gathering in his quarters, the SS officers came out and took nearly a dozen men, women, and young boys into the *Gruppenführer*'s quarters. That night, there was no mistaking the screams; children begging for their lives, women pleading that *they* be tortured instead of the children, men weeping and wailing. We saw blood spatter on the inside of the windows. We saw shadows jerking back and forth, some of them flipping, fluttering, but always there was the blood, and the wailing, and the screaming . . . and then the not-quite-silence, the muffled noise of many throats releasing something between a whimper and a grunt.

"That was late April 1945. The Germans had received word that the Americans were coming. You have to understand, rumors that the war was ending soon—was perhaps even over—had been whispered for weeks, but that night was the first time that I allowed myself to think that maybe, just maybe, the end was finally here. If that meant my death, then so be it. I was so hungry and sick by then that I almost didn't care.

"The next morning all of the Germans left the camp but made certain to lock the gates so none of us could escape, as if any of us had that much strength or hope left. They gave us what they called a 'generous' amount of food—one cube of sugar to each person, and one loaf of moldy bread for every seven people. There were nearly as many of us dead as there were still alive, if you can call what we were 'alive.' Men, women, children so drawn and weak and starving they could barely walk, but that didn't stop them from trying when the Americans arrived. The Seventy-First Infantry Division shot through the locks and entered Gunskirchen on the morning of May 1, 1945. By then we'd been trapped in the abandoned camp for over a week. What little rancid food we'd been left was gone, and we had been without water for several days even before that. I can still hear the cries from the throats of those who could still speak, calling out, '*Wasser!*' and '*Ich habe Hunger!*' One child whose legs had been broken and were now blackened with infection used her elbows to pull herself through the mud toward an American soldier. I saw her die in his arms as he gave her a drink from his canteen. All around me, skeletons crawled or shuffled through stinking, ankle-deep mud and human excrement. I saw the decayed bodies of horses and dogs that lined the road, carcasses that had been torn into by the teeth of the starving as they wandered from the camp days before, after the Germans had abandoned it; physicians, lawyers, people of education, men of letters, rabbis, women and children . . . all reduced to chewing on rotting animal intestines like beasts.

"It was then I felt a hand on my shoulder and looked up to see my friend Uri, still alive and standing. I hadn't seen him in months and had assumed that he was dead. He smiled at me—his teeth were rotted, many of them missing, but it was still one of the most beautiful smiles I had ever seen. I hugged him and wept. As the Americans moved into the camp, many of the prisoners lined the way, hands outstretched to touch the sleeves of our saviors. Uri took my hand and led me through the throng toward the *Gruppenführer*'s quarters. The Americans were too concerned with ministering to the prisoners to bother then with going through the buildings. I did not want to see whatever it was that waited in there, but I was too weak to resist, and—I hate admitting this—a part of me wanted to know if there had been any truth to the hideous, perverted images that the sounds had helped put into my head. If there were horrors waiting in there that were worse than those I had imagined, then perhaps my soul wasn't forever tainted. Perhaps God had given me a glimpse of something horrible to prepare me for something even worse. In such ways is spiritual strength tested and achieved."

He fell silent after this for a few moments as he finished up ministering to Annette's wounds. He completed what could only be called an expert job of bandaging her hand, turning it first to the left, then to the right. "Does it still hurt?"

"Not in the least. Thank you for being so kind."

The bookseller gave a tight smile that contained no joy in it whatsoever and nodded his head. "I am truly sorry this happened."

Annette shook her head. "I shouldn't have taken the book from under the bell jar."

The bookseller held up a hand in protest. "No, that was my fault. I should have taken the book as soon as it appeared. At the very least, I should have made sure the CLOSED sign was in place and the door locked." He looked once again toward the two books at the end of the counter: the new one under the bell jar, and the volume of Fitzgerald whose pages had so cut Annette's fingers and hand.

She leaned forward and touched the bookseller's arm. "What was in there? What did you and Uri see?"

The bookseller nodded toward the bell jar. "That. It was on a lovely oak table in the corner of Steiner's office. There was a book inside, in Arabic. The paper was old, thick, and stiff. Neither Uri nor I ever knew what the book was. It was filled with symbols and writings in verse that Uri thought might be incantations. It *felt* like something evil that was being imprisoned under glass. And it was the only book there.

"The floors of the *Gruppenführer*'s quarters were littered with the bodies of those prisoners who had been taken there the night before the Nazis fled. They were not only decomposed, they were . . . deflated. Their flesh was gray, drained of any moisture. I remember how Uri knelt down next to several of the bodies and shook, pointing to their wounds. Hundreds, *thousands* of tiny cuts—paper cuts. And not a single drop of blood anywhere. I think Uri knew then what unholy rites the *Gruppenführer* and his Thule had been practicing on those nights of singing and soft glowing lights. But I couldn't grasp it. I felt sick and dizzy and more afraid at that moment than I had been during the years I'd been in the camp. I tried to turn and run out, to find an American who would give me a drink or a taste of his K-rations, but as soon as I turned around the world went black.

"I awoke in a makeshift hospital, inside a massive tent. The Americans had established a camp just outside Lambach, not that far from Gunskirchen itself. I opened my eyes and saw glass bottles hanging next to me, saw clear tubes running into my arms. I turned my head and saw Uri sitting on the floor next to my bed. He was sleeping, his head resting on his bended knees. I reached out and touched the top of his head. He shuddered, made a terrible wet sound, but then lifted his head and blinked his eyes. I could see that he had been in the midst of a nightmare, and the phantom images of it still reflected in his eyes told me how horrible it must have been. I never asked him to recount any part of it.

"He gave me a sad and tired smile—his teeth were now gone, having been removed by an American dentist; what an old man he looked like! But I loved seeing that old-man smile. Did I mention that Uri was only nineteen? He looked fifty, and stayed that way until the day he died.

"He took hold of my hand and kissed the palm, then held it against his cheek. 'I have secured the evil vessel,' he whispered to me. 'It can harm no one ever again.'

"I asked him how he'd done this, how did he know it was evil, and several other questions that seemed to confuse him as much as they did me. He told me that an American soldier had helped him to remove the bodies of the prisoners and give them a decent burial, and that this 'Yank'—that's what Uri called the Americans—had helped him to find a crate and blankets and secure the bell jar and its contents. 'The Yank will help me send it to what family remains to me in the States,' he said. 'I don't know what the Yanks did when they saw the interior of the quarters. If it ever was reported, I never heard anything about it. In my letter I will ask my family to not open the crate, and I know they will honor my wishes.' He then squeezed my arm. 'When we get to the States, my friend, you will be with me. I have told them that we are brothers, and we are—if not by blood, then by choice, by loyalty, by our having survived this madness, by our love and friendship.'

" 'Brother,' I said to him. 'My brother. Thank you.' "

"How could Uri have had such strength when he found you? Didn't you think it was odd that—?" Annette cut off her words before the question could be completed. Looking at the bookseller's expression, she knew the answer.

"Yes," whispered the bookseller. "Uri had become a *kapo*. He did so in order to ensure that I would not be harmed. He never told me what acts he participated in, and I never asked.

"He never left my side after that day in the hospital. I remember when I awoke, it was V-E Day. The war was at last over. I felt almost reborn." The bookseller looked up at the clock on the wall. "My goodness, I've been talking your ears off for a while, haven't I."

"I don't mind," said Annette.

"If your friends didn't mention it, this is not the type of neighborhood where one wants to be caught on the streets after the streetlights come on—*if* the streetlights come on. It's always something of a crapshoot around here."

"Please," she said, "tell me the rest. I have to know. I'm the one who bled on the thing. It's because of me that another book's appeared. I saw the expression on your face. You were terrified . . . and a little sickened, I think."

The bookseller gently took her unbandaged hand in both of his and said: "Do you believe in such a thing as evil? Wait, before you answer, I'm not talking about evils like starvation, or genocide, rape, torture—as horrific as those things are; I'm talking about a power that transcends what we know as 'nature' to dwell in a space not only that we *cannot* comprehend, but that our five senses are powerless to recognize in its purest form."

"Are you asking me if I believe in supernatural evil?"

"I suppose I am, yes."

"I don't know," she replied. "I mean, I guess I've wondered like everyone else if there's something more than just this life, a force that guides everything, holds all matter together, but I never . . . I never tried to imagine much beyond that. It scares me. Usually I have a hard enough time just getting through the *day*, you know?"

"Don't you have friends?"

"Not any close ones, not really. I've always been a bit solitary.

That's why I love books so much. I can lose myself in another world, another time, another person's adventure. I always liked pretending when I was a child, and I guess that hasn't changed much over the decades. I read a book and it's like it actually comes alive. The story's a living thing and the pages are . . . I don't know . . . like the thing that gives the story its voice. Does that make sense? Probably not. I just love reading."

"Don't you find it lonely?"

Annette considered the question for a moment. "I try not to think in terms like that. I figure as long as the same old sun rises to greet me, and the same old moon is there at night, then things are okay. It helps."

The bookseller nodded his head and patted her hand. "I really like you. You're quite sweet and kind."

"I think you're a pretty nice person yourself. *Colorful*, but nice."

The bookseller laughed. "Oh, you're a quick study, you are. Hey—why did you come in here in the first place?"

"I want that copy of *Reflections in a Golden Eye* in your display window."

"Ah, McCullers! Exquisite writer. Died far too young." He rose from his chair. "Come on, then. Let's get your book while I finish my story. You know, it's interesting that you talk about books like they're living things. What would you say if I told you some of them are?"

We savored the sensations of every moment as we were cut into dozens of large, heavy sections and loaded onto gigantic flatbed trailers; we admired the world our human bodies had not lived to see as our pieces were driven to mills, where they were split into logs; we drank in the cool goodness as the logs were treated in a steady flow of chemically enriched water made steady and constant by grindstones; we tingled with wild, unbound excitement as the logs were turned into wood chips and then treated under pressure with a solution of sulfu-

rous acid and calcium sulfite, followed by caustic soda, carbon, and sodium sulfide; we centered our collective consciousness and began to focus our thoughts as the lignin contained in the chips decomposed, allowing f-dextrose to form as our cellulose was purified; we briefly flashed on the smug expressions our executioners wore as they staked us, dismembered us, blinded us with bodkins or acid, but those images vanished and were replaced by exhilaration as the wood chips were pulped and then immersed in water; the water molded the pulp into fibers; the fibers were felted together as the water was purposefully agitated; then, at last, after centuries of patient waiting, the felted fibers became sheets as they were lifted from the water by a wire screen.

And we lived again as the mammoth rolls of virgin paper were loaded onto trailers and hauled away to the waiting presses and binderies. We were given our new forms. Words were imprinted on us, emblazoned on the covers used to hold us together. We lived the stories on our new flesh, every word, every feeling, every dream and pain and agony and glory and triumph and defeat and tragedy. They made it easier to wait a little longer.

Because eternal life means eternal, whether you live inside a puppet of meat or the materials used to produce the pages of a book. Eternal life means eternal.

And our eternal life means the hunger never goes away. We have been very, very hungry. We've waited. And some of those meat puppets have helped to find more of our brothers and sisters of the night. And we wait. And wait. And wait.

But something about this night, this night, *vibrates deep within our yearnings and whispers, "Soon . . ."*

Annette stared at the volume of Fitzgerald on the counter, now back to its original size and thickness, and then glanced at the book now inside the bell jar: *Heraclites' Theory and Modern Social Thought.*

"You seem . . . stunned," said the bookseller.

"It's just . . . you're right, if you had told me this earlier, I would have thought you were crazy."

"Imagine my reaction when Uri first showed it to me. We came back here to live with his aunt and uncle, who owned this bookstore, and after a decade and a half, when his uncle grew too sick to continue working, the bookstore was passed to us; *then* he finally opened the crate and removed the bell jar and the book inside. 'Living demons,' he told me. 'Something evil was scattered into the earth, and became part of the trees and plants that were used to create certain books. These books are demons. They live. I have seen what they can do. They hunger. They demand a blood sacrifice.' Yeah, I nearly ran screaming from the premises myself. And then he proved it to me.

"He lifted the bell jar, opened the book, and I *saw* its pages bend, I *saw* the corners turn into teeth, and I *saw* them bite into his flesh and drink his blood. I don't know what kind of monsters these things were when they walked the Earth, but just because their bodies were burned and buried and became part of the trees that were used in the making of these books . . . good God, I sound crazy to myself right now. But that's the truth. I don't know how—Uri and I were never able to agree on a theory, we argued about it until the day he died and left this store to me—but when one of these books feeds, it somehow . . . it somehow *communicates* with others of its kind, acts as a kind of beacon, and another of them follows its . . . its *signal*, and appears on the display block. That is why anyone taken into the *Gruppenführer*'s quarters was never seen again. Steiner and other members of the Thule Society were sacrificing them to these demons—or whatever they are—in order to ensure victory for their supreme *Führer*. When I trick one of those books into appearing here, it remains beneath that bell jar until it feeds and another of its kind arrives to take its place."

"H-how . . . how do they feed?"

The bookseller held up his hands. For the first time, Annette noticed the dozens of healing paper cuts on the old man's fingers.

"I feed them my own blood," said the bookseller. "It doesn't take that much to slake one of them, but I've never given one more than a few drops. About the same amount the Fitzgerald took from you."

Annette took a step back from the book. "What do you do with them? How do you protect yourself—protect *others*—from them?"

"When Uri and I realized what we were dealing with, we had a vault installed in the back of the store. There are *banks* in this city that don't have vaults this impenetrable. When you came in I was back there, saying a protection prayer as I unlocked it. I was going to put the Fitzgerald in there as soon as it fed and then close and seal it again. You beat me to the first part."

Annette stared at the small man with the Wild Turkey voice and wondered if, like her, he was alone and isolated in his own skin. She felt a sudden, surprising rush of affection for the bookseller that she could not find the words to express.

"Why?" was all she could manage. "Why do this?"

The bookseller's eyes seemed to be looking at something a thousand feet away, something filled with misery and desperation and hopelessness and, perhaps, near its edge, a hint of redemption, a dim, nebulous promise of salvation. "When I was a child, I watched men in crisp black uniforms and shiny dark boots stomp the faces of people I loved into the mud. I watched them bury sick children in deep graves of feces and gore. I watched as these men laughed and drank and goose-stepped their way across continents in a zealous effort to turn this planet into a graveyard filled with the bodies of those they deemed less pure, less worthy, less deserving of life and dignity than their own blond-haired, blue-eyed Aryan ideal. I watched this evil and was powerless to do anything to stop it. All I could do was watch, and weep, and pray to a God I wasn't certain was even *there* any longer. 'Make it stop,' I would pray. 'Please, make it stop. Make them see the evil they do.'" He shook his head and wiped at his eyes. "Never again. I promised myself that I would never again watch as evil took the blood of the innocent. I promised myself that I would never allow that kind of suffering to continue, not as long as I have strength in these hands and breath in this body." He looked at Annette, his gaze nailing her to the spot. "So I do this. I don't know what it is I help to prevent by these actions, but I know—I *pray*—that I am, in some small way, as only one old, weak man can, preventing another evil from being set loose upon the world.

"I can sleep at night, and the nightmares aren't as frequent or as terrible as they once were. So I think maybe I'm doing the right thing."

Annette nodded her head. "May I . . . may I come with you and watch you put this book away?"

"Of course. It would be an honor for me. Since Uri's death, I have had no one to share this secret with. Sometimes it weighs on me. It will be nice to have a friend with whom I can share this, if just for one evening. I thank you for it." He removed a large, pristine white handkerchief from his pocket. The material was heavy, thick, and when he snapped it open, the smell of starch was almost overpowering. He placed the handkerchief over the cover of the Fitzgerald book and quickly folded it around until the entire volume was enshrouded in cloth.

"Blessed by a rabbi," he said, picking it up. "Here, take this, please." He offered her a thin gold necklace from which dangled a lovely but oddly shaped charm of some sort. "It's called a hamsa. It protects against forces of darkness."

Annette smiled her thanks and put the hamsa around her neck, hoping he wouldn't see the crucifix she wore and possibly be offended.

The bookseller nodded. "Now we are safe. Come, you really must see the vault. It's quite impressive."

"I'll bet it's fuckin' impressive," said a voice behind them.

Annette and the bookseller turned to see a tall, thin, and pale young bald man pointing a gun at them. Annette didn't know much about guns, but she'd read enough detective novels and seen enough movies and television shows to recognize that whatever its make, it was equipped with a silencer.

"Just give me the money, old man, and I won't hurt either one of you."

The bookseller calmly walked over to the register, hit a few of the keys, and the cash drawers popped out with a loud *ding!* He stepped back from the register and pointed at them. "There's about three hundred dollars there, maybe another twenty in change. Please take it and leave."

The gunman moved toward the register and began yanking out the bills, stuffing them into the pockets of his black leather jacket, never moving his gaze from the bookseller. When he finished emptying the drawers, he slammed them closed and pointed the gun directly at the bookseller's chest; it was only then that Annette noticed all of the tattoos that covered the gunman's neck, but the one that stood out among the images of blood and violence depicted on his flesh was the large, dark swastika.

"Now," said the gunman, "how about we all go back and take . . . take a look at that vault of yours?" He was shaking and seemed to be in pain.

"Are you all right, son?" said the bookseller, taking a step toward him and reaching out, his sleeve moving up to reveal his prison camp number.

The gunman looked at the number and sneered. "I ain't your son, you fuckin' kike!"

The bookseller stopped moving. If he was afraid, it didn't show on his face or in his eyes.

" 'Kike'?" he said to the gunman. "You've got to be kidding me.

'Kike'? That's the best you can do? Oh, I admit, it has the tinge of nostalgia to it, but really? 'Kike'? Is that all you've got?"

"Don't," said Annette. The gunman momentarily spun in her direction, pointing the gun at her shoulder, but then turned back to the bookseller.

"You r-really don't want to mess with me, heeb!"

The bookseller clapped his hands together. "*Heeb!* Now we're getting someplace. What's next—oh, wait, don't tell me, let me guess—um . . . how about 'himey' or 'shylock' or 'matzo-gobbler' or—oh, no, I've got it! '*Arbeit Macht Frei!*'! Haven't heard *that* golden oldie since my camp days!"

The gunman clenched his teeth; whatever he was hurting for, it was getting bad.

The bookseller shook his head sadly. "Just take the money and leave."

The gunman moved closer. "Not until you sh-show me what you've got stashed in that vault."

Annette was so scared she could barely breathe. What the hell did the old man think he was accomplishing, provoking a robber like this?

The bookseller stood silent for a moment and then said, "That's it? 'Not until you sh-show me what you've got stashed in that vault'? No racial slur at the end?" He made a *tsk*-ing sound and shook his head. "Losing your edge, son. What would your Aryan brothers say at the next meeting if they knew you dropped the ball like this?"

"*Shut up, motherfucker!*"

"Oh, *that's* original."

The gunman moved closer, but the bookseller didn't budge from his spot. "Last chance, half dick. Let's go back to the vault."

The bookseller shook his head. "I'm afraid I can't do that. Trust me, son, there's nothing back there that'll be of any value to you."

The gunman started laughing. A thin patina of perspiration covered his head and face, making him almost glow under the lights. "Ain't that just like a Jew? They'd rather die than part with any of their wealth." A sudden spasm ripped through his body and he started to double over. As a result, the gun went off and shot the bookseller.

The round blew through the old man's shoulder with such ferocity that his blood spattered onto the gunman's face and hands. For a moment, the bookseller remained standing, looking at the wound as it bled out, and then he looked at Annette with an unreadable expression and slowly sank to his knees.

Her fear suddenly gone, Annette rushed over and knelt beside the bookseller, holding him in her arms.

"Oh, Lord," croaked the old man. "I'd forgotten how much that *hurts.*"

"Don't move," she said, grabbing the edge of the handkerchief the old man used to wrap the Fitzgerald volume and pulling it. The book spun out and away, freed from its wrapping. Annette crumpled the handkerchief into a tight wad and used it to stanch the flow of blood from the bookseller's shoulder. "You'll be all right, you will."

The bookseller smiled his thanks to her and then looked up toward the gunman. "*Please,*" he said. "You *need to leave now.*"

"Not until you open that vault!"

The bookseller closed his eyes and sighed in resignation, then looked at the gunman, pity in his gaze. "You poor, misguided son of a bitch. It's already open."

The floor began to vibrate; it was just a low rumble at first—more of a thrum than an actual physical manifestation—but it quickly grew in strength and intensity.

The gunman looked around in panic. "What the—? Is this a goddamn *earthquake*?"

"Not exactly," said the bookseller. His eyes were filled with tears as he looked once more at the gunman and said, "I tried to get you to leave, son. I am truly sorry."

"For what?"

All around the store, shelves began to tremble as their books shuddered, pushing against one another until there was no more room and they began falling, scattering over the floor as the glass-fronted cases began to shake and rattle, a few of the panes making loud crunching noises as spiderweb cracks spread out from their centers. The cash register was shaking, its bells sounding softly but continuously, and as more shelves began to collapse Annette felt the floor beneath her shudder as if something large and fast like a subway train were roaring underneath them.

The vault, she thought. *They can communicate with each other. Oh, dear God.*

The roar of a freight train thundered up from the floor and became a deafening snarl as somewhere farther back in the store a door was splintered into a thousand pieces and its glass shattered, blowing outward with such force Annette could feel a few slivers of it hit the back of her neck.

"I'm so sorry," whispered the bookseller in her ear.

"I know," she whispered back, kissing the old man's forehead.

There was nothing they could do.

Our eternal life means the hunger never goes away. And we have been very, very hungry. And we have waited, here in this cramped, dark place. And we have found more of our brothers and sisters of the night. And they have waited with us.

But now . . . the scent. Brief and sweet, but enough to make our hunger all-consuming.

Our waiting ends again.

Now we feed.

A sea of books hurtled themselves through the air from the back of the store, pages snapping, dog-eared teeth chewing, filling the small bookstore with the sound of a thousand paper wings flapping in rage, flying around like panicked birds released from their cages for the first time in their lives, the prolonged *hissssssss!* of a hundred thousand turning pages becoming almost deafening. The only sound louder was coming from the young man with the gun; he was screaming.

But the sounds of the books' snapping, gnawing pages quickly drowned out even that hideous noise as each dog-eared page found purchase in his flesh and slashed down, slicing, cutting, biting, tearing through skin, shredding the material of his coat and the clothing beneath, each set of teeth puncturing deeper to make room for the next page's teeth to find fresh meat, fresh blood, fresh sustenance after so long imprisoned in dusty shadows where never a hand caressed their covers, never an eye read their words, never a warm fingertip stroked their sharp, waiting, numbered corners.

For one brief moment, the pile of raw hamburger that was once a young man with a gun staggered around, eyes not yet dropping from ruined sockets, and looked straight at Annette. There was pleading in its gaze, confusion, maybe even remorse.

Annette managed to say, "So sorry . . . ," before her throat hitched and she couldn't speak.

The meat pile opened what might have been a mouth to issue something that might have been a scream, but nothing came out; no sound, no meat, no blood.

It took only a few more minutes, but soon there was nothing left of the young man with the gun except his weapon and the shredded rags that had once been the clothes he'd worn. Even his bones had been consumed.

After a few moments, the bookseller reached up and took hold of Annette's hand. "We need to . . . to clean up."

Shaking the tears from her eyes, Annette shook her head. "Screw that—we need to get you to a hospital."

Annette stood up and gently pulled the bookseller up with her. "Put your weight against me."

"It's not *that* bad."

"Tell that to my coat and blouse." Both were soaked in the bookseller's blood.

They made their way over to the counter and the bookseller sat down on a small stool. "Thank you for being so kind," he said.

Annette touched the hamsa around her neck. "Thank *you* for protecting me."

The bookseller reached under his tie and behind his shirt collar, pulling out a similar hamsa. "Don't leave home without it. Hey . . . will you . . . will you come back tomorrow and help me? The books have gorged themselves. They'll be sleeping for a good while. You won't be in any danger. Will you come back?"

"Come back? What the hell makes you think I'm going to leave your side any time soon?" Annette found the telephone—a rotary-dial, it figured—and began dialing 911. They'd get their stories straight before the police and EMTs arrived.

The bookseller smiled. "Uri once said the same thing to me."

"Yeah, well . . . just don't ever call me that. My name is Annette."

"Mine is Saul."

"Nice to meet you."

"The pleasure is mine, dear lady. The pleasure is most definitely mine." He waited until she hung up the phone before asking, "What was that about not leaving my side . . . ?"

"Seems to me you could use an extra pair of hands around here."

The bookseller grinned. "Now that you mention it, there are only *so many* paper cuts one person can take . . ."

—For Nanci Black

MISS FONDEVANT

CHARLAINE HARRIS

"The class will be seated," Miss Fondevant said clearly, and the twenty-two sixth graders sat down at their desks. Miss Fondevant looked around her domain, Room 2. Susan Langley held her breath, and she knew she wasn't the only child who did.

Miss Fondevant nodded approvingly, and Susan relaxed. "Taylor Oswalt, turn over the calendar." Taylor left his desk and hurried to the calendar, a big one by the teacher's desk. He flipped it over to read *Friday, September 25, 1970*. Then he went back to his desk just as quickly, his shoelaces flopping around and his black hair flying.

"Please get out your spelling and vocabulary books," Miss Fondevant said. She was wearing a skirt and blouse, as always. She favored pastels in the hot months, oranges and greens in the cold months. Though she was rather stout and pale, Miss Fondevant had beautiful skin and smooth brown hair pulled back into a bun, an old-fashioned hairstyle that suited her.

The other teachers thought it looked out-of-date. Susan knew this because her own mother was a teacher.

"You have five minutes to look over the words before we have the test," Miss Fondevant told them. Miss Fondevant glanced at the little clock on her desk. All of the faces but one were bent intently to the lists of twelve words.

"Miss Fondevant, can I go to the bathroom?" James Phillip Farmer asked. There was a suppressed snicker from Ricky Cannavale behind him, because when you're twelve years old, any bathroom reference is funny.

"James Phillip, you had ample time to go to the bathroom before the bell rang," Miss Fondevant replied, with no smile of any sort. "You must wait."

"But, Miss Fondevant—"

"I said no, James Phillip."

James Phillip Farmer looked rebellious . . . and uncomfortable. He wriggled in his seat. "I been sick, Miss Fondevant. Please!"

Miss Fondevant's lips pressed together, an expression that meant she was displeased—or rather, that she was more displeased than usual. "All right, James Phillip. Tomorrow, no more excuses. If you are sick, you must stay home. If you're at school, you should be well enough to abide by the rules."

"Yes, ma'am. I'll get the note." James Phillip, who was a small boy with a shock of pale hair, fumbled with his backpack for a second before giving up the attempt. He fairly jumped from his seat and ran out into the hall, looking almost as pale as Miss Fondevant. While Susan and the other children looked at their spelling lists, Miss Fondevant went to the classroom door to watch for James Phillip's return. She was very conscientious.

Susan, to her chagrin the tallest child in the room and therefore always conspicuous, very cautiously turned her head a little to watch Miss Fondevant. It was a good idea to always know the location of her teacher, she'd found. Her mother had been so happy when Susan had found her own name on Miss Fondevant's class list! Her mother had said, "Honey, she's only been here for three years, but her reputation is solid. Everyone behaves in her room. You can really learn because she keeps order. You're going to love it."

After the tumult of her fourth-grade classroom and the horror of her fifth-grade year, Susan had found the first few weeks in Miss Fondevant's room blissful, just as her mother had predicted.

Kids just *minded* this teacher.

This was all the more extraordinary because Miss Fondevant's face seldom wavered from its expression of calm benevolence. She never said she would paddle them or that she would send them to the principal or that she would call their parents. Miss Fondevant didn't *threaten*.

She gave you one warning.

If that warning was not heeded, she'd walk by the offender's desk, kind of casual, and grip the child's shoulder, and after that, she'd be obeyed. After the first month of school, somehow even the worst kid, Taylor Oswalt, had bent to Miss Fondevant's will— though the previous year, he'd talked back to Mrs. Stoker, deemed the most terrifying woman in the world by the kids at Vivian G. Anderson School, which housed the fifth, sixth, and seventh grades.

Taylor was a quiet boy now, not the whirling dervish he'd been since he'd been born. Even his father had commented on the change at Teacher Conference Night. Though it was intended for parents to talk to the teacher without the student present, Susan's mom was a single parent, rare in Schulzberg. So Susan, who was able to be relied on to sit quietly outside the classroom, had trailed along. On their drive home, her mother had muttered, "I never knew Larry Oswalt realized he had a kid named Taylor, much less knew how bad he was." Then Susan's mother had said, "Susan, you forget I said that. Larry has his own problems."

"Yes, ma'am," Susan had said. And she had repeated her mom's comment to only one person—Frieda Parker, her best friend. Frieda clearly didn't want to criticize Susan's mom, but she'd said, "Who could forget he had a kid like Taylor?"

"I think my mom meant that Mr. Oswalt is always in trouble himself." Susan, who was a much better listener than her mother had ever imagined, had no problem putting two and two together. And Susan was certainly smart enough to realize that Frieda was not the sharpest knife in the drawer.

"Wow. He must be pretty awful," Frieda said. "Taylor's the worst kid I've ever met."

Susan agreed. Taylor *was* the worst. Though he did not talk back or act out violently, he could not sit still. He had trouble concentrating. He seemed to daydream all the time, or at least he didn't pay attention to what the teacher was saying.

Taylor had been assigned Miss Fondevant's room as a last resort, Susan had overheard her mother say. Susan's mom, Merlie, taught at a different school, the elementary. Since Susan's dad had died, Merlie Langley had spent a lot of time on the phone, mostly with her own best friend, Donna Lynn Strasbourg, who also taught at the elementary school.

Susan heard a lot of gossip about the other teachers, since her mother seemed to forget Susan was listening. Susan was pretty good at keeping her mouth shut. It was part of being smart. If she talked about what she'd heard, she wouldn't hear any more. Susan liked to know stuff. It kept her safe. Since Susan didn't have a dad, safety was a big issue to her.

Merlie Langley had told Donna Lynn, "I guess they gave Emily Fondevant both Susan and Taylor to kind of balance each other out."

Susan hadn't been able to hear Donna Lynn's reply, but Merlie had laughed and said, "No, Susan's always been naturally obedient. She's no saint, but she's got that sense of order. Her dad had nothing to do with *that*, I can tell you."

Susan had her own opinion about her dad's effect on her character. He'd been a fun-loving man from way up in Wisconsin, a place so far from Arkansas and so cold in the winter that Susan couldn't even imagine it. He'd adored Susan. He'd loved Merlie. He'd had a good job at the bank. And then he'd died.

Susan, taking her vocabulary test now that James Phillip was back from the restroom, didn't want to think about it. She glanced over at Frieda, whose lips were moving as she matched the vocabulary words with their definitions.

Miss Fondevant was walking up and down the rows of desks. She, too, seemed to be watching Frieda's lips move. Frieda was olive skinned where Susan was fair, and her brunette hair came down to the point of her chin and bounced in exuberant waves, while Susan's was flaxen and fell straight down her back. Frieda's dad often slapped Frieda's big brother, and Frieda, too. Susan had learned a lot about the Way Things Were from Frieda.

After the vocabulary test (Susan had gotten every word right, as usual), it was reading time. All the children had books from the school library. They were supposed to take them out from their desks and read them, while smaller groups took turns working on sentence structure with Miss Fondevant. The first small group was made up of James Phillip, Taylor, Frieda, and Susan. They took their chairs at the small round table by the door. Miss Fondevant was too big to get right up to the low table, so she sat back a little. To Susan's anxiety, James Phillip was twitchy again, and tense all over.

Susan thought, *There's something wrong with him.* Otherwise, the fear of Miss Fondevant would have kept the boy still. Even Taylor Oswalt took his seat in an orderly way.

Miss Fondevant frowned at James Phillip. She leaned forward to put her hand on his shoulder, as if to remind him that he must be quiet and still. But though his body was less tense as he perched in his chair, his mouth was drawn to one side.

Susan thought, *He hurts.* She was reminded of how her grand-mother had looked when she'd had one of her upset stomachs.

However, she began to hope everything would go smoothly when James Phillip read his paragraphs. He did well enough, though he gasped once or twice. Just as it was time for Taylor to tell what word in the next sentence was the subject, James Phillip blurted, "Miss Fondevant, I have to go again."

"No, James Phillip."

"Miss Fondevant. Something's wrong with me."

"There certainly is. You seem intent on disrupting this class." And there was not anything benevolent about Miss Fondevant's face any longer. She was quite angry.

"I'm sick, Miss Fondevant."

"I received no note from your mother, or the doctor, or the school nurse."

James Phillip said, "I have a note . . ." But something terrible seemed to happen inside him just then, because he looked like no boy should look: in pain and terrified. He bent over and vomited. He pitched off his chair and onto the blue area rug.

Miss Fondevant acted immediately. "Frieda, run to the office. Tell Mrs. Fallon to call an ambulance." As Frieda dashed out, the teacher knelt by James Phillip. "Sit in your places and keep quiet," she told the other children, sounding quite savage. Too frightened to return to their desks, Susan and Taylor remained at the round table. Since James Phillip and Miss Fondevant were on the side of the table closest to the door, Susan and Taylor were the only ones who had a clear view. James Phillip had froth coming from his mouth.

Frieda ran back into the classroom to tell Miss Fondevant that the ambulance was on its way. She stood by the doorway, panting. The principal, Mr. Kosper, stepped around her to enter.

"How is he?" asked Mr. Kosper. He was very worried. His normally good-humored face was serious, and his glasses had slid down on his nose. "What happened? Didn't you get the note?"

Miss Fondevant didn't shift her gaze from James Phillip as he lay on the carpet. He was breathing noisily. In a voice like ice slivers, she replied, "I received no note. I had no way of knowing something was wrong with the boy."

Susan thought, *She's setting out her case.* Miss Fondevant was preparing to defend herself. She'd heard her own mother do the same thing when she'd written a check on an account she'd known was overdrawn.

Mr. Kosper, looking down at James Phillip, said, "Mrs. Fallon is calling his parents." He turned to look at the doorway. "I can hear the ambulance coming." He lurched to his feet and went to look out into the hall, ready to wave the stretcher to the right room.

Miss Fondevant remaining kneeling by James Phillip, whose eyes were closed. The boy was looking whiter and whiter. Susan couldn't look away, though she wanted to. So she was watching when—with a jerky motion, as though she couldn't help herself—Miss Fondevant put her hand on James Phillip's forehead. His body rippled from head to foot as though a wave had picked him up, and the breath escaped his lungs in a little "aaaaaa."

Then he was still. Susan knew he was dead.

Susan and Taylor looked at each other. Then they turned to Frieda. It was the most complex silent exchange Susan had ever had since she'd looked into her grandmother's eyes at her dad's funeral. None of them dared to look at Miss Fondevant, for fear she would look back. Without speaking a word, they went to their desks, walking as silently as they possibly could. Aside from the blare of the ambulance just outside the school doors, there was not a single sound in Room 2.

The children who could go home early were picked up by their parents. Room 2's other kids were divided among the rest of the sixth-grade teachers. Susan, whose mom had to work, spent the remainder of the day sitting at the back of Mrs. Sullivan's room next door along with Frieda, whose mom hadn't been home when the school called.

Though Merlie wanted to spend that Saturday talking about what had happened and comforting her daughter, Susan had other fish to fry. She told her mother she felt fine, and she rode her bike to the library as soon as her mom got on the phone with Donna Lynn to talk about her daughter's intransigence.

Susan had consulted the set of encyclopedias in the bookcase in the dining room. She took a notebook with her and wrote many interesting points in it, gleaned from her research. She also checked out several books. "This is a new interest for you, Susan," Mrs. Prentiss said. She frowned. "Not a healthy one."

"You know I have a good head on my shoulders, Mrs. Prentiss," Susan said. "My mom always says so." She smiled at the older woman. She was secretly afraid that the librarian would call her mom, but as Mrs. Prentiss shook her head and turned to the next patron, Susan could tell she wasn't going to.

On Sunday, Susan and Merlie went to church in their nice dresses, and then they ate Sunday lunch at Gary's Golden Grill along with lots of other church people.

Susan did not sleep well Sunday night. Tomorrow she'd be back in Room 2.

On Monday, Mr. Kosper was going to have an assembly to talk about what had happened. Merlie had explained to Susan that some of the town ministers would be there to answer children's questions about James Phillip's "passing." This was a new and revolutionary concept to everyone in Schulzberg.

Merlie said, "They'll help you put James Phillip's passing in a faith context." Merlie sighed. "I think we've already been through this, though, haven't we, honey?" Merlie missed Susan's dad awfully, just like Susan.

"Mom, I'm scared," Susan said.

Her mother looked at her with sympathy and said, "Sweetie, I know it seems awful wrong when someone your age passes away, even worse than when we lost your dad, maybe, but it's part of life. You need to go to school and face it. Everyone else is very sad, too. They'll understand."

"I'm not scared about that," Susan said, trying desperately to find a way to tell her mother the truth. "At least, not of dying like James Phillip. I know he's in heaven, Mom." (At least, she sort of believed that might be true.) "It's the *way* he died." But there she stalled. Susan just couldn't tell Merlie that Miss Fondevant had murdered James Phillip. Her mother would never believe it.

Susan was simply resigned when Merlie dropped her at the middle school, giving Susan an extra kiss and saying, "I'll be thinking of you, honey," before she drove off to the elementary school.

Since the bell hadn't rung and the weather was sunny, a lot of the kids were staying outside until the last minute. Susan sat on the low wall around the schoolyard. Frieda joined her there. Taylor ran by, his shirt untucked and his shoelaces undone. He gave them a wild look. Susan could tell he wanted to talk but didn't dare stop. Boys who stopped to talk to girls (at least some boys who talked to some girls—it was a complex system) got teased. A lot.

When the bell rang, Frieda and Susan trudged silently to Room 2. Miss Fondevant was standing at the door, so they were obliged to greet her as they passed inside. There was a big black bow on James Phillip's desk, as though he'd gotten the most awful birthday present ever. Susan rolled her eyes at Frieda, who stared back like a frightened rabbit.

All the children gave the empty desk sidelong glances. Susan noticed the compartment under the seat was completely cleaned out: all James Phillip's drawings and old papers and books and notebooks, gone. The desk looked as if it had been scrubbed.

No black for Miss Fondevant; she wore powder blue and tiny gold earrings to match the gold ring she always wore on her right hand, the one with the three pink roses on it. Susan had always admired the ring. She wondered if Miss Fondevant would say anything about what had happened on Friday, but she didn't. She took attendance just as usual, her voice calm and cool.

The intercom crackled on. Mr. Kosper's voice announced, *"Teachers, please take your classes to the auditorium."* Jillian, who had the desk to the right of James Phillip's, was already tearful.

Because they were in Miss Fondevant's class, they were in the position of being chief mourners. None of the children jostled or joked in line on their way to the auditorium.

The teachers had all had special instructions, Susan could tell, because none of them sat with their children. Instead, they all stood against the auditorium wall close to their classes. Susan wondered if they stood apart so they could watch their students better. She'd managed to maneuver next to Frieda in line so they could sit together. Since Miss Fondevant was looking at the stage, Susan felt free to look at her teacher. She whispered, "She doesn't look upset."

"Shut up," Frieda whispered back urgently.

Susan had never been spoken to like that, especially not by her best friend. She almost replied, but she saw that Miss Fondevant's gaze was moving in her direction. She looked straight ahead and kept her lips pressed together.

Mr. Kosper stepped up to the podium. He was tall and skinny with big black-framed glasses, and he was not married, which made a few single teachers hopeful. Susan kind of liked Mr. Kosper, who usually wore bright ties with cartoon characters on them and usually smiled a lot. Today, Mr. Kosper wore a black tie and a somber look.

"Most of you knew James Phillip his whole life," he said. "Some of you went to church with him at Our Lady of Sorrows Catholic Church. Some of you played with him. What you didn't know about

James Phillip was that he had just gotten diagnosed with a serious illness. His doctor thought James Phillip had a Wilms' tumor." Mr. Kosper had been looking down to read the unfamiliar term. He missed the startled flicker of movement from many of the students. None of them had known.

"James Phillip was taking medicine," Mr. Kosper continued. "In his math book, he had a note for Miss Fondevant from his mom, describing his illness and requesting Miss Fondevant to let him go to the restroom any time he needed, or to the nurse's room to see Mrs. Marks. And James Phillip's mother called the school Friday morning and talked to Mrs. Marks and to me." Mr. Kosper took a deep breath. Mrs. Marks, the school nurse, was patting her eyes with a tissue. "But James Phillip got sicker faster than anyone expected. He forgot to give his note to Miss Fondevant. And everything went wrong after that. Now we're all going to miss James Phillip."

Without turning her head, Susan slewed her eyes to the left to look at Miss Fondevant.

Though it would have been easy to believe that her teacher was so stern faced today from grief and regret, Susan knew that she was simply angry about all the to-do. Miss Fondevant had murdered James Phillip when she'd put her hand on his forehead. Susan felt the knowledge settle into her, as immutable as the multiplication tables.

After Mr. Kosper finished speaking, a woman Susan had never seen before told them how important their feelings were. It was certainly the first time any of the children had heard this, and they gaped at her. Then there was a long announcement about how Father Perry and the Reverend Hutchins were going to stay in the auditorium to talk to any kid who asked to leave class to speak to them. That was kind of weird and exciting.

Even kids who hadn't liked or known James Phillip were unsettled by the time the assembly was over. None of the kids in Miss

Fondevant's class asked to return to the auditorium except Jillian, the girl who'd cried that morning.

Miss Fondevant let Jillian go without even a stern look. And she didn't touch anyone all day.

Susan's mom asked her that night if she'd talked to any of the counselors.

"No," Susan said. She turned her head back to the television. She loved *Gunsmoke*. Matt Dillon was always right, and Miss Kitty was always supportive.

"Are you feeling sad?" Merlie sat on the couch by Susan. "You know you can tell me about it."

Susan turned to look at her mom. For one second, she hoped she could. But then she went through the conversation in her mind. *Mom, Miss Fondevant put her hand on James Phillip's head and killed him. She just couldn't stop herself. The kids in her class are good because she makes us be good.* "I'm not feeling sad," she said hesitantly. "But I'm pretty mad."

Her mom looked surprised. "That's not what I expected," she said. "What makes you mad?"

"Miss Fondevant," Susan said.

"But, sweetie . . ." Her mom took a deep breath. "It's not James Phillip's fault, exactly, that he didn't give her the note. I think his mom should have called Miss Fondevant at home to explain. If only he hadn't forgotten the note. Or maybe he thought it would make him stand out, and he was embarrassed."

Susan, who saw she simply couldn't tell her mother the truth, struggled to frame a question about something else that had bothered her. "He didn't have a dad, James Phillip. I mean, he has a dad, but his dad is in the army and he doesn't get to come home much. And I don't have a dad. But I'm not sick, right?" Miss Fondevant had been able to kill James Phillip so easily because he was already ill.

Immediately, her mom's face got that wounded look, the one Susan had learned to dread. "You are just right as rain, baby girl," she said very quietly. "Your dad . . . well, the doctors weren't able to find out what happened inside his body. But you and me, we're okay." For a moment, Susan's mom looked unlike the naturally lighthearted woman that Susan instinctively knew her mom to be. "Honey," Merlie went on, "I've known Miss Fondevant for two years. She's always kept a quiet classroom, and she's always known every kid very, very well. It's just crazy, the way she can tell you about each and every child in her room. She's a marvelous teacher."

"Right, Mom," Susan said, turning back to the television.

The day after the assembly was a little more normal than Monday had been. Miss Fondevant removed the bow from the desk. Wednesday was even better. A new kid entered the school, and she took James Phillip's place. Of course the other children told her that she had a dead boy's desk, and JerriDell pretended to be terrified, but Susan could tell JerriDell didn't have a lot of imagination. James Phillip didn't seem real to the new girl.

That was actually good for the other kids in the class. JerriDell fit in very easily.

Now it was Frieda's willful ignorance that worried Susan. When she tried to talk to her best friend at their usual meeting place at recess, Frieda said, "We probably just thought we saw something." Frieda was trying to sound grown-up, but instead sounded unbearably condescending. Susan glared at her, keenly feeling the betrayal. Frieda recognized Susan's anger and became more adamant. "Everything is *all right*," she told Susan defiantly, and then she ran off to play jump rope with the Lucky Girls. The ones who had dads *and* moms *and* nice houses *and* clothes. Susan had fallen out of that group when her father had died and they'd had to move to a smaller house. To Frieda's (and Susan's) astonishment, the Lucky Girls let Frieda in the game.

In her despair, Susan did something she had never, ever imagined she would do. She waited by the outside water fountain for Taylor, and she voluntarily spoke to him. She'd taken great care to time it so they were by themselves. "Hey. Taylor. Do *you* understand what happened to James Phillip?" she said.

"Yeah. She killed him," Taylor said, holding still with an effort. He glanced from side to side, reassuring himself they were not being watched. "And when she puts her hand on my shoulder, sometimes I think she'll kill me, too." The manic light in his eyes was gone, as was the overabundance of energy that had made him move constantly before Miss Fondevant had gotten a hold on him. For a moment, he seemed like a ghost of himself. Then his face reanimated, he grimaced grotesquely, and Susan felt a great relief.

"We have to stop her," Susan said.

And then JerriDell ran up to get a drink, and Susan and Taylor split away in opposite directions.

For the next two weeks, the odd conspirators met at snatched moments, each terrified the other children would detect and publicize their partnership. Susan continued to reign as the class smart person, and Taylor continued to be the just-reined-in bad boy, thanks to Miss Fondevant's shoulder squeezes. Sometimes Susan wondered if Miss Fondevant suspected something, because her shoulder squeezes became more frequent. One day, she gripped Taylor's shoulder twice. He found a chance to talk to Susan behind a tree on the playground. "I don't get it," he said. "She doesn't come to my house at night and drink my blood."

"She's not drinking blood," Susan said, "she's stealing your energy."

He nodded. "Yeah," he said wearily. "Maybe she'll take it all." He trudged away.

One evening as they were driving home, Susan's mom asked, "Does your teacher . . . grab people by the shoulder?" She was trying so hard to sound casual that Susan was instantly alerted. She had a flash of hope. Someone suspected!

Susan nodded vehemently.

Merlie looked straight ahead. She said, "Mrs. Costello was telling me that." Mrs. Costello taught in Room 1, right across the hall. Merlie took a deep breath before she continued. "Do you . . . has she ever done that to you? I would hate to think she . . . when she became your teacher, I just figured how nice it would be for you to be in a quiet room, after last year." The fifth grade had been awful for Susan, and her teacher had not been any kind of disciplinarian.

Susan thought hard about how to respond. "Miss Fondevant doesn't grab them to make their shoulders hurt," Susan said, trying to tell her mother the vitally important thing without mentioning the word she knew would make her mom quit listening. "She squeezes some, and they get really quiet. Like she's draining them." She waited, hopeful.

"She just touches their shoulder, huh?" Susan's mom looked vastly relieved. In fact, she laughed a little. "Well. Okay. As long as she's not hitting kids, or paddling them." Merlie shook her head. "I know that woman's sixty, and she doesn't look a day over forty. I'll have to ask her what her secret is!"

"No, Mom, don't!" Susan's cry was involuntary and from the heart.

Merlie looked right at Susan then. "You think that would be rude? Well, maybe. No reason to get all in fuss, Susan."

Susan was desperate. "Mom, you know what her secret is," Susan whispered. How could Merlie not understand?

For the second time, Merlie shied away from the truth. She laughed far too shrilly. "Oil of Olay? Pond's Cold Cream? I've tried 'em all, honey, and I haven't looked a day younger."

Susan's disappointment was so sharp that she almost summoned up the cruelty to ask her mother why her father had died. That was a question that always made her mother get quiet and sad. Susan knew only that her father had been found crumpled by his car in Lake Crystal Park, at the west end of town. When her grandmother had come for the funeral, she'd also been silent about the way her own son had perished.

After her grandmother had gone home, her mother had said to Donna Lynn, *I know what people are saying behind my back. They're saying he didn't go there to run, he went there to meet some other woman.* Susan had been angry that no one had thought of telling *her* that. Surely she should know what people were saying about her own father? There was no way at all that her dad would meet up with some other woman in the park.

But now, Susan knew she should be kind to her mother, who couldn't help being blind. Susan said, "Mom, you always look pretty, Oil of Olay or not. I can tell Mr. Kosper thinks so."

Merlie looked startled. "Really?" she said. "He said something to you?"

"Yes, ma'am," Susan said. "He said he wished you taught at his school."

The rest of the way home, Merlie was thoughtful, cheerful, and (most importantly) diverted.

Susan missed her father something awful. Maybe she could have made him understand.

That night, for the first time in fourteen months, Susan opened her father's box.

Though Susan thought of it as a sacred object, it was just a brown cardboard box stuffed into the back of the shelf in the hall closet, where her mother kept the vacuum cleaner. It had always been very hard for Susan to reach, and she had to be very quiet while she did it.

She managed that this evening. Merlie was working on student evaluations, and she'd put on a record album (Three Dog Night) to listen to while she worked. So Susan was able to set up the folding steps, reach the shelf, and pull the box forward. It was much easier than it had been the last time she'd done it—a measure of how much she'd grown the past year.

She crept to her room with her burden. By now the objects in it were very familiar. The largest one was her parents' honeymoon photo album, which her mother couldn't bear to see these days. And there were framed things: certificates, commendations, and diplomas earned over her dad's thirty-five years. Underneath those was a small shoebox of pictures of Howard Langley's childhood, spent in a baffling world of deep snow and canoes in mysterious waters, and relatives Susan had seen only a couple of times. Wisconsin seemed like another world to her.

But after a quick glance, she put all these things aside for her favorite memento: her dad's high school yearbook. It was almost magical to her, her dad so young and handsome, the clothes so different. Howard Langley had played a game called lacrosse. Susan had never heard of it, but she'd looked it up. The yearbook showed Howard in his lacrosse uniform, and decorating the school for the Winter Carnival (whatever that was), and in a group of athletes giving a talk to younger kids. Those kids were the size of Susan now, so she enjoyed that picture more than all the others. She turned to it now. It was a whole half page.

Her dad was controlling a puppet, its wooden feet against the teacher's desk, and another brawny boy was manipulating his own puppet to engage in battle with her dad's, and the kids were laughing, and even the teachers way in the background were smiling . . .

Susan clapped a hand over her own mouth to smother a yell.

One of the teachers was Miss Fondevant.

No, Susan thought. *It can't be.* She took a deep breath, clamped her lips together, and looked at the picture again.

The teacher's hair was in a different style, but not that different. Her clothes were a different style, too, but looking at the other teachers in the picture, they were right for the time and place. Her figure was the same. The way she held her head was the same.

She wanted to run to the TV room to show her mother. But Susan thought, *Sit for a minute before you do something. Think about it.* She took some deep breaths. She read the caption under the half-page picture.

Lacrosse seniors Howard Langley and Dave Parnell demonstrate their puppeteer abilities to Miss Franklin's seventh-grade class.

Miss Franklin was Miss Fondevant.

In that crystalline moment, Susan understood how her father had died. He had gone to run at Crystal Lake. He *had* gone there to run. But that evening, Miss Fondevant had been there as well. He must have seen her at his job at the bank. He had let her know that she reminded him—what an amazing coincidence!—of a teacher from his youth back in Wisconsin, of all places! How shocked she must have been to be starting over in a new place, far away, and be recognized. What had Susan's father thought when she grabbed ahold of him and wouldn't let go? Had he not wanted to hit a woman, especially an older one? But then realized she was killing him . . . too late?

The enormity of it made her almost as weak as her father must have felt. Though she returned the box to its place before she went to bed, she kept the yearbook and hid it in her room in an old satchel on her closet floor.

It took Susan two days to recover. She was carrying around something too big for a person her age, too big for a person any age. She told herself that it was good Frieda was not her best friend anymore because she would have had to ignore her while she tried to get back to normal. She missed Frieda bitterly, in every sense of the word.

On the second day after she'd opened her father's yearbook, Miss Fondevant gripped her shoulder.

Susan had gotten careless, hadn't been paying the careful attention she'd given the teacher ever since the James Phillip incident.
Since James Phillip died, she told herself harshly. She'd been thinking
of the picture again, a terrible mistake when she was actually in Miss .
Fondevant's presence.

"Susan!" said the teacher. "Pay attention." For the first time,
Susan felt Miss Fondevant's hand on her, felt the cold of it pulling
the warmth out of her . . . felt a strange lassitude creep over her.
Susan called it "sleepiness" to herself, but it was both more and less
than that. For the rest of the school day, Susan was able to cope only
because she feared the consequences. She did everything Miss
Fondevant told her to do, because otherwise Miss Fondevant would
touch her again.

As Susan watched Miss Fondevant make her way to the teachers'
lounge, after the lunch bell, Susan came to a horrible realization.
Miss Fondevant was able to walk and talk because she had stolen
some of Susan's life from her.

That afternoon, she got into her mother's car like a puppet with
slack strings. "Are you all right?" Susan's mother asked, her face worried.

"Miss Fondevant touched my shoulder," Susan said. She looked
directly into her mother's eyes.

"She hurt you?" Susan's mom said incredulously. "I'll tell her not
to put a goddamned finger on you again. Just you wait."

"And what's she going to say?" Susan asked, her voice merely
tired.

Susan's mother was disconcerted. "What do you mean?"

"She's going to say, 'Oh, Merlie, I just tap them on the shoulder
to make sure they're listening to me.' And you're going to say,
'Emily, something you're doing to those kids is really having an
effect on them. I wish you'd find some other way to make your dis-
cipline felt in the classroom.' And for a while she'll lay off, but it
won't last forever."

Susan's mother looked at her strangely. Susan could see her struggling with what to say. As they got out of the car at their house, her mom said, "We'll talk about this tomorrow, okay?"

If Merlie hadn't gone right to the kitchen to use the telephone, Susan might have had some hope. But Merlie was calling Donna Lynn. After a moment they would laugh, and the problem would shrink. They'd think of something else to talk about, and the problem would shrink some more.

The next day in a far corner of the playground, where Susan pretended to be making a clover blossom chain while Taylor was bouncing a ball off the fence and catching it—just within hearing distance—they talked over ways and means. "If we could figure out how to do it," Susan said, "we could hook her up to something that would drain *her*. She would lose all her energy and die."

"My dad has a gun," Taylor said. "I don't know if I could take it without him knowing, but I bet I could. We could just shoot her."

Susan stared at him, her hands lying limp in her lap full of clover blossoms. "I never thought of that." She mulled it over for a minute. "It would make a big noise, like it does on TV, I guess," she said uncertainly. "And it would be real messy. And people would come running."

"Yeah, it'd be hard to act like we didn't know anything about it," Taylor said. "My dad's gun, after all."

"She drinks coffee all the time—maybe I could put something poisonous in her coffee. Like the stuff we put out to kill roaches."

"That stuff has a pretty strong smell," Taylor said. "My dad uses it in his shop."

Susan pictured a flower shop, full of sweet scents and beautiful blooms. "What does your dad do?"

"He fixes cars, sometimes. He works for a construction company, sometimes. What does your dad do?"

"My dad is dead. Miss Fondevant murdered him, too."

"He died out at the park, right?"

"Yeah, but she was there. They knew each other from before, and she looked the same. She couldn't let him live."

They looked at each other briefly. Then Taylor went back to bouncing the ball.

Susan had to say something. "What about your mom?" Of course, Tyler would know that her mother was a teacher.

"She married someone else. She's got three kids with her other husband. She doesn't need me." Blessedly, Taylor did not ask her any questions about her father. At that moment, Susan came close to genuinely liking Taylor.

"We have to keep thinking," Susan said, and she did.

Susan carpooled to gymnastics class that afternoon. When she returned, she found her mother sitting in the kitchen with her dad's yearbook open before her on the table. It was turned to the page Susan had marked with a torn piece of paper—the picture of Susan's dad with Miss Fondevant.

Susan stopped in the doorway, uncertain of what to say or do. Her mom was not crying, and that was good. Susan couldn't stand it when her mom cried.

"Susan, I'm sorry," her mother said.

Susan came a little farther into the kitchen, still waiting to be sure she understood.

"It's Miss Fondevant, isn't it?" her mother said, and Susan's heart soared with joy. Merlie believed her! But her mom looked wrong, not "avenging angel" but more like "soft mama."

"This woman looks so much like her," Merlie said, "I can see why . . ."

The crush of the disappointment made Susan run past her mom down the hall to her little bedroom, slamming the door behind her. Susan didn't know whom she hated more—Miss Fondevant or her mother.

It was a bad night in the Langley household.

Susan didn't sleep well, and she was in a grim mood the next morning. Susan wasn't sure if she ever wanted to be a grown-up, if grown-ups were that stupid.

She was glad when Taylor passed her a grubby note on his way to his desk that morning. It read *I thought of a way.*

It took some elaborate maneuvering for Susan to engineer a moment to talk to him. She sat on a bench on the playground, apparently absorbed in a piece of paper, and he sat on the other end facing in the opposite direction, studiously taking off a sneaker and shaking it upside down to get out an imaginary pebble.

"My dad showed me a stick of dynamite," he said over his shoulder. "I remembered a couple of days ago. It took me until now to find it. He keeps it at the back of his shop in a lockbox. I found the key last night."

"But we can't blow up our classroom."

"We can blow up her car. While she's in it."

"Okay." That seemed simple enough to Susan. "Is it like the cartoons? You just light the thing at the end?"

"Pretty much. That's what my dad told me, back when he was showing it to me. He stole it off a demolition job."

Though they were planning to kill Miss Fondevant, Susan was still shocked when Taylor confessed so casually that his father had stolen something. She didn't want Taylor to see it, so she instantly created a crime for herself. "I'll take the lighter my mom uses to light candles," she said firmly. It was an old Zippo that her father had used for his rare cigarette. "We'll have to put it under her car when she gets into it."

"So we need to watch to see when she goes to her car," Taylor said. "I catch the bus."

"Okay," Susan said, understanding. Since she waited at the school for her mom, she was the obvious choice for the job.

Even this would take some doing. Before today, she'd waited inside the school at the main entrance, so she could watch for her mother's car to pull up. "Tomorrow," she told her mother that night, "I'm going to wait at the side entrance by the teachers' parking lot."

"Why? Not that it really makes any difference, but . . ."

"I had a fight with Frieda, and I don't want to wait with her." It was the most childish reason Susan could think of, and it worked like a charm.

The next day it was raining, and Susan sat on the floor just inside the glass doors. Miss Fondevant was the second teacher to leave. She stopped beside Susan.

"Is everything all right, Susan?" she asked in her formal way.

"Yes, ma'am. My mom told me to wait at this door today." Susan hoped she was imagining the gleam of suspicion in Miss Fondevant's eyes, behind the glasses. The gold ring seemed to wink at Susan in the fluorescent light.

"All right, then. See you tomorrow," Miss Fondevant said, and went down the steps and to her car, a Ford Fairlane. It was 4:02 p.m., Susan ascertained by glancing up at the big hall clock. For the next three days, Miss Fondevant left at the same time. The fourth day, she stayed longer for a teacher meeting. Susan's mother got used to picking Susan up at the side entrance, and she even said it was a little easier than the front.

While she waited to execute her schoolteacher, Susan tried to remember what it had been like before she knew about Miss Fondevant, about her father. Frieda and her other classmates seemed like real children to her now, while Susan was not. She began wearing sweaters or jackets with pockets, so she could put the lighter in them. Since the weather was cooling off, her wardrobe was not peculiar, but if she'd been caught with the lighter, the consequences would have been dire.

Taylor seemed almost buoyant that Thursday, running on the

playground and playing basketball with his buddies like a demon, energy flying off in all directions. When he came in from lunch recess, sweaty and disheveled, he dropped his geography book while Miss Fondevant's back was turned, and she jumped. Some of the children laughed; it was so strange to see Miss Fondevant surprised by anything.

Miss Fondevant turned, smiling, and instantly all the laughter died away. "Taylor," she said, "please come up here." Taylor looked across the room at Susan and she saw the fear in his eyes. Taylor, who really had no choice, got up and walked to the front of the room. Susan held her breath. Surely Miss Fondevant wouldn't dare to kill him? Susan thought, *She can't, he's healthy.* And she had the vague conviction that two dead kids in one room would be very suspicious, even for someone as respectable as Miss Fondevant.

Taylor's hands, dangling, were visibly shaking. Daniel (who sat to Susan's left) opened his mouth to jeer, but Susan glared at him. Daniel's grin faded and he looked down.

Miss Fondevant put her hand on Taylor's shoulder. He looked sick almost immediately, so Susan knew the teacher was gripping hard to cause pain as well as to suck the life out of Taylor. The children watched, their eyes wide, though some looked away and behaved as if nothing were happening.

Susan tried desperately to think of something to stop the teacher. She looked at the door, with its big glass pane, and she said, "Mr. Kosper!" in a voice designed to carry.

When Susan looked back at Miss Fondevant, the teacher was standing a couple of feet away from Taylor, who had put one hand to the corner of her desk to keep upright. Miss Fondevant looked from the door to Susan when Mr. Kosper didn't appear. Her teacher's face was smooth but Susan could see under her skin now, and she knew the look. It was like when her always-dieting mom pushed away her dinner plate before she was satisfied.

Susan knew she was doomed. Miss Fondevant would never forgive and forget.

Luckily for Susan, there was a peremptory crackling from the public address system, and the school secretary's voice said, "*Miss Fondevant, Mr. Kosper says it's time for your class to go to their exams.*"

The scoliosis exam. Everyone had it when they were in the sixth grade. Today was their room's time slot. Susan exhaled, unaware she'd been holding her breath until she let it out. And the mention of Mr. Kosper's name had somehow made it seem as though he *had* looked into Room 2.

"Line up," Miss Fondevant said briskly. "We're going to the PE classroom over in the gym."

Miss Fondevant made sure they formed a line silently, and then she started them marching in the right direction. The halls were full of kids returning from and going to the exam site. The other classes were jostling and talking, and in some cases the children were laughing out loud.

But the kids in line behind Miss Fondevant were silent. Taylor was walking under his own power, but his face was white as a sheet. Susan could see that he'd thought he was going to die. As he went past Susan, he said, "The lighter?"

She nodded.

"Today."

She must have gotten through the scoliosis exam without doing anything very strange, though she saw Frieda looking at her funny once. It touched her in a tender part, that Frieda still knew enough about her to tell when something was wrong.

When the final bell rang for the end of school that day, Taylor headed for the school bus pickup door, as always. She wanted to scream at the idea of being abandoned. She was the only one who noticed, she hoped, when he ducked inside a boys' bathroom. He stayed inside until after his bus left, and then he walked down the hall to where Susan stood waiting at the door to the teachers' parking lot. He looked like an old little boy, Susan thought, and then she couldn't figure out what she'd meant.

But it was true. Taylor's dark hair looked dusty and tousled, and his shirt was rumpled, and one of his sneakers had a loose sole. But there was something scary in his brown eyes. He had his ancient backpack slung on one shoulder as he always did. She fell into step beside him, her own books clasped in her arms, as they walked into the parking lot together.

One large tree had been left standing in the parking lot, and Miss Fondevant got there early enough to park underneath it. They hid behind it; if another exiting teacher saw them, she would certainly feel obliged to do something about their presence in an odd place.

Taylor put his backpack on the ground and unzipped it. He pulled out a recognizable stick of dynamite. It didn't look exactly like it did in the cartoons (it was brown instead of red), but Susan never doubted that what Taylor held was the real thing. She shuddered at the sight of it.

In turn, she got the Zippo out of her pocket.

"So we wait till she gets inside the car," Taylor said, becoming the boss by virtue of possession of the dynamite. "You light it, I roll it under her car, and we both run like hell." He tacked on the *hell* defiantly.

"We need to put our books farther away, so we won't have to grab them," Susan said, trying to have some input.

"Good idea."

When Taylor didn't move, Susan grabbed the strap of his backpack and scooped up her own stack of books. She toted them a few yards away against the fence. She put hers some distance away from Taylor's.

"Why'd you do that?" he asked.

"Why would we be standing together out here?" she said. "You can say you came to ask me if my mom could give you a ride home. Since you missed your bus." It didn't seem strange to either of them to be thinking about explaining Taylor's presence when they were planning on killing their teacher.

They waited behind the tree, Susan clutching the Zippo and Taylor gripping the dynamite. Neither had a watch. At last someone came out, one of the seventh-grade teachers. She climbed into her car and pulled away without a glance in their direction. Next came familiar footsteps. The children didn't look at each other. They watched the car from their meager concealment. The car door unlocked and opened, and the seat squeaked a little as Miss Fondevant got in.

Susan took a sharp, frightened breath, fired up the Zippo, and touched it to the dynamite. Taylor stepped forward and rolled it under the car, and they both took off running. There was a terrible count of four while nothing happened, and then the world rocked from side to side.

Susan screamed, she couldn't help it, and she crouched with her hands over her ears, too late. Taylor sprawled to the pavement beside her. Hot bits of things shot past her, one landing in her long hair and burning. She reached up, clawing to get it out, and it tinkled to the pavement, a sound she could barely hear. It was bright and glittery in the sun, and she found herself reaching down to pick it up.

It was Miss Fondevant's ring. Clutching it in her hand, she turned around to see the smoking ruin of the prim gray sedan. Something alien and unrecognizable had flopped out of the place where the driver's door had been, something smoking and flaking in the sunlight. As she stared at the thing, Taylor turned over, groaning, blood running down his cheek from a cut on his head.

"What happened?" he said. "Is that her?"

The smoking, flaking thing twitched.

Susan screamed again, but the sound was so tiny, so faint, that she wasn't sure she had heard it herself. She took a step closer, then another, though she could hear Taylor shout, "No! No!" She watched her own loafers cross the pavement, arrive at a streaked and blackened area, keep going. She looked down at the twitching thing.

She could tell it was Miss Fondevant. And she understood after a second that the dynamite hadn't killed her, but the sunlight was. The explosion had blown off Miss Fondevant's fingers and one of those fingers had been circled by the ring. The finger was gone. The ring remained. In Susan's hand.

Susan did something previously unthinkable. She bent over Miss Fondevant to say, "Look, bitch, I got your ring."

And what was left of Miss Fondevant smiled. Smiled. Before she crumbled away to nothing.

And then there was just lots of screaming and shouting, and the sounds of the ambulance and the fire truck.

Mr. Kosper was so relieved no one else had been killed or hurt that Taylor's explanation for his presence was easily digested. He and Susan were in the same classroom, so it only made sense to an adult that Taylor would ask Susan's mom for a ride home after he'd missed the bus. To the other kids, that didn't seem feasible, and good-girl Susan and bad-boy Taylor underwent a lot of teasing, after the horror had worn off. To Susan's own surprise, she just laughed when kids accused her and Taylor of being in loooooove, and gradually the teasing stopped.

It wasn't just Susan's cool reaction to the teasing but the fact that Taylor stayed as far away from Susan as he could that finally squelched the jokes that had been flying around. No one would ever have suspected Susan and Taylor of conspiring to do anything, they so clearly did not want to be in each other's presence.

As Taylor had expected, his father didn't even seem to remember that he'd ever had a stick of dynamite. He never accused his son of stealing it.

The police found the explosion very suspicious, of course. And the fact that both students present were from Miss Fondevant's class made the situation even more questionable. But Susan was where she was supposed to be, and Miss Fondevant was following her own routine, and both were above reproach. Taylor and his dad were questioned very carefully, but there was no reason at all to suspect either of them had a reason to kill Miss Fondevant. In fact, Taylor's dad had never even met his son's teacher. That made him a crappy dad, but it did not make him a murderer.

Susan's mom was horrified by the whole thing. When Mr. Kosper asked her to marry him six months later, she said yes faster than you could ring a dinner bell. Mr. Kosper gained a pleasant bedmate who smiled often and enjoyed her meals, and a stepdaughter who was bright and pretty and well behaved.

Susan needed time to recover from the mortal fear she'd felt back on that day, and she needed time to understand that last smile Miss Fondevant had given her.

Miss Fondevant was never nice, not even a little bit, so her smile could not have meant anything good. And Susan had told her that she now had the ring.

So the ring must be bad.

Consumed with curiosity, Susan read more about vampire lore than a girl her age, of any age, should ever read. Susan's mother, absorbed with being Mrs. Kosper, figured this vampire craze was just an adolescent thing Susan was going through. She made the wise decision not to ride Susan about it. It would die away in time when Susan found something more interesting to obsess about, as adolescents did.

In some of her deeper reading, Susan discovered legends that suggested that energy-sucking vampires have to stay out of the light, just like regular blood-sucking vampires did. Unless they had a magical talisman, which sounded like it was something from a game. It was clear, even if you were dumb (which Susan was not), that the gold ring with the roses was Miss Fondevant's talisman.

And now it was Susan's. She'd earned it in combat. She kept it in a secret place, and pulled it out from time to time to admire the dull gleam of the gold and the three pink roses. The ring had given Miss Fondevant a terrible ability.

Susan wondered what else the ring could do.

What power it could give her.

IN A CAVERN, IN A CANYON

LAIRD BARRON

Husband number one fondly referred to me as the Good Samaritan. Anything from a kid lost in the neighborhood to a county-wide search-and-rescue effort, I got involved. If we drove past a fender bender, I had to stop and lend a hand or snap a few pictures, maybe do a walk-around of the scene. A major crash? Forget about it—I'd haunt the site until the cows came home or the cops shooed me away. Took the better part of a decade for the lightbulb to flash over my hubby's bald head. He realized I wasn't a Samaritan so much as a fetishist. Wore him down in the end and he bailed. I'm still melancholy over that one.

Lucky for him he didn't suffer through my stint with the Park Service in Alaska. After college and the first kid, I finagled my way onto the government payroll and volunteered for every missing-person, lost-climber, downed-plane, or wrecked-boat scenario. I hiked and camped on the side. Left my compass and maps at home. I wanted to disappear. Longest I managed was four days. The feds were suspicious enough to send me to a shrink who knew his business. The boys upstairs gave me a generous severance check and said to not let the door hit me in the ass on the way out. Basically the beginning of a long downward slide in my life.

Husband number three divorced me for my fifty-fourth birthday. I pawned everything that wouldn't fit into a van and drove from Ohio back home to Alaska. I rented a double-wide at the Cottonwood Point Trailer Park near Moose Pass, two miles along the bucolic and winding Seward Highway from Cassie, my youngest daughter.

A spruce forest crowds the back door. Moose nibble the rhododendrons hedging the yard. Most folks tuck in for the night by the time Colbert is delivering his monologue. Cassie drops off my infant granddaughter, Vera, two or three times a week and whenever she can't find a sitter. Single and working two jobs, Cassie avoided the inevitability of divorce by not getting married in the first place. Wish I'd thought of that. Once I realized that my nanny gig was a regular thing, I ordered a crib and inveigled the handsome (and generally drunken, alas) fellow at 213 to set it up in my bedroom.

On the nanny evenings, I feed Vera her bottle and watch westerns on cable. "Get you started right," I say to her as Bronson ventilates Fonda beneath a glaring sun, or when a cowboy rides into the red-and-gold distance as the credits roll. She'll be a tomboy like her gram if I have any influence. The classic stars were my heroes once upon a time—Stewart, Van Cleef, Wayne, and Marvin. During my youth, I utterly revered Eastwood. I crushed big-time on the Man with No Name and Dirty Harry. Kept a poster from *The Good, the Bad and the Ugly* on my bedroom wall. So young, both of us. So innocent. Except for the shooting and murdering, and my lustful thoughts, but you know.

Around midnight, I wake from a nap on the couch to Vera's plaintive cry. She's in the bedroom crib, awake and pissed for her bottle. The last act of *High Plains Drifter* plays in bad 1970s Technicolor. It's the part where the Stranger finally gets around to exacting righteous vengeance. Doesn't matter that I've missed two rapes, a horsewhipping, Lago painted red and renamed HELL . . . all those images are imprinted upon my hindbrain. I get the impression the scenes are *always* rolling down there against the screen of my sub-conscious.

I am depressed to recognize a cold fact in this instant. The love affair with bad-boy Clint ended years and years ago, even if I haven't fully accepted the reality. Eyes gummed with sleep, I sit for a few seconds, mesmerized by the stricken faces of the townspeople who are caught between a vicious outlaw gang and a stranger hell-bent on retribution. The Stranger's whip slithers through the saloon window and garrotes an outlaw. I've watched that scene on a dozen occasions. My hands shake and I can't zap it with the remote fast enough.

That solves one problem. I take the formula from the fridge and pop it into the fancy warmer Cassie obtained during a clearance sale. The LED numerals are counting down to nothing when it occurs to me that I don't watch the baby on Sundays.

The night in 1977 that my father disappeared, he, Uncle Ned, and I drove north along Midnight Road, searching for Tony Orlando. Dad crept the Fleetwood at a walking pace. My younger siblings, Doug, Shauna, and Artemis, remained at home. Doug was ostensibly keeping an eye on our invalid grandmother, but I figured he was probably glued to the television with the others. That autumn sticks in my memory like mud to a Wellington. We were sixteen, fourteen, eleven, and ten. Babes in the wilderness.

Uncle Ned and I took turns yelling out the window. Whenever Orlando pulled this stunt, Dad swore it would be the last expedition he mounted to retrieve the "damned mutt." I guess he really meant it.

Middle-school classmate Nancy Albrecht once asked me what the hell kind of name was that for a dog, and I said Mom and Dad screwed on the second date to "Halfway to Paradise," and if you laugh I'll smack your teeth down your throat. I have a few scars on my knuckles, for damn sure.

Way back then, we lived in Eagle Talon, Alaska, an isolated port about seventy miles southwest of Anchorage. Cruise ships bloated the town with tourists during spring, and it dried up to around three hundred resident souls come autumn.

Eastern settlers had carved a hamlet from wilderness during the 1920s, plunked it down in a forgotten vale populated by eagles, bears, drunk teamsters, and drunker fishermen. Mountains and dense forest on three sides formed a deep-water harbor. The channel curved around the flank of Eagle Mountain and eventually let into Prince William Sound. Roads were gravel or dirt. We had the cruise ships and barges. We also had the railroad. You couldn't make a move without stepping in seagull shit. Most of us townies lived in a fourteen-story apartment complex called the Frazier Estate. We kids shortened it to Fate. Terra incognita began where the sodium lamplight grew fuzzy. At night, wolves howled in the nearby hills. Definitely not the dream hometown of a sixteen-year-old girl. As a grown woman, I recall it with a bittersweet fondness.

Upon commencing the hunt for Orlando, whom my little brother, Doug, had stupidly set free from the leash only to watch in mortification as the dog trotted into the sunset, tail furled with rebellious intent, Dad faced a choice—head west along the road, or troll the beach where the family pet sometimes mined for rotten salmon carcasses. We picked the road because it wound into the woods and our shepherd-husky mix hankered after the red squirrels that swarmed during the fall. Dad didn't want to walk if he could avoid it. "Marched goddamned plenty in the Crotch," he said. It had required a major effort for him to descend to the parking garage and get the wagon started and pointed in the general direction of our search route. Two bad knees, pain pills for said knees, and a half-rack-a-day habit had all but done him in.

Too bad for Uncle Ned and me, Midnight Road petered out in the foothills. Moose trails went every which way from the little clearing where we'd parked next to an abandoned Winnebago with a raggedy tarp covering the front end and black garbage bags over the windows. Hoboes and druggies occasionally used the Winnebago as a fort until Sheriff Lockhart came along to roust them. "Goddamned railroad," Dad would say, despite the fact that if not for the railroad (for which he performed part-time labor to supplement his military checks) and the cruise ships and barges, there wouldn't be any call for Eagle Talon whatsoever.

Uncle Ned lifted himself from the backseat and accompanied me as I shined the flashlight and hollered for Orlando. Dad remained in the station wagon with the engine running and the lights on. He honked the horn.

"He's gonna keep doing that, huh?" Uncle Ned wasn't exactly addressing me, more like an actor musing to himself on the stage. "Just gonna keep leanin' on that horn every ten seconds—"

The horn blared again. Farther off and dim—we'd come a ways already. Birch and alder were broken by stands of furry black spruce that muffled sounds from the outside world. The black, green, and gray webbing is basically the Spanish moss of the Arctic. Uncle Ned chuckled and shook his head. Two years Dad's junior and a major-league stoner, *he'd* managed to keep it together when it counted. He taught me how to tie a knot and paddle a canoe, and gave me a life-time supply of dirty jokes. He'd also explained that contrary to Dad's Cro-Magnon take on teenage dating, boys were okay to fool around with so long as I ducked the bad ones and avoided getting knocked up. *Which ones were bad?* I wondered. Most of them, according to the Book of Ned, but keep it to fooling around and all would be well. He also clued me in to the fact that Dad's vow to blast any would-be suitor's pecker off with his twelve-gauge was an idle threat. My old man couldn't shoot worth spit even when sober.

The trail forked. One path climbed into the hills where the under-growth thinned. The other path curved deeper into the creepy spruce where somebody had strung blue reflective tape among the branches—a haphazard mess like the time Dad got lit up and tried to decorate the Christmas tree.

"Let's not go in there," Uncle Ned said. Ominous, although not entirely unusual, as he often said that kind of thing with a similar laconic dryness. *That bar looks rough, let's try the next one over. That woman looks like my ex-wife, I'm not gonna dance with her, uh-uh. That box has got to be heavy. Let's get a beer and think on it.*

"Maybe he's at the beach rolling in crap," I said. Orlando loved bear turds and rotten salmon guts with a true passion. There'd be plenty of both near the big water, and as I squinted into the forbidding shadows, I increasingly wished we'd driven there instead.

Uncle Ned pulled his coat tighter and lit a cigarette. The air had dampened. I yelled, "Orlando!" a few more times. Then we stood there for a while in the silence. It was like listening through the lid of a coffin. Dad had stopped leaning on the horn. The woodland critters weren't making their usual fuss. Clouds drifted in and the darkness was so complete it wrapped us in a cocoon. "Think Orlando's at the beach?" I said.

"Well, I dunno. He ain't here."

"Orlando, you stupid jerk!" I shouted to the night in general.

"Let's boogie," Uncle Ned said. The cherry of his cigarette floated in midair and gave his narrowed eyes a feral glint. Like Dad, he was middling tall and rangy. Sharp-featured and often wry. He turned and moved the way we'd come, head lowered, trailing a streamer of Pall Mall smoke. Typical of my uncle. Once he made a decision, he acted.

"Damn it, Orlando." I gave up and followed, sick to my gut with worry. Fool dog would be the death of me, or so I suspected. He'd tangled with a porcupine the summer before and I'd spent hours picking quills from his swollen snout because Dad refused to take him in to see Doc Green. There were worse things than porcupines in these woods—black bears, angry moose, wolves—and I feared my precious idiot would run into one of them.

Halfway back to the car, I glimpsed a patch of white to my left amid the heavy brush. I took it for a birch stump with holes rotted into the heartwood. No, it was a man lying on his side, matted black hair framing his pale face. By pale, I mean bone-white and bloodless. The face you see on the corpse of an outlaw in those old-timey Wild West photographs.

"Help me," he whispered.

I trained my light on the injured man; he had to be hurt because of the limp, contorted angle of his body, his shocking paleness. He seemed familiar. The lamp beam broke around his body like a stream splits around a large stone. The shadows turned slowly, fracturing and changing him. He might've been weirdo Floyd, who swept the Caribou after last call, or that degenerate trapper, Bob something, who lived in a shack in the hills with a bunch of stuffed moose heads and mangy beaver hides. Or it might've been as I first thought—a tree stump lent a man's shape by my lying eyes. The more I stared, the less certain I became that it was a person at all.

Except I'd heard him speak, voice raspy and high-pitched from pain, almost a falsetto.

Twenty-five feet, give or take, between me and the stranger. I didn't see his arm move. Move it did, however. The shadows shifted again and his hand grasped futilely, thin and gnarled as a tree branch. His misery radiated into me, caused my eyes to well with tears of empathy. I felt terrible, just terrible, I wanted to mother him, and took a step toward him.

"Hortense. Come here." Uncle Ned said my name the way Dad described talking to his wounded buddies in 'Nam. The ones who'd gotten hit by a grenade or a stray bullet. Quiet, calm, and reassuring was the ticket—and I bet his tone would've worked its magic if my insides had happened to be splashed on the ground and the angels were singing me home. In this case, Uncle Ned's unnatural calmness scared me, woke me from a dream where I heroically tended to a hapless stranger, got a parade and a key to the village, and my father's grudging approval.

"Hortense, please."

"There's a guy in the bushes," I said. "I think he's hurt."

Uncle Ned grabbed my hand like he used to when I was a little girl and towed me along at a brisk pace. "Naw, kid. That's a tree stump. I saw it when we went past earlier. Keep movin'."

I didn't ask why we were in such a hurry. It worried me how easy it seemed for him and Dad to slip into warrior mode at the drop of a hat. He muttered something about branches snapping and that black bears roamed the area as they fattened up for winter and he regretted leaving his guns at his house. *House* is sort of a grand term; Uncle Ned lived in a mobile home on the edge of the village. The Estate didn't appeal to his loner sensibilities.

We got to walking so fast along that narrow trail that I twisted my ankle on a root and nearly went for a header. Uncle Ned didn't miss a beat. He took most of my weight upon his shoulder. Pretty much dragged me back to the Fleetwood. The engine ran and the driver-side door was ajar. I assumed Dad had gone behind a tree to take a leak. As the minutes passed and we called for him, I began to understand that he'd left. Those were the days when men abandoned their families by saying they needed to grab a pack of cigarettes and beating it for the high timber. He'd threatened to do it during his frequent arguments with Mom. She'd beaten him to the punch and jumped ship with a traveling salesman, leaving us to fend for ourselves. Maybe, just maybe, it was Dad's turn to bail on us kids.

Meanwhile, Orlando had jumped in through the open door and curled into a ball in the passenger seat. Leaves, twigs, and dirt plastered him. A pig digging for China wouldn't have been any filthier.

Damned old dog pretended to sleep. His thumping tail gave away the show, though.

Uncle Ned rousted him and tried to put him on Dad's trail. Nothing doing. Orlando whined and hung his head. He refused to budge despite Uncle Ned's exhortations. Finally, the dog yelped and scrambled back into the car, trailing a stream of piss. That was our cue to depart.

Uncle Ned drove back to the Frazier Estate. He called Deputy Clausen (everybody called him Claws) and explained the situation. Claws agreed to gather a few men and do a walk-through of the area. He theorized that Dad had gotten drunk and wandered into the hills and collapsed somewhere. Such events weren't rare.

Meanwhile, I checked in on Grandma, who'd occupied the master bedroom since she'd suffered the aneurysm. Next, I herded Orlando into the bathroom and soaked him in the tub. I was really hurting by then.

When I thanked Uncle Ned, he nodded curtly and avoided meeting my eye. "Lock the door," he said.

"Why? The JWs aren't allowed out of the compound after dark." Whenever I got scared, I cracked wise.

"Don't be a smart-ass. Lock the fuckin' door."

"Something fishy in Denmark," I said to Orlando, who leaned against my leg as I threw the dead bolt. Mrs. Wells had assigned *Hamlet*, *Julius Caesar*, and *Titus Andronicus* for summer reading. "And it's the Ides of August, too."

My brothers and sister were sprawled in the living room in front of the TV, watching a vampire flick. Christopher Lee wordlessly seduced a buxom chick who was practically falling out of her peasant blouse. Lee angled for a bite. Then he saw, nestled in the woman's cleavage, the teeny elegant crucifix her archaeologist boyfriend had given her for luck. Lee's eyes went buggy with rage and fear. The vampire equivalent to blue balls, I guess. I took over Dad's La-Z-Boy and kicked back with a bottle of Coke (the last one, as noted by the venomous glares of my siblings) and a bag of ice on my puffy ankle.

The movie ended and I clapped my hands and sent the kids packing. At three bedrooms, our apartment qualified as an imperial suite. Poor Dad sacked out on the couch. Doug and Artemis shared the smallest, crappiest room. I bunked with Shauna, the princess of jibber-jabber. She loved and feared me, and that made tight quarters a bit easier, because she knew I'd sock her in the arm if she sassed me too much or pestered me with one too many goober questions. Often, she'd natter on while I piped Fleetwood Mac and Led Zeppelin through a set of gigantic yellow earphones. That self-isolation spared us a few violent and teary scenes, I'm sure.

Amid the grumbles and the rush for the toilet, I almost confessed the weird events of the evening to Doug. My kid brother had an open mind when it came to the unknown. He wouldn't necessarily laugh me out of the room without giving the matter some real thought. Instead, I smacked the back of his head and told him not to be such a dumb ass with Orlando. Nobody remarked on Dad's absence. I'm sure they figured he'd pitched camp at the Caribou like he did so many nights. Later, I lay awake and listened to my siblings snore. Orlando whined as he dreamed of the chase, or of being chased.

From the bedroom, Gram said in a fragile, singsong tone, "In a cavern, in a canyon, excavatin' for a mine, dwelt a miner forty-niner and his daughter Clementine. In a cavern, in a canyon. In a cavern, in a canyon. In a cavern, in a canyon. Clementine, Clementine. Clementine? Clementine?"

Of the four Shaw siblings I'm the eldest, tallest, and surliest.

According to Mom, Dad had desperately wanted a boy for his firstborn. He descended from a lineage that adhered to a pseudo-medieval mind-set. The noble chauvinist, the virtuous warrior, the honorable fighter of rearguard actions. Quaint when viewed through a historical lens; a real pain in the ass in the modern world.

I was a disappointment. As a daughter, what else could I be? He got used to it. The Shaws have a long, long history of losing. We own that shit. *Go down fighting* would've been our family motto, with a snake biting the heel that crushed its skull as our crest. As some consolation, I was always a tomboy and tougher than either of my brothers—a heap tougher than most of the boys in our hick town, and tougher than at least a few of the grown men. Toughness isn't always measured by how hard you punch. Sometimes, most of the time, it's simply the set of a girl's jaw. I shot my mouth off with the best of them. If nothing else, I dutifully struck at the heels of my oppressors. Know where I got this grit? Sure as hell not from Dad. Oh, yeah, he threw a nasty left hook, and he'd scragged a few guys in 'Nam. But until Mom had flown the coop she ruled our roost with an iron fist that would've made Khrushchev think twice before crossing her. Yep, the meanness in my soul is pure-D Mom.

Dad had all the homespun apothegms.

He often said, *Never try to beat a man at what he does.* What Dad did best was drink. He treated it as a competitive event. In addition to chugging Molson Export, Wild Turkey, and Stoli, Dad also smoked the hell out of cannabis whenever he could get his hands on some. He preferred the heavy-hitting bud from Mexico courtesy of Uncle Ned. I got my hands on a bag those old boys stashed in a rolled-up sock in a number-ten coffee can. That stuff sent you, all right. Although, judging by the wildness of Dad's eyes, the way they started and stared at the corners of the room after he'd had a few hits, his destination was way different from mine.

Even so, the Acapulco Gold gave me a peek through the keyhole into Dad's soul in a way booze couldn't. Some blood memory got activated. It might've been our sole point of commonality. He would've beaten me to a pulp if he'd known. For my own good, natch.

Main thing I took from growing up the daughter of an alcoholic? Lots of notions compete for the top spot—the easiest way to get vomit and blood out of fabric, the best apologies, the precise amount of heed to pay a drunken diatribe, when to duck flung bottles, how to balance a checkbook and cook a family meal between homework, dog-walking, and giving sponge baths to Gram. But above all, my essential takeaway was that I'd never go down the rabbit hole to an eternal happy hour. I indulged in a beer here and there, toked some Mary Jane to reward myself for serving as Mom, Dad, chief cook and bottle washer pro-tem. Nothing heavy, though. I resolved to leave the heavy lifting to Dad, Uncle Ned, and their buddies at the Caribou Tavern.

Randal Shaw retired from the USMC in 1974 after twenty years of active service. Retirement didn't agree with him. To wit: the beer, bourbon, and weed, and the sullen hurling of empties. It didn't agree with Mom either, obviously. My grandmother, Harriet Shaw, suffered a brain aneurysm that very autumn. Granddad had passed away the previous winter and Gram moved into our apartment. By day, she slumped in a special medical recliner we bought from the Eagle Talon Emergency Trauma Center. Vivian from upstairs sat with her while I was at school. Gram's awareness came and went like a bad radio signal. Sometimes she'd make a feeble attempt to play cards with Vivian. Occasionally, she asked about my grades and what cute boys I'd met, or she'd watch TV and chuckle at the soaps in that rueful way she laughed at so many ridiculous things. The clarity became rare. Usually she stared out the window at the harbor or at the framed Georgia O'Keeffe–knockoff print of a sunflower above the dresser. Hours passed and we'd shoo away the mosquitoes while she tunelessly hummed "In a cavern, in a canyon, excavatin' for a mine" on a loop. There may as well have been a VACANCY sign blinking above her head.

After school, and twice daily on weekends, Doug helped bundle Gram into the crappy fold-up chair and I pushed her around the village, took her down to the wharf to watch the seagulls, or parked her in front of the general store while I bought Dad a pack of smokes (and another for myself). By night, Dad or I pushed the button and lowered the bed and she lay with her eyes fixed on the dented ceiling of the bedroom. She'd sigh heavily and say, "Nighty-night, nighty-night," like a parrot. It shames me to remember her that way. But then, most of my childhood is a black hole.

The search party found neither hide nor hair of Dad. Deputy Clausen liked Uncle Ned well enough and agreed to do a bigger sweep in the afternoon. The deputy wasn't enthused. Old Harmon Snodgrass, a trapper from Kobuk, isolated footprints in the soft dirt along the edge of the road. The tracks matched Dad's boots and were headed toward town. Snodgrass lost them after a couple hundred yards.

In Deputy Clausen's professional opinion, Randal Shaw had doubled back and flown the coop to parts unknown, as a certain kind of man is wont to do when the going gets tough. Uncle Ned socked him (the Shaw answer to critics) and Claws would've had his ass in a cell for a good long time, except Stu Herring, the mayor of our tiny burg, and Kyle Lomax were on hand to break up the festivities and soothe bruised egos. Herring sent Uncle Ned home with a *go and sin no more* scowl.

"How's Mom?" Uncle Ned stared at Gram staring at a spot on the wall. He sipped the vilest black coffee on the face of the earth. My specialty. I'd almost tripped over him in the hallway on my way to take Orlando for his morning stroll. He'd spent the latter portion of the night curled near our door, a combat knife in his fist. Normally, one might consider that loony behavior. You had to know Uncle Ned.

"She's groovy, as ever. Why are you lurking?" The others were still zonked, thank God. I hadn't an inkling of how to break the news of Dad's defection to them. I packed more ice onto my ankle. My foot had swollen to the point where it wouldn't fit into my sneaker. It really and truly hurt. "Ow."

"Let's go. Hospital time." He stood abruptly and went in and woke Doug, told him, "Drop your cock and grab your socks. You're man of the house for an hour. Orlando needs a walk—for the love of God, keep him on a leash, will ya?" Then he nabbed Dad's keys and took me straightaway to the Eagle Clinic. Mrs. Cooper, a geriatric hypochondriac, saw the RN, Sally Mackey, ahead of us, and we knew from experience that it would be a hell of a wait. So Uncle Ned and I settled into hard plastic waiting room chairs. He lit a cigarette, and another for me, and said, "Okay, I got a story. Don't tell your old man I told you, or he'll kick my ass and then I'll kick yours. Yeah?"

I figured it would be a story of his hippie escapades or some raunchy bullshit Dad got up to in Vietnam. A tale to cheer me up and take my mind off my troubles. Uh-uh. He surprised me by talking about the Good Friday Earthquake of '64. "You were, what? Two, three? You guys lived in that trailer park in Anchorage. The quake hits and your dad's been shipped to 'Nam. My job was to look over you and your mom. Meanwhile, I'm visiting a little honey out in the Valley. Girl had a cabin on a lake. We just came in off the ice for a mug of hot cocoa and *boom!* Looked like dynamite churned up the bottom muck. Shit flew off the shelves, the earth moved in waves like the sea. Spruce trees bent all the way over and slapped their tops on the ground. Sounded like a train runnin' through the living room. Tried callin' your mom, but the phone lines were down.

"I jumped in my truck and headed for Anchorage. Got partway there and had to stop. Highway was too fucked up to drive on. Pavement cracked open, bridges collapsed. I got stuck in a traffic jam on the flats. Some cars were squashed under a collapsed overpass and a half-dozen more kinda piled on. It was nine or ten at night and pitch-black. Accidents everywhere. The temperature dropped into the twenties and mist rolled in from the water. Road flares and head-lights and flashing hazards made the scene extra spooky. I could taste hysteria in the air. Me and a couple of Hells Angels from Wasilla got together and made sure people weren't trapped or hurt too bad. Then we started pushing cars off the road to get ready for the emergency crews.

"We were taking a smoke break when one of the bikers said to shut up a minute. A big, potbellied Viking, at least twice the size of me and his younger pal. Fuckin' enormous. He cocked his head and asked us if we'd heard it too—somebody moaning for help down on the flats. He didn't hang around for an answer. Hopped over the guardrail and was gone. Man on a mission. Guy didn't come back after a few minutes. Me and the younger biker climbed down the embankment and went into the pucker-brush. Shouted ourselves hoarse and not a damned reply. Mist was oozin' off the water and this weird, low-tide reek hit me. A cross between green gas from inside a blown moose carcass and somethin' sweet, like fireweed. I heard a noise, reminded me of water and air bubbles gurglin' through a hose. Grace a God, I happened to shine my light on a boot stickin' outta the scrub. The skinny biker yelled his buddy's name and ran over there."

Uncle Ned had gotten worked up during the narration of his story. He lit another cigarette and paced to the coffee machine and back. Bernice Monson, the receptionist, glared over her glasses. She didn't say anything. In '77 most folks kept their mouths shut when confronted by foamy Vietnam vets. Bernice, like everybody else, as-sumed Uncle Ned did a jungle tour as a government employee. He certainly resembled the part with his haggard expression, his brooding demeanor, and a partialness for camouflage pants. Truth was, while many young men were blasting away at each other in Southeast Asia, he'd backpacked across Canada, Europe, and Mexico. Or *went humping foreign broads and scrawling doggerel*, as my dad put it.

Uncle Ned's eyes were red as a cockscomb. He slapped the coffee machine. "I didn't have a perfect position and my light was weak, but I saw plenty. The Viking lay on top of somebody. This somebody was super skinny and super pale. Lots of wild hair. Their arms and legs were tangled so's you couldn't make sense of what was goin' on. I thought he had him a woman there in the weeds and they were fuckin'. Their faces were stuck together. The young biker leaned over his buddy and then yelped and stumbled backward. The skinny, pale one shot out from under the Viking and into the darkness. Didn't stand, didn't crouch, didn't even flip over—know how a mechanic rolls from under a car on his board? Kinda that way, except jittery. Moved like an insect scuttling for cover, best I can describe it. A couple seconds later, the huge biker shuddered and went belly-crawling after the skinny fellow. What I thought I was seeing him do, anyhow. His arms and legs flopped, although his head never lifted, not completely. He just skidded away, Superman style, his face planted in the dirt.

"Meanwhile, the young biker hauled ass toward the road, shriekin' the whole way. My flashlight died. I stood there, in the dark, heart poundin', scared shitless, tryin' to get my brain outta neutral. I wanted to split, hell yeah. No fuckin' way I was gonna tramp around on those flats by myself. I'm a hunter, though. Those instincts kicked in and I decided to play it cool. Your dad always pegged me for a peacenik hippie because I didn't do 'Nam. I'm smarter, is the thing. Got a knife in my pocket and half the time I'm packin' heat too. Had my skinning knife, and lemme say, I kept it handy as I felt my way through the bushes and the brambles. Got most of the way to where I could see the lights of the cars on the road. Somebody whispered, "Help me." Real close and on my flank. Scared me, sure. I probably jumped three feet straight up. And yet, it was the saddest voice I can remember. Woeful, like a lost child, or a wounded woman, or a fawn, or some combination of those cries.

"I mighta turned around and walked into the night, except a state trooper hit me with a light. He'd come over the hill lookin' after the biker went bugshit. I think the cop thought the three of us were involved in a drug deal. He sure as hell didn't give a lick about a missing Hells Angel. He led me back to the clusterfuck on the highway and I spent the rest of the night shivering in my car while the bulldozers and dump trucks did their work." He punched the coffee machine.

"Easy, killer!" I said, and gave an apologetic smile to the increasingly agitated Bernice. I patted the seat next to me until he came over and sat. "What happened to the biker? The big guy."

Uncle Ned had sliced his knuckles. He clenched his fist and watched the blood drip onto the tiles. "Cops found him that summer in the water. Not enough left for an autopsy. The current and the fish had taken him apart. Accidental death, they decided. I saw the younger biker at the Gold Digger. Musta been five or six years after the Good Friday quake. He acted like he'd forgotten what happened to his partner until I bought him the fifth or sixth tequila. *He* got a real close look at what happened. Said that to him, the gurglin' was more of a slurpin'. An animal lappin' up a gory supper. Then he looked me in the eye and said his buddy got snatched into the darkness by his own guts. They were comin' outta his mouth and whatever it was out there gathered 'em up and reeled him in."

"Holy shit, Uncle Ned." Goose pimples covered my arms. "That's nuts. Who do you think was out there?"

"The boogeyman. Whatever it is that kids think is hidin' under their bed."

"You tell Dad? Probably not, huh? He's a stick-in-the-mud. He'd never buy it."

"Well, you don't either. Guess that makes you a stick-in-the-mud too."

"The apple, the tree, gravity . . ."

"Maybe you'd be surprised what your old man knows." Uncle Ned's expression was shrewd. "I been all over this planet. Between '66 and '74, I roamed. Passed the peace pipe with the Lakota, ate peyote with the Mexicans, drank wine with the Italians, and smoked excellent bud with a whole lot of other folks. I get bombed enough, or stoned enough, I ask if anybody else has heard of the Help Me Monster. What I call it. The Help Me Monster."

The description evoked images of *Sesame Street* and plush toys dancing on wires. "Grover the Psycho Killer!" I said, hoping he'd at least crack a smile. I also hoped my uncle hadn't gone around the bend.

He didn't smile. We sat there in one of those long, awkward silences while Bernice coughed her annoyance and shuffled papers. I was relieved when Sally Mackey finally stuck her head into the room and called my name.

The nurse wanted to send me to Anchorage for X-rays. No way would Dad authorize that expense. No veterinarians and no doctors; those were ironclad rules. When he discovered Uncle Ned took me to the clinic, he'd surely blow his top. I wheeled a bottle of prescription-strength aspirin and a set of cheapo crutches on the house and called it square. A mild ankle sprain meant I'd be on the crutches for days. I added it to the tab of Shaw family dues.

Dad never came home. I cried, the kids cried. Bit by bit, we moved on. Some of us more than others.

I won't bore you with the nightmares that got worse and worse with time. You can draw your own conclusions. That strange figure in the woods, Dad's vanishing act, and Uncle Ned's horrifying tale co-alesced into a witch's brew that beguiled me and became a serious obsession.

Life is messy and it's mysterious. Had my father walked away from his family or had he been taken? If the latter, then why Dad and not me or Uncle Ned? I didn't crack the case, didn't get any sense of closure. No medicine man or antiquarian popped up to give me the scoop on some ancient enemy that dwells in the shadows and dines upon the blood and innards of Good Samaritans and hapless passersby.

Closest I came to solving the enigma was during my courtship with husband number two. He said a friend of a friend was a student biologist on a research expedition in Canada. His team and local authorities responded to a massive train derailment near a small town. Rescuers spent three days clearing out the survivors. On day four, they swept the scattered wreckage for bodies.

This student, who happened to be Spanish, and three fellow countrymen were way out in a field after dark, poking around with sticks. One of them heard a voice moaning for help. Of course, they scrambled to find this wretched soul. Late to the scene, a military search-and-rescue helicopter flew overhead, very low, its searchlight blazing. When the chopper had gone, all fell silent. The cries didn't repeat. Weird part, according to the Spaniard, was that in the few minutes they'd frantically tried to locate the injured person, his voice kept moving around in some bizarre acoustical illusion. The survivor switched from French to English, and finally to Spanish. The biologist claimed he had nightmares of the incident for years afterward. He dreamed of his buddies separated in a dark field, each crying for help, and he'd stumble across their desiccated corpses, one by one. He at-tributed it to the guilt of leaving someone to die on the tundra.

My husband-to-be told me that story while high on coke and didn't mention it again. I wonder if that's why I married the sorry sonofabitch. Just for that single moment of connectedness, a tiny and inconstant flicker of light in the wilderness.

High noon on a Sunday night.

Going on thirty-eight haunted years, I've expected this, or something like this, even though the entity represents, with its very jack-in-the-box manifestation, a deep, dark mystery of the universe. What has drawn it to me is equally inexplicable. I've considered the fanciful notion that the Shaws are cursed and Mr. Help Me is the instrument of vengeance. Doesn't feel right. I've also prayed to Mr. Help Me as if he, or it, is a death god watching over us cattle. Perhaps it is. The old gods wanted blood, didn't they? Blood and offerings of flesh. That feels more on the mark. Or it could be the simplest answer of them all—Mr. Help Me is an exotic animal whose biology and behavior defy scientific classification. The need for sustenance is the least of all possible mysteries. I can fathom *that* need, at least.

A window must be open in my bedroom. Cool night air dries the sweat on my cheeks as I stand in the darkened hall. The air smells vaguely of spoiled meat and perfume. A black, emaciated shape lies prone on the floor, halfway across the bedroom threshold. Long, skinny arms are extended in a swimmer's pose. Its face is a smudge of white and tilted slightly upward to regard me. It is possible that these impressions aren't accurate, that my eyes are interpreting as best they can.

I slap a switch. The light flickers on but doesn't illuminate the hall or the figure sprawled almost directly beneath the fixture. Instead, the glow bends at a right angle and gathers on the paneled wall in a diffuse cone.

"Help me," the figure says. The murmur is so soft it might've originated in my own head.

I'm made of sterner stuff than my sixteen-year-old self. I resist the powerful compulsion to approach, to lend maternal comfort. My legs go numb. I stagger and slide down the wall into a seated position. Everybody has had the nightmare. The one where you are perfectly aware and paralyzed and an unseen enemy looms over your shoulder. Difference is, I can see my nemesis, or at least its outline, at the opposite end of the hall. I can see it coming for me. It doesn't visibly move except when I blink, and then it's magically two or three feet closer. My mind is in overdrive. What keeps going through my mind is that predator insects seldom stir until the killing strike.

"Oh my darlin', oh my darlin', oh my darlin' Clementine. You are lost and gone forever, dreadful sorry, Clementine." I hum tunelessly, like Gram used to after her brain softened into mush. I'm reverting to childhood, to a time when Dad or Uncle Ned might burst through the door and save the day with a blast of double-aught buckshot.

It finally dawns upon me that I'm bleeding, am sitting in a puddle of blood. Where the blood is leaking from, I've not the foggiest notion. Silly me, *that's* why I'm dead from the waist down. My immobility isn't a function of terror, pheromones, or the occult powers of an evil spirit. I've been pricked and poisoned. Nature's predators carry barbs and stings. Those stings deliver anesthetics and anticoagulants. Have venom, will travel. I chuckle. My lips are cold.

"Help me," it whispers as it plucks my toes, testing my resistance. Even this close, it's an indistinct blob of shadowy appendages.

"I have one question." I enunciate carefully, the way I do after one too many shots of Jäger. "Did you take my dad on August fifteenth, 1977? Or did that bastard skip out? Me and my brother got a steak dinner riding on this."

"Help me." The pleading tone descends into a lower timbre. A satisfied purr.

One final trick up my sleeve, or in my pocket. Recently, while browsing a hardware store for a few odds and ends, I came across a relic of my youth—a black light. Cost a ten-spot, on special in the

clearance bin. First it made me smile as I recalled how all my childhood friends illuminated their Funkadelic posters, kids as gleeful as
if we'd rediscovered alchemy. Later, in college, black light made a
comeback on campus and at the parties we attended. It struck a
chord, got me thinking, wondering . . .

Any creature adapted to distort common light sources might be
susceptible to *uncommon* sources. Say, infrared or black light. I
hazard a guess that my untutored intuition is on the money and that
thousands of years of evolution haven't accounted for a ten-dollar
device used to find cat-piss stains in the carpet.

I raise the box with the black light filter in my left hand and
thumb the toggle. For an instant, I behold the intruder in all its malevolent glory. It recoils from my black light, a segmented hunter of
soft prey retreating into its burrow. A dresser crashes in the bedroom. The trailer rocks slightly, then is quiet. The moment has
passed, except for the fresh hell slowly blooming in my head.

The black light surprised it and nothing more. Surprised and
amused it. The creature's impossibly broad grin imparted a universe
of corrupt wisdom that will scar my mind for whatever time I have
left. Mr. Help Me's susurrant chuckle lingers like a psychic stain.
Sometimes the spider cuts the fly from its web. Sometimes nature
doesn't sink in those red fangs; sometimes it chooses not to rend
with its red claws. A reprieve isn't necessarily the same weight as a
pardon. Inscrutability isn't mercy.

We Shaws are tough as shoe leather. Doubtless, I've enough juice
left in me to crawl for the phone and signal the cavalry. A quart or
two of type O and I'll be fighting fit with a story to curl your toes.
The conundrum is whether I really want to make that crawl or
whether I should close my eyes and fall asleep. *Did you take my dad?*
I've spent most of my life waiting to ask that question. Is Dad out
there in the dark? What about those hunters and hikers and kids
who walk through the door and onto the crime pages every year?

I don't want to die, truly I don't. I'm also afraid to go on living. I've seen the true, unspeakable face of the universe, a face that reflects my lowly place in its scheme. And the answer is yes. Yes, there are hells, and in some you are burned or boiled or digested in the belly of a monster for eternity. Yes, what's left of Dad abides with a hideous mystery. He's far from alone.

What would Clint Eastwood do? Well, he would've plugged the fucker with a .44 Magnum, for starters. I shake myself. Midfifties is too late to turn into a mope. I roll onto my belly, suck in a breath, and begin the agonizing journey toward the coffee table, where I left my purse and salvation. Hand over hand, I drag my scrawny self. It isn't lost on me what I resemble as I slather a red trail across the floor.

Laughing hurts. Hard not to, though. I begin to sing the refrain from "Help!" Over and over and over.

WHISKEY AND LIGHT

DANA CAMERON

No one had settled here for a long time, maybe forever, before us.

The wild savages who were living nearby when we arrived never came within eyesight of the rocky mound and ruin of an oak, and wouldn't talk about it, neither. And the first ones of us who came after them, well, it was either war, or disease, or the curse of the place that kept the area around the mound from being settled right away.

Our kind came from a seagoing people, and that natural harbor a few miles from the mound—sheltered, wide, and deep—was too good to leave unused. When there were too many people near the harbor and not enough room, a deal was struck: take the land close to the mound, farm it free of taxes, but the men stay there, in perpetuity. It was, easy enough to see, Stone Harbor's way of keeping a barrier between itself and the mound, but with the hunger for land being what it was, Farmington soon became a going concern. The folks who lived here were the kind who weren't welcomed elsewhere and didn't have the money to look for a better living than that rocky inhospitable land. But it could be farmed, and it was. Every year, Stone Harbor sent a priest to say the rituals that kept the evil of the mound at bay. Farmington wasn't a prison colony, but it might as well have been, the folks it attracted.

The mound was spit up out of the ground at the edge of the fields like the earth itself couldn't bear to keep it inside anymore, a rocky outcropping with a wide, flat stone perched on top. The dead oak that marked the outcrop stood bare against the sky, a little humped, like a miser cackling over his hoard. Its back had been braced against the wind and the salt for two hundred years, some said; it had been a mature tree when Gammer Avon was small, and she could remember back then better than she could remember last week. Maybe there had been other trees on the hill then, but the oak—or maybe the demon—had smothered them all, leaving bare branches thrown against the sky, defying decay, denying defeat.

There was a rusty iron pike fence around the base of the rocky mound, like at the burying ground behind the church, to keep the animals from rooting about where they shouldn't. The tumbledown stone wall marking our plot's boundary was just before that. Repairing the stone line would have required getting nearer the mound than anyone was brave enough to do. No reason to go there anyway, as nothing grew out of the soil along that boundary.

One day, my little sister, Jenn, who is the light in my life, found her way out there, peering through the iron pickets. Da caught her, and thrashed her within an inch of her life. I didn't interfere, didn't protest, even though it meant I'd catch a beating too, for not keeping an eye on her. She had to learn. Better a beating than death and damnation.

No one had ever seen the demon, so maybe there wasn't one living in that dead, blasted spot between the last of the fields and the untamed woods, as some, almost always kin from outside, claimed. But the men who lived in Farmington, tough enough to endure a monthlong sea crossing and eke out a life from that unforgiving soil, avoided the mound like it was the plague; they grew more fractious and violent as the blessing time drew near, and were downright dangerous until the priest arrived and the ritual was completed according to book and verse. The animal was marked with the warding glyphs in indigo dye on its shaved skin and left bleating by the flat rock perched on lower boulders in the afternoon. The next morning, nothing more than broken bones and matted hair would be found. I knew it wasn't bears. Bears, like the savages and anyone else with sense, didn't go near the place.

The *priest being late* was one of the favorite stories at harvest time, when the days were still long enough and bright enough to celebrate and there was plenty of food and the endless winter nights were still months away. Tales about the demon itself, to warn the children and scare them into obedience, were told only in summer, when there were hours of evening light. Some said it was a serpent, or a great worm, and others said it was a beast more like a lion or a giant boar, but *teeth* figured in all the stories, and everyone agreed that the demon craved live flesh, live blood. It didn't take anyone as old as Gammer Avon to remember the winter when the blessing time was delayed a day or two. The screams of the slaughtered goats and pigs could be heard through shuttered windows during a gale.

It was only in the summer, too, that the men would show their tattoos, parts of the glyph patterns and wards put on the sacrificial animal, a kind of drunken taunt, a fractional gesture of defiance against a safely contained evil. It was never the entire glyph they made, in indigo and ash, but more than enough to prove their defiance of the large needle and mallet, and their parents, if not of the demon itself.

But the stories became fewer with fall, and were gone entirely long before winter drew down, and feasting was over, and supplies got thin. In those last dark months, until the priest arrived, the men stayed up later, drank more. Drinking led to fights, and offers to *finish the mark* and *leave you at the stone* were counted as bad as a threat of death. Drinking led to rash proposals to storm the rocky hill and confront the demon there with fire and tar. But there was not enough whiskey in Farmington or Stone Harbor or even the whole of the world to get the men to take on what they feared in the first place. So they redoubled their drinking and tried to put the shadows behind them. Because they were scared, because they didn't have the courage to kill the thing and wanted to crawl under the blankets. There was always too much whiskey and never enough light.

Trudging through the snow and frozen mud, we gathered in the church on Sabbath, to hear when the priest would arrive. The ship had never been so late as this year, and while annually it seemed to be a closer thing than any of us liked, with the weather and the tides against us, talk started to get ugly, blossoming into tauter nerves and sharper tempers than usual. No fewer than three black eyes in the church, and more than a dozen bandaged fists. I liked the church. No fights here, at least for an hour during sermon, and the big space was filled with light. Whitewashed walls reflected the one stained glass window over the altar—salvaged from another church that burned in Stone Harbor—which was about the only colors we'd see until spring. Blue and red and green and gold—I wished I could curl up inside those colors. The cross in the center of it was pretty, too, if a little stark in its silver and black and a little crooked from the botched repairs.

Da, his friend Mr. Minter, and Mr. Daggett escorted the stranger to the steps just in front of the big stone altar. They didn't look happy, and he didn't look like no priest. The man was dressed oddly, even odder than the folk in Stone Harbor, with bold colors—bright red and rich blue—that seemed ridiculous compared to our gray wool and brown homespun, and a little irreverent, as if he were trying to compete with the stained glass.

"I'm Captain Thrupp," the man announced to the congregation.

"And I'll tell you right off, I have bad news. The priest died during the passage from Southport."

A stifled scream from the back, followed by sobbing. Jenn's hand pinched mine, she held on so tight. I looked at Aunt Lize; she'd gone pale, but she held up a finger. The captain wasn't done yet.

Captain Thrupp held up his hands. "I'm going to make a quick run down the coast to Port Providence."

"That's two days away!" Miss Minter shouted. "That's not fast enough."

"It's close, but not impossible," the captain said. "We'll get him back in time."

Da nudged him. Captain Thrupp looked abashed. "We can't leave for another day, though. Weather's against us and we've a spar needs repairing. But we can get the work done and be back in time. No worries; Stone Harbor is paying me well for the extra trips and the repairs, as well as a bonus if—when—I return with the priest."

There was muttering in the church, and it took the lay deacon, Mr. Turner, a good five minutes to get everyone quiet and reciting a prayer.

I watched as Da and his friends hustled Captain Thrupp out of the church. Aunt Lize nudged me, hard, so I'd bend my head and pray.

We'd need something more than prayers, I thought.

That night, I finished collecting the bowls from dinner. The whiskey jug had gone around once again, and Da and them were getting raucous.

Aunt Lize hissed at me. "Get over here, girl!"

She grabbed my arm and yanked me to the other side of the kitchen's curtain door. "What are you doing, loitering out there! It's not safe, not with them in this state." She relented, though, and took the bowls from me, scraping the scraps—scant as they were—into the bucket for our last remaining pig. "You were just doing as you ought, and a good little housekeeper you'll make someday. But you don't want to be in the way of them, when they're like this. You look in on Jenn, and I'll take these out to the sow."

I nodded thanks; the wind was howling, whipping snow under the doors and piling it up against the windows. I shivered; I didn't like to think what else might be out there, for the Minters had lost a horse just the night before. No one was sure if it was the demon or just the madness of people cooped up and living with fear and hunger.

If she was right about the men, Aunt Lize was wrong on another score; I was already a good housekeeper. It was no sin to say so if it was true. It was our secret conspiracy, me and Aunt Lize; she would have run to Stone Harbor and found a place there, if my mother hadn't died. As I was so small, and Jenn just a baby, she put that thought aside and came to help Da, much as she hated him and Farmington. She couldn't leave us, her sister's children, not when she could do something about it.

So: her free life for mine. Whenever she made a coin or two extra, she put it aside without Da's knowing. She and I weren't overly fond of each other, but she knew my skills, and when she determined to do a thing, she did it right, spitting in the eye of the deal that kept the men tied to the land. I helped other women in the village, with cooking, with looking after their babies, with cleaning. Not out of the goodness of my heart, oh, no. I hated Missus Daggett's nasty gossip, Missus Foyle's mean cheapness, and the way that cowlike Miss Minter let her widower brother look on me in ways he shouldn't, not when I was still a good year off from any thought of marrying. Their nastiness was another curse upon Farmington, demon or no. But Missus Daggett made the best bread, Missus Foyle knew a trick with laundry that took out any stain, and Miss Minter would give me a penny more than she should; it was those skills and coins I wanted, because as soon as Jenn was old enough to manage on her own, I would shake the thin dust of Farmington from my skirts forever. When I made more money, away in Stone Harbor, I'd send for Jenn, and maybe Aunt Lize, too, if she'd come.

Not long now.

I pushed the curtain aside and went to the back room, where Aunt Lize, Jenn, and I slept, barring the door behind me. Jenn sat up.

"It's only me. Go back to sleep."

"I can't." Her voice was small, no more than a mouse's squeak. "Tell me about 'Away.' Please."

"You don't need to think about 'Away,'" I said, even though I'd just been comforting myself with the very same thoughts. "You need to go to sleep."

"Please, Marr." There was an unevenness in the door's planking that let a sliver of light through, glancing off Jenn's dark hair and bright eyes. She took my hand. "Please."

I sighed and told her the other story she knew by heart, the one where we heard the fine bells of the church in Stone Harbor, walked the five miles to the town, following them. We'd live in a large house, or get on a ship and sail far away.

She fell asleep a moment later. I heard Aunt Lize come back into the house, slamming the door shut against the weather behind her. We were as safe as we could be, for now. I curled up next to Jenn's warm little body and fell asleep myself.

I was on my way back from a long morning's work at Missus Foyle's four days later, my knees worn out with scrubbing floors, but an old and much-begrudged coin in the pocket under my skirts. The sky was dull as wash water. The roads were clear of snow but rutted awful with the frozen mud that recorded the tracks of every person and horse and cart that came along this way. It was as bad clambering over those uneven ridges as it would be going through snow.

So my head was down, and I didn't even see him until we bumped into each other. The sea captain, Thrupp.

"I'm sorry, I didn't mean— Is he here? Has the priest come?"

"No."

I felt the blood rush from my face. "Then why—how are you here?"

"There was no luck at Providence Port, but I sent my ship's boat up the river. There's a man there can do the job, they say."

I didn't believe him, but I couldn't afford not to.

Close up, I had a chance to examine the captain more thoroughly. Thrupp was only as tall as me, but broad enough, stout enough to stand against a gale, I thought. An ugly mug of a face, with one eye scarred and a little closed, the result of an accident or a fight. He had a canny, honest air about him, a bit of the hell-raiser, all ginger hair and whiskers and a voice suited for shouting orders over nature, if not quiet city life. Maybe his crew would save us after all.

"I'm only out to stretch my legs while they're gone. It was a chance to get the smell of tar and salt and dirty men out of my nose, to stretch my legs a bit on ground that didn't move beneath me."

I raised an eyebrow, an unspoken query.

"And given the air of this village, I'm eager to be back among the dirty men and bilge water." He laughed, a little nervously, I thought. "I have the notion that I shouldn't stay in this place too long. There's . . . so much bad feeling around here, and I don't like superstition I ain't been brought up in."

I nodded dully and suddenly he realized he was speaking to a resident of this ill-favored place.

He had some manners, at least enough to be embarrassed by his gaffe. His honesty. "That's not to say— I mean—"

"Don't trouble yourself. I'd be away, too, if I could. I *will*, when I can," I said, correcting myself a little too insistently. "Someday."

His face cleared. "Why wait? Be at the ship no later than noon-tide tomorrow. We return to Southport, and my sister Bonne needs a smart girl to help in the house. You can do that, I suppose."

I nodded, eager but still knowing that all life is a bargain, as Aunt Lize had said often enough. "How much? For the passage, I mean?"

"My sister will pay *me*, if I can bring her reliable help." He laughed. "She'll kiss my boot, if I make her life easy with the twins, those two hellion boys."

I scowled at his so casually invoking hell, here, now.

"And she'll pay you, too, every week. Labor's scarce, 'round our parts. How's that?"

I nodded again, even more hastily, and felt the unfamiliar upturn of my lips into a smile. Suddenly ashamed, I remembered Jenn. "I have . . . I have a little sister. Just seven. I can't leave her."

"Bring her. Bonne's just lost her girl; she's pining for someone to dress in ribbons, and she'll treat her decent, teach her the running of a house. You have my word; Bonne's a good lass, and her husband knows I'll beat the shit out of him, he does her—or me—wrong."

Maybe there was a sister in Southport, I thought, or maybe there was just an auction block and the captain's purse to be filled once I was got away from . . . well, not the safety of Farmington, but the constant prying eyes of it. It didn't matter, I decided suddenly, it was time for us to get out of here. No more waiting. Tomorrow, early, I'd take Jenn, leave breakfast for Da and a note for Aunt Lize. Then we'd walk the five miles to Stone Harbor and the docks. Five miles to freedom, or at least a change of dread, which would be near enough. After that, we'd see.

I nodded. "Tomorrow, noon. What ship?"

He laughed. "She's the only one there!" Then he saw that I knew nothing and said, "The *Fraunces*. She's a fine lady for a bowsprit—that's a kind of statue, on the, er, front of the ship. You won't miss her."

I returned home quickly, but less quickly than a rumor flies.

My da met me at the door, hot whiskey breath hanging sour on the cold air. "Been making a spectacle of yourself, have you? Not even the decency to sneak out in night, you have to go out in broad day."

Broad day was too kind a description. There were six hours of daylight, these days, and it made falling snow look more like ash with the sun so hidden amid the clouds.

I knew better than to ask *what?* Mr. Minter had seen me talking to the captain and flew here across his field. Get me cheaper, if I was damaged goods. "No, sir, I wasn't—"

"Liar." A flash of gold, a crack-slap to my face, stinging like a switch. "I'll just have a word with Thrupp myself. Teach him to—"

"Gar, she won't have had time to get herself into trouble," Aunt Lize said. "She's just come from Jaine Minter's now. Look at her clothes—there's no mud, no straw in her hair, nothing of the round-heel about her. You." She turned to me. "Get inside and fix the noon meal. Now!"

"Yes'm."

I was able to slip past her, avoiding another crack. I felt a warm trickle of blood against my cold cheek; the ring had drawn blood again.

Arguing outside, muffled voices raising and lowering, my father shouting, spoiling for any fight, and my aunt trying to keep him from making more of a show for the neighbors.

I put the bowls out and stirred the pot; the door slammed open, the cold rushed in and made the flames dance unevenly.

Aunt Lize shut the door behind her, leaned against it. "Girl, you can't afford scandal. Nobody can, especially now, when tempers are running high and people are looking for someone, something, to lash out at. Don't give them a target. And you, yourself . . ." She sighed. "It's a small village, and if you don't get out of here, you have to marry as best you can. Make the best bargain, that's the only way. You don't want another woman in the house—there can only be one queen in a hive. That's just one more reason you don't want Mr. Minter, apart from his bad breath, loose hands, and goggle eyes— there's also his sister. So better to hope she lives a long, long life, the better to have an excuse to avoid marrying him."

A small chuckle. A lightening of the mood on our side of the smoke-and-gloom-filled room.

"Once winter's done, we'll see where we stand, but until then . . . mind yourself."

She was thinking we'd survive winter. She was thinking we'd survive the week. I didn't say anything; she was giving herself a worry over which she had some control.

Or so she thought. I was leaving, with Jenn, tomorrow just before dawn.

I kept my head down and myself out of the way the rest of the afternoon and into the evening. Dinner was thin that night, and would be worse tomorrow; we were down to the scrapings on the inside of the storage barrel. But tomorrow night, there'd be two fewer mouths to feed, so I didn't feel guilty when I put the last of the bread in my pocket to take with us when we left, right next to my small stash of hoarded coins.

I washed the bowls, but between the thin commons and the hunger with which we scraped them, it was hardly necessary.

I put Jenn to bed, kissed her forehead. I ran my finger down the scratch on her arm, the result of a scuffle with our last chicken. "This is healing well," I whispered. "Sleep tight."

As soon as her eyes closed, I took her two shirts, coat, and skirt under one arm, and put her stockings and underthings in my pocket. Pitiful, how little there was to take with us, but it would make it easier to smuggle out.

I picked up my work basket and sat down on our side of the room, as close to the firelight as I could, but still in the shadows.

Aunt Lize unlocked the cupboard and brought out the jug and two cups.

"We need another one." My father's voice was gruff; he'd already started at Mr. Minter's house, and now that neighbor was here and it was Da's turn to supply the liquor.

"Who's coming?"

"No one. It's for my daughter. For Marr."

I looked up, and then Aunt Lize and I looked at each other. "No, thank you, Da."

"Pour it." He took the mug from Aunt Lize and gave it to me.

"There's a priest coming tomorrow. Turns out, Thrupp heard of someone farther north, up the coast, and sent his boat to make inquiries, despite the weather. They will bring him tomorrow."

"Tomorrow," Mr. Minter repeated, already drunk. "Tomorrow, it's all done."

"It'll be nothing but a bad memory, after then."

Aunt Lize whooped and clapped her hands. Da tried a smile, but he was worn out with worry and fear. We all were; there's a fatigue that comes with them both. "Drink it up. You . . . you earned it, after all. It was your . . ."

Da paused so long, I wondered whether he'd say *forwardness* or *sluttishness*.

". . . doing," he said. "You're the reason we'll all be safe. Go ahead, before I change my mind."

I took it and drank, making a face. It was far bitterer than I expected, and it burned my throat. I sputtered and coughed. No laughter, as I expected, just that sad smile.

"You're getting so grown up," Da said. "You're slipping away from me."

I frowned and opened my mouth to reply. The floor fell away

beneath me; the rafters of the ceiling, draped in dried herbs, spun crazily.

"Church bell—" If the priest was really coming, why were there no bells? No celebration?

"Is it done?" It was Mr. Minter's voice. "How long?"

"Another minute or two, before she's all the way gone."

"A pity. For the best, though. For everyone."

I grabbed at the table leg, the closest thing to me, to try to pull myself up. I grabbed the wrong one of three wheeling around in front of me and felt my hand slam to the floor, leaden and disobedient.

Aunt Lize screamed, but the last thing I heard that made any sense was Da saying: "Get the needles and ink, then."

I awoke, my head silted up with brick dust and coal clinkers and aching as if I'd been sleeping on the smith's anvil while he was working. Movement brought dry heaves and the notion that the earthen floor was moving beneath me. I closed my eyes again, and slept.

When I woke the second time, it was light, and I felt much better. The unexpected quiet of the neighborhood was a blessing, and this time, I was able to push myself upright and onto a stool, my head resting against the table.

The quiet of the neighborhood . . . bright daylight, or what passed for it.

Not even the deepest snow on the darkest days could muffle *every* sound of Farmington.

I started, remembering what had happened the night before. My clothing was intact. I shoved my sleeves up, hauled up my skirts above my knees—nothing but pale skin.

My hands flew to my face—I couldn't feel the ache I should have, had the needle marks been made on me there, but I sought the cloudy and speckled glass on the mantel anyway.

Not a mark on me, save the bruise on my cheek.

Not sold in marriage to Mr. Minter, not marked with the glyphs, the invitation to the demon to depart. Then why the whiskey, that'd hit so hard?

The quiet of the neighborhood, the quiet of the house—

Jenn.

"No! Jenn! No, no, no, nooo!"

I ran to the bedchamber. Empty save for crumpled sheets and the same bitter smell of whatever had been in my whiskey.

A tiny drop of blood on the sheet. The needle and mallet, a small dish of ink and ash, almost empty.

I felt the world spin around me and clutched the door. "Jenn!"

No one was anywhere in the house. Back into the kitchen, all was empty, a chair knocked over, and the table askew, probably from my own collapse.

The door was not on the latch and hung ajar. It was the cold air that revived me.

I shoved it open, nearly tripped over Aunt Lize, lying just outside. The puddle of blood on the paver beneath her head expanded sluggishly, seeming to pause against a patch of grass before breaking around it.

I pinched her cheek; she mumbled incoherently, agitatedly, and did not recognize me.

The spreading red puddle slowed to a stop, warming the frozen mud just enough to begin to seep into the ground. Her eyelids fluttered open and then were still.

I leaned to her face but felt no warm breath on my cheek. There was blood on her lips and a swelling.

Had the demon come this close? No, she was too . . . intact.

I looked around for answers.

There.

Jenn's blanket lay on the frozen mud. A few threads of its gray wool were snagged on Aunt Lize's fingernails.

I saw it all then, with a terrible clarity. Aunt Lize had fought for Jenn, because she was either misdosed or presumed to be in agreement. A blow across her jaw had sent her back, with Jenn's blanket—a warm woolen thing against the frozen ground—wrenched from her grasp, and fallen from my little sister.

They'd been so drunk, they'd left Aunt Lize there to bleed to death, lest stopping to help her, they lose their nerve to do what they intended.

I picked up the blanket, crushed it to my face to stifle my screams.

It took me a long time to get up the courage to move from where Aunt Lize's body lay—it felt like forever, but the sun hadn't moved much in the sky before I realized I had to see for myself, and maybe I'd be able to stop them. Maybe I could save Jenn.

The village was so quiet. I heard a door banging, once, twice, but it was the wind. An unlatched door in Farmington was unheard of. Rather than see what had caused it, I sped up, my eyes straight ahead, my fists balled up under my apron, my reluctance to go where I must overwhelmed by my fear of what I'd see there.

I followed the disturbed path to the one place none of them would ever have gone if they'd been in their right minds. The stones were cold and rough under my hands as I scrambled over the low wall.

After an age, I found myself closer to the mound than I'd ever been and pushed open the rusty iron gate that surrounded its base. The lock that secured it lay on the ground; the gate had never been left unlocked or unlatched in my lifetime.

I looked up at the mound and began to run toward the rocky outcropping. I did so without a thought, without a hesitation, and not even the old tales, told in high midsummer, slowed me. Not the warnings of my mother, my father, my aunt, and every elder I knew could stop me.

I'd seen a tiny stripe of white against the mud by one of the granite boulders. It was not rock—it was flesh, as white as birch bark.

There was a slight movement that was no stirring of the wind, no bleached-out part of the demon. It was human.

I hurled myself up the hill, sliding on the scree, my hands cut by the granite chips. "Jenn!"

As if in response, a small, chubby hand reached out. As I drew closer, I could see a familiar scar across the back of the hand, covered with the hastily, crudely wrought tattoos of lye and ash, colored with blood. The same as I'd seen on Mr. Daggett and Mr. Foyle, covered up since fall.

Jenn was still alive.

I screamed and raced toward the stone, the loose rock and mud keeping me from going all the way under that flat outcropping. I grabbed at her hand, felt it clutch at mine. Then there was a jerk, and Jenn's hand slid through my fingers, slick with . . . mud? Blood, mixed with a noxious black ooze.

Without thinking, I reached in under the flat rock, straining to grab Jenn. My shoulders jammed under the rock. A sharp bite, a dagger through my palm, and I snatched my hand back. Blood streamed across my wrist, and a yellow-white foam lined the wound. My skin there felt as if it was burning off.

I tore my apron to rags. Wiped off as much of the foam as I could. Bound up my hand with the rest, once the burning had stopped and the blood was flowing freely. I sat back heavily, woozy from whatever poison had found its way inside me. I fell over onto the cold granite scree.

I might have only imagined the last little gasping whimper, the

crunch of birdlike bone, another effect of the poison, before unconsciousness took me.

Or maybe I was awake. I couldn't move, not even to shut my
eyes, but perhaps I slept and dreamed or my mind wandered, as if
in a fever. I couldn't feel the wind, the cold, my body, but saw greenish clouds speeding over the sky, racing a sun the color of the
stormy sea.

I woke hours later, freezing cold, stiff, and aching, my eyes gritty,
pain like a spear through my forehead. My muscles felt as if they
were knotted ropes, my joints like soggy bread. Once my head
cleared, only enough to realize what I'd seen, and failed to do, I
turned and vomited until I thought my ribs would crack.

I wiped my mouth with the back of my hand, and my eyes with
the corner of my cap—the only thing left that wasn't fouled with dirt
and blood—and turned toward the stones. Nothing there, no sound,
no smell, no movement, no hint of anything amiss. Indeed, there
was a bird hopping idly at the edge of the brown, burned grass,
pecking halfheartedly for seeds. It was something I had never seen
before; animals never came here.

It could only mean that the demon was gone.

Too much to believe that it was gone for good. It had only found
a new nest, maybe one closer to the village itself for better feeding.

Why hadn't it taken me?

I was rooted to the spot, a foolish logic whispering that if the
demon hadn't taken me here, I must be safe. Finally, the urge to run
overwhelmed my fear and drove me to speed with the notion *I might
survive.*

Without thinking, I ran, sweating and slipping and tripping
over the churned-up mud, my breath coming in hitches, sight
blurred, my limbs moving unguided by anything but panic. More
than once, I stumbled, and once, catching my foot on a root, I fell,
the wind knocked from me. My wounded hand felt as though the

bones had turned to shattering glass, shearing through the muscles.

When I could catch my breath again, my eyes focused, and I saw something on the ground, not ten feet from me. At first, I thought it was cloth and old leather, and then I saw the pink and white of cleaned bone. Mr. Minter's skull had been staved in, his face flattened, the meat and marrow sucked from his bones. What was left of him was flat, wrinkled, and brown, like a cowpat that had dried out in the sun for a month or two.

It was almost enough to get me up and running, but a prey's instinct stopped me. A rustling high up in a fir tree, movement in the shadows. A glint of gold.

Da's ring flickered in the dull sunlight, and his hand jerked slackly, as if it were on a puppeteer's string. I could not make out the rest of him. He made no noise, but as I strained to see, I heard a wet sound, like a smacking of lips. Then a rustling, and it was as if a curtain had been drawn back.

Clawed fingers held on to Da's shoulders, talons digging into his flesh. The demon's head moved and I saw two teeth like silver daggers fastened on Da's neck, blood running down his shriveling corpse.

I must have made a slight noise, for suddenly my father's head lolled away and two pale eyes glared at me. The demon's face was otherwise featureless, but for a mouthful of pointed teeth, those two fangs, and those wide, malevolent eyes.

The demon hissed, then returned to its feeding.

I found myself running with no memory of getting up. I was at our house before I knew I had gone so far, and shut the door behind me, the image of Aunt Lize's body burning into my mind.

This place wasn't safe, it never had been, and certainly not against the demon. I grabbed a few things, found the whiskey jug and a small, sharp knife, a lamp, and a blanket. Some guardian angel reminded me of my hoard of coins, and I put them into my pocket.

The church was the only answer. The only safe place. I fled to there, barely feeling my feet beneath me.

The door to the church creaked open, and my heart sank; I'd hoped to find the rest of the villagers here.

The quiet was not because they were safely hidden, but because they were all dead.

I barred the door behind me and only then struck a light against the glowing dark of late afternoon. I sank onto one of the benches, and then, feeling too exposed, moved deeper into the building, to the front of the church. Even sitting on the steps before the great stone table of the altar was not enough, and with a reverence, I climbed underneath, the wine and water set on the top, ready for the blessing next service. Finally, the space was small enough to reassure me. I lit the lamp I'd taken and left it just outside my hiding place, and too tired to eat the crust I'd hidden, I tried to keep awake, not certain what I'd do if it tried to get in. Eventually, my eyes closed as the sunlight faded through the stained glass cross.

I dreamed of nothing but woke the next morning exhausted and freezing. Crawling out from under the altar, I stretched, still sore, and my wounded hand, and the arm above, felt swollen and tight. The daylight streamed in and I knew it would keep me safe; the demon still needed the clouds and shadows.

The daylight streamed in because the stained glass was gone. I had woken freezing because there was no window to keep out the night's winter air.

A swish, a rustling, up high in the corner, and I saw it.

The demon nestled there, dormant, between the wall and the ceiling like a moth's cocoon. Granite gray and brown, its bony wings were wrapped around its body. They were nearly translucent, naught but a bat's thin membrane over a butterfly skeleton, stretched thin for a hundred years of near-starvation. I fancied I could see its belly beneath the wings, distended now; a pile of cracked bones and bloodied cloth beneath it told that it had brought its kill into the church along with it.

The wind scattered a few dried leaves across the filth, and I saw how the demon had entered this once-holy place: the fragile lead of the window smoldered with an acrid stench like a failed batch of lye soap, the glass broken and scattered across the altar and surrounding floor. All the demon had to do was wait on the roof and let its ichor drip down, dissolving the bonds of the lead. With the glass went the cross, and so there was no impediment to stop its invasion.

I had to get past it while it slept. I took my knife and stepped out, cautiously.

As soon as the broken glass crunched under my boot, it woke. The demon screeched and spread its wings. Short, bird-like legs extended from its body, and the wings ended in taloned claws.

I turned away when I saw the distended belly move. I could not tell whether it was a still-struggling victim or some diabolical off-spring.

As I turned, I saw the bottle of wine on the altar. I snatched it up and flung it at the demon, and before it could react, I threw my lamp at it.

The light was low and guttering but was enough. The wine, and the last of the lamp oil, spattered and caught against the gray speckled skin. Shrieking like a thousand pigs at slaughter time, the demon fell heavily to the ground, as the fire ate up its flesh like sugar melting in water.

On the stone floor, the demon continued to scream, its mouth opening wider and wider, until finally it split, the jaw hanging slack from its skull.

There was no movement for a moment, then a popping noise: flesh pulling away from flesh. A white slug-like creature, the very heart and soul of the demon, squirmed out of the broken mouth, leaving a dark green slime behind it. The only similarity between it and the body it had inhabited was its large eyes; this changed creature was small, translucent ivory, veined, its head at one end, diminishing to a small tail at the other. Like a larval creature or a misshapen snake, it kicked away from the ruin of a body and advanced on me.

A buzzing in my head: I knew immediately, I had to grab it and never let go until it was dead. I grabbed behind what I assumed was the head. It immediately wriggled, slick and elastic within my grasp. I felt the body contract and lengthen, all muscles within a thin membrane of slippery skin.

When I finally got two hands and a firm grip on it, the head lashed around, and before I had a chance to cry out, the monster's mouth opened. Two long fangs seemed to uncurl from within it—how could they be so long and still fit into that evil little head?

Another contraction and it almost got away, but I held on. The head reared back, and the fangs, like two of the finest, sharpest embroidery needles, sank into my hands. Blood dripped, acid venom burned, and I wanted to scream. Instead, I gritted my teeth and devoted all my energy, every fiber of my being, to holding on to that creature and crushing it. Unless I could kill it, it would claim me.

The tighter I held, the more it curled and contorted and bit. My hands felt as if I'd stuck them into the hottest coals of the hearth, and I felt the poison work its way up my arms, weakening them. Still, I held fast, spots and threads of lightning blurring my vision.

Slowly, I moved to the altar and, careful never to loosen my grasp, crabbed up the stairs sideways. I twisted suddenly and tried to stuff the wriggling demon into the chalice of would-be holy water; it hissed and twined around my hands. My fists were too big to immerse the creature, so I knocked it over, a small sacrilege to stop a greater evil. I slammed my hands on the puddle of water and felt the thing writhe violently. Even unblessed, it had some virtue against the monster. Still not enough; as the water slid away, grew shallower, the thing redoubled its attacks, stretching and snapping at my eyes now.

The pain in my hands gave me a desperate idea. If not water, then fire.

So careful not to fall—because if I fell, I would drop the demon— I kicked over my jug of whiskey. The long trailing altar cloth soaked up the whiskey, and the growing puddle caught the flame that still consumed the thing's previous body.

The altar cloth caught ablaze immediately, and suddenly, the altar was a perfect rectangle of fire. Before it could consume the thin material, I plunged both of my hands, and the demon, into the inferno.

A thin, shrill cry, another flurry of resistance, and finally, I felt the creature droop. Refusing to believe this was not a ruse, I held on, pressing my clenched fists into the flames, until I felt nothing but numbness.

The flames died. The demon did not move.

Cautiously, I opened one hand, still pressing down with the flat of my palm. No movement but the sliding of my hand against greasy soot where the demon had been. I opened the other, in the same fashion, scarcely believing my eyes.

A smear of oily green against the dying embers on top of the stone altar was all that was left of it.

I'd killed it. I stepped back, made a reverence, and only then felt the pain that had been blotted out by my concerted efforts. My eyes stung from smoke, my hands looked like ground meat, and I was infernally tired. My head ached, from clenching my teeth in concentration and from Da's drink and his blow to my head.

Then I didn't hurt. The numbness I'd felt returned, flooding my body, and for one excruciating moment, I thought I'd somehow caught fire. I looked down, and the charred and shredded flesh of my hands fell away, showing new, pink flesh beneath. I undid the bandage on my hand, and the roughness of my torn wool dress against the new skin was the only discomfort I felt.

I understood. In defeating something so unclean, I'd received a measure of grace.

I heard the Stone Harbor church bell tolling the hour. Could it really be only noon? I ran from there, not caring that I was in bloody rags, not caring who saw me going about without a cap, my hair untied and streaming behind me. There was a strength to the pale winter sun that I'd missed, and I laughed aloud to feel its warmth.

Spring was finally here. Spring was here, the demon was dead, and there was light in the world again.

I tripped across new, deep furrows: someone, in a fit of optimism or desperation or drunkenness, had begun to plow early. As I stumbled, still laughing, the fresh, honest scent of the earth filled my lungs, and as I reached the other side of the field, the ground began to climb. I knew I was at the edge of Farmington, and Stone Harbor was not two miles away. Another rise, cross the beck, and I'd be there. I had my small store of funds and I could sell my labor for a term or two, and be no worse off than I had been in the village. Captain Thrupp had told me there was a need for workers, and I believed him to be an honest man.

As I started up the second rise, I began to breathe heavily. Thinking on all that had occurred in the past few days, it only made sense to be weary. The liveliness that follows extended effort wore away, and my pace slowed. But I could see the steeples of Stone Harbor now, and my heart was light.

I'd won. I'd survived.

I slowed further as I reached the stream. It was wider and deeper than I ever remembered seeing, and I paused at this last boundary between my old life and my new. I was sweating now, and itched all over, alternately shivering and feverish. Just cross the stream, and an easy walk to town, and I would be safe.

The stream was swollen from the winter snows beginning to melt up in the mountains. The water rushed and roared, such a monstrous racket for a small stream. But it seemed no longer a minor obstacle to be traversed by wading or going from smooth stone to stone. I felt myself shrink before it, almost, afraid to risk crossing when I was exhausted and feeling sickly. Drowning, being swept away, and a memory of the spilled holy water made me frightened.

One last step, I told myself. *That's all. Put a foot, a hand, in the water, and you'll see it's nothing,* an unfamiliar voice deep inside me said faintly. *Do that, and you'll find the courage to cross. All will be well.*

The sun beat down as if at midsummer, and my head seemed filled with the roiling chaos of the current, until I could not think clearly. Fear welled in me, and I was as stone.

The brutal sun overhead, the confusion of the river that threatened to drown me even as I stayed on the shore. I was filled with terror, unable to move. The other side of the stream seemed an ocean away, the tumultuous waves as high as the bell tower.

That thought calmed me. The distant bell tower. That brought peace; I felt my head clear. The wind shifted, carrying the sound of Stone Harbor's tolling bell—had I really spent two hours here, by that roaring torrent, amazed? The sound grated on my ears; there must have been a crack in those lovely bells I had loved so much, for they now seemed hateful and shrill. Doom-laden.

The wind picked up, and I caught again the scent of the tilled earth behind me. Perhaps I didn't need to leave after all. Everything I'd feared in Farmington was gone now. I had a house, I had my housewifely skills.

I could feed myself as well in the village as in some far-off town. I knew how to work, I wasn't afraid of hard work. I'd never be afraid again.

A kind of mellowing happiness settled over me as I turned away from the consuming flood of the stream. My fatigue and illness lifted. I'd made the right decision.

I trudged, wearily, happily, and decisively, back up to Da's house—my house, now. I kept going, until I crossed the field and found myself at the mound. I began to climb it. The intensity of the sun—when had the first month of spring ever been so hot?—was like the flames on the altar. I crawled under the flat rock, smelling the dampness and feeling the cold of the ground soothe me. I settled myself comfortably, curling around until I was a snug little ball.

Maybe just a nap, then I'd search for food. And then, who knows? Perhaps I'd find my way across that stream, when it was frozen over, and visit Stone Harbor after all. Plenty to eat there, too.

As I settled into my slumber, away from the hateful sun, I heard Jenn singing to me. She was happy, I could tell, because we were together again, just as we'd been promised.

Besides, this was my village. No one else belonged here. There can be only one queen.

WE ARE ALL MONSTERS HERE

KELLEY ARMSTRONG

After decades of movies and TV shows and books filled with creatures by turns terrifying and tempting, it was a guarantee that the real vampires could never live up to the hype. We knew that. Yet we were still disappointed.

When the first stories hit the news—always from some distant place we'd never visited or planned to visit—the jokes followed. Late-night comedy routines, YouTube videos, Internet memes . . . people had a blast mocking the reality of vampires. The most popular costume that Halloween? Showing up dressed as yourself and saying "Look, I'm a vampire." Ha-ha.

Then cases emerged in the US, and people stopped laughing.

While vampirism was no longer comedy fodder, people were still disillusioned. They just found new ways to express it. Some started petitions claiming the term *vampire* made a mockery of a serious medical condition. Others started petitions claiming it made a mockery of long-standing folklore. There was actually a bill before Congress to legislate a change of terminology.

Then the initial mass outbreak erupted, and no one cared what they called it anymore.

I first heard about the vampires in a college lecture hall. I couldn't tell you which course it was—the news made too little of an impression for me to retain the surrounding circumstances. I know only that I was in class, listening to a professor, when the guy beside me said, "Hey, did you see this?" and passed me his iPhone. I was going to ignore him. I'd been doing that all term—he kept sitting beside me and making comments and expecting me to be impressed, when all I wanted to say was, "How about trying to talk to me *outside* of class?" But that might have been an invitation I'd regret. So I usually ignored him, but this time, he'd shoved his phone in front of me and before I could turn away, I saw the headline.

The headline read REAL-LIFE VAMPIRES IN VENEZUELA. The article went on to say that there had been five incidents in which people had woken to find themselves covered in blood . . . and everyone else in the house dead and bloodless.

"Vampires," the guy whispered. "Can you believe it? I'd have thought they'd have been scarier."

"Slaughtering your entire family isn't scary enough for you?"

He shifted in his seat. "You know what I mean."

"It's not vampires," I said. "It's drugs. Like those bath salts."

I shoved the phone at him and turned my attention back to the professor.

Two years later, I was still living in a college dorm, despite having been due to graduate the year before. No one had graduated that term, because that's when the outbreak struck our campus. Classes were suspended and students were quarantined. The lockdown stretched for days. Then weeks. Then months. The protests started peacefully enough, but soon we realized we were being held prisoner and fought back. The military fought back harder. The scene played out across the nation, not just in schools, but in every community where people had been "asked" not to leave for months on end. Martial law was declared across the country. The outbreaks continued to spread.

Given what was happening in the rest of the world, soon even the college's staunchest believers in democracy and free will realized we had it good. We were safe, living in separate quarters equipped with alarms and dead bolts so we could sleep securely. Otherwise, we were free to mingle, with all our food and entertainment supplied as we waited for the government to find a cure.

One morning I awoke to the sound of my best friend, Katie, banging on my door, shouting that the answer was finally here. I dressed as quickly as I could and joined her in the hall.

"A cure?" I said.

Her face fell. "No," she said, and I regretted asking. I'd known Katie since my sophomore year, and she bore little resemblance to the girl she'd been. I used to envy her, with her amazing family and amazing boyfriend back home. It'd been a year since she'd seen them. Three months since she'd heard from them, as the authorities cut off communications with her quarantined hometown. She'd lost thirty pounds, her sweet nature reduced to little more than anxiety and nerves, unable to grieve, not daring to hope.

"Not a cure," she said. "But the next best thing. A method of detection. We can be tested. And then we can leave."

A method of detection. Wonderful news for an optimist. I am not an optimist. I heard that and all I could think was, *What if we test positive?* At the assembly, I was the annoying one in the front row badgering the presenters with exactly that question. "What will happen if we have the marker?"

That's what it was—a genetic marker. Which didn't answer the question of transmission. Two years since the first outbreak, and no one knew what actually caused vampirism. It seemed to be something inside us that just "activated." Of course, people blamed the government. It was in the vaccinations or the water or the genetically modified food. What was the trigger? No one knew, and frankly, it seemed like no one cared.

Those who had the marker would be subjected to continued quarantine while scientists searched for a cure. The rest of us would be free to go. Well, free to go someplace that wasn't quarantined.

The next day, the military lined us up outside the cafeteria. There were still people who worried that the second they got a positive result, the nearest guy in fatigues would pull out his semiautomatic. Bullshit, of course. The semiautomatic would make noise. If they planned to kill us, they'd do it much more discreetly.

To allay concerns, the testing would be communal. As open as they could make it. I had to give them props for that.

They took a DNA sample and analyzed it on the spot. That instant analysis wouldn't have been possible a couple of years ago, but when you're facing a vampire plague, all the best minds work day and night to develop the tools to fight it, whether they want to or not.

My results took eight seconds. I counted. Then they handed me a blue slip of paper. I looked down the line at everyone who'd been tested before me. Green papers, red, yellow, purple, white, and black. They didn't dare use a binary system here. So we got our papers and we sat and we waited.

When Katie came over clutching a green slip of paper, she looked at mine and said, "Oh," and looked around, mentally tabulating colors.

"They say the rate is fifteen percent," I said. "There are seven colors. That means an equal number for each so we don't panic."

Once everyone was tested, they divided us into our color groups. Then we were laser-tattooed on our wrists.

I got a small yellow circle. When I craned my neck to look at the group beside us—the reds—they were getting the same. So were the blacks to my left. I exhaled in relief and looked around for Katie.

A woman announced, "If you have a yellow circle, you are clear and you may—"

That's when the screaming started. From the green group. I caught sight of Katie, standing there, staring in horror at the black star on her wrist. I raced over. A soldier tried to stop me, but I pushed past him, saying, "I'm with her."

A woman in uniform stepped into my path. "She's—"

"I know," I said. "I'm staying with her."

It wasn't a particularly noble sacrifice. That circle on my wrist meant I could leave at any time. Katie could not. I had nowhere to go anyway. My family . . . well, let's just say that when I got accepted to college, I walked out and never looked back and don't regret it. I won't explain further. I don't think I need to.

I would stay with Katie because she needed me and because I could and because—let me be frank—it was the smart thing to do. I'd heard what the world was like beyond our campus. I was staying where there was food and shelter and safety and a friend.

Assemblies and a parade of officials and psychologists followed, all reassuring the others that their black star was not a death sentence. Not everyone who had the marker "turned." Those who did were now being transported to a secure facility, where they'd continue to await a cure.

There were private sessions that day, too, with counselors. During those, I sat in one of the common rooms with the other yellow suns. Yes, I wasn't the only one. We all had our reasons for staying, and most were like mine, part loyalty, part survival. We sat and we played cards, and we enjoyed the break from being hugged and told how wonderful and empathetic and strong we were, when we felt like none of those things.

Night came. Before today, the locks had been internal, meant to protect us while reassuring us that in the event of an emergency, we *could* leave. Now the doors had been fitted with an overriding electronic system. Perhaps it's a testament to how far things had gone that not a single person complained. We were just happy for the locks, especially now, in a building filled with dormant monsters.

I woke to the first shot at midnight. I bolted up in bed, thinking I'd dreamed it. Then the second shot came. No screams. Just gunfire. I yanked on my jeans and ran to the door, in my confusion forgetting about the new locks. I twisted the knob and . . .

The door opened.

I yanked it shut fast and stood there, gripping the knob.

Was I really awake? Was I really me? How could I be sure?

People who "turned" were not usually killed on sight, not unless they were caught mid-rampage and had to be put down. Studies said that when vampires woke in the night, they later had no memory of it. People took comfort in that—at least if you turned, you'd be spared the horror of remembering you'd slaughtered your loved ones. I took no comfort because it also meant there was no way of knowing what it felt like to turn. Would you be conscious in that moment? Did it seem real at the time?

I looked at the unlocked door. My gaze swung down to the yellow sun on the back of my wrist.

Another shot, this one so close that I ducked, the echo ringing in my ears. The shot had come from the other side of the wall. Katie's room.

I threw open my door and raced to hers, and finding it open, I ran through and . . .

Katie lay crumpled on the floor. In her outstretched hand was a gun.

I ran to her and then stopped short, staring. She lay on her stomach, and the side of her chest . . . there was a hole there. No, not a hole—that implies something neat and harmless. It was bloody and raw, a crater into her chest, just below her heart. I dropped to my knees, a sob catching in my throat.

She whimpered.

There was a moment when I didn't move, when all I could think was that she'd come back to life, like a vampire from the old stories and Hollywood movies. Except that wasn't how real vampires worked. They weren't dead. They weren't invulnerable. I grabbed her shoulders and turned her over.

Blood gushed from her mouth as I eased her onto her back. I tried not to think of that, tried not to let my brain assess that damage. It still did. I was pre-med. I'd spent enough hours volunteering in emergency wards to process the damage reflexively. She'd tried to shoot herself in the heart, not the head, because she didn't know better, because she was the kind of person who couldn't even watch action movies. So she'd aimed for her heart and missed, but not missed by enough. Not nearly enough.

I shouted for help. As I did, I heard other shouts. Other shots, too, and screams from deep in the dormitory, and I tried to lay Katie down, to run out for help, but she gripped my hand and said, "No," and "Stay," and I looked at her, and as much as I wanted to believe she'd survive, that she'd be fine, I knew better. So I shouted, as loud as I could, for help, but I stayed where I was, and I held her hand, and I told her everything would be fine, just fine.

"I couldn't do it," she whispered. "I couldn't wait to turn. I couldn't make you wait."

"I would have," I said, squeezing her hand as tears trickled down my face. "I'd have stayed for as long as you needed me."

A faint smile. "Just a few more minutes. That's all I'll need. Then you can go."

I told her I didn't want to go, to just hold on, stay strong and hold on and everything would be fine. Of course it wouldn't and we

both knew that, but it gave us something to say in those final minutes, for me to tell her how brave and wonderful she was, and for her
to tell me what a good friend I'd been.

"There," she whispered, her voice barely audible as her eyelids
fluttered. "You can go now. Be free. Both of us. Free and . . ."

And she went. One last exhalation, and she joined her family
and her boyfriend and everyone she'd loved and known was dead,
even if she'd told herself they weren't.

I sat there, still holding her hand. Then as I lifted my head, I realized I could still hear shouts and shots and screams. I laid Katie on
the floor, picked up the gun, and headed into the hall.

How many times had I sat in front of the TV, rolling my eyes at the
brain-dead characters running *toward* obvious danger? Now I did
exactly that and understood why. I heard those shots and those
screams, and I had to know what was happening.

I got near a hall intersection when the guy who'd shown me the
news of the first reported deaths two years ago came barreling
around the corner. He skidded to a halt so fast his sneakers
squeaked. He stared at me, and there was no sign of recognition because all he saw was the gun. He dropped to his knees and looked up
at me, and even then, staring me full in the face, his eyes were so
panic filled that he didn't recognize me. He just knelt there, his
hands raised like a sinner at a revival.

"Please, please, please," he said. "I won't hurt you. I won't hurt
anyone. I couldn't do it. I just couldn't. I need to say good-bye. My
mom, my sister, my nephew . . . please just let me say good-bye.
That's all I'll do, and then I'll do it, and if I can't, I'll go away. I'll go
far, *far* away."

I lowered the gun, and he fell forward, convulsing in a sob of
relief, his whole body quaking, sweat streaming from his face, the
hall filling with the stink of it.

"Thank you," he said. "Oh God, thank you. I know I should do it—"

"Where did the guns come from?"

He looked up, his eyes finally focusing. "I know you. You—"

"My friend had this gun. I hear more. Where did they come from?"

He blinked hard, as if shifting his brain out of animal panic mode. Then his gaze went to my yellow sun. "You aren't . . . So you don't know. Okay." He nodded, then finally stood. "When the black stars had their private counseling session, they gave us guns. Access to them, that is. They told us where we could find them, if we decided we couldn't go on. Except . . ." He looked back the way he came. "Not everyone is using theirs to kill themselves first."

"They're killing the other black stars?"

He nodded. "They think we should all die. To be safe. They're killing those who didn't take the guns."

Footsteps sounded in the side hall.

"I need to go," he said quickly. "You should, too."

I lifted my hand to show my tattoo. "I'm not a threat."

He shook his head but didn't argue, just took off. I waited until the footsteps approached the junction.

"I'm armed," I called. "But I'm not a threat. I've got the yellow sun—"

"And I don't really give a shit," said a voice, and a guy my age wheeled around the corner, blood spattered on his shirt, his gun raised. "Kill them all and let God sort them out."

I dove as he fired. He shot twice, wildly, as if he'd never held a gun before tonight. When he tried for a third shot, the gun only clicked. I ran at him but didn't shoot. I couldn't do that. I smashed the pistol into his temple and he went down. Then I heard running footsteps and more shouts, and I raced down the hall, taking every turn and running as fast as I could, until I saw the security station ahead. I fell against the door, banging my fists on it. When no one answered, I held my wrist up to the camera.

"Yellow sun!" I shouted. "Let me in!"

A guy opened the door. His gray hair had probably been cut military short a couple of years ago, but no one enforced those rules now and it stood on end like porcupine quills.

"Get in," he said.

I fell through. When I got my balance, I saw a half dozen military guards watching the monitors. Watching students killing each other.

"You need to get out there," I said. "You need to stop this."

The gray-haired guy shrugged. "We didn't give them the guns."

"But you need to—"

"We don't need to do anything." He lowered himself into a chair. "You want to, girlie? You go right ahead. Otherwise? Wait it out with us."

I hesitated. Then I turned away from the monitors and slumped to the floor.

I was released the next day. That was their term for it: *released*. Cast out from my sanctuary. They escorted me back to my room to get my belongings and gave me a bag to pack them in. Then they walked me to the college gates, and for the first time in over a year, I set foot into the world beyond my campus.

It was fine in the beginning. Better than I dared to hope for. The entire college town had been tested, the black stars already rounded up and taken away, and while families grieved and mourned their loved ones, there was a sense of relief, too. Was it not better that their loved ones be taken somewhere safe . . . so the remaining family members would be safe *from* them, if they turned? That's what it came down to in the end. What left us safe.

I boarded with an elderly couple who'd lost their live-in nurse and declared that my medical experience was good enough for them.

It was four months later when we heard the first report of a yellow sun turning into a vampire.

No one panicked. The story came from California, which might only have been across the country but was now as foreign to us as Venezuela had been. The reports kept coming though. Yellow suns waking in the night and murdering their families. Then rumors from those who worked in the nearest black-star facility, that they'd had only a few occurrences of the dormant vampires turning. Finally, the horrible admission that the testing had failed, that the stars seemed to indicate only a slightly higher likelihood of turning.

That's when the world exploded, like a powder keg that'd been kept tamped down by reassurances and faith. People had been willing to trust the government, because it seemed they were honestly trying their best. And you know what? I think they were. As much as my early life had taught me to trust no one, to question every motive, I look back and I think the authorities really did try. They simply failed, and then everyone turned on them.

I lived with the elderly couple for almost a year before their daughter came and kicked me out. She said I was taking advantage of them, pretending to be a nurse without credentials. The fact that her town had been taken over by militants had nothing to do with her decision to move home. No, her parents—whom she'd not contacted in years—needed her, so she'd be their nurse now.

The old couple argued. They cried. They begged me to stay. Their daughter put a gun in my face and told me to leave.

A month later, after living with some former classmates in a bombed-out building, I went back to try to check up on the old couple. I heard the daughter had turned. She'd killed her parents. Killed their neighbors too, because these days, no one was watching. Unless someone reported them, the vampires just kept killing, night after night. Some committed suicide. Some surrendered. Some ran off into the wilderness, hoping to survive where they'd be a danger to no one. The old couple's daughter just kept living in their house while her parents' bodies rotted and a growing swath of neighbors died.

I thought about that a lot. The choices we made. What it said about us. What I'd do if I woke covered in blood. I decided if that happened I'd head for the wilderness. Try to survive and wait for a cure. Or just survive, because by that point, no one really expected a cure. No one even knew if the government was still trying. Or if there still was a government.

I spent the next year on the streets, sometimes with others, but increasingly alone. I was lucky—none of my companions turned on me in the night. I hadn't even seen a vampire. That wasn't unusual. Unless you spotted one being dragged from a house to be murdered in the streets, you didn't see them. And even those who were hauled into the street? Well, sometimes they weren't vampires at all. No one asked for proof. If you wanted shelter, you could cut yourself, smear the blood on some poor soul, drag him out, let the mob take care of him, and move into his house. Two of the groups I was with discussed doing exactly that. I left both before that thought turned into action.

I'd been walking for six months. That was really all there was left to do: walk. Wander from place to place, seeking shelter where you could find it. The cities and towns weren't safe, as people reverted to their most basic animal selves, concerned only with finding a place to spend the night and food to get them through the day.

It was better in the countryside. No one could be trusted for long, but that was the curse of the vampirism. That kindly old woman who offered you a warm bed might rise in the night, kill you, and go right on being sweet and gentle when she woke up. Until she saw the blood.

In the country, there were plenty of empty homes to sleep in and flora and fauna to eat. I met a guy who taught me to trap and dress game. I returned the favor with sex. It wasn't a hardship. He didn't demand it, and in another life, it might even have turned into something more. It lasted six weeks. We would meet at our designated place to spend the day together, walking and hunting, and talking and having sex. Then we'd separate to our secret spots for the night, for safety. One morning, he didn't show up. I went back twice before I accepted he was gone. Maybe he turned, or he met someone who had. Or maybe someone had fancied his bow and his knife and his combat boots and murdered him for them. He was gone, and I grieved for him more than I'd done for anyone since Katie. Then I picked up and moved on. It was all you could do.

I found a house a few days after that. Not just any house—there were plenty of those. The trick was to find exactly the right one, hidden from the road, so you wouldn't need to worry about vampires or fellow squatters. Even better if it was a nice house. "Nice" meant something different these days, as in not ransacked, not vandalized, not bloodied. The last was the hardest criterion to fill. There'd been so many deaths that after a point, no one bothered cleaning up the mess. You'd find drained bodies left in beds, lumps of desiccated flesh and tattered cloth. But other times, you'd just find smears of old blood on the sheets and on the floor, where some squatter before you had been too tired to find other lodgings and simply dragged the rotting corpses to the basement and settled in.

But that house? It was damned near perfect. Out in the middle of nowhere, hidden by trees, so clean it seemed the family had left voluntarily and no one had found it since. The pantry was stuffed with canned and dry goods, as if they'd stocked up when things started going bad.

I lived there for three weeks. Read half the books in the house. Even taught myself to use the loom in the sitting room. Damned near paradise. But one day I must have been sloppy, let someone see me return from hunting. I woke with a knife at my throat and a man on top of me. There was a moment, looking up at that filthy, bearded face, when I thought, *Just don't fight*. Let him have what he wanted and let him leave. Just lie still and take it and he'd go and I'd have my house back.

That's when I saw the others. Three of them, surrounding the bed, waiting their turn. And it was as if a pair of scales in my head tipped. I fought then. It didn't do any good, and deep inside, I knew it wouldn't. I don't even think I was fighting to escape. I was just fighting to say, *I object*, and in the end, lying there, bloodied and beaten, I took comfort in that, when every part of me screamed in pain. *I fought back*. No matter what had ultimately happened, I'd fought back.

It was a week before the leader—Ray—decided he'd broken me and I could be allowed out of that room. It took another week to build their confidence to the point where they left me alone long enough for me to escape that place, because of course they hadn't broken me. As a child, I'd been inoculated against far more than mumps and measles. They did what they would do, and I acted my part: the cowed victim who comes to love the hand raised against her. An old role that I reprised easily.

Which is not to say that those two weeks didn't leave their mark, and not simply physical ones. But I survived, and not for one moment did I consider *not* surviving, consider taking Katie's way out. I respected her choice, but it was not mine. It never would be.

As I walked along a deserted country road a day after my escape, I remembered an old TV show about a zombie apocalypse. I'd been too young to watch it, but since those hours in front of the TV were the best times I had with my family, I took them, even if it meant watching something that gave me nightmares.

That show had endless scenes just like this one, a lost soul trudging along an empty road. While I didn't need to worry about the undead lurching from the ditches, at least in that world you knew who the monsters were. In ours, the existence of vampires was almost inconsequential. In the last year, I'd had a gun to my head twice, a knife to my throat three times, and been beaten and raped repeatedly. And I had yet to meet an actual vampire.

When I heard the little girl singing, I thought I was imagining it. Any parent worth the title had taken their children and fled long ago. There were fortified communities of families run by the last vestiges of the military, sanctuaries you couldn't enter unless you had a kid. That's another reason parents kept them hidden—so no one stole their children to gain entry.

But this really was a girl. No more than eight or nine, she sang as she picked wild strawberries along the road. The woman with her took off her wide-brimmed straw hat and waved it, calling "Hello!" and I cautiously approached.

"You're alone," the woman said. She was about thirty. Not much older than me, I reflected.

I shook my head. "I have friends. They're—"

"If you're not alone, you should be," she said, waving at my black eye and split lip.

I said nothing.

"Do you need a place to stay?" she asked. "Somewhere safe?"

"No, I—"

"I can offer you a room and a properly cooked meal." The woman managed a tired smile. "I was an apprentice chef once upon a time, and I haven't quite lost the touch."

"Why?" I asked.

She frowned. "Why do I still cook?"

"Why give me a bed and a meal?"

She shrugged. "Because I can. I have beds and I have food, and as much as I'd love to share them with whoever comes along this road, most times I grab my daughter and hide in the ditch until they pass."

"And I'm different?"

"Aren't you?"

The little girl ran over and held out a handful of strawberries. I took one and she grinned up at me. "We have Scrabble."

"Do you?" I said.

"And Monopoly. But I like Scrabble better."

"So do I," I said, and followed her to the strawberry patch to continue picking.

If I thought the last house was heaven, that only proves how low my standards had fallen. With this one, even before the vampires, I'd have been both charmed and impressed. And maybe a little envious of the girl who got to grow up in this cozy sanctuary, like something from an old-timey English novel, the ones where children lived charmed lives in the countryside, spending their days with bosom friends and loyal dogs and kindly grown-ups, getting into trouble that really wasn't trouble at all.

The house itself was as hidden by trees as the one I'd left. The woman had seeded the lane with weeds and rubble, so it looked as if nothing lay at the other end. There was a greenhouse filled with vegetables, fruit trees in the yard, a chicken coop, even goats for milk. The pantry was overflowing with home-canned goods.

"Keeps me busy," the woman said as she took out a jar of peaches for afternoon tea.

For dinner, we had a meal beyond any I'd dared dream of in years. Then we played board games until the little girl was too tired to continue. After that, her mother and I read for an hour or so. Finally, we headed off to bed, and I was shown how to lock myself in. There were two dead bolts, one fastened on either side of the door. As to be expected these days.

I said good night. Then I went inside, turned my lock, and climbed into bed.

I lay there, in that unbelievably comfortable bed, with sheets that smelled of lemons and fresh air. I lay, and I waited. Hours later, when I heard footsteps in the hall, I closed my eyes.

The woman rapped softly on my door and whispered, "Are you awake?"

I didn't answer. She carefully unbolted the lock on her side. Then came a rattle as she used something to pop mine. The door opened. Eyes shut, I waited until I heard breathing beside my bed. When I pinpointed the sound, I leaped.

I caught the woman by the throat, both of us flying to the floor. I saw a blur of motion and heard a muffled snarl and turned to see the little girl with a canvas sack over her head. Her mother swung at me. I ducked the blow and slammed her against the wall. The girl was snarling and fighting against the sack. As I pinned her mother, the girl got free of the bag.

The child's eyes didn't glow red. Her fingers weren't twisted into talons. Her canines weren't an inch long and sharpened. She looked exactly like the girl I'd just played Scrabble with for two hours. But the look in her eyes told me I'd guessed right. Yes, I'd hoped it was still possible for a stranger to be kind to me, to take me in and feed me and give me shelter because we were all in this hell together. I'd taken the chance, because I still dared to hope. But I'd known better.

If I was surprised at all, it was because I'd presumed the mother was the vampire, and she'd been locking her daughter in each night to keep her safe. But this made sense.

"She's my daughter," the woman said. "All I have left."

I nodded. I understood. I really did. In her place, maybe I'd have done the same, as much as I'd like to think I wouldn't.

I looked at the little girl. Then I threw her mother at her. The woman screamed and tried to scramble away. The girl pounced.

It was not over quickly. I'd heard stories of how the vampires killed. The rumor was they paralyzed their victims with a bite. But the girl kept biting and her mother kept struggling, at first only saying the girl's name and fighting to control her. Then came the panic, the kicking and screaming and punching, any thought of harming her child consumed by her own survival instinct. The girl bit her mother, over and over, blood spurting and spraying, until finally the woman's struggles faded, and the girl began to gorge on the blood while her mother lay there, still alive, still jerking, eyes wide, life slowly draining from them.

I walked out of the guest room and locked the door behind me.

The next morning, I hit the road, back the way I'd come. I walked all morning with the little girl skipping beside me, then racing off to pick wildflowers and strawberries. She'd woken in her own room, her nightgown and face clean.

I'd woken her at dawn, seemingly panicked because I couldn't find her mother. Something must have happened, and we had to go find her.

The girl followed without question. Now she walked without question. I'd told her that her mother had vanished, and she still skipped and sang and gathered flowers. Proving maybe a little part of her *was* still that monster after all.

At nightfall we reached my old sanctuary, the horror I'd escaped two days ago. I led her right up to the porch and rang the bell.

One of the guys answered. Seeing me, he stumbled back, as if a vengeful spirit stood on the porch.

"I want to see Ray," I said.

He looked at the little girl. "Wha . . . ?"

"I want to see—"

"Hey, girlie." Ray appeared from the depths of the dark hall.

"I want to come back," I said.

He threw back his head and laughed. "Realized it's not so bad, compared to what's out there, huh?"

"I brought a gift," I said. "My apology for leaving."

That's when he saw the girl. He blinked.

"You can use her to get into a refugee camp," I said. "We'll say we're her parents, and the guys are your brothers."

"Huh." He thought for a moment, but it didn't take long before he smiled. "Not bad, girlie. Not bad at all."

"I just want one thing," I said.

He chuckled. "Of course you do. Gotta be a catch."

"I'm with you," I said. "Just you. None of the others."

The smile broadened to a grin. "You like me the best, huh? Sure, okay. I accept your condition and your apology . . . and your gift. Come on in."

After midnight, I slipped from under Ray's arm and crept out. I tiptoed down the hall, unlocking doors as I went. It was an old house, the interior locks easily picked. The last one I opened was the little girl's. Then I continued along the hall, down the stairs, and out the front door to begin the long walk back to the other house, my new home.

I got as far as the road before I heard the first scream. I smiled and kept walking.

MAY THE END BE GOOD

TIM LEBBON

Things went ever from bad to worse.
When God wills, may the end be good.
—UNKNOWN MONK, WORCESTER, ENGLAND, 1067

As dawn broke, it started snowing again, and Winfrid saw a body hanging from a tree.

He paused downhill from the grisly display, catching his breath and shrugging his habit and sheepskin in tighter. Nothing could hold back the shivers. They were mostly from the cold, but over the last ten days he had seen things that set a terror deep in his bones. Fear of God he had, as did any monk; a complex, rich emotion that seemed to both nurture and starve. But this fear was something new. He had yet to define it fully.

Perhaps the body in the tree would feed him another clue.

As he crunched through the freshly fallen snow, softly layered over the previous week's falls, several birds took flight from the corpse. A rook he expected, but some of the smaller creatures—finches, a robin, several sparrows—were a surprise. With fields of crops burned, villages put to the torch, and the dead more numerous than ever before, perhaps these previously cautious birds were taking whatever they could get.

"Even the animals are against us," he muttered as he moved cautiously uphill. He didn't truly believe that, because the animals served only themselves. But if they *had* turned, it would have been the fault of the French. This brutality, this scourging of the land, was all their doing. William the Bastard and his mounted armies had not stopped when they defeated the English uprising in the north. They had carried on, shifting their attention from soldiers to farmers, peasants scraping a living from the land. The cattle fell beneath the sword first, then homes were put to the flame. Anyone who objected received the same—sword, flame, or sometimes both.

Winfrid had seen a child speared onto the side of a burning home. A man split from throat to crotch and seeded with the torched remnants of his stored harvest. Women tortured and raped, left as barren as the land. Whole villages destroyed, populations massacred or left to fend for themselves from a blasted landscape where nothing would grow, no livestock remained alive, and no building was left standing.

The north had paid a hundred times over for rebelling against he who called himself king, and that debt was still being gathered.

The body was relatively fresh. A man, stripped of clothing and hanged from his neck, which was stretched thin and torn, head blackened and tilted to one side. His swollen tongue protruded from his mouth like a final scream.

Winfrid muttered some prayers and tried to unsee the signs of scavenging. He had witnessed them on several bodies over the past few days, and rumors of cannibalism were muttered in the darker parts of his mind. Prayers would not hide them away.

The man's legs were mostly stripped of flesh, bones plainly visible in several places, knife marks obvious. His cock and balls were gone, his stomach slack and drooping, and his sticklike fingers seemed unnaturally long.

Winfrid's prayers froze when he heard a sound. It might have been a song being sung in the distance or a whisper from much closer. He stared up at the dead man's face and saw no movement there, but still he hurried on, pleased when the trees and snow finally hid the grotesque sight from view.

"Just the wind," he said. His voice was muffled in the landscape, the white silence of snow and woodland showing only scattered signs of life. Birds pecked ineffectually here and there. Rabbits scampered from shadow to shadow. He saw prints that might have belonged to a fox but then found larger marks that were undoubtedly those of a wolf. Winfrid had heard that wolves had ventured north and east from the borderlands between England and Wales, but he was surprised that they had come this far. The slaughters in the north would have left little for them to eat.

He would have to be careful. Hungry wolves had been known to take down a grown man, and with the snows falling later this year, a pack might become desperate.

He heard the sound again, from ahead and above, drifting down the hillside and twisting between the trees. Perhaps it *was* the wind, but it had a haunting quality that stopped him in his path. It lured him in and scared him at the same time. *I believed I was away from the horror*, he thought, but perhaps he never could be. The body hanging from the tree was yet another sign of that, and he had no way of knowing just how far King William's fury might extend.

The wind, the voice, suddenly ceased, and the silent snowscape surrounded him once again. Frightening though the sound was, in a way the silence was worse. He moved on, listening for more sounds and keeping alert for movement.

It was difficult. He was cold and tired, and a man in his fifth decade was not meant to be wandering the landscape, especially one as harsh as this. He had spent his younger years spreading the Word, and now in his old age he should have been comfortable in the monastery, waking early to pray, tending the gardens, brewing mead, and waiting for that approaching hour when God would call him home. But instead the monastery had been sacked, riches plundered, and the monks turned out to fend for themselves. Never a material man, even so he had cried at the sight of French knights and their horses trampling the fields he had toiled in for so long.

Winfrid started a low, soft prayer, the whispered words calming and comforting. It reminded him of friends and peace, and right then he would have given anything for either.

"Did you hear her?"

The voice shocked him and he started upright, staggering into a young tree. The impact shook dead leaves and snow from a fork in its branches, and he saw the man through a haze of falling leaves and ice.

"You. Did you hear her?" The man seemed frantic, head jerking left and right like a chicken's. He had one hand cupped behind his ear.

"Did I hear who?" Winfrid asked.

"My Lina. My sweet girl Lina, singing so that we can find her, though we never can, we *never* can!"

"Who's there?" a woman's voice called. Winfrid saw them both more clearly now that the falling leaves had settled. The man was twenty steps away, the woman close behind him, and he had seen healthier-looking people dead by the trail. How they could still be alive he did not know.

"My name is Winfrid," the monk said. He offered them a prayer in Latin, aware that they would not understand yet eager to ensure they knew who he was. They looked hungry. And Winfrid could neither forget nor unsee the signs of cannibalism he had seen.

"So you *did* hear her," the woman said.

"No, I—"

"You're praying to bring her back to us. So keep praying. Tell God to give her back!"

"I can't tell God to do anything," Winfrid said.

The man and woman stared at him for a while, the snow floating between them doing little to soften their skeletal forms. Then the man began to cry. They were dry tears, but his shoulders shook, and his chest emitted a *click-click* like bone tapping against bone.

"Will you eat with us?" the woman asked. She held out her hand even though they were twenty steps apart.

Winfrid's stomach rumbled. He could not recall the last time he had eaten anything resembling good food, and as if bidden by her invitation, he caught the scent of cooking meat on the air. *They'll attract wolves*, he thought. *Or Frenchmen might still be close, looking for survivors to kill for fun.*

"Eat what?" he asked.

"Rabbit," the woman said past her husband's shuddering, shriveling form.

It was through hunger that Winfrid let himself believe her.

They had a weak fire burning on a small, rocky plateau shielded by a steep hillside. Several sticks spanned the fire, with chunks of speared meat spitting fat into the flames. Snowflakes hissed into oblivion in the smoke. Burning logs jumped, settled, coughed ash.

Winfrid's mouth watered at the smell. "There are wolves. I've seen their tracks."

"We'll die if we don't eat," the woman said. They stood round the fire. It was too cold and wet to sit down. The man was a shaking statue, staring at his shoes and dribbling from his mouth. Even with thick clothing, he was barely there. His wife was just as thin, but she seemed stronger. More present, less close to death.

"And with Lina still out there, we can't just go on," she said. "We lost our other children. Our three boys, two girls, dead and gone . . ." She stared into flames.

"The French?" Winfrid asked.

"Some of them." She stretched her hands out to be warmed. "The things I've seen . . ."

And the things I *have seen*, Winfrid thought. The murders and rapes, the fury and wretchedness, the inhumanity. And sometimes the pity and love. That kept him going. God's love, always, but even more affecting was the love he saw between people. Not everyone was given over to violence. It provided hope.

He prayed that this sad couple might also give him hope.

"What happened?" he asked.

"We were leaving our village," she said. "Four weeks ago."

"More," the man said. Winfrid had not even thought he was aware, but now he saw that the man's shivering had lessened, and he leaned against his wife, still looking down at his feet. "Six weeks, maybe seven. Forever."

"Maybe," she said. "They were burning the village. The cattle had been slaughtered. The knights had killed anyone with a weapon or farming tool in their hands, and their blood was up. They wanted more. Some of them stayed . . . in the background. Just killing things. But one of them, the one in charge, he was bigger than them all."

"Bigger than any man," her husband said.

"It just seemed that way," she whispered. "He was taking the girls and raping them. I ran with Lina, crawling through a muddy field, and Eadric here met us a day later on the other side of the woods."

"I saw what else they did," Eadric said. He stared into the weak flames, then knelt and ripped a chunk of meat from one stick. He handed it to his wife, then tore off a scrap for himself. They both started eating, noisily, slurping at running fat and grunting in satisfaction as the hot, chewed meat slipped down their gullets.

Winfrid's hunger turned from pang to pain, and he swayed where he stood. A fat snowflake landed on his nose and remained there, as if he gave off no heat. As if he were dead.

"Ten days, it took, to get this far," the woman said, chewing and swallowing as she spoke. "Meat?"

"Yes, I . . . ," Winfrid said. He leaned forward and fell to his knees. Coldness ate through his clothes and surrounded his legs. Heat stretched the skin of his face, and as he reached forward, his hands tingled, burned. He touched the hot meat on one stick, then drew his hand back again.

"Where did she go?" he asked. Their daughter Lina kept them here, and suddenly he wondered how. The singing he might have heard could have been the wind, or perhaps it was this woman's own madness. Or this man's. Neither seemed all there.

"The shadows," the woman said. Her eyes went wide and she stopped chewing, staring off past the fire into the shady woods. Snow continued to fall, dulling any sound, making even the crackling flames sound weak and distant. "She walked into them and never came back."

"She got lost in the woods?"

"She is not lost," Eadric said, looking up at last. He followed the woman's gaze. "*We* are lost." He started to sob, going to his knees and clasping her clothing all the way, trying to keep himself upright. "We are *lost!*"

"How do you catch rabbits?" Winfrid asked. "Where are your spears? Your snares?"

"We find them dead," the woman said. "Hanging from the trees."

Winfrid stood and backed away from the fire. The remaining meat was blackening beneath the flames, and it would be dry and tough now, hot. Rabbit, that was all, and he had eaten rabbit a thousand times before. But though hunger squirmed in his stomach and writhed in his bones, he no longer had an appetite.

"God help you," he whispered. Eadric smiled at him then, displaying several teeth and the dark gaps between them, and shreds of meat speckling his tongue. The woman smiled as well. "God help you both, because your daughter is dead, and—"

From somewhere higher up on the hillside, there came singing.

A sweet, light voice rose and fell. Winfrid could not hear the words, but the music they made drove through him like the sharpest blade.

"Lina!" Eadric shouted.

"She sings to us," the woman said. "Every day she sings, and we go to find her, and we never do . . . but one day we will, one day when the snows end and life returns to the land and Lina sings us closer and closer, we'll find her, and in the end everything will all be good."

"Lina!" Eadric shouted again. The singing faded in and out, seeming to shimmer through the falling snow. Flakes danced to the voice.

Eadric ran. There was no warning, no tensing of muscles. One moment he was still clasping his wife's clothing, the next he leapt past Winfrid and darted across the small clearing. He scrambled up the steep slope and soon disappeared among the trees and falling snow. Winfrid watched him go. He breathed lightly because Eadric had come so close, and he had smelled of death.

When Winfrid turned back to the woman, she was also gone. He searched for her footprints in the snow and then saw movement across the slope as she dashed between trees.

Logs settled on the fire with a shower of sparks. A chunk of meat fell into the flames, spitting and letting off black smoke. The singing drifted in from somewhere far away, and though Winfrid turned left and right, he could not tell which direction it came from. But there was something about the song that terrified him. Though high and light on the surface, it was sung with a mocking humor, and not with the voice of a little girl.

This voice sounded ageless.

In a land like this, with snow falling and cold seeping through his thick habit and woolen undergarments, a fire would be the safest place. But this one no longer felt safe. It poured sick smoke at the sky, and as he turned to flee he tried to summon a prayer, a plea, to help him on his way. He muttered to God and then shouted at Him. It seemed that the more he prayed, the closer the silent surroundings crowded in around him.

He stumbled across the slope toward the west, slipping eventually down a steep hillside toward a valley bottom. The singing had ceased, left behind or faded away. He slipped several times, falling onto his back and escaping injury when his bag broke his fall. Everything he owned was in there, the material things at least. His heart contained his true riches: a knowledge of God, and a soul given over to goodness. *I am good*, Winfrid kept telling himself, and in that mantra he found courage. A sense of evil hung dense all around him. It hid behind tree trunks, hunkered down beneath rocks tumbled from the heights an endless time before, danced from snow-flake to snowflake, daring him to find it. And though he feared this evil—unknown though it was, and more awful because of that—he also felt secure in his beliefs. The worst could happen to him and God would be there on the other side.

At last he reached a place where he thought he could rest. It was gone midday, the smear of sun in the sky already hidden behind the western hills, and his pounding heart had begun to settle.

A stream gurgled merrily along the valley floor, the flat ground on both banks smoothed by virgin snow. Winfrid crouched beside the water and enjoyed the sound. Better than his own heavy breathing, the crunch of his feet through snow and fallen leaves, his grunts as he'd slipped and fallen. Better than the singing.

"God's voice," he said as the stream ignored him.

"God does not speak."

Winfrid fell onto his behind, hands sinking into the snow to find wet, muddy ground beneath. He clasped at the mud, securing himself to the world.

Across the stream, in a spread of snow unmarred by footprints, stood a little girl. She wore a simple dress made of rough, gray material, poorly fitting across her shoulders and dropping almost to her ankles. It was thin and holed. She did not appear cold. Not her body, at least.

But her eyes were ice. Their glimmer was frozen as if at the moment of death, and her pale skin was mottled blue.

"God speaks through me," Winfrid said, and the little girl laughed. It animated her face and shook through her body but gave her no semblance of true life. *Lina*, he thought. *This must be Lina the singer, and her voice is even more terrible than her song.*

"Your pride pulsates within you," she said. "You take your vow and assume too much."

Winfrid pushed himself to his feet. The mud was wet and slick between his fingers. "And you speak well for a farmer's little girl."

"I'm not little anymore." Her laughter had ceased, but the smile remained. Like a slash in dead flesh.

"Then what are you?"

The girl tilted her head to one side, a wolf observing its prey.

"Your parents mourn you."

She looked him up and down. He felt her gaze upon him, rough beneath his clothing. Wherever she looked, he was colder than ever.

"I'll return to them soon."

"Did they hurt you? Whoever took you, did they . . . do things to you?" he asked, already knowing this was wrong. The French had had no hand in this.

"You don't even know who *they* are."

"Then tell me."

She ignored him, finishing her assessment and then turning to walk away.

"Wait!"

Across the other side of the stream, Lina strode toward the trees. Winfrid could have gone after her. But that would have meant splashing through the icy waters, and if he did that, he would risk freezing if he did not stop to dry his clothes. He had seen plenty of weak, sick people dead from the cold, and he had no desire to lie with snow filling his glazed eyes.

Besides, he could do nothing for her. The way she moved, the disregard, her calmness in this cold, brutal landscape, all seemed so unnatural. So unholy. He went to call her again, but then the singing recommenced, and he had the disconcerting sense that it did not come only from her.

Just before she disappeared into the forest, the girl paused and looked back at him. Squinting through the flitting snow, he just made out her mouth moving. It did not seem to match the strange words of the haunting song.

Then she was gone, and the thick mud between Winfrid's fingers was starting to dry and grow hard. It showed that he exuded the heat of life, at least.

Where Lina had stood, there were no marks in the snow.

He believed he was fleeing the song. There was nothing Winfrid wanted more than to lose himself to any place where that monstrous girl was not, and as he struggled through the snow, he craved his simple room in the monastery. Away from there, he was lost. Until recently, life at the monastery had been peaceful, calm, and safe, and Winfrid had rarely considered traveling farther than the next village. Now, with so much destruction and murder in the land, with hopelessness almost manifest in the marsh mists and the silent landscapes of snow, he had no idea what dark things were abroad.

Such a time might attract horrendous things.

The snow fell heavier. Any hint of the sun was obscured in the uniform gray. Perhaps it was late afternoon, but he could not be sure. The heavy gloom seemed intent on confusing him. The landscape, too. One patch of woodland looked the same as another, and when a breeze blew up, whisking snow into the air and driving it in drifts against trees and rocks, he lost his way completely. He might have been traveling in circles, but drifting snow covered his tracks.

I should have stayed with her, tried to help her! The child was lost and alone, terrified by her ordeal, and he had probably scared her more than anything. But though guilt inspired such thoughts, truth shoved them aside with a sneer that might have suited the girl's own face. He could not fool himself. The realization that she was something unnatural assuaged the guilt, but in its place was his own harsh, growing fear.

So he hurried on, hoping that he would see no place he recognized, praying that he would not hear that song again. He was leaving Eadric and his wife to some unknown fate, but he could do nothing for them. Even if he knew what their girl had become, he was useless. *God does not speak,* the girl had said, and the memory of her voice caused him to shiver, his vision growing hazy and unsure. He leaned against a tree and closed his eyes, but in memory there was only her.

Staring at him with those dead, cold eyes.

"God save me," he muttered, pushing away from the tree and moving on. The snow was deep here, coming almost up to his knees in places, and the long habit grew heavy where snow and ice stuck around its hem.

He struggled on through a dense forest, the stark tree canopy offering little shelter from the snowfall. A while later, as light began to fade and shadows emerged from their daytime hiding places, he found a place to rest.

It was barely an overhang, but the rocky lip of a shallow ravine offered some shelter from the weather, and the snow cover was lighter than elsewhere. He dragged a log into the sheltered area to sit on, then went about building a fire. He carried a flint and kindling in his bag, and was relieved to find them still dry. But to find other wood to burn, he had to root around on the sheer walls of the ravine, reaching up onto narrow ledges to rescue fallen leaves and twigs that had gathered there. Though damp, they would be his best hope for a constant flame.

He hoped the practicalities of survival would divert his mind from what had happened. But he found himself pausing every few moments and cocking his head, listening for the one thing he dreaded hearing. The breeze remained, but it carried only the gentle patter of snowflakes against the rocky wall above him, and the creaking of trees.

God does not speak. The words echoed back at him, however much he cast them aside, however hard he disbelieved them. She had been not only mocking but confident, a certainty in herself that belied her years. *I'm not little anymore.*

It took Winfrid a long time to light the fire, and by the time he had an ember and nursed it into flame, dusk had settled around him.

The growing fire made the night even darker. He welcomed the crackling of the flames, but for the first time in his life he feared what lay beyond. Darkness had rarely troubled him, because he had always been surrounded by safety at the monastery. Even fleeing the French and the devastation they had left in their wake, God had been with him to soothe any doubts about what might lie beyond his nightly fire.

Now he saw glimmering eyes among the trees, heard the creak of snow compacting beneath cautious feet, smelled the carrion rot of creatures stalking the shadows just beyond the reach of his fire's light. He sat close and took comfort from the heat, but he could not sleep. Weary though he was, each time he closed his eyes, something jarred him awake. He hoped it was memory. He feared it was something else.

Winfrid tried to position himself as close to the steep slope as he could, but even then, his back felt exposed. He prayed. He stood and circled the fire, realized that the snow had ceased, looked up at the clearing sky and the stars and moon silvering the landscape.

When the breeze died out and moonlight revealed the deserted woodland around him, he began to settle. He ate the last chunk of stale, hard bread from his bag and drank the final dregs of ale, thankful that the bottle had not been smashed. Thirst and hunger attended, if not sated, he finally closed his eyes to sleep.

The screams shattered his dreams and scattered them across the snow. He stood quickly and staggered as his sleeping legs tingled back to life. Snatching up a burning log from the fire, he turned a full circle, wondering whether he had heard anything at all.

Maybe I just imagined—

Another scream, long and loud, sang in from some distance. It changed to a series of short, sharp cries that seemed to echo from the cleared sky.

"Not wolves, not foxes," he whispered, comforting himself with his voice. "Nothing like that. That's human pain."

He shouldered his bag and started through the woods. Away from the screams, the agonies, and whatever might be causing them. He imagined Lina smiling in the shadows, her childlike shape hidden beneath the trees and as ancient and uncaring as the hills. Guilt pricked at him but he was only a man, a monk who had never raised a hand against another. How could he help?

There was movement ahead of him. Shadows shifting, flitting from one tree to another, and when he paused and stared they grew motionless. He held his breath, heart thumping in his ears. Edging sideways, downhill and away from the shadows, he came to an old trail heading through the trees and down into the valley. He followed, glancing over his shoulder and seeing movement behind and to his right.

Following him.

Winfrid tried not to panic, running at a controlled rate instead of a headlong dash that would wear him out, trip him up, injure him and leave him prone and vulnerable to whatever—

Another scream, and this was much closer, coming from just ahead of him past where several trees had fallen across the trail. He skidded to a halt and pressed in close to the splayed branches, hunkering down so that his habit and cloak gathered around his knees and thighs.

Ducking down lower, he saw beneath one tilted trunk to what lay beyond. His breath froze. His heart stuttered. His vision funneled so that all he knew, all he saw, was the grotesque, moonlit scene playing out not thirty steps away.

A man was impaled on a tree several feet above the ground. A broken branch protruded from his chest, bloody and glistening, and he was clasping it, trying to pull or push or twist himself away. He writhed and kicked against the tree, every movement bringing fresh pain, inspiring another scream.

Who put him up there? Winfrid thought, and then Eadric and his wife came into view, running to the tree, reaching up, and for an instant Winfrid believed he was going to see the man saved. It was the natural thought, the only good one, and it lasted less than a heartbeat.

Because he remembered the dead man he had seen hanging from a tree the afternoon before, and what had been done to him.

Eadric tugged at the scraps of clothing the man still wore, ripping them away. The man kicked feebly, and the woman caught his foot, pulled his leg straight, and hacked at it with an ax.

The man screeched.

Eadric sliced at his other leg with a knife, cutting away a chunk of flesh as big as a fist and dropping it into the snow. Blood spattered and sprayed, drawing sickly curves across the ground. Moonlight blackened the blood.

Winfrid wondered how they could both still look so thin, so weak, considering the meat they had been ingesting.

But perhaps the flesh of your own was poison.

"No!" Winfrid shouted, pushing his way through the branches and clambering over the trunks of the fallen trees.

The woman glanced back at him, surprised, but Eadric continued cutting. He worked only on the man's thigh, and already the victim was bleeding out. He cried now rather than screamed, shaking uncontrollably so that Winfrid heard his ribs creak and break against the snapped branch.

"What are you doing?" Winfrid shouted. He ran toward the couple, and the woman turned on him with the ax raised.

"We've got to eat," she said. "Got to stay strong so we can find Lina."

"Lina is gone!" Winfrid said.

"No!" Eadric said, still slicing, dropping gobbets of meat to the ground and wiping blood from his face. "She's still with us. We hear her singing."

"That's not your daughter you hear," Winfrid said. Tears filled his eyes, then anger dried them away.

"Stay out of our business," the woman said.

"Killing people to eat is a work of evil, so it *is* my business."

"We don't kill them. We *find* them."

"Then who—?" Winfrid said, and then the singing began. At his back, perhaps as close as the trees he had just been hiding behind, the song floated across the small clearing and seemed to freeze the scene in place.

In Eadric's and the woman's eyes, delight and disbelief as they looked past Winfrid.

The dying man saw only horror.

Winfrid turned and saw Lina approaching him. Three others were with her, two women and a man, and Winfrid knew that he was in the presence of the unholy, the monstrous. They presented themselves as human—scraps of clothing, pale skin marked with dirt and scars, an air of insolence—but they were clearly something else. Their eyes betrayed that.

"Lina," her mother whispered.

Winfrid went to his knees and began to pray, and Lina stared at him. Her mouth was not quite in time with her song.

They passed him by.

"Lina, we knew, we waited, and you've come back to us," Eadric said.

The singing ceased. Winfrid found his feet again and backed toward the fallen trees. Before him, Lina and the three adults. Beyond them, her desperate and insane parents, hands marred with the dying man's blood, chunks of meat from his wretched body melted into the snow at their feet. The hope in their eyes was grotesque.

But it did not last.

Lina and one of the women took her mother down. The other man and woman pounced on Eadric. Neither of them screamed as the beasts bit hard into their throats, their necks, opening them up and gasping in the sprays of blood that arced into the starlit night.

Winfrid tried to back away farther, but his feet would not move, his legs would not carry him. He was as bound to witness this horror as the dying man stuck on the tree. For a second, the two of them locked eyes but then looked away again, the terror drawing their attention.

A new song began. It held nothing of Lina's previous tune, which, though unsettling, had been light and musical, singing of uncomfortable mysteries best left untouched. This new song was made up of grunts and sighs. The sounds of gulping and swallowing. And then the sickly groans of ecstasy as Lina and the others bit, lapped, and raised their faces to the stars, their bodies squirming in intimate delight as blood flowed across their pale skins and into their heavily toothed mouths.

What monsters are these? Winfrid thought, but he could dwell only on what he saw. It horrified and fascinated. The victims on the ground were thrashing beneath the weight of their attackers, and he caught sight of the mother's face only once. Eyes wide in disbelief. Throat wide and gushing. Her daughter dipped her head down again, seemingly lowering her face for a kiss but then pressing herself into her mother's open neck.

She drank and groaned, and the woman died.

Winfrid still could not move. He had to watch, and he saw the moments when Eadric and the man on the tree perished also. That left him alone with them, and when Lina stood and turned, he thought she was coming for him.

But she paused, only looking his way.

"Because I'm a man of God!" he shouted. "Because He *does* have a voice, and you hear Him in me! That is not pride. That is faith."

"Your blood is weak, your flesh bland," Lina said as she turned her back on him. "Holy man."

She and the others disappeared into the trees, shadows swallowed by the night, and he saw that the truth should have been obvious to him long before. That Eadric and his wife had been fed and nurtured for this moment, eating the human flesh presented to them to make their own that much more . . . delectable.

Winfrid remained there for a while, unable to move, slumped down against the fallen trees. A chill seeped into his bones, though his soul was already colder.

As dawn broke and color came into the world, most of it was red.

MRS. POPKIN

DAN CHAON AND LYNDA BARRY

I.

A new family moved in across the road and their name is Popkin. A mom, two big teenage boys, and a boy and girl about my age. I like to walk down the hill to their house because I enjoy the company of other children.

But my mother has somehow gotten the idea that the real reason I go is because of Mrs. Popkin. Whenever I go over to their house, my mother teases me about it. *Mrs. Popkin,* she says in an exaggerated sexy voice. *Oh! Mrs. Pop! Kin!* I don't know when she decided this, but she thinks it's hilarious.

"Todd's on his way to see his girlfriend tonight," she tells Old Lady Hotchkiss over the phone. I am sitting at the kitchen table reading *Watership Down* and she regards me for a moment. I act like I'm not even listening.

"The family that moved in across the road," she says. "The woman and her seven dwarves."

"Four," I say under my breath.

"Ha!" my mother says to the phone. "It's so cute; you should see how he looks at her."

I am thirteen years old and small for my age and the word *cute* is not a word that I particularly like, but I don't say anything. I just turn the page of my book.

My mother is currently in the process of trying to be happy. This is her new thing. She had been very low for a while, for a year or two, I think—so low that she didn't think she wanted to live anymore. But we are going to put that behind us, she says.

Live life to the fullest! That is her new motto. She has ideas about JOY! SPONTANEITY! To somersault in the grass, for example. To take a moment to TRULY EXPERIENCE the world of nature around us, looking at birds, for example, and spreading some birdseed out in the yard where our late dog used to be tied up. RECONNECT TO YOUR CREATIVE SELF, which might include, for example, a tea cozy crocheted in the shape of a ball gown, with a plastic doll head at the top of it. The two of us made it together one afternoon.

This tea cozy is sitting on the counter by the sink and staring at us as my mother talks on the phone to Old Lady Hotchkiss and I read *Watership Down*.

We live outside of town off of Highway 30. On our side of the road, houses are about a mile apart, sometimes more. On the other side of the road are fields of wheat, alfalfa, and pastures where white-faced Hereford cattle wander around, grazing.

I never understood why people want to live out of town. There is no cable television, no one to play with, nothing to do. I remember reading a book about some children who lived in a city and they went down to the corner store to get a Popsicle. I loved that idea. *The corner store.*

When my mother tried to kill herself, there was nowhere to go for help. She had told me never, ever to call the cops. Under any circumstances. I didn't know whether I should call Old Lady Hotchkiss or not.

I went outside, and the circle of the porch light extended only part of the way down the gravel driveway. Beyond that was pitch darkness, no streetlights, not even stars. There was nowhere to go.

Then the Popkins moved into the old farmhouse down by the creek. That house had been empty ever since a fire had killed a family there the year before, but it wasn't uninhabitable. Most of it was still intact. Must have been cheap to buy it, my mother said.

Mrs. Popkin put the teenage boys to work immediately once they arrived, and soon they had planted flower beds and grass in front of the house, and they had painted the rooms where the smoke damage was, and patched up the hole in the roof where the fire had broken through and licked up toward the sky. The younger two—a boy named Bernard and a girl named Cecilia—built a rabbit hutch, and one day it was filled with rabbits, rabbits of all colors, and one white rabbit with red eyes. Magenta, like the color of the crayon.

When the farmhouse had burned, so had one of the trees, but the skeleton of the tree still stood, just along the bank of the creek. The Popkins put a rope on the tree and swung themselves into the water. I watched from the window of my house as the older boys dove off the swing, still wearing their work clothes and boots, and splashed like boulders into the creek. Cecilia and Bernard stood on the bank, observing.

II.

His name is Todd. The kid of the house up the hill. The standing-there kid. The staring kid. Staying on his side of the gravel road that runs between our two houses. Watching us watching him. We didn't even know there *was* a kid in that house. The whole time we were moving in, there was no evidence of him. No bike, no swings, no toys lying in the yard. The only one I thought lived there was the lady who came out in her nightgown to water her hanging begonias. She had bad veins on her legs. Mom pointed that out.

Now there he is, staring at our house, dressed in school clothes like he's going somewhere, but it turns out, no, he's dressed in school clothes because those are the only kind of clothes he can stand to wear.

Mom tells me to get her cigarettes and when I come back, she is standing in my spot at the front room window, pointing through the drapes at him. "I feel kind of sorry for that one."

"Why?"

"Oh, I recognize the type."

"What type?"

Then Bernard starts walking across the yard toward him fast with a rock in his hand.

Mom steps to the screen door and hollers his name.

"Bernard!"

"What?"

"Don't you dare!"

"I wasn't!"

"Go find out his name," she says to me.

"Make Bernard."

"Cecilia," she says.

"Why do I have to do it?"

"I shouldn't have to tell you why."

When I come back to tell her his name is Todd, Mom repeats it. "*Todd*," she laughs. "Todd, Todd, Todd. What was your mother *thinking*?"

Then she's at the screen door calling his name, and the kid turns. "Hello! Todd! Come in and join us for some lemonade! Todd."

I say, "We don't have lemonade."

Mom says, "Oh, he won't care."

It's late in the afternoon and I'm walking with Todd and Bernard along the gravel road to a cutoff Todd wants us to see. It's hot and Bernard keeps kicking gravel at my legs to show off. He runs way ahead and kicks up a huge dust cloud and dives in and out of it. "Gas attack! Poison gas! Gas mask! Ahhh! I don't have a mask!" and I'm embarrassed by his babyishness. Todd isn't babyish. He moves back from the dust. He's the type that doesn't like to get dirty.

The cutoff leads to a part of the creek that is deeper and when we get there, Todd says, "There is something you need to know," and he starts telling us that the people who lived in our house before us died in a most terrible way.

"It was most terrible!" says Bernard, making fun. "I say, old boy! Most terrible!"

"You think I'm joking, but I'm not," says Todd.

"No one died in our house," says Bernard. "Psych."

We follow Todd through some brush. "Five people died in your house," says Todd. "One father, one mother, three kids."

Cause of death: fire. "But it wasn't the burning that did it," says Todd. "In fact, they were hardly burned at all."

"From what, then?" says Bernard.

"From the fire sucking their lungs out."

"*Super* psych!" says Bernard. "Sure, Todd."

"It's the nature of fire," Todd says. And he's very calm as he describes the instantness of the vacuum caused by the fire sucking away all the oxygen. How you can't escape—the fire will suck it out of you. It will suck it right out of your own mouth.

"You're supposed to crawl on the floor!" says Bernard. "The stupids. Anybody knows that."

"Wouldn't matter where you crawled," says Todd. "Not in this case."

"Okay," says Bernard, "so how come the house didn't burn down?"

"It was a very special case," says Todd.

And I remember the first day of moving in, the smell of burned wood that was so strong that Mom said not to bring it up. That we would get used to it faster if we didn't mention it. Now I can hardly smell it at all, even if I try.

III.

Mrs. Popkin! says my mother that morning. Something is wrong with her eyes, and her hair is not quite combed right. People stare after her as she walks through the supermarket, stepping slightly too fast for normal.

Ooooh, Mrs. Poppy-kins! she says, and tries to pinch my cheek.

Which is almost too embarrassing to even think of it.

"There's something wrong with you," I say to my mother.

I don't actually. But I think it.

Later, Mrs. Popkin and I are sitting at her kitchen table and I watch as she lights a row of pink candles that smell of rose perfume. On the biggest candle, in gold lettering, it says:

LORD, bless our door, that opens wide
To welcome those who come inside!
And bless our house, dear LORD above
That we may share YOUR peace and love!

Mrs. Popkin loves blessings, she says. Also angels, miracles, the works of God.

"I don't believe in forcing my religion on people," she says. "I'm not a holy roller like some of them."

She puts the ham of her foot up on the edge of the table and flexes out her toes.

"Don't tell your mother you saw me putting my foot up on the table like this," she says. Smiles. Unscrews the cap of her nail polish.

I watch as she dips the brush into the nail polish and lifts it. She presses the hairs of the brush against the mouth of the nail polish bottle until the excess paint has squeezed off. Drip. Drip. Then she brings the applicator slowly toward her pinkie toe. I don't say anything. In the kitchen doorway stands the girl Cecilia, with her weird small mouth and staring eyes. She is very still on the threshold, observing us, holding a rabbit in her arms like it's a cat.

"I got my first baby when I was fifteen years old," Mrs. Popkin tells me. "Only a few years older than you. That must seem so strange. Does it?"

"Not really," I say.

I watch as Mrs. Popkin fans her toes with a letter, a piece of junk mail I guess, and Cecilia watches too. Very still, holding her rabbit and petting it in long slow strokes.

"It's just old-fashioned," Mrs. Popkin says. "That's the way the people always used to do it. Back in the olden days, fifteen wasn't even considered young. And I'm actually glad I started early because I love babies. Some women don't like it, but I do."

"That's good," I say, and Cecilia and I glance at each other. There is a little bit of smoke lifting up from the candle, vanishing before it gets very far. But when I look upward, I can see all the smoke stains running along the surface of the ceiling, gray-black smoke stains from that long-ago fire, I guess. The stains are like figures and shadows and branches. A thicket.

"Um," Cecilia says, after there has been a little silence. "Todd, Bernard is looking for you."

"Oh, Cecilia," Mrs. Popkin says, and she leans toward me and gives a wink. "That girl. Always interrupting," she whispers, as if she doesn't want Cecilia to hear us.

IV.

The way Mom talks to him:

I am noticing their deal with each other where she talks to him like a person, like she talked at our before-house, when we still had cousins and aunts and uncles coming over, when she would tell people the door was always open, our door was always open.

The way she pours him coffee. When she puts his cup down along with Coffee-mate and the sugar bowl and says, "You don't have to drink it—it's just that one cup of coffee looks so by-itself." I am looking at Todd, the way he drinks it like a person. Not like a kid. If he was a midget, if he was like Romey, then okay. I would say okay. But he is for sure not a midget, although he slightly acts like it.

The way he doesn't show his personality to her. Where with us he will talk about the people who died in our house and it makes you nervous but you still keep listening. Like how there was no screaming because with your oxygen sucked out, you can't scream. You can only silent scream.

And that the silent scream is the worst scream of all.

But to Mom, he says he didn't know the dead people that well when she asks if the house is more attractive inside now. He says he didn't come inside all that much before because his mother didn't like the old family, but he knows it was way darker because they kept their drapes shut.

Then later I walk up the hill—I will admit I wanted to spy on his house a little—but I did not expect his mom to instantly come out. I keep walking, but his mom says, "Are you a Popkin? Are you one of the Popkin brood?"

So I stop and she says, "You think your mother would trade me one of her big boys for my son? He seems to be over there enough. Think she could send over a boy to be infatuated with me?"

She laughs in the direction of my house. She says she saw we had rabbits and that she loves rabbit and Todd also loves rabbit and do we sell them cleaned?

We don't sell them, I say.

She says to ask my mom if she would consider it. The people before us weren't stingy with *their* rabbits and is Mom my natural mother? Because I don't look like her at all and do I know there was a girl named Karen about my age who used to live there? And that Todd about died when that family moved away.

"He was so close to that Karen," says Todd's mom.

I say I have to go, but she keeps talking. I walk away and she follows. When I run, she laughs. "Oh, I don't bite, for heaven's sake!" she calls.

Later I'm with Todd and Bernard walking back to the cutoff.

I say to Todd: "Your mom said the people who lived in our house moved."

He says: "They did. They moved to the cemetery."

Bernard is laughing very hard at this. He says it's a good one. "That's a good one," he says.

V.

When I walk back home up the hill, I think about how I could confront Mother. *How dare you!* I think about saying.

It is the sort of thing that Bernard makes fun of, like I'm trying to sound like some kind of professor or from England, he says, but I like the dignity of it. *How* dare *you!* I think, and I like the way the words feel, like the Statue of Liberty holding a torch aloft over the ocean. *How dare you, Mother! How dare you tell* lies *to my friends!*

But when I come in, she is asleep on the couch in that position, her knees pulled up and her shoulders hunched and her hands loosely covering her eyes. In my encyclopedia, there are pictures of the ancient Romans who died in Pompeii, cowering in such a position, turned to statues as the ashes covered them.

I go into the kitchen and make myself a peanut butter sandwich for dinner. Peanut butter on one piece of bread. Margarine on the other piece of bread. Slices of apple in the middle. I am making this sandwich and pretending that I am building something.

But I can still hear her in the next room. Breathing, breathing.

When Karen and her family died, when their house burned and they died, my mother said, *Oh, honey, please don't be sad, please please don't be sad.* I was lying there facedown on the bed with the pillow against my eyes and she put her hand on my back and rubbed along my spine.

Do you know what I think? she said at last, very softly. *I think that they moved away. That's what I think. I think they moved away to someplace far away like—I don't know—Washington or Oregon or California.*

I felt her long fingernail trace its way up between my shoulder blades, up the back of my neck to the place where my spine connected to my skull. I didn't move.

And even though they are gone, my mother said, *even though they are gone and we will miss them, we know that they are having a good time in—Oregon. And we can write them a letter, if we want.*

"That's stupid," I said. I whispered under my breath.

I have the address right here, she murmured. *Karen's mom left it for me. Here, I'll write it on your back.*

And I felt her tracing out the numbers and letters with her fingernail.

When the house where Karen and her family lived caught on fire, my mother was in one of her manic states. She was up all night for several days, drawing pictures, trying out horrible recipes for things like aspic or haggis, making artworks from twigs and leaves and nature items that she found outside. She woke me up in the middle of the night and the light of the fire was flickering in my window. The wind had carried the bits of ash up the hill and it drifted through the air like the fluff from cottonwood trees.

"Todd," my mother said, and she shook me awake; it must have been three thirty in the morning. "Todd—Todd—Todd—" she whispered.

I sat up in bed and she was already outside again, standing in the yard in her T-shirt with no pants on. She was doing a kind of dance, like she was a cheerleader, shaking her hands as if she had pom-poms in her fists. "Hi!" she called—up toward the sky, and skipped forward, then back. "Hi! Hi!" Like maybe she was saying hello to God, or the stars, or a UFO. Ash was coming down. "Hi!" she said rhythmically. "Hi! Hi!"

VI.

Mrs. Hotchkiss comes over in her Hotchkiss Farms station wagon and we all sit very still watching through the sheers as she looks around and calls hello.

Hello hello!

And it looks as if her eyes are right on us, but Mom says she can't see a thing through the sheers during the day because they trap the shadows. Mrs. Hotchkiss reaches her hand in the driver's window and taps the horn. Why doesn't she just come to the door and knock?

Why doesn't anyone come to the door? They just stand there until you come out. Except Todd. *He* knocks at the door. He knocks even though Mom has said he doesn't need to. He is always welcome. But he likes to knock. He likes her opening the door for him.

Hello?

Old Lady Hotchkiss is about ready to leave, she is getting back in the station wagon, when Mom jumps up and opens the door and invites her in.

The coffeepot is heaving, they are at the table smoking, Mrs. Hotchkiss brought by her extra seed potatoes and tomato starts in case we could use them, and she wants us to know she could use berry pickers in about a week and she preferred girls—Dee sent her girl, Dee, the name of the lady, Dee, the former mom of this house, she assumes we've heard the story, and Mrs. Hotchkiss says history does repeat itself because here she is smoking in Dee's kitchen again, and isn't life a mystery? They know it wasn't arson for a provable fact, but people still say that something feels not all the way right. Well, time marches on, and it's good to have people here again and are you keeping rabbits just for enjoyment? Well, that's a luxury! And then Todd knocking.

I'm going to answer the door and Mom does it instead.

"Why, Todd! Come in! Bernard's around here somewhere. Cecilia, help Todd find Bernard."

Todd looks disappointed as he follows me through the kitchen and out the back door.

I head down to the hutch to get Ivan.

Behind me is Dee's Place. Mrs. Hotchkiss said we shouldn't take it wrong if people called it Dee's Place even now. I am thinking of the fire and holding Ivan and getting the shivers—a fire that killed the people but left the house standing, a fire at Dee's Place.

And then Todd is there beside me saying, "What did Old Lady Hotchkiss tell you?"

Me: Nothing.

Todd: She tell you my mom set the fire?

Me: No.

Todd: What'd she tell you?

Me: That history repeats itself.

Todd: Better let that rabbit go, then. Better let all your rabbits go.

VII.

Bernard, Cecilia, and I walk along the banks of the creek, and Ivan the Rabbit lopes along beside us. I ask them what if he runs away and Cecilia says don't worry, he won't. It's late morning on a Saturday and there are patches of clover that the rabbit stops to nibble in his quick, scared rabbity way, but he seems to keep an eye on us. When we begin to walk forward he quits eating the clover and follows us. He's wearing a little blue sweater from one of Cecilia's dolls.

We are looking for the cat I saw that night when I stayed over, the pale cat that must have come in through the open window while we slept. I was in the bedroom with Bernard and I woke up and everyone was asleep, and a cat was sitting on my chest, purring.

"We don't have a cat," Mrs. Popkin told me the next morning. "I can't abide them." The other kids were still asleep, and we sat at the kitchen table in silence.

"Don't tell your mother you saw me taking down my curlers in my kitchen," Mrs. Popkin said. "It's unsanitary. But I like looking out this window.

"Why don't you go play on that old tire swing," Mrs. Popkin said. "It'll give me something to watch while I'm doing my hair."

We both looked out at it, turning in the breeze.

"Go on," she said. "I'll watch."

It must have been a stray cat, Cecilia says now.

I do not tell them that it has occurred to me that the cat was a kind of *ghostly manifestation*.

I do not say that maybe it is a spirit connected in some way to Karen, who died in the fire, my friend Karen who suffocated, the oxygen sucked out of her so she couldn't even make a sound.

Maybe it has kittens somewhere around here, Cecilia says.

I think about what it felt like to wake up with the weight of the cat on my chest. The cat had been sitting there looking down at me; its eyes were hooked onto my face as if it was waiting for a mouse to come out of my mouth.

Here, kitty, kitty, kitty, Bernard calls. *Unless Todd's psyching us.*

Here, kitty, Cecilia says also, and then she glances over at me.

But personally, I am quiet. Up at the house, the older brothers have come home in the pickup, and I watch as they start unloading heavy rocks from the back, thick and trudging as mules. I don't think I have ever seen them without a frown; I don't think I've even heard them talk except to grunt at one another moodily. But Mrs. Popkin exclaims at them in her jolly way: *It's about time you boys got back! I was about to send out the search party!*

For a while as we are walking along, we talk about the fire.

What did Old Lady Hotchkiss tell you? I ask. I can hear my own voice as if I am listening in another room. *She tell you my mom set that fire?*

I can feel my face getting red and my voice like something that a ventriloquist put inside of me. *It's just because my mom is a little eccentric*, I tell them, *people suspected her.*

"What's *excentric*?" Bernard says, and they both look at me. Ber-

nard scrunches his round, freckled face, and Cecilia eyes me skepti-
cally, fingering the plastic barrette in her short-cropped hair, and
Ivan puts his ears back and I am reflected in his magenta eye.

"It means . . . ," I say. "It just means different. Very, very different
from other people.

"She had to go down to the police station and take a lie-detector
test," I tell them, which actually isn't true. They never took her down
to the police station, though I wished they had.

"She passed the lie detector," I tell them. "So that should have
been the end of it but some people still gossip," I say. "Certain people
hate my mother."

And that, at least, is true. I don't really know if people like Old
Lady Hotchkiss think that she started the fire at Karen's house, but
whenever we are in town I can see the way their eyes rest on us. They
are suspicious of her, uncomfortable, and why shouldn't they be?
Even when she is trying to be normal, you can sense a force coming
out of her in ripples, like radiation. Sometimes we are standing in
line at the supermarket or the post office and I will feel it. *Repellent.*

We are repellent, and I feel my face getting hot just thinking of it.
I put my hand on my chest because I can almost feel that cat sitting
there, that weird kind of pressure.

We come at last to the place on the edge of the creek where Karen
and I used to like to play. There is the crab-apple tree where we
nailed wooden slats to the trunk so it was easier to climb up into the
branches. There is the soft, loamy ground where we buried pieces of
our old toys—a plastic tea set, Matchbox cars, GI Joe legs, a bent
Slinky—because we liked to pretend that we were archaeologists and
we were going to find a forgotten civilization. There is the place
where Karen and I saw the poisonous mushrooms, the Destroying
Angel, *Amanita virosa* is the Latin name of the mushroom. Once
Karen and I had talked about putting some of those mushrooms into

my mom's food, and standing here now, I wonder what would have happened.

VIII.

Eating a rabbit. Todd has done it. My mom has done it. My brothers and even me. I am told when I was little I did not mind it. When Mawmaw fixed it, I ate it.

And I don't remember it or the taste of it, but the thought of it is in my mouth and in my teeth and when Mom tells the story of how I loved Mawmaw's stew before I knew what was in it and how I screamed bloody murder when I realized it—she always tells it in the same way and she does not skip a word when she tells Mrs. Hotchkiss—as I try to sneak off the back porch steps she says

Cecilia.

And how she says it in the accent of a doctor asking for a scalpel.

"Cecilia. Mrs. Hotchkiss needs a fresh ashtray," she says.

"Oh no, no, I really do have to get going, I just wanted to ask about your girl for the berry pick—"

"Oh, she was screaming bloody murder. Have you seen that movie *The Miracle Worker*?"

"Well, I really have no time for watching movies this time of year! It was good talking with—"

"She screamed bloody murder and tore the room up worse than Helen Keller. I told her, you'd make a good Helen Keller, you know that? We learned all kinds of things on that day, didn't we, Ceci? Even Mawmaw learned something."

"Well! Good-bye then, let me know about the—if she—if your girl wants to pick with us. Thanks again for the—"

Screamed bloody murder because it was bloody murder.

I have made certain vows to Ivan. Certain swears upon my honor to live as his guard and be willing to die saving him. I play movies of it in my head, how I give my life. And movies of what I do to anyone who hurts him. *Miracle Worker*, only very bloody. And if I should die before I get my revenge, I will come back, come back from the dead, and I will be violent. I have written these things in pencil on the wood of Ivan's pen but you can only see it if you tilt your head just right. It is not obvious, but to certain kinds of people it will be visible.

And Todd asks Bernard about Mawmaw, why we say it, why not Grandma?

Bernard says we had a grandma and a mawmaw. "Before she passed," says Bernard.

Todd: Died. Dead.

Bernard: We have to say *passed*. Unless you want a slap. Do you want a slap?

Todd: No.

Bernard: Mawmaw would go, You want a slap? You want a slap?

And I see Bernard remembering, about to say it, and I step toward him.

Bernard: Todd! Wanna see Ceci go crazy? Put your hands like claws and say—

SAY IT, BERNARD! Say how I just kicked you so hard between your legs, perfectly and very on purpose. SAY! SAY! Tell Todd the magic words that will make me kick his nuts too, because you know I will do it. I will do it if you say my name and just three other words.

Cecilia. *Mawmaw wants Ivan.*

It is the worst place to kick a person and I must get the belt for it, but Mom says the belt isn't working for me anymore. So what will work for me? There were slaps and Bernard snot-faced crying, "Kill Ivan, Mom! She doesn't deserve him!" and my other brothers come in, see there will be no dinner, and slam out.

Mom sits at the table and lights a cigarette. She points to the chair across from her.

Scalpel.

I sit.

IX.

"So," Mother says to me. "What was all that screaming about?"

I am sitting with my microscope by the window, with some creek water on a glass slide, trying to adjust the microscope's mirror so it catches the sun and illuminates the amoebas and protozoans and things.

"Down there at your girlfriend's house," she says. "Your wonderful Mrs. Popkin."

There are four lenses on a revolving nosepiece that magnify 4x, 10x, 40x, and 100x. I turn my lenses and then I look into the tube and adjust the focus. All I can see is a gray, swimmy blur that feels like a hair on my eyeball.

"I could hear that little girl screaming all the way up here," Mother says. "Screaming like she was out of her mind."

The proper way to focus a microscope is to start with the lowest-power objective lens first and, while looking from the side, crank the lens down as close to the specimen as possible without touching it. Now look through the eyepiece and turn the focus knob upward until the image is sharp.

"She must be a really terrific mother, your Mrs. Popkin," Mother says. "Did she eventually kill the child? What's that girl's name? Cecille?

"You sure came running home awfully fast, didn't you?" she says. Mother is so happy. I don't think I have seen her this happy in a long time. "Maybe your boring old home and your boring old mom aren't so bad after all!"

I believe I have located a ciliated protozoan, which looks like a transparent grain of rice. It's got three black round spots inside it that almost look like a face, eyes nose mouth. A ghost going: "Ooooooh."

One night there was a dream where I went down to the creek by the Popkin house.

It was the clearing where Karen and I used to play, where we saw the crab apple with *Amanita virosa* mushrooms growing underneath it and the creek is deep where it curves into a meander pool beside the tree. And in my dream, there was Mrs. Popkin bathing in the creek pool. She was standing in the water up to her waist but I could see that she was naked. Her skin very buttery white and nipples on her breasts pink like a cat's tongue.

The only women I have ever seen nude are the women in actual art, in encyclopedia entries about, for example, Botticelli.

Except that in Botticelli the lady is gentle and dreamy-eyed, and in my dream Mrs. Popkin looked up and saw me standing there in the clearing and she was not gentle at all. Her expression was cold and fierce and my legs were frozen from the force of her gaze. It threaded through my bones in a thin, quivering line, like a noise so high-pitched it was almost inaudible, and I could feel my arms and legs getting thinner and tighter and shrinking away. I could feel my face narrowing and my vocal cords shutting off. My ears grew long and I was running away, and dogs or teenagers were chasing me, and I was running home and then my mother bent down and grabbed me by my long ears and yanked me up.

"Gotcha!" she said, and then I woke up.

This is not a dream that you would tell to anyone, not ever, but I couldn't help but think of it again when Mrs. Popkin came out of the house.

Cecilia kicked Bernard, and Bernard went down on all fours hollering and vomited up an amoeba of milk and cereal. Cecilia fell onto his back and began to try to rip up his shirt with her clawed fingers.

She was biting him. Screaming. She was small and thin and Bernard was bulky and big for his age, but he was the one who was crying for his mom.

I just stood there over them. I watched them rolling around on the ground, Cecilia clawing into Bernard like someone drowning.

"You guys," I said.

And then Mrs. Popkin came out of the door.

She had that look on her face, the way that her green eyes looked in my dream, the kind of glare that could go straight through metal, that could disintegrate you so that your cells fell into a mass of wriggling protozoans.

"Cecilia," she said.

"Bernard," she said.

Just those two words.

And I didn't turn and run but I did leave, I left as silently and stealthily as possible. I didn't ever want to hear my name spoken in that voice, the kind of voice that stripped your name down to shivering bones.

Oh, Todd, my mother used to say. *Will I always be lonely?* This was back when she was at her worst, back when we were good friends, back when she thought we should commit suicide together. *Oh, Todd, I am so afraid that I will always be alone like this. Do you think I will always be lonely?*

I don't know, I'd said, but now I find myself thinking about it.

Will I always be lonely? I think, and maybe the answer is yes.

I think of Karen, gone almost a year now, Karen who I loved; and I think of my mother, and how much I loved her back when I was seven or eight, how I would have gladly died with her back then; and I think of Mrs. Popkin, who seems so pretty and interesting, and how I will sit at her kitchen table and drink coffee and pretend that something is happening.

Some kind of relationship. We talk about books, and our philosophies of life, and she tells me about her childhood and maybe I can someday tell her a little about mine.

I don't know. *Will I always be . . .* I don't know what I'm doing wrong . . . *lonely?*

I am sitting here at the window of my bedroom and it is almost midnight and Cecilia is still screaming.

"*Ivan! Ivan! Ivan, I love you I am sorry I love you I am sorry . . .*" And it is pretty steady, her voice is hoarse but she doesn't seem like she's ready to give up.

If Ivan is dead, his eyes will no longer be the distinctive magenta color associated with albino animals. The eyes of an albino animal appear red because the color of the red blood cells in the retina shows through where there is no pigment to obscure it.

I can feel my mother standing in my doorway.

"Quite a set of lungs on that girl," she says.

X.

Once we do what we must, it's over. It's done. And then, like my mom says, the Lord gives us a new day.

And I wake up to Todd's mother and my mother talking in the kitchen, and Todd sitting on the end of my bed, staring at Ivan. Ivan is standing on his hind legs, standing right next to my head, right next to the Bundle as if he's guarding it, and he and Todd are having a stare-off. Todd looks like he wants to say something but he can't. His mother is laughing loudly at something. The kitchen is directly beneath us.

We can see stripes of them through the vent. Their cigarette smoke curls up through the chipped slats.

Todd: My mom wanted me to give you this.

Action: he hands me an envelope and inside is a card, a picture of a mouse holding a blue umbrella in a rain shower. It says: HEARD YOU WERE UNDER THE WEATHER.

Todd: She has a card for everything.

Inside the card are two dollars and a poem about getting well soon.

Todd: She said we better check on you.

Me: Thank you.

Action: my mother laughs at something Todd's mom says, and then they both laugh and they are getting along and Todd's mom starts to talk about Todd's screaming fits, how he would howl! Screaming his head off about nothing!

"About me hanging a new set of drapes while he slept," she says. "About the sound his lamp made when it was off. It was a good lamp. And he buried it! I saw him doing it from the top-floor window and I dug it back up. No damage. I've never heard it talk, but Todd . . . ha-ha-ha . . . he swears it murmurs!"

Mom: Murmurs?

Todd's mom: Isn't that Todd all over? Murmurs! His vocabulary!

Action: Todd is staring straight at me and I am staring straight at him and there is light falling from a side window that hits his eyelashes in a way that makes them look white. For a moment there is red-eye, a red eclipse, and then normal eyes.

Human eyes. They blink at me.

And now the two mothers are talking about last night's screaming.

More jolly laughing coming up the vent.

I say to Todd this: We don't mention it.

Todd: No.

I sit up and he sees it, the Bundle I have kept under my pillow the way Mom told me to. *Keep it warm all night long,* she told me. *My good brave girl.*

XI.

We are sitting there together on the bed in her room, Cecilia and I, and Ivan is right there in the bed with her, wearing his little blue sweater. He stands on his hind legs and his nose works up and down like he is trying to send me a message in code.

"Hi, Ivan," I say.

It's a relief. After all that screaming, I was sure that Ivan was dead. Butchered. I don't want to believe that Mrs. Popkin would do such a thing, but last night it was all I could think of. *Mawmaw's stew*, Bernard said, and then Cecilia screaming Ivan's name. I didn't want to believe it could happen, but I have seen the kinds of things that mothers will do. *For your own good*, they will say. *To teach you a lesson*. Knowing that you can't stop loving them. Even now, the sound of her laughter downstairs is musical.

"Are you feeling better now?" I say. And Cecilia makes her lips very small.

I guess that this probably means "no."

"We don't mention it," she says.

"No," I say, at long last.

It's so weird to sit in a girl's room on her bed, especially when the girl is in it. I watch as she turns and gazes out the window, and then I think that *gaze* might be a word, like *murmur*, that my mother and Mrs. Popkin would laugh at.

"Where are your brothers?" I say. "It's so quiet in the house."

Cecilia shrugs and she looks at me for a second and I stare down at my knees.

"They're not even my brothers," she says after a long time. "Not really. Every time we move somewhere, my mom finds a new one. She likes boys better than girls."

"Oh," I say.

I watch as she shifts the lumpy package under her covers like she's trying to make it comfortable. It's wrapped tight as a mummy, with a blanket turbaned around and around it. A stuffed animal, I guess. But then I think I see it move beneath its swaddling, and I watch Ivan smell it and put his ears down flat.

For just a moment she pulls back a flap of blanket, and I imagine I see a mouth, a wet tongue clutched between teeth. Then she covers it quickly and our mothers' laughter comes rising up again through the vent.

"She's not half-bad," my mother says as we are walking home. She swings the clear plastic grocery bag that Mrs. Popkin gave her back and forth, forth and back. "I don't mind her."

"Mmm," I say.

"She's funny. She has a nice sense of humor."

I nod.

"I can see why you have a crush on her," my mother says.

"No, I don't," I say.

She smiles. In the grocery bag, I can see a package wrapped up in aluminum foil, a little smaller than a baby, but it seems to have about the same weight.

My mother whistles for a little while, and then stops whistling.

"So," she says. "Guess what we're having for dinner tonight?"

XII.

Three days later. Standing on a chair next to the stove, pouring a box of elbow macaroni into a pot of boiling water. And then a second box.

"Cecilia," Mom says. "Get me my cigarettes."

She is making balls of meat with her hands. *The catchall grind*, she calls it. Into the metal funnel of the silver grinder screwed hard onto the kitchen table. Rough-chop your meat scraps, throw in anything else you want, salt the hell out of it, let it sit, and run it through.

Throw in the meat, all kinds, torn-up stale bread, leftover pancakes, mashed potatoes, oatmeal, peeled-off chicken skin. Layering everything just so.

"Well. Todd's not hers," Mom says. "She got him somewhere."

Into a small frying vat she drops a test ball of catchall. She eats one raw.

On the radio, singing is interrupted by static. Then a signal. Mom walks toward the radio, picking something out of her mouth. "Tickles," she says, and keeps trying to grab whatever is there, which seems to be moving quickly down her throat. She coughs into her palm.

"Hair," she says.

The warning signal stops. It is only a Test of the Emergency Broadcast System, the man on the radio says. If it was a real emergency, there would be better instructions.

Mom says: "When it's done, you'll run a covered dish up to Todd and his mom."

And until it is done, I am free. Go. There is a part of grinding catchall that no one is allowed to see. The part Mom calls *the binder*. What is it?

Mom turns from the stove and looks at me and even now I love how beautiful she is. Could have been a pinup girl, she's done the pose for me, Mom asking me do I know why she looks so good?

Because she never had any natural children.

XIII.

Around dinnertime, Cecilia Popkin shows up at our door with a covered dish. "Just some meatballs and sauce and elbow macaroni," she tells my mom.

It has been three days since I spoke to Cecilia, and she doesn't look at me. She just stands there at the door like a little girl who delivers a package in a play. "My mom said to tell you that it would go good with that bread she made," she says.

"Oh, how nice," my mother says. That bread! When I first saw the bread that Mrs. Popkin made, it was wrapped up in aluminum foil and it was in a clear plastic grocery bag. I watched the bag swinging back and forth in my mom's loose hand, the foil glinting, and I had the terrible image of a skinned naked rabbit inside of it, I thought of Cecilia screaming and her mom with a knife. Not Ivan, at least, I thought—just one of the others. But I definitely imagined that when Mother undid the foil, we'd see the glistening pink muscle, the feet and hands and head removed.

I think my mom had thought that too, because when she unwrapped it she seemed disappointed. It was just a loaf of brown bread. The shape of the bread was a *little* like a rabbit, I thought, a hiding rabbit with its ears tucked down and its body held close.

"Oh, that bread! It was so wonderful!" my mother says now to Cecilia. "So dense . . . and seedy!"

Actually, she threw it in the garbage. After we unwrapped it and she cut it open, we saw that it was full of tiny white shells and nuts and my mother made a face.

Ugh, she'd said, and handed it to me. *Why don't you scatter it out in the backyard. Birds might eat it.*

Now she says to Cecilia: "Your mother likes starches, doesn't she?" She gives Cecilia that smile she sometimes makes. "It's so thoughtful of your mother. She must think all we eat is peanut butter and jelly. Mrs. Popkin is thoughtful, isn't that right, Todd?"

"I guess," I say.

But Cecilia still won't look at me. She leaves as my mother takes the casserole, or whatever it is, and my mother puts it in the oven.

XIV.

I am about halfway down the hill when Todd catches up with me. The moon is up; his lips look blue-gray. They say, *Hey*. White eyelashes flick, his pale lids lower and raise, his nose is wider than Bernard's.

I say, "Hey," and keep walking. "Bye," I say. "See ya." But he's following me, crossing the gravel road behind me, saying, "Wait a sec, Cecilia."

The way he says my name like I'm a person. Sometimes in the beginning, they do that. They think I'm a person like Karen was a person. A person they can talk to. Or if they had a sister, maybe they will think that. And they start to feel very friendly. And Mom does not understand why I don't use this to my advantage. It's a natural talent. It's a gift. And I waste it.

Todd touches my arm and we stop. He's looking past me to our dark front porch. There are no lights on in the house. Even so, he wants to come over.

I remember Mom standing at the front window when she first saw him, saying, *I feel kind of sorry for that one.*

I feel her looking at us, I feel her standing at the window, watching us, but I'm wrong. She's standing on the porch.

"*Cecilia?*"

"Go!" I whisper to Todd. "You gotta go. GO!" And I shove him.

"*Cecilia?* Bernard needs your attention." And then, "Todd? Is that you?"

Me: GO!

Action: shoving him back across the road and him shoving back.

Todd: Why are you doing this?

Mom: *Cecilia?*

Action: digging my fingers into Todd's bare arm and scratching him as hard as possible, digging in until he yells and his mother steps out to save him.

XV.

After being scratched and yelled at, I am not really in the mood to eat the casserole, but my mother insists, and she even takes a few of the meatballs herself. I don't want to like them, though they are actually really good.

"Hmmm," my mother keeps saying as she takes small bites. "Interesting flavor."

And then after we do the dishes and put them away, I go upstairs to my room. I feel sad that it's summer, and I don't have any homework to do. So I read my book about dragonflies, and then I read in the encyclopedia about rabbits. The family Leporidae of the order Lagomorpha. Cottontails. Pikas. Hares.

Out my window, I can see Cecilia's house. There is one light on, and I imagine it is maybe Cecilia's. Maybe she is sorry, maybe she just lost her temper. I imagine I could send her a signal with a flashlight. If she knew Morse code. *Friend*, I could say.

But then, just as I get out my penlight, I see movement in the frame of the window. The thick, hulking shape of one of the big brothers stares out, stares up toward me. For a minute, it feels as if he senses me, but then the other brother comes in, the one who wears the baseball cap backward, and I can see the two of them begin to dance. I can see their silhouettes, their hands in the air and their hips grooving.

"What are you doing?" my mother says.

And when I turn from the window, she is standing there in the doorway.

"Nothing," I say. "Just reading."

"Memorizing the encyclopedia again," she says when I show her the book. "R for *railroad*. R for *Rembrandt*. R for *running away*."

"Why do you even say that?" I say, and I watch as she sits down on my bed with her glass of wine. "I never try to run away anymore," I say.

"That's true," my mother says. "You don't."

For a second, I have a little flash of memory—how long ago, how many years? It's actually more like a dream: I am running through dark high grass. I don't believe that she's my mother. I am calling: Mom! Dad! Help me!

And then, in my dream, she catches me by the back of my hair and pulls me to the ground and pushes my face deep into the wet mud.

"Hmmm," she says, and she sips her wine, settling back against my pillow. *Hmmm*: this is what she likes to say when she's lost in thought, or when there's nothing else.

It was a sound that she made a lot right before the fire.

And so I am silent, and I glance at the yellow light down the hill, and I say, "Are you okay?"

"Hmmm," she says.

"You're not mad at me, are you?" I say.

And she lowers her head. "Oh, Todd," she says. She sips her wine, grimaces.

"Don't be sad," I say. "Mom." And she gazes at me for a long time with her big eyes.

Then she moves her fingers softly: *come. Come.* Her fingers waving like sea plants. Anemones.

I lie down in her lap the way she likes, and she puts her arms around me, cradling, like I am a baby, and she rocks a little as she lowers her mouth to my neck.

I feel her sharp tongue poke me, and then I get sleepy, of course. I close my eyes. I can hear the soft sounds that she makes as she's nursing. *Hmmm. Hmmm. Hmmm.* Almost as if she's crying.

XVI.

We don't sell our rabbits because we need them for things. You learn things when you dress them, like how when they are skinned they all look the same, and then you eat what can be eaten and you keep the feet for luck and you use the head for thinking.

Tonight, my mom needs to think.

I'm holding the bundle. She's in her robe and curlers holding the birdcage containing Ivan. Did I follow the instructions? Keep it with me, keep it warm, make sure there is enough air, the bundle needs the same tender care that Ivan does, Mom says. She sets Ivan on the floor and reaches for the bundle. How is our project coming along?

She puts the bundle on the table and begins to unwrap it. "Have you seen my cigarettes?" And yes, they are on the kitchen counter next to the sink, and I put them on a plate and carry them to her and she says, "Don't be a smart-ass."

It was my job to dress it, to wash and comb its hair, slice off its eyelids, remove its nose and lips. Those were, Mom said, the best parts. The ones she wanted most. But she became impatient with how I was detaching the nose and took over. "You're scaring him!" She said I'd ruined the freckled skin of his cheeks with my antics as she cut the little lips away.

And now the face peers out at us. The mouth opens and the tongue comes out and licks the bare teeth. We hear it draw air through its nose hole. The gelatin eyes rake back and forth. I can tell how bad Mom wants to be alone with it, to take it on a TV tray up to her room and close the door.

She begins the prayer and I repeat it. This time of year comes with the buzzing of certain insects with rasps on their legs that make a sound that rolls along underneath our chanting. Mom hands me a cigarette, strikes a match. "Have you been practicing?" I have, I say. And it's true. I can smoke like her. Just like her when I want to.

The bundle opens and closes its mouth, its tongue wiggling, its eyes shocked. Mom takes a long, long sip of her cigarette and then she lowers her mouth to the nose hole and exhales. I watch as the smoke curls out of its mouth, out of the ragged hole of its throat where the neck is severed. Then she tells me it's my turn. She tells me it's a different kind of smoking.

When I lift my face away, I watch the eyes grow dim and the freckles on the cheeks fade out.

Bernard.

In reality, Bernard is not a name. In reality it's a place, a hutch, which a boy needs to occupy for a certain amount of time.

We chant and we clap as the pink candles glint, Mom gathers the bundle and heads up the stairs, and I take Ivan out of his cage. We open the door for the new Bernard. And we do not mention what I did to the last one's face.

XVII.

Mrs. Popkin laughs when she sees me. "You don't have to knock, Todd," she says. "You're family." I am standing at the screen door holding the dish, my mom said that I should throw it away but why would you do that, it belongs to Mrs. Popkin. And so while she was sleeping, I washed it along with the other dishes and I dried it and then I mopped the kitchen and dusted and then I thought, *All right. I'm going to go up there. I don't care what Cecilia says.*

And now I can see Mrs. Popkin through the screen door, coming toward me, barefoot, wearing a very thin nightgown. Smoking her cigarette. You can see her nipples blurrily through the sheer of her garment. The dark of her pubic hair. She comes close to the door but doesn't open it.

She just presses her palms against the mesh of the screen and bends down. She wets her lip with her tongue and then she closes her lips around her cigarette and her chest expands as she draws on it and I see the lit tip grow brighter.

"Have you ever played this game?" Mrs. Popkin says. She tells me to press my face up against the screen, and I do.

Back at the house, my mom is asleep on the couch with her arms folded over her chest and the TV on low volume and I can picture her flinching, I can picture the way she softly grimaces when she is dreaming.

"Push your lips up to the screen," Mrs. Popkin says, and I do. There is a dusty, chalky taste to the meshed wires, but I do what she says. I feel my lips making a damp print.

"Close your eyes," she says, and I do that too. I know that it is the stupidest thing that a boy like me can do. When you are a nerd, kids at school are always telling you to close your eyes. *Open your mouth and close your eyes and you will get a big surprise*, they say.

"Are you brave?" Mrs. Popkin whispers, and I think

Why are you doing this you shouldn't be doing this

And then I taste the hot smoke as she breathes it into my mouth and I gasp and it goes into me.

In the dream, there is a girl sitting beside my bed when I open my eyes. She is holding a rabbit in her arms, and staring hard at me, and I think she is going to tell me something.

I think that she is trying to tell me with her face that I should get up. She is trying to tell me that I should run away.

The rabbit's nose moves rhythmically, as if it's smelling something over and over.

"Mom!" the girl calls out. "He's awake!"

"Bernard, sweetheart," the mother says. She leans over me, and I can smell her breath, the scent of old smoke and sweet beer and bread. The mother leans down and kisses me on the lips, gently, and draws a little air out of my lungs and into hers.

Then she places a washcloth on my forehead.

"Oh, I've been so worried about you, baby," she says. "I think you've been delirious."

And when I open my mouth to speak, she says *sshhhhhhhh*. She presses a cup to my mouth. I can see the liquid, which is like thin gruel, a grayish brick-red color like hamburger when it is spoiled.

"Drink," she says. "Drink."

XVIII.

While Mom feeds him, I take Ivan out back to the rabbit hutch, and then I go to the garden and pull some carrots. They are small enough and thin enough that I can push them through the chicken-wire mesh, and Ivan lopes over to nibble at orange whisker roots at the end of the carrot.

The other rabbits watch warily. They know that I won't be giving them any treats, and they let out nervous little turds, round as marbles, which fall through the wire floor of the pen and onto the ground. Those are the ones whose names I try not to remember. It's better if you don't think of them as anything.

All that carrying on for nothing, Mom said. *See? It wasn't so hard, was it?*

Well. It would have been harder not to keep my promise. Another carrot to Ivan.

In the earliest days, back when we were living with Mawmaw and Romey, I remember when Ivan was my real brother. We were twins, and he had short hair and I had long hair, but otherwise we were identical. We were six years old.

And one day Mawmaw was asleep in the bedroom and Romey was sitting on the couch watching TV, his midget legs splayed out, and they didn't even reach the edge and he was wearing nothing but jockey shorts and he said, "Your mom is looking for you."

I remember I met her in the backyard, and she showed me what it meant. *Think of it this way,* she said, and I saw two pictures in my mind. On the one hand here was Ivan, skinless, no hands or feet or head, no guts inside his stomach, hanging by his feet from a rope. On the other hand was a little white rabbit in a hutch.

I thought I was making the saving choice, but actually it was the trapping choice. My pledge. My vow.

"We've got a new Bernard, Brother Rabbit," I tell Ivan now. "You're going to like him. He won't throw rocks at you or yank you up by the ears or any of that. He's nicer." And Ivan keeps nibbling thoughtfully, and the other ones make their bodies tight and huddled and glare at me and shiver.

None of them had been *just right,* as Mom says. None of them just right enough to be Bernard. None of them strong enough to be one of the big boys. None of them loved enough to be protected, like Ivan. They know that one late night the hutch door will open, and a fist will clutch their ears. They know about the hammer and the skinning knife.

They are not one of the Seven: the big boys. Bernard. Mom. Me. Ivan.

Once upon a time there was a family, that is the story I tell Ivan. *And the family had a rabbit,* I whisper to him.

XIX.

Up the hill is this crazy woman who comes to her door every night at dusk. Thin as a skeleton. She is in a torn, dirty nightgown even during the day. "Todd," she calls. Sometimes for ten or twenty minutes, she hollers. Sometimes screeching. Sometimes crooning in a loud way. Sometimes wailing. *"Todd! Tooooooooooddddd!"*

She won't be around much longer, Mom says. She's very old, and this is what happens when they start to pass.

Mom sits at the kitchen table, smoking, tapping her cigarette against the ashtray. "That's how God works," she says, and winks at me. "He takes your strength, and then he takes your mind, and then he takes your breath. Not necessarily in that order."

And then she blows a stream of smoke toward the ceiling.

"Todd," the crazy woman keeps calling. "*Todd!*" And upstairs my brothers are grunting and grumbling about it.

And Cecilia is standing at the doorway, holding Ivan, and his ears shift back and forth like the antennae of insects.

"Bernard," Cecilia says, "come on, let's go to the cutoff."

But Mom says no. "You go on, Cecilia," Mom says, and she sits down beside me and puts her arm around my shoulder. We look out together at the old tire swing. "Bernard can stay here with me and keep me company in the kitchen."

Upstairs, the big boys are packing our things into boxes, because we'll be moving soon, and their heavy boots thump as Mom lets her fingernails trace along the edge of my hair. I lean against her shoulder and close my eyes. *I love my mom*, I think, and I feel how soft her arm is when I rub my cheek against it. *I love my mom.*

DIRECT REPORT

LEIGH PERRY

Another morning, another rape.

Actually, it could have been any time of day. There were no windows, clocks, computers, or cell phones. The lamp on the ceiling was always on, and even the line of light coming in from under the door was artificial. So in the absence of other data, I'd decided it was morning. The point was that I was awake and starved.

And that I'd been raped. Again.

My nose wrinkled at the stench of sweat and sex, and the stickiness between my legs disgusted me. There was soreness from the invasion, too, but the tactile evidence of his presence on me bothered me more. The pain would fade quickly, but it would take a good hour under the shower before I could feel clean again.

Relatively clean.

I hadn't felt completely clean since the first time I awoke in that room, the first time I'd smelled him on me. Him being Claudio.

I hated to admit it, but I'd lost track of how long that had been. Days, without a doubt; quite likely weeks; perhaps even months. But most likely weeks, since my hair wasn't noticeably longer and the curl was holding.

I climbed out of bed and looked down to see what ridiculous outfit he'd picked for me this time. Today it was a long white dress, with a pale pink corsage on one wrist, as if I were some virginal prom queen. Ludicrous, but hardly the worst set of clothing I'd found myself in. I'd woken up in a push-up bra, garter belt, and fishnet stockings; a filmy negligee; a schoolgirl's plaid kilt with black patent-leather shoes and bobby socks. Once, I'd been dressed in an obviously expensive Supergirl costume, complete with cape. The first time, I'd been humiliated to find myself dressed like a doll. The next few times, I'd been angry. Now I just sneered at his pitiful attempts at kinkiness.

I pulled the dress off, wadded it up, and threw it into the wicker clothes hamper in the adjoining bathroom. The corsage went into the trash can.

The bed linens varied just as widely as the clothes: black satin, red silk, even camouflage once. Today was a pink flowered girly pattern, no doubt to coordinate with the prom gown. I stripped the bed, and the sheets went into the hamper with the dress.

All according to Claudio's instructions.

The rules for my captivity had been left for me the first day, a printed sheet of paper placed on the table.

1) Bathe.
2) Place soiled sheets and clothing in the hamper.
3) Drink your meal.

Of course, I hadn't obeyed. After a fruitless attempt to break through the door and screaming my throat raw, hoping I'd be res- cued, I'd ripped the list into pieces, shoved the dirty clothes into the toilet to stop it up, ripped the surprisingly fragile bedsheets, and de- stroyed the hamper.

The only instructions I'd followed were to bathe, because I stank of him, and then to drink the "meal" that had been left for me, because I was insanely thirsty. I'd have made do with drinking from the faucet if I could have, just to defy him, but he'd done something to the water. I could bathe in it, but every time I tried to drink it, the foul taste made me spit it out again.

The next morning, there'd been a new note.

If you cause damage, you will be punished.

I hadn't taken it seriously. After all, who was going to punish me? I hadn't seen a living soul while awake during those endless hours. So I'd repeated my performance, and broken the table into bits for good measure.

The morning after that, I'd awoken chained to the bed. Unable to clean myself, I'd had to smell that stink on myself all day, plus the inevitable result of not being able to get to a toilet. There'd been less of my meal that day, too, and I'd grown so thirsty that I'd imagined I could see my skin getting drier before my eyes and after a while, my screams for help were nothing but croaking.

Since then I'd followed Claudio's instructions to the letter, hoping for a loophole.

I'd first met Claudio in his home. I'd been expecting an office building when I got the call to set up the appointment, but it turned out that he did business out of his Manhattan brownstone. I was wary—I was hungry for a job, not stupid—but I'd relaxed after seeing other people bustling around the requisite amount of office equipment. Besides, I'd known professionals ranging from literary agent to lawyer who conducted business out of their homes. It was, however, an indication that this might not be the kind of corporate-career job I was hoping for. The next was Claudio's response when his secretary escorted me to his private office.

"Mr. Mendoza?" I said, offering my hand.

He blinked several times. "You're Taylor Blake?"

I suppressed a sigh, realizing that he'd assumed I was a man. "That's right." I was still holding out my hand, and he rose to take it limply, as if my female bones might snap from a firm grip.

He was shorter than I was, even if I hadn't been wearing high-heeled pumps, and not particularly attractive. His teeth were yellowed, and his skin pale and pockmarked. If I'd met him socially, I would have passed him by, but I was there to interview for a job, not to choose a lover, and his clothes, watch, and overdone jewelry said money.

I needed a job. Badly.

I'd taken two pay cuts in order to survive multiple rounds of lay-offs at my old company, only to be out of work anyway once the place shut down, and with only a skimpy severance package. The ones who'd been laid off earlier turned out to be the lucky ones—they had first shot at the jobs in our field. By the time I hit the market, I was burned out by that last year of frantically trying to keep the company going and tainted by association with a failed firm. Now that my job hunt had stretched into its ninth month, I was more than a little desperate.

Claudio and I sat, and he referred to the résumé on the desk in front of him to go through the usual queries about background and previous experience. I wasn't overly impressed with him. For one, he needed me to explain common business terminology like *downsized* and *outsourced*. For another, he asked too many questions about my personal life.

I shouldn't have answered of course, but he had an accent, South American I thought, and I knew that business was run differently in other countries. I'd once had an elderly Swiss man ask why he should hire me when I was going to quit my job to get married and have babies within a couple of years, and a British headhunter had wanted to know what my father did for a living, as if he could determine my place in the class system that way. So telling Claudio that I was single and without close family didn't seem too far out of the ordinary.

I did dodge his questions about other relationships, but that wasn't so much observing proper boundaries as it was not wanting to admit that my friends were primarily work-related. That meant I'd had to lay off many of those I'd socialized with, hardly a recipe for bonding. As for the rest, contacts who couldn't help me find a job were of no use to me. Once I had my career moving forward again, I would make time for such things.

Finally, Claudio got down to describing the position he was filling, and I knew immediately that it wasn't what I'd hoped for. I'm an executive, and I'm at my best when working with a large staff and a good number of direct reports. What he wanted was a business manager—a high-level one, given what he told me about his finances, but hardly something to help build my future. The person he hired would be working directly for him, sharing his secretary, without a single direct report.

Still, it was a job I could do in my sleep, and I tried to wax poetic about what I would be able to accomplish for him, but I could tell he wasn't enthused. I knew damned well it wasn't my résumé, because if anything, I was overqualified, and since Claudio was so out of touch with business, I couldn't imagine he was bothered by my association with a dead firm. When he remarked that the previous manager had been a man, I could only conclude that he was uncomfortable with the idea of having a woman handle his money.

Since I wasn't planning a sex-change operation, I didn't really expect to hear from Claudio again, so I was elated when he called two weeks later and asked for another meeting. Apparently he'd reconsidered the idea of working with a female business manager, because he requested that I come back to the brownstone late that afternoon. I hesitated just long enough to make it sound as if I were juggling other appointments, when in fact none of the headhunters I'd spoken to were even returning my calls.

The brownstone was much quieter that day, which I assumed was because of the hour, but I was too excited to worry about it, even when the secretary popped in during the meeting to announce that she was on her way out. The discussion with Claudio went for two solid hours as he posed specific questions about what I would do in various circumstances. He gave me far more detailed information about the businesses he owned than he would have if he hadn't already decided to trust me.

At last, Claudio said that he'd found no one whose business acumen could match mine. Moreover, he needed someone he could work with closely, on a personal level, and he was sure he and I would be completely compatible. I could hardly believe my luck when he handed me a formal offer letter, with a salary better than what I'd made at my previous job and substantially beyond what I was willing to settle for at that point.

I told him that I'd have to think it over—I knew better than to sign a contract without reading it carefully. There was one provision I immediately had concerns about: a probation period of up to six months. I was going to suggest that I come back the next day to discuss final questions but then thought of the pile of overdue-payment notices waiting at my condo. The sooner I signed, the sooner I could pay those bills. So even though it was a rookie mistake, I said, "Actually, I've changed my mind. I'm extremely excited about this position, and I'm happy to accept right now." I signed on the dotted line.

"Splendid!" he said, looking delighted. "Why don't we have dinner tonight to celebrate?"

One rookie mistake was enough. Going out with the new boss was no way to start a professional relationship. "I wish I could," I lied, "but I have plans tonight. Maybe drinks instead?" I'd passed a likely-looking bar half a block away, so I wouldn't even have to get into a car with him. And of course, had we made it there, I would have known better than to leave my drink unguarded with a man I didn't know well.

All my common sense added up to no protection at all.

Claudio said, "A drink would be perfect." Then he stood and looked into my eyes.

The next thing I knew, I was in that room in that bed, smelling Claudio all over me.

I went to the shower. My breakfast was waiting, and though my stomach rumbled at the sight of the pouch on the table, I knew if I slurped it down, I might not stay awake long enough to finish bathing. Claudio was drugging me, though either he was using progressively less or I was developing a tolerance, because I stayed up longer and longer each day. Still, I didn't want to take the chance.

The bathroom was small, with a shower stall instead of a tub, but I'd never run out of hot water and there was always plenty of high-end soap, shampoo, and towels. A couple of times I'd found perfume, but I'd decided I'd be damned if I'd make myself smell good for him. So I poured it down the toilet, then peed on top of it before flushing, a meaningless act of defiance that had cheered me for all of ten seconds. Apparently perfume was optional, because I hadn't been punished for it. So far, it was the only loophole I'd found in the instructions, but that didn't stop me from trying to find more.

I spent my usual hour in the shower, took my time drying off, and brushed my teeth thoroughly, even though there was no sign that Claudio had taken me in the mouth the previous night. Then I put on the short red robe hanging in the bathroom. The only other choices were going naked or wrapping a towel around myself.

Back to the room, where my choices were nearly as limited: sit on the bed, sit on the floor, sit on the chair. Or I could run around the room, screaming and yelling and generally going berserk. I'd tried that more times than I cared to admit. Unless I destroyed something in the process, no notice was taken, so I'd given up that approach.

Mostly I sat in the plain wooden chair and read.

There was a stack of magazines on the equally utilitarian nearby table, all months-old issues of the *Harvard Business Review*, *Bloomberg*, *Fortune*, *Forbes*. They were the kinds of magazines Claudio would want a business manager to keep up with, so my inclination was to ignore them, but it was either read them, stare at the walls, or cry some more.

I was sick to death of crying. I read.

When I could stand the thirst no longer, I picked up the plump, silver pouch that held my meal. It looked like nothing so much as an oversized kids' fruit-flavored drink, without the colorful label. There was even a straw taped to one side that I punched into it. I had no idea what the drink was. I'd spilled some on my finger once so I could look at it, but it was just red liquid, like fruit punch or something. But the taste . . . Ambrosia. Liquid crack. Pure, orgasmic pleasure. And apparently unexpectedly nutritious, because I never felt hungry afterward, though I wouldn't have minded something to chew on.

I could have made a fortune in a matter of months if I'd been allowed to develop that drink as a product—with nothing better to do, I toyed with new business models, marketing plans, advertising ideas. Of course, it was addictive as hell, which would be a negative in the marketplace, but I thought we could get around that. Maybe that was why I was there—a lab rat to see how long I could survive on the stuff. It had occurred to me that the rape was only incidental to Claudio, which infuriated me. I should have poured my meal down the toilet, but I couldn't force myself to do it. Drinking it was the only bright spot in my day.

If I ever got out, I'd see if there was an applicable twelve-step program. In the meantime, I squeezed every last drop into my greedy mouth, and licked my lips afterward.

Some interval later, I realized that I'd read through most of the magazines, so a large part of the day must have gone. Yet I was just starting to feel the inevitable lethargy. It was definite. I was indeed becoming accustomed to the drug Claudio was using on me. I wasn't sure what difference it made to my situation, but it still felt like a victory of sorts.

I left the magazines stacked on the table, then stretched out on the floor, knowing I would be asleep in seconds. It wasn't particularly comfortable, but I never went willingly to that bed.

When I awoke, for the first time in ages, I wasn't alone. Somebody was beside me in bed.

No, he was on top of me.

In me.

I screamed, and to my shock, so did he. I jerked back, and once he was out of me, I shoved him away as hard as I could. He seemed to almost fly off the bed, and his head slammed against the wall. His eyes rolled back in his head, and he slumped to the floor.

It wasn't him.

It was a man, but it wasn't Claudio.

I stared at him. I'd known other people came into the room while I slept because somebody had to clean, empty the hamper, restock the towels and toiletries, and of course dress me in those Halloween-party clothes. And I'd assumed it was someone other than Claudio because I couldn't picture him mopping a floor, but it had never occurred to me that he wasn't the one violating me.

When the man didn't move, I cautiously scooted out of bed, finally noticing that my costume du jour was a cheerleader getup. The panties that went with my bright-red-and-white uniform were on the floor, and I stopped to pull them on. I craved that small measure of protection.

The rapist was naked. He was also out cold, and I saw a good-quality pinstripe suit, dress shirt, and boxers folded neatly on the chair. Still keeping one eye on the man, I rummaged through his belongings and could have cried when I found a cell phone. It had a password set, but of course every phone allows for emergency calls.

Only there was no reception, none at all. I carried it to every corner of the room, even into the bathroom, hoping for one lousy bar, but there was nothing.

I also had his wallet, and that gave me his name—Martin James—and a glimpse of some family photos. To my disgust, there was a picture of him and a teenage girl dressed much as I was at that moment. Of course I'd already known he was a sick bastard, so that wasn't particularly useful information.

Since I was fairly sure that my actions would be deemed worthy of punishment, even if the instructions hadn't specifically said not to coldcock a rapist, I decided there was no reason I couldn't continue to break rules.

I ripped Martin's powder-blue shirt into strips so I could tie him up. It tore easily—his clothes must have been cheaper than they looked. Even with him bound, I felt the need for a weapon, so I broke the leg off of the chair. It, too, was ridiculously easy to destroy. I was surprised it had held my weight as long as it had.

Martin started to come to just a few minutes later, and the pained groans he made would have made me feel sorry for him if he weren't a rapist. As it was, I was tempted to beat on him with my chair leg. I would have, if I hadn't wanted answers.

He finally managed to focus on me, and turned white. "You're alive."

"No thanks to you. Was killing me the next part of your plan?"

"What? No! You were already dead!"

"Obviously not."

"Anemone & Lime guarantees dead women! What kind of rip-off is this?" He was actually indignant.

"I'm so sorry to disappoint you," I said as insincerely as I could manage. "Where are we?"

"Are you kidding me? Look, I don't know what you people are trying to pull, but you damned well better give me my money back."

"You actually paid to rape me?"

"*No*, I paid to have sex with a dead woman. You're not dead, so I want a goddamned refund."

"Anemone & Lime is a whorehouse?" Suddenly I pictured a whole procession of men taking turns with me—that was even worse than Claudio using me repeatedly. My stomach roiled, and I was grateful I hadn't eaten solid food for so long.

Martin continued to rant. "Just because I was late for my appointment doesn't mean you can get away with cheating me. I paid big bucks—up front—for this service, and I want what I paid for." He jerked at his tied hands. "I'm not some pathetic bottom paying for Mommy to spank me, so you're going to untie me right now!"

"What I'm going to do," I said calmly, "is ram this chair leg up your asshole unless you answer my questions. Is that perfectly clear?"

He swallowed visibly, twice. "Uh . . . yeah. I mean . . . yes, Mistress."

Fine, let him think I was a dominatrix gone rogue, as long as I got the information I needed. "So, Martin James, you're a necrophiliac?"

"Yes, Mistress."

"And it was your understanding that I was dead, and available for your use. Correct?"

He nodded.

"I don't suppose it occurred to you to ask how this facility had obtained such a fresh specimen?" As he struggled to come up with an answer that wouldn't result in immediate sodomy, I said, "No, strike that. It's not important. The fact is that I was *drugged*, not dead."

But he shook his head. "Lady . . . I mean, Mistress, I drove an ambulance to get through college, and I can tell a dead body from a live one. You weren't breathing. You had no pulse. Your limbs were completely loose. You were *dead*. And then, all of a sudden, you weren't."

"That's impossible," I scoffed. He started to say something, but I held up one hand to shush him so I could think. Martin had been completely convinced that I was dead, and given his background and proclivities, he wouldn't have been easy to fool. Besides, I'd never heard of a drug that would be convincing enough—certainly nothing that could be used repeatedly without horrifying side effects—and I'd been drugged every night for as long as I'd been in that room, however long that was. I remembered Martin's phone, and checked it. Then I blinked. "Is this date right?"

He looked confused but nodded.

If he was telling the truth—and I thought he was too afraid of my chair leg to lie—I'd been in that room for nearly six months. *Six months*. And in all that time, I'd been subsisting on nothing but a liquid diet. Even now, I was craving a pouch of that red liquid. "What time is it?"

"Um, you've got my phone."

"Right." I picked it up and checked it. It said five thirty-eight. "You came to a whorehouse the first thing in the morning?"

"What? No, it's nighttime. My appointment was at three, but—"

I held up my hand to quiet him again. Had that been my real schedule all along? Drugged to sleep all day, awake only at night?

If there's one thing I've learned in business, it's to face the facts. What I had were the following: one, I'd appeared dead and suddenly

I wasn't; two, I was awake during the night and sleeping all day; three, I'd apparently survived for nearly six months with no food other than a liquid. A red liquid.

It was impossible, unbelievable, but either I was insane or it was true. And I refused to believe that I was insane.

Before I could ask anything else, there was a knock on the door and a male voice said, "Mr. James? Time's up! I've fudged it for as long as I could."

Catching Martin's eye, I whispered, "Tell him you're almost ready to go. Nothing else!" Then I brandished the chair leg to remind him of what would happen if he disobeyed.

He nodded and in a loud voice said, "Just putting on my pants."

"Put 'em on in the corridor, man. I'm going to get fired if I don't get you out of there before lockdown."

I pressed myself against the wall so I wouldn't be seen right away, and for the first time, I saw the door open. A big burly man stuck his head in, and as soon as he saw Martin wriggling on the floor, he hissed, "*Shit!*" and started to pull back. But he was too slow. I grabbed his shirt and yanked him the rest of the way into the room.

In retrospect, I should have left the two men there and run for it, but at the time, I had no idea what was outside the door or how many others might be nearby. I needed information about what was going on before I leapt from the frying pan into the fire.

So I let the door shut behind us as I pushed the new man across the room, where he slammed up against the wall. He was wearing a maroon smock with gray trim, with pants to match. Embroidered in flowery letters on the front of the shirt were the words *Anemone & Lime*, and underneath it said *George*.

George was staring at me, saying, "Shit shit shit shit shit," over and over again, while Martin yelled, "Untie me, you idiot!"

"Quiet, both of you," I snapped.

They obeyed as quickly as if I'd flipped a switch.

"You," I said, pointing at George. "Who else works here?"

"There's a crew of like twenty guys out there, and they're going to be in here in a minute if you don't let us out right now."

"You're a terrible liar," I said in a conversational tone. "How many, really?"

He looked rebellious but said, "Just two of us in this wing, this time of day. You've got to let us out!"

"I don't think I do." A moment later, a loud buzzer went off, and I heard something click in the door. "What was that?"

"Lockdown," he said, and now he was sweating. "The door won't open until morning."

"You must have a key," I said.

He shook his head. "If I had a key, I swear I'd let you out. I don't want to be in here with you!"

While I kept an eye on him, I tried the door, pulling at it as hard as I could, with far more strength than I'd ever had before, but it wouldn't budge.

"I'm telling you it won't open," George said. "Not until dawn."

Martin said, "Somebody must know we're in here. They have to let us out."

George shook his head. "Nobody is going to risk letting *her* out, not when she hasn't had a meal."

"It's because they're afraid of me, isn't it?" I said.

George nodded. Clearly he was petrified.

"Then I am . . . I've become . . ."

He nodded again.

"How?"

"Somebody . . . you know . . . *bit* you."

"Claudio," I said.

"What are you talking about?" Martin asked. "You mean, you didn't drug her to play dead? She isn't just a whore?"

I said, "No, I'm starting to think that I'm more than that. And George here is going to tell me everything he knows about what I can do."

It took a couple of hours, and several more threats, to drain George dry. Metaphorically, that is, as I posed question after question.

The literal draining started immediately thereafter.

Afterward, I took off the cheerleader clothes, showered, put on my regular robe, and spent the rest of the evening rereading magazines. When I felt tired, I used the bed for the first time. The floor was too dirty.

Nothing in the room had changed when I woke. I was assuming my room was still on lockdown—George had said it was protocol in case one of the "girls" couldn't be controlled. Yes, there were other women with other gifts being held at Anemone & Lime—some were even willing. I just happened to be the only one with my particular gifts currently in residence.

I checked Martin's phone, pleased when I saw it was five minutes earlier than I'd woken the day before. Apparently I was progressing much faster than those in my situation usually did.

I showered again quickly, then looked at the available clothing options. Definitely not the cheerleader outfit. I could have made do with George's smock and pants, though the fit would have been loose, but he'd pissed himself the night before. That left Martin's suit. There was no shirt, since I'd used it to tie him up, and his undershirt smelled too much like him for me to stomach wearing it. But if I kept the jacket buttoned and belted the pants tightly enough to keep them up, I'd be decently covered. For shoes, I had the cheery red-and-white oxfords.

With that done, I sat down to wait. I wasn't hungry yet, and I'd already finished with the magazines, but Martin had some games on his phone to keep me amused until I felt the call George had warned me would be coming.

Call was far too mild a word. It was more of a pull, an urgent compulsion—I knew I had to get to Claudio as soon as possible. The door was still locked, and being blocked was physically hurting me. I was ready to try beating it down with my bare hands when a note was slipped through the crack underneath it.

When the door opens, follow the path. A car will be waiting.
Drive to Claudio.
DO NOT STOP OR YOU WILL BE PUNISHED.

I had to smile. Even knowing that Claudio was calling me, the employees of Anemone & Lime were frightened of what I might do. They had nothing to worry about, at least for the time being. I picked up the souvenirs I was taking with me and waited until the door clicked open. Sloppily taped-up arrows showed the way, and I saw no one and nothing but closed doors until I reached an open one that led to an underground garage. Just past the door was a car, keys in the ignition and the motor already running, and in a few minutes I was on my way.

I didn't know where Anemone & Lime was in relation to Claudio's brownstone, but I didn't need to know. I just followed the call. As long as I kept going toward Claudio, I felt fine. If I stopped, even for a traffic light, I started to feel a constricting pain in my throat. To go in a different direction or to pause any longer than absolutely necessary was unthinkable.

An hour and a half later, I pulled up in front of the now-familiar brownstone. A man I'd seen in Claudio's offices was holding a parking place on the street for me, but he stayed far away as I pulled in. The call was so strong that I was nearly running as I went in the door and up the stairs to where Claudio was waiting.

Only when I saw him in front of me did the call stop.

The bastard was smiling.

He held both hands out to me. "My dear Taylor, you have so impressed me. Not even six months since I brought you over! I would never have been out of reach at such a delicate time had I suspected such a thing would happen. You were destined for this life. None of my children have ever regained their senses so soon."

"Your children?"

"The children of my blood. Those whom I have raised, the ones who answer to me."

"Then you're a—we're both—"

"Don't be afraid of the word. Vampire."

I'd known since the previous night, of course, but knowing it and hearing it were very different. "And now I answer to you?"

"Think of yourself as my *direct report*, if you prefer." He waggled his finger at me. "I know I should be angry at you for what happened last night, but how can I be? You've regained yourself so quickly and can soon begin your work for me."

"After you—" I stopped myself. I'd planned what I was going to say and do, and I wasn't going to go off script now. "Why did you put me in that place?"

"A newly born vampire is a rapacious thing, more appetite than person, difficult to control and expensive to feed. Though you were and always will be incapable of harming me, anyone else would have been in grave danger until you recovered yourself. So some years back, I made an arrangement with a man who caters to a certain kind of clientele. He feeds and houses my new ones, and in return makes use of them." He cocked his head. "Surely you're not angry about events that took place when you were insensible? There was no permanent damage—that is part of our arrangement."

"An arrangement that impresses upon your children that you are completely in charge. A probation of sorts."

"Of course, it's not really necessary. You have no choice but to obey me." His voice sharpened. "On your knees."

I complied instantly, without thought. And hated him for it.

"You see? From this moment on, as long as you continue to exist, you must obey any order I give you. If I tell you to crawl to me, you will do so. If I tell you to return to Anemone & Lime and service men while you're fully aware, you will do so. If I tell you to walk into the sun, you will not rest until you are destroyed. Is that clear?"

"Perfectly. May I rise now?"

"Of course." He even offered a hand to help me. "You must be hungry, and you'll want to see your quarters. Tonight is for recuperation—tomorrow night will be soon enough to begin your duties."

"I wouldn't dream of delaying any further," I said. "You've waited nearly six months for someone to take over—there's no need to wait another night."

"Ah, you are remarkable, Taylor," he purred.

I did accept a meal of blood—poured from a crystal decanter and sipped from a goblet rather than sucked out of a pouch—but then went right to work. First was a tour of the brownstone and an introduction to the servants. All were human—Claudio's other "children" were scattered around the country. He hinted that they were taking care of other activities for him but would say no more. Nor would he say what had happened to my predecessor, the vampire who'd previously managed his money. I knew better than to push.

Claudio had already arranged an office for me, but we worked in his as he showed me reports about his financial holdings. Though I'd wanted to get started immediately for my own reasons, I could see why he was eager to take me up on the offer. The six months of my "probation" had left some items in a precarious position. He claimed he had no interest in such matters, but I suspected the real answer was that he had no understanding of how money needs to be looked after in a modern world and was all too happy to hand over all his account numbers and passwords, even his safety-deposit key and the combination to his safe. As long as his assets continued to grow, he said, he was happy to leave it all under my control. What he'd do to me if those assets didn't grow was left unspoken, but I had no doubt that he'd have plenty of ideas.

Having something meaty to think about after all those months was nearly as satisfying as drinking blood, but not so much so that I didn't detect something stirring within me a couple of hours later. I mentally reviewed the mass of information I'd been given and decided that it would be enough for me to take the next step. If I was missing anything, I'd just have to track it down afterward.

I resisted the impulse to smile, not wanting to tip my hand, and instead rubbed my eyes even though I wasn't sure my eyes could get weary anymore.

"Tired, my dear?" Claudio asked.

"Yes, and no." I stretched as alluringly as I could manage, stood, and unbuttoned the suit coat I was wearing far enough that he could see I was wearing neither bra nor shirt under it. "I do have a question. Do we . . . ?" I smiled, as if embarrassed by being so forward. "Do *vampires* make love?"

"Indeed we do," he said.

I slowly took off my clothes, letting everything fall to the floor except those red cheerleader panties, which I twirled on my finger a moment before letting them slip onto the desk.

"Shall we go to my room?" he said, but since it was an invitation rather than a command, I could resist.

"No, here. Here is where we met, here is where you brought me into this life. Let's do it here." I pushed papers and folders onto the floor and leaned up against the desk.

He sauntered over, and I began to caress him through his clothes as I sent out my own call. Claudio's touch was sure and practiced, and I writhed against him, moaning loudly and crying out to make him think I found him as skilled a lover as he thought he was. So he never heard the commotion from outside the room as it came closer.

At the very last moment, I grasped his head with both hands and pulled his mouth to mine, kissing him so hard that I tasted his blood.

That's when George burst through the door.

Claudio had described a new vampire as rapacious, and George certainly looked the part. Not one spark of intelligence was left in his eyes, only hunger. I was almost afraid at first, even though I knew I was the only one on earth safe from him.

I'd made him.

"Kill this man, now!" I ordered.

Claudio opened his mouth, no doubt ready to command me to defend him or to stop the other vampire or . . . Whatever he'd intended, it didn't matter. As soon as George made his entrance, I'd grabbed the red panties from the desk and now I rammed them into Claudio's mouth. Of course he tried to pull them out, but before he could, George was on him.

I'd noticed that Claudio was small when I first met him, and I suspected he used his vampire wiles far more often than he did actual strength. George, on the other hand, was a big man and intent on tearing and ripping and pulling the other vampire apart.

I hadn't specified a method for killing Claudio—apparently I hadn't needed to.

There was an odd twinge in my neck, as if a necklace had tightened before breaking loose. Then Claudio burst into dust, and the red panties dropped to the carpet.

George was panting, and I quickly found the decanter of blood from which Claudio had poured my meal and helped the starving vampire drain it. Then he collapsed, replete. If a vampire could snore, he would have been doing so.

I'd bitten Martin the night before, too, but he was just dead. That was to be expected. George hadn't been positive how vampires were made—all he'd known was the gossip Anemone & Lime employees had shared while slurping coffee in the break room. One theory was that anyone drained to death would rise again. Another said that the sire had to nearly drain a person and then make the victim suck some of his blood in return. Since I'd had two subjects available, I'd tried both methods.

I hadn't been completely sure which man would rise, so I'd brought both. Dragging the bodies behind me hadn't prevented me from answering Claudio's call, and the Anemone & Lime employees hadn't dared to interfere. When I arrived at Claudio's home, I left the men in the trunk of the car, safely covered with a blanket. As soon as I felt the new vampire stir, I'd begun my seduction of Claudio.

I made a mental note to have Martin's body taken care of, but for the moment, I had more urgent concerns. I needed to see if any of the servants had survived, and to inform those survivors that the brownstone was now mine.

I also had to reach out to Claudio's other so-called children. They'd probably felt him die just as I had, and it was my guess that they'd be grateful for their deliverance. If not, I'd point out that I already had control of Claudio's finances. Surely, arrangements could be made.

My highest priority was to find a safe place for George to complete the six months of his probation period. After all, for the time being he was my only direct report.

SHADOW AND THIRST

JOHN LANGAN

The tower was there when they returned from their early-morning dog walk. August saw it first, squatting in the meadow at the foot of the hill behind his father and stepmother's house. It was round, dun colored, maybe ten feet high, ten wide. "Hey," he said, "what's that?"

Tony, his father, looked up from Orlando the pit bull, who was rolling in the damp grass, grunting happily. "What?"

"Down there." August pointed. "That's still your property, right?"

"All the way to the stream and halfway up the other side." Tony squinted; he wasn't wearing his glasses. "That looks a bit too elaborate for your little brother to have built by himself. Huh. Guess I'd better have a look at it. You want to come, Officer?"

August had yet to decide whether his father's use of his job title was ironic or conciliatory, a sign of displeasure at his decision to drop out of college and join the Newark city police department or an indication of Tony's acceptance of his choice. "Sure," he said, "let's check it out."

"It's probably something the neighbors' kid put up," Tony said. "The boy's quite the budding filmmaker; we've let him shoot a couple of his movies here. I played King Arthur in one of them. I bet this is connected to his latest project. Come on, Orlando." He tugged the dog's leash. Orlando snorted and twisted to his feet.

When they started down the hill, however, the dog planted his feet firmly and would not move. "Orlando, come," Tony said. "Come on, big guy, move." Orlando whined and pulled backward. "Orlando," Tony said, more sharply. "Orlando, come!" In response, the dog's whines were succeeded by a chain of high-pitched barks, almost yelps.

"Man," August said, "he does not like that thing."

"Apparently," Tony said.

"You want me to take him inside?"

"If you wouldn't mind," Tony said, passing him the end of the leash. "I'll go check out the round, squat turret."

"The what?"

"It's from a poem by Robert Browning, 'Childe Roland to the Dark Tower Came.'"

August nodded at the dog, who was straining toward the house. "Doesn't look like this Roland read it."

Tony laughed. "Just as well. Things don't turn out so well for the guy in the poem."

"Give me a minute and I'll come with you."

"Don't worry about it. I think Rebecca said she was making waffles. Get started and I'll join you in a minute."

"All right, Professor," August said. He watched his father start toward the prop, a heavyset, middle-aged man wearing white karate pants and a white T-shirt, his bald spot pinkly visible through the hair he kept long to conceal it. Unexpectedly, August's throat was tight, his eyes burning. *What the hell?* But before he could answer his own question, Orlando lunged in the direction of the back door, almost yanking him off his feet. "Okay, okay," he said to the dog, "we're going."

Inside the house, Orlando didn't wait for his leash to be unclipped; instead, toenails clacking on the tile floor, he scrambled through Tony's office to the kitchen. Dressed in a fuzzy purple robe and pink pajamas, her curly hair gathered in a bun, Rebecca, Tony's second wife, was whisking batter in a white ceramic bowl. Orlando danced around her. "Good morning, baby," she said, craning her head toward him. "What was all that barking about? Did you see a squirrel?" Orlando dropped at her feet. "Hi, August," she added.

"Good morning," he said, moving past her to the refrigerator, from whose top shelf he removed the orange juice.

"Where's your dad?"

"He went to check out something at the foot of the hill. Actually, that was what set Orlando going. Someone put up a building down there." August stepped to the other side of Rebecca and took a glass from the cupboard.

"A building?"

"It's for a movie. That's what Tony thinks." He placed the glass of orange juice on the kitchen table and returned the carton to the fridge. "He said one of your neighbors shoots his films on your property."

"Nate, yes." She nodded. "Last summer, he constructed a small castle in the meadow."

"Well, maybe he's making a sequel, because he built a tower this time—not much of one, really, just a single story. Tony called it a round, squat turret."

"That sounds like your father." Rebecca wiped the whisk off on the rim of the mixing bowl and placed it in the sink, then plugged in the waffle maker. "Ever the teacher."

"He said it was from a poem by Robert Browning."

"One of his favorite poets. He taught a special topics course on him a couple of years ago."

"Who's one of Dad's favorite poets?" Forster said. At ten, August's half brother had already left behind pajamas for gray sweatpants and a red Minecraft T-shirt.

"Robert Browning," August said.

"Oh." Forster went to the cupboard for a plastic cup.

"So how do you like police work?" Rebecca said. She opened the waffle maker and ladled batter into it.

August shrugged. "It's okay."

"You're keeping safe?"

"As much as I can."

"August," Rebecca said, "those kinds of statements do not fill me with confidence. I know Newark's a dangerous place; I want you to tell me you're being careful in it."

"Have you shot anybody?" Forster said.

"Forster!" Rebecca said.

"What?" He finished filling his cup with white grape juice. "I was only asking."

"My firearm has remained in its holster," August said. "Fortunately. Which is not to say there haven't been a few times I thought I might have to draw it."

"Really?"

Rebecca's frown stalled the anecdote forming on his lips. "Nah, not really."

"Awww," Forster said.

"I figure I'll stay in Newark for a few years, then see about going federal."

"The FBI?" Rebecca said.

"What's the FBI?" Forster said.

"Or the US Marshals," August said.

"*FBI* stands for 'Federal Bureau of Investigation,'" Rebecca said to Forster. "They're like the police, only, they work for the government in Washington, DC." To August, she said, "I imagine the benefits are great."

"Oh yeah," he said, "but you may have to move around a lot, which I'm not sure how I feel about. It's the same thing with the Marshals."

"You're young. You should see the country. Besides, it would give us the excuse to visit you wherever you're stationed. Is that what they say, *stationed*?"

"I think it's *assigned*."

"Right. So make sure you're assigned somewhere nice."

"Okay," August said. "Any requests?"

"I'm still lobbying for your father to take me to Hawaii," Rebecca said.

"Can you go to Wyoming?" Forster said.

"Wyoming?" August said. "What's in Wyoming?"

Forster shrugged. "I don't know. I just want to go to Wyoming."

"Fair enough," August said. "I'll see what I can do, buddy."

Forster smiled into his juice.

Throughout their conversation, as the smell of warm vanilla threaded the air, Orlando had remained at Rebecca's feet, his eyes lifted to her while she prepared breakfast, his tongue darting out to lick his lips and nose. All at once, he was up, his eyes on the back door, a growl rumbling his chest. Rebecca looked down at him and said, "What's—" but the rest of her question was drowned out by the barks that burst from the dog. These were not the anxious yelps Orlando had voiced earlier; these were deeper, louder, full of the same aggression that was evident in the dog's stance, legs squared, quivering; chest out; heavy head forward. He'd positioned himself between Rebecca and the back door, which, August saw, his father was pushing open. There was just enough time for him to register something different about Tony, something off, and then Orlando sprang from his position and in one snarling bound was on the man.

Rebecca and Forster screamed simultaneously, she, "Orlando! Tony!" he, "Dad!" She stepped toward the back door, which Tony had been forced most of the way out of by Orlando, who scrambled up him, tearing his clothes with his claws, snapping at his neck and face. August ducked in front of his stepmother, trying to work out how he was going to haul eighty pounds of pit bull off his father. Maybe the dog's collar . . .

His hand was almost at the blue band when he heard a pair of sharp cracks, like wet branches being snapped, and Orlando's snarls gave way to howls. Something was still growling—*Tony?* It wasn't the dog, whose wails continued as August's fingers hooked his collar. Before he could pull Orlando away from Tony, there was a tearing sound; the dog's cries were swallowed by a liquid choking, and Orlando flew against August with sufficient force to knock him off his feet. His head smacked tile. Stars flared in front of his eyes, dissipated in time for him to see his father leaping over him into the kitchen. Rebecca said, "Tony?" and screamed.

August rolled Orlando off him, noting as he did the splintered bones protruding from the dog's forelimbs, the great, bloody hole in Orlando's not-inconsiderable throat. Tony was standing with his back to him, bent forward, his arms out. Rebecca had retreated to the other side of the kitchen table, where she'd grabbed Forster from his chair and had pulled him against her. Her face was bloodless white, Forster's wide-eyed, tearful. "What happened to Dad?" Forster said. His mother answered with a groan.

Tony clearly heard the squeak of August's sneakers on the floor behind him but didn't turn fast enough to evade his son's tackle. The impact carried both men stumbling across the kitchen, Tony's right arm sweeping the waffle maker and bowl of batter into the sink. August caught the shoulders of his father's T-shirt and wrenched them to the left, steering Tony into the refrigerator with a crash. Tony rebounded into August, forcing his left hip into the kitchen table's nearest corner. Though dimmed by adrenaline, the pain was enough to loosen August's grip on his father, who twisted around, swinging his left hand in a sloppy backfist that scraped August's ear. Now that it was plainly in view, August saw that there was indeed something wrong with his father's features, beyond the blood and bits of flesh smeared around the mouth. It was as if he were looking at Tony's face in a smashed mirror, the particulars arranged in cubist angles. He was sufficiently startled not to track Tony's left hand coming back the other way for a punch to the jaw that jolted August's head. He released his hold on Tony entirely, striking his hip against the table a second time as he stepped back. *Who knew the old man could hit so hard?* For that matter, who knew he could rip out the throat of the family dog with his teeth?

August's hand trailed over the plate set out for him as Tony rushed at him. One of the good plates that Rebecca brought out whenever he visited, it shattered against Tony's head, driving him to August's right. August pivoted and snapped his right fist into Tony's solar plexus. With a hoarse gasp, Tony collapsed against the sink, his eyes bulging. August considered a follow-up chop to the neck, to the vagus nerve, but the combined plate to the head and shot to the midsection appeared to have quieted whatever had animated Tony. His legs had given out, and unable to prop himself up on the sink, he sagged to the floor. His face was still different—wrong—but August needed to call 911 before worrying over it.

Obviously, his father had suffered a psychotic break and required immediate medical attention. The cordless was in its cradle on the other side of the refrigerator. He lifted the phone with a hand suddenly trembling so violently the device almost slipped from his fingers. In an instant, the shaking spread to the rest of his body, accompanied by a combination of nausea and dizziness. He leaned against the fridge, closing his eyes to keep from vomiting at the bloody mess that was his father, the ruin of Orlando beyond him. The coppery stink of blood mixed with the vanilla odor of the waffles. From somewhere behind him—the bathroom, he guessed—he heard Forster murmur, Rebecca hush him. August swallowed, called out, "You guys okay?"

"We're all right," Rebecca answered. "Are you?"

"I'm okay," August said. "A little shaken up, but all right."

"Is Tony . . ." She let the remainder of the question hang.

"He's . . ." August glanced at his father, slumped at the base of the kitchen counter, his pants and T-shirt torn and soaked with blood, his chest heaving as he struggled to breathe. "I have to call 911," August said. "He's okay, but we have to get him some help. I want you guys to stay where you are for the moment."

"Did you kill my dad?" Forster's voice was high, frightened, full of tears waiting to spill.

"No," August said, "I just . . . subdued him. But he's okay, buddy, I promise. I'm going to phone for an ambulance, all right?"

"All right," Forster said. "What about Orlando?"

August grimaced. "I'm not sure. He's hurt pretty bad."

Forster wailed, his cries ringing on the bathroom's tiles. "Shhh," Rebecca said.

The 911 operator was brisk, efficient. There would be help at the house shortly, she said. August was reasonably certain he remembered a firehouse nearby; all that remained was for him to keep an eye on his father and offer what assistance he could to the EMTs when they arrived. He returned the phone to its cradle, thinking that the remainder of his visit was going to be radically different from what he had anticipated. Once Tony was on his way to the hospital, August would have to tend to Orlando's remains, carry the dog outside if he could, cover him if he could not, in either case, do what he could to ensure that Forster was not confronted with the sight of his dog's mutilated corpse. No doubt, Rebecca would want to be at whatever hospital accepted Tony, even if, as August suspected, his father was headed for a locked ward. He couldn't imagine she would want Forster with her, but neither could he picture her leaving his younger half brother here, amid the bloody wreck of Tony's rampage. Something else that would have to be seen to—

Faster than August would have predicted possible, Tony heaved himself onto his feet and ran for the back door. He was through it by the time August was halfway across the kitchen. *Son of a bitch.* The old man was full of surprises today, wasn't he?

At the threshold, at the top of the four stairs that led down to the back lawn, August paused, sweeping his gaze from side to side. If Tony still had his sights set on Rebecca and Forster, then he might feint, lead August outside while he circled to the front door and gained readmittance to the house that way. But no, there he was, racing down the hill behind the house, in the direction of the neighbor kid's prop. Had he been in uniform, standard procedure would have dictated August remain where he was until help arrived. He weighed doing so. Through the woods beyond the meadow at the foot of the hill, wasn't there another house? Hadn't Tony and Rebecca complained about its owners allowing their dog to roam off-leash, provoking Orlando? By the time the help August had requested appeared, Tony could be done with his neighbors and their wandering dog.

Cupping his hands around his mouth, he turned toward the kitchen. "Tony just ran out of here," he called. "I'm going after him. There's help on the way; someone should be here in a minute. Don't come out until they arrive."

Without waiting for an answer, he leapt down the stairs and sprinted after Tony.

His third week in the academy, one of August's instructors— Officer Bennett, a tall, sparse man in charge of the recruits' daily exercise—had delivered a speech about running. *The first time someone runs from you,* he had said, *and they will run, because they see you're new, or because they panic, or because they are, in fact, guilty of something—that first chase, you must catch them. If you do not, word will get around—word will fly around—that you can be outrun, and in short order, every time you approach anyone, they will take to their feet. You cannot permit that to happen.* August had taken the instructor's words to heart, adding a two-mile run—the last fifty yards of which he sprinted—to his daily workout. In the seven months since he had graduated the academy, the extra training had served him well: in fourteen foot chases, including one through the aisles of the enormous IKEA near Newark-Liberty, he had not been beaten once. Even with his father's head start—even with his hip throbbing from its collisions with the kitchen table—August had little doubt he would catch him, and quickly, at that.

Tony, however, proved to be fleeter of foot than August would have predicted of a man his age and with his physique. Already, his father was two-thirds of the way down the back hill, his apparent destination the short tower in the meadow. How was the old man doing it—any of it? The blows he'd taken should have kept him on the kitchen floor. Conceivably, he could have regained his feet, but for him to cover ground like an Olympic sprinter seemed beyond the realm of possibility. Yet there Tony was, drawing closer to the prop while August barreled downhill in pursuit. Whatever had broken in Tony's mind, it had opened reserves of fearsome strength. August thought of the tube of pepper spray clipped to his car keys, lying on top of the dresser in the guest room, and wished he'd brought it with him.

As Tony approached the tower, he veered left. Once beside it, he turned right and plunged into the structure. August slowed, waiting to see whether his father would come hurtling out of the prop the same way he'd gone into it, crash through the opposite side, or remain within. Tony had to know he was behind him, didn't he? How could he not?

While he was still a good ten yards from the tower, August circled right. From the top of the hill, the prop had appeared amateurish, if ambitious, a frame wrapped with heavy brown paper whose surface had been covered with hundreds of rectangles executed in black Magic Marker. Seen up close, the structure was considerably more substantial and impressive. It consisted of at least one layer of actual bricks, laid together with a neatness that suggested extensive workdays for something this size. The bricks were composed of reddish-brown material that gave the impression of incredible age, an effort August guessed might have been produced with the use of certain tools, which added to the amount of time it must have taken the neighbor kid—and his assistants, surely—to build it. How could Tony and Rebecca have missed it for so long? How could Forster have failed to notice it?

Coming around to the place where Tony had disappeared into it, August saw a narrow entrance in the brick. No doubt it was a consequence of the morning sun, which saturated the air with hazy brilliance, but the doorway to the tower appeared too dark, as if the kid had draped it with a thick black cloth. August walked all the way past the opening, but no matter what angle he surveyed it from, the aperture remained impenetrably dark. Had he not witnessed Tony passing through it, he would have been tempted to assume it was painted on. Tony was likely concealing himself to either side of the entrance, seeking to evade, and possibly ambush, August.

If his father was waiting for him to charge in after him, however, his wait was going to be a long one. Standard procedure in a situation such as this one, where Tony was safely contained—alone—within a building with a single doorway, was to remain outside and wait for backup, and that was exactly what August intended to do. Once properly equipped officers were on scene, August would apprise them of the situation and they could decide how best to proceed. He had not yet picked a spot at which to station himself when the screaming started.

It poured from the doorway, a single ragged note that extended long past the limits of what August would have judged possible. August jumped as the scream was succeeded by another, and another, the cries echoing on the tower's brick, lingering, so that each new scream overlapped the ones that had preceded it, strata of pain. He couldn't discern whether all the screams were Tony's. He recognized the tones of his father's voice in certain of the cries, but others sounded different, distinct. *Oh, Christ, is there someone else in there with him?* If there was, then SOP did a one-eighty and you entered the building in question immediately.

Of course there was something wrong with it, with all of it. The time span didn't work. From the construction of the tower in the first place, to Tony's abrupt and catastrophic psychic collapse, to his father's bringing a third party into the tower and hurting them sufficiently to drag the screams of the damned out of their throat, the last thirty minutes' events should have required much longer to happen. Tony and Rebecca should have been walking to the top of the hill to watch the neighbor kid build his tower for weeks on end, and Tony's mental break should have been forecast by warning signs for at least as long. (Shouldn't it? August was no expert in the psyche; that was his mother, and at the moment, he could not consult with her.) As for Tony's kidnapping someone and dragging them to the tower—that, too, should have been a lengthier process.

Unless this had been occurring for more time than August had realized. Perhaps his father had been sliding into madness for weeks, months. Tony could have put up the tower on his own, with the neighbor kid available as a convenient explanation. After the structure was done, he could have brought someone to it . . . no, none of that worked, either. Rebecca was on sabbatical this semester, making it difficult for the kinds of activities he was imagining Tony engaged in to have escaped notice.

Whatever explanation arranged the morning's details into coherence, it would have to wait. The screaming was now a chorus, blending its agonies. Although he had assumed Tony was lurking to one side or the other of the door, the screams called into question that assumption. Wherever the old man was waiting, August was going into the tower.

For a moment—an instant—as he was rushing across the threshold, August had the sensation of striking and passing through a liquid, as if the doorway framed a fall of black water. By the time he was reacting, clamping shut his mouth, attempting to conserve whatever air remained in his lungs, August was on the other side of the entrance, inside a room whose brick walls and dirt floor were bare, near the top of a flight of stairs that corkscrewed into the earth. A circular opening in the ceiling admitted sunlight into the space; none appeared to have followed him through the door. The knot of screaming wound up the stairs; August hurried down them.

There had been, he thought, a wellhead at the foot of the hill, in the tower's approximate position. During August's first visit here, Tony had pointed it out to him, a concrete tube a foot and a half high, three feet in diameter, with a lid that extended another couple of inches all the way around. There was a spring in that spot, Tony had said. The old guy who had owned the property before them had dug out the spot, gone down ten, fifteen feet, poured concrete walls to keep it from caving in. Once he was finished, he had a well for the garden he planted in the meadow, and for himself and his family, should they ever have need of it. Tony supposed it was a good resource, though it became a hazard during the winter, when a decent snowfall transformed the hill into a sledding course for Forster and his friends. He and Rebecca had not figured out what to do about the thing.

August felt reasonably sure that excavating the well further and installing a set of stairs would not have been among his stepmother's choices. Already, August had descended at least fifteen feet, the air dimming as he went. Where had Tony found, or stolen, the time for such a project? The stairway had been cut into the rock below the shallow topsoil, each step topped with a flat slab of stone. It was difficult to picture his father hefting slab after slab into place; although, was it any more extraordinary than Tony crippling and killing an angry eighty-pound pit bull with his bare hands and teeth?

But that wasn't the point: in truth, neither action made sense in relation to Tony, to the existence he and Rebecca and Forster had here. Yes, that was what the family members of criminals always said, wasn't it? Not my father/son/brother/whatever. This was more than the standard denial, though. The rock of the stairway's walls was smooth, polished as if with the passing of many hands over it, and not the rough surface of recent excavation. The screams below rang off it, almost seemed amplified by it. The air was dry to the point of parched, rather than the heavy damp of a well. All of it was more of the wrongness August had recognized outside the tower, a kind of warp to everything that he felt as a pressure behind his eyes, an ache in his molars.

The stairs ended in an archway cut in the rock. While the light had faded to a faint glow, August's vision had adjusted to it, which allowed him to distinguish the tunnel opening in front of him. From somewhere within the thicker darkness farther down the passage, Tony and whoever was with him continued their screams. August wasn't certain how long they'd been screaming—probably not as long as it seemed—but surely, his father and the other person or people should have screamed themselves hoarse by now.

Trying to move slowly enough for his eyes to grow accustomed to the steadily diminishing light, but quickly enough to reach Tony and his companions, August stepped through the archway and moved along the tunnel. In low light, peripheral vision picked up a lot of the slack: was it Tony who'd told him that? He thought so. It sounded like the kind of quasi-interesting fact with which his father had peppered their phone conversations during the middle stretch of August's adolescence, when he'd been angry at Tony all the time, for not staying married to August's mother, for agreeing to her having full custody of him, for staying in New York while he and his mother moved to Pennsylvania. Tony would deliver some nugget of information, and if August didn't snarl at him, his father was off and running, stretching that nugget into as much more conversation as he could manage. The tactic had served its purpose, which was to keep the two of them talking, and subsequently, August had proved an asset during trivia night at the bar he and a few of his fellow officers frequented.

And here was his peripheral vision kicking in, showing the walls to either side of him carved with a series of unfamiliar characters, each the size of his hand. Most of them were combinations of loops and swirls that wrapped around and doubled back on themselves, forming arabesques whose precise design defeated his passing glance. In their midst, however, he found a pair of simpler characters, a circle, broken at about nine o'clock, and a square whose interior was filled by a line that drew in toward its center in a series of right turns—a maze, he thought. Both the incomplete circle and the maze repeated at irregular intervals. With so little light, and his ears crowded with screaming, it was difficult to be sure, but the characters did not appear recent. He trailed his right hand over the wall; the edges of the figures were even with the surrounding rock.

August was losing track of the number of details for which he was unable to account. Could all of this, the stairs, the passageway, the carvings, have been here before Tony and Rebecca had bought the place? Had his father ever verified that what he'd been told was a well was, in fact, a well? Why would he have, though?

Ahead, the tunnel branched left, right, and straight on. Screams poured from each opening. August leaned in each direction, attempting to locate the source of Tony's cries. *Left?* He couldn't decide. *Pick one. Left.* He turned and started that way.

Almost immediately, the air was clouded with a stench that forced him back a step, coughing. He had smelled it previously, when he had assisted a raid on a drug house out near the airport. The three guys who ran the place had suspected one of their regular customers of being a criminal informant. The guy wasn't, but his general twitchiness had appeared to belie his protestations to that effect, with the end result that two of the dealers had tortured him to death with a pair of carving knives. Afterward, there had been great pools of blood, which one of the murderers had had the inspired idea of using a wet-vac to clean up. This had worked reasonably well, except that the men had not gotten around to emptying the blood, so when August and his fellow officers swarmed the house five days later, the wet-vac was sitting in a corner, full of something that swished suspiciously. That something, as the cops found out once one of them unclipped and removed the lid, was spoiled blood. Already, August had smelled some foul odors on the job, but this was especially vile, rotting meat mixed with copper. It was a point of pride with him that he had not vomited, but he alone knew what a close thing that had been.

That same smell hung around him now. The orange juice he'd drunk earlier boiled at the back of his throat. He swallowed, continuing forward. *Oh, Tony*, he thought, *what did you do?* Maybe it was an animal. *Please let it be an animal.*

It was not. Dressed in filthy rags, the man was lying on the opposite side of the modest chamber into which the tunnel emptied. From a small hole in the middle of the ceiling, a shaft of light stabbed the floor. August blinked at its brilliance. Ten feet away, the heat it threw off raised sweat from his skin. August circled to the right, keeping close to the room's brick walls. Undiminished, the screaming continued. The man in front of him had been the victim of incredible violence, his chest split open, ribs broken and pushed to the sides as if for some brutal anatomy lesson. The heart was missing, the object, presumably, of whoever had exposed it in the first place. At some point in that process, the assailant had splashed the man's blood on the walls, from which it had run down into puddles that had darkened and decayed. Estimating time of death was not part of August's job, but it was plain the man had been here for, at minimum, several days.

Which meant nothing good, as far as Tony was concerned. Not to mention Rebecca and Forster: how would they react to learning that the man they loved had committed such a savage murder? Sick at the prospect, August leaned against the wall to his right. The slight change in perspective this produced brought into focus the dead man's face, tilted up and back, the mouth open in a final cry, the eyes bulging, and August saw that the corpse sprawled at his feet was that of his father.

His heart kicked. Everything in him seemed to rise up, as if threatening to exit his body through the top of his head, then to drop, carrying him to the floor. His mind was a blank, all other thoughts blown to its margins by Tony's ravaged body. That blank, he understood a moment later, was a grief so immediate and profound it doubled him over, flooding his eyes with tears, forcing sobs from his lips. No matter that one part of his brain had resumed the this-doesn't-make-sense complaint (as the blood demonstrated, the man in front of him had been dead for days, at least; even if there were another explanation for that detail, August should have heard the sounds of his father's murder, despite the screaming that vibrated the air). Tony's corpse made all of that seem inconsequential, irrelevant.

August had wondered, upon occasion, what his response to the death of a family member would be. It was the catalyst in so many of the crime and police dramas he had watched growing up—the hero's wife or husband or mother or father is killed, often in a horrifying manner, and in response, the hero seeks out and has revenge upon those responsible. While it was possible that, later on, he would be overcome by the desire for vengeance, all August wanted right now was to remove his father's remains from this strange and terrible place. He wiped his eyes, his nose, used the wall to help himself to his feet. His legs wobbled. If he crouched, he could slide his hands under Tony's back to his armpits, hoist him up from behind and half carry, half drag him out that way. Not the most graceful method, but it would allow for the gaping wreck of Tony's chest.

The arm slipped around August's throat and was dragging him backward almost before he knew it. Strong—it was monstrously strong, its muscles tight against his neck as it squeezed. August didn't bother grabbing for the hand. His feet were still on the floor. He backpedaled hard and fast, going with the choke, overbalancing his attacker. His assailant's feet slipped and he went down, pulling August with him. August twisted as he fell, gripping his left hand with his right to brace the left elbow he drove into his attacker's ribs. He heard a grunt, another when he brought the elbow in a second time. His assailant's grip had slid, placing his right hand in easier reach. August seized it with both of his hands and twisted it off him, maintaining his hold on it as he scrambled to his feet, yanking the arm straight and torquing the wrist into a lock. His attacker cried out. August kicked him in the ribs he hoped were already broken. "Who are you?" he shouted. "Why did you kill my father?"

The man moaned.

August applied more pressure to the joint lock. "I will snap your goddamned wrist," he said.

"August," the man said.

"How do you know my name, huh? Did he"—he flicked his head toward Tony's body—"tell you before you cut out his fucking heart?"

"August," the man said.

"Do not say my name," August said. "Who are you? Why did you kill my father?"

"August," the man said, "it's me."

Though his voice was hoarse with pain, some note in the man's words caused August to stare at his face more intently. Both the man's long beard and ponytail were white, and his nose looked to have been broken at least once, but August recognized Tony looking up at him—albeit, a Tony from twenty, twenty-five years in the future. The room around him appeared to shimmer, but August retained his grip on the man's wrist. He stole a glance at the dead man. As surely as he could tell from where he was standing, it was Tony lying there. August looked at the man who had choked him. The resemblance was uncanny. "Who are you?" he said.

"It's me, Tony," the man said.

"Sorry," August said, "you're about two decades too old for the part. Try again." He pressed the man's wrist.

The man grimaced. Voice tight, he said, "The last big fight your mother and I had—the two of you had moved. I came down for the weekend to see if we couldn't work things out. We couldn't. She told me she was going ahead with the divorce. I accused her of lying to me, of leading me on. She was standing at one end of the dining room table. I was near the front door. You ran out of your bedroom, which was on the other side of the kitchen. How long you had been listening, I'm not sure. You were in your short pajamas. Your face was red; you were crying. You screamed at the two of us to stop it, which I guess we did. Afterward, I came to see you in your bedroom before I left. You were inconsolable. I kept telling you it was nothing to do with you, I just had to go, but you knew better. You knew everything had changed."

"Jesus." August released the man's hand, stepping away from him.

"I know." The man he could not yet think of as his father struggled to stand. Clothed in a loose gray shirt and black pants, the slight curve in his spine worse, he was thinner than August had ever known him, as thin as he'd been in some of the old photos he'd shown August. His eyes, though—his eyes were the same steel blue.

Rubbing his side where August's elbow and foot had found it, he said, "I've thought about how I would explain all of this to you if I had the chance. There was a quotation I was going to use, from Stevenson, *Dr. Jekyll and Mr. Hyde*: 'I hazard the guess that man will be ultimately known for a mere polity of multifarious, incongruous, and independent denizens.' It seemed perfectly applicable to me, but I wasn't sure if you'd agree on the relevance."

"Oh my God," August said, "it is you." His vision doubled, blurred; he swayed drunkenly. The screaming seemed to be happening inside his head as much as outside it.

Tony's hands were on his shoulders. "Hey," his father said, "hey." August's mouth opened, but there were too many questions, tripping over one another in their haste to be asked. "I understand," Tony said. "It's a lot to absorb. Nor is this the worst of it."

"I don't understand."

"Would you come with me so I can show you something?" Tony dropped his hands from August's shoulders.

"What?"

"It's better if you see it for yourself." Already, Tony was backing toward the doorway. "I'm not going to try to hurt you," he added. "I only did that as a, a . . . precaution. You'll have to forgive me. I've been down here a long time."

"You didn't recognize me?"

"It took me a moment," Tony said. "I'm sorry. Come this way." He spun on his heel and exited the room.

Staying in place was hardly an option. August followed Tony out of the room into darkness and cool, the short distance to the junction of the four passageways. There, Tony turned left. This tunnel sloped steeply down. Whatever faint remnant of the sun's glow had accompanied August's initial progress was long gone, despite which, he could discern the general details of the passage, whose walls bore the same weird graffiti he'd observed earlier. In fact, it was these markings—the Möbius characters, the broken ring, the maze—that were responsible for what illumination there was. They didn't glow; rather, so black were they that they caused the surrounding darkness to appear lighter, as if they were drawing it into themselves. The air was dry and full of screaming.

"Who is that?" he said.

"Who's what?"

"Doing all the screaming."

"Oh. That's me. And others."

On the right, the tunnel wall was interrupted by a succession of rough openings, each about five feet high by three wide. Tony stopped at the fourth and ducked into it. Mindful of his head, August went after him.

The space into which they emerged was more cave than proper room. Approximately circular, it was illuminated by a series of holes drilled in the center of its high ceiling, through which beams of phosphorous-white light slanted to the floor. The odor of dust mixed with that of rotten blood. The cave's circumference was studded with ledges and outcroppings, a dozen of which supported human bodies. As far as August could discern, every one of the figures was in the same condition as the one he'd discovered in the smaller room, the chest wrenched open, the heart taken.

Nor did the resemblance end there. "Come." Tony waved him to the right, where the nearest corpse lay prostrate. Were Tony not standing in front of him, he would have identified the man dead on the rock shelf as his father. Dressed in worn and bloodied karate pants and a torn white T-shirt, he appeared far closer in age to Tony as August had last seen him than did the white-haired figure watching for his reaction. August cleared his throat and said, "If I checked the other bodies in here, they'd all look like this one, wouldn't they? Like you."

"They would."

"You realize how fucked-up this is."

Tony frowned. "Language."

"Seriously?" In spite of the body broken and violated before him, of the ever-increasing horror of the entire situation, August laughed. "Since when did you become such a prude?"

"Since I spent twenty years in here," Tony said, flinging his hand to take in the cave and what lay beyond it, "in the tower."

"How is that possible?" August said. "How is any of this?"

His father leaned against the outcropping that held what appeared to be the corpse of his younger self. "This place, the tower, is a prison. Except it's also the prisoner. Never mind that part. The point is, it contains an extremely dangerous man. To be honest, *dangerous* doesn't begin to cover it. Nor does *man*, for that matter. The tower houses a monster, and I mean that in the most literal way. It was a man, once, a long, long time ago. Now he's more shadow than flesh, shadow and thirst. As long as he thirsts, he suffers terribly. Whenever he satisfies his thirst, he earns a respite from his pain."

"What's he so thirsty for?"

"Blood—human blood."

"You make him sound like a—"

"Like a vampire, yes."

"Fuck," August said. "No fucking way. I mean—just—fuck."

This time, Tony did not reproach his cursing. "After everything you've seen—after me . . ."

"Jesus, Dad," August said. "Why—ahh, shit." He could feel his lip quivering, his eyes growing moist.

"I'll take the 'Dad,'" Tony said.

The chorus of screaming went on. After a moment, August said, "You were saying."

"The . . . prisoner can't leave the tower, so he has to wait for someone like me to come blundering into it. Complicating matters for him, the tower doesn't remain in one place for any length of time. It shifts, changes location every few minutes. Based on what I've learned, I believe it moves through time as well as space. Though I may be mistaken. Regardless, what this means is, the prisoner's victims are few and far between. He has to find a way to . . . prolong each one. To this end, he employs a device. It resembles a full-length mirror, but its surface is black. The prisoner positions his victim in front of it, and the mirror splits part of them off. Not an arm or a leg, but a self. One of that multitude of selves Stevenson wrote of, a constituent of the aggregate that is each and every one of us. That new self serves the prisoner's immediate needs. Once he's . . . calmer, in better control of himself, he cuts more selves away and sets them loose inside the tower."

"What for?"

"To hunt them. It's a form of amusement for him. The original, the prisoner keeps alive for as long as he can, recapturing them when he needs to slice more selves away from them, until the person is little more than a husk. Unless, that is, a new victim wanders in, in which case, he drains the previous one immediately."

"Why?"

"What do you mean, why?"

"I mean, why not have a couple of food sources available?"

"I'm not certain, but I believe the prisoner is afraid they would find a way to overpower him, destroy him. He's powerful, but not all-powerful. Together, a dedicated pair of individuals might be able to accomplish what one could not."

"But what about the copies, the other selves the guy sends off into this place? Isn't he worried about them ganging up on him?"

"Have you encountered any of them yourself?"

"As a matter of fact, I have. That was what brought me here, actually. He got into the house and killed Orlando. He looked like he was going for Rebecca and Forster next, but I stopped him. He ran, and I chased him here."

"Orlando's dead?"

"Yeah."

"But your stepmom and little brother are okay?"

"Pretty freaked out, but they're all right."

"Poor Orlando!" Tony said. "He was such a sweet dog. Not a mean bone in his body, I swear."

"I don't know if it'll make you feel any better, but he was protecting Rebecca and Forster from you—your double."

"God, how awful for them."

"They're okay, really. What about the other selves?"

"Yes, yes. I'm sure you noticed that that version of me was somewhat less articulate."

"To put it mildly."

"That tends to be the result of the mirror's process. Occasionally, one is produced who's capable of coherent speech, but they're mad in a different way. In either case, the prisoner doesn't have anything to worry about from the mirror's children."

"Is this what your vampire does when he catches one of them?" August nodded at the corpse.

"No," his father said, "that was me."

"You did this?"

"I did all of this." Tony glanced at the room's grisly contents. Was the screaming louder in here, more concentrated?

"Jesus Christ."

"You know how savage the creatures are."

"I get that," August said. "Believe me. One of these guys jumps you, you have to do whatever's necessary. It's . . ." He waved his hand at the broken ribs fencing the chest cavity, the missing heart. "This seems a little premeditated, you know?"

"It was." Before August could respond, he said, "I'm trying to starve him."

"All right," August said. "I can understand that. Why remove the hearts, though? Does the vampire eat them?"

"No," Tony said, "I do."

"What?" August's stomach lurched. "What the fuck are you talking about?"

"I read about it. There's a library in the tower. I was looking for a way out of here, and I thought I might find information about it there. The books on its shelves . . . they're what you'd expect to find in a monster's keeping. They're full of . . . darkness. I found what I was looking for pretty quickly, but I kept reading. It had been so long since I had held an actual book in my hands, turned its pages, let my eyes take in its sentences, its paragraphs. Imagine having been without running water for a month, and then being able to sink into a hot bath. Or picture sitting down to a filet mignon after a year of stale crackers. I luxuriated in the act of reading. When the contents of the pages under my scrutiny became clear, I didn't credit them. Isn't that ridiculous? Eventually, I learned that there was something to them."

"You ate someone's heart because you read about it in a book?"

"Not someone's heart," Tony said, "*my* heart. My heart sectioned and sectioned again, grown coarse with the use. I've lost count of the number of times I've faced the black mirror, watched another piece of me step forth from its darkness. Frankly, I'm amazed there's any of me left. Consuming the heart was supposed to be a way of taking what I'd lost back into myself."

"Christ," August said. "You make it sound so reasonable."

"It isn't," Tony said, "not at all. It's insane and obscene. But so is the tower. And the prisoner."

"Has it worked?"

"I'm still here."

"You said you found a way to escape this place."

"I did. It took me some time to map out the directions to it, but I should be able to get us there fairly quickly. My God, August, how I've missed you. How I've missed all of you."

"I—"

"I know. It hasn't been that long for you. However, we need to start moving, or you're going to find out how much time it's possible to spend in here." Tony pushed himself off the ledge on which he'd been leaning and strode past August, toward the cave entrance.

With a last look at the carnage his father had wrought, August followed. Tony turned right. After the room's beams of light, the passageway was dim to the point of blackness. August fell into step beside Tony. "The tower," he said, "the prisoner: do you know where they come from?"

Tony nodded. "I do. I have to tell you, though, that none of this was what I planned to talk to you about. Were we to meet again, I had a list of things to say to you."

"Oh yeah?"

"Yes. We weren't going to spend our time on the origins of the tower and its occupant. We were going to discuss . . . important things."

"Well, it's a bit late for the sex talk, so you don't have to worry about that one."

"Very funny. I assumed your mother and stepfather saw to that."

"They did. There was a book."

"A book?"

"It was pretty horrifying."

"I'm sure it was."

"So. Why didn't you try to leave before this?"

Tony glanced away. "I was afraid to. What I told you about the black mirror—there's a reason the prisoner kills the first of its creations right away. He does it to intimidate his captive, which it absolutely does. Long before the books I read in the tower's library, I knew about vampires; I taught *Carmilla* and *Dracula*. I had a good idea how to destroy one. Yet there's a difference between theory and praxis, isn't there, especially when a monster is involved. Thus my plan for starving the prisoner until he became weak enough to risk confronting."

"All right. Well, what about the prisoner?"

"His name is Mundt," Tony said, "Edon Mundt. He's from a very old city that stood on the shores of a black ocean."

"You mean, like the Black Sea?"

"I mean an ocean whose water is black. It isn't anywhere on Earth; it's on another plane of existence . . . another dimension."

"But there are people there."

"More or less. Mundt was a member of the city watch, the police force. He was good at his job, excelled at it, in fact. His performance came to the attention of his superiors, and he was offered a position on the night watch. This was a group tasked with safeguarding the city's libraries and cemeteries. It was no ceremonial post. The books in the libraries were of the same nature as the ones I discovered here, while the cemeteries were full of all manner of strange things. Mundt accepted the offer and was made part of the night watch, a process that involved his transformation into a vampire. I'm not clear on all the details, but it involved his having to walk out into the dark. Not the night, or a dark room, but something like death, if death were a place. Mundt entered the dark, and this allowed the dark to enter him. There's a passage about a vampire in one of Byron's poems: '*And fire, unquenched, unquenchable, / Around, within, thy heart shall dwell; / Nor ear can hear nor tongue can tell / The tortures of that inward hell!*' From what I've been able to learn, that seems a fairly apt description of his state."

"Makes you wonder why he did it in the first place."

"Power. The price he paid bought Mundt enormous power."

On their left, a gap in the wall: the entrance to another tunnel. Tony took it. Carved from rock, this passage was shorter and curved to the left. Its walls were inscribed with the broken circle and the maze, set one after the other. The tunnel ended in a shallow cave, against whose back wall August distinguished a pale form slumped. At the sound of their approaching footsteps, the figure raised a head that was too long and said, "Help me." August slowed, but Tony caught his elbow and hustled him to the left, into the next passage. August cast a glance back at the white form but could not make out any details. "Who was that?"

"Not who," Tony said, "but what. I told you the tower jumps around in space and possibly time. Although a person doesn't always wander in, other things do. Animals, mostly, which helps anyone alive inside it to survive. Sometimes, other . . . creatures show up. That"—he gestured behind them—"is one of them."

"What does it do?"

"It hollowed out one of the mirror's children. Left him looking like an old, empty costume. I'm not sure how."

Shorter than the last, this tunnel's walls were also marked with the repeating maze and broken ring. It, too, curved counterclockwise, until it met bare rock face. August saw the passage on their left before Tony could guide him toward it. "You never told me what happened to the prisoner, to this Mundt guy. I mean, after he became a vampire."

"He committed a crime," Tony said. "I don't know what it was, but obviously, it was severe. The penalty was imprisonment in the tower, which was cast loose through the cosmos. The tower is . . . Mundt and the tower are connected, in the most fundamental of ways. Its contains all of him, all of his pain. It traps all the pain of his victims, too."

"The screaming."

"It's supposed to heighten his punishment, though I'm not certain how well it's worked."

"That sounds pretty harsh."

Tony shrugged. "He's a monster."

As had been the case with the previous tunnels, this one's walls were carved with the broken circle and maze, and bent left. "How is it that we can keep going this way without running into the other tunnels?" August said.

"The spatial relations in here are not always consistent," Tony said. "It's the same with the passing of time. Depending on your location, time runs more slowly or more quickly. You've been down here for what? An hour?"

"Roughly, yeah."

"Yet for anyone standing at the tower's door, I'd guess no more than two or three minutes have elapsed."

The passage ended in a narrow archway, through which a flight of stairs led up. Tony halted at its foot. The blended screams of Edon Mundt and his victims poured down it. "These," he said, "will take us to the tower's central chamber. Directly across from the top of the stairs, there is a doorway out of the tower. It has a black frame. That is our destination. The chances are excellent that Mundt will be somewhere in the room. As far as I know, he hasn't fed in some time. He should be weak enough for me to occupy while you make your escape."

"While I—what are you saying?"

"At the door, touch the frame with your right hand and concentrate on where you want to go."

"Where we want to go," August said. "You're coming with me."

"We'll see."

" 'We'll see'? What do you think I am, five? I am not leaving you here. I—I didn't realize how long I'd lost you. Shit, I didn't know you were missing to begin with."

"You know I love you, right?"

"Stop," August said. "Do not say that. You think I don't know what you're doing? That's the kind of shit you say when you're preparing for the big sacrifice. No. You are not doing that. No way."

Tony smiled. "Here we are, arguing again." With his left hand, he reached behind his back and withdrew a sizable knife from the waistband of his pants. "But we're wasting time."

"Where did you get that?" August said. The blade of the knife was a foot and a half long, grooved up the center; its handle was bone.

"One of the mirror's children. I'm not sure how he obtained it. There are still parts of the tower I haven't explored. It's possible it was in one of them."

"You know how to use it?"

"Did you think I killed my doubles with my bare hands?"

"I guess not. Lucky for me you didn't stab me before you knew who I was."

"I almost did," Tony said. "At the last minute, something stopped me."

"Well, that's reassuring."

"All right; we'd better get a move on."

Here, the walls were cut with a single character, the maze, repeated every few feet. The lines of the symbol shone, as if they opened to a blackness more total than August had known. He was overcome with the desire to speak to Tony, to tell him he loved him, too, he enjoyed their intermittent phone conversations, he no longer held his divorce from August's mom against him, all the platitudes brought shuffling to the fore by extremity. However, the words could not find their way out, because they were drowned by the almost-visible wave of fear that swept through the stairway and over him. The temperature might have dropped fifty degrees. His legs shook; goose bumps roughed his skin; the hair on the back of his neck stiffened. Worse, it was as if the cold had passed into him, freezing his heart, his gut, his balls. The screaming seemed to be his own, except his mouth would not open.

On the job, August had experienced moments of intense fear. His second month on duty, he'd been part of a three-man team that searched a condo in whose upstairs bedroom an old woman lay a week dead. The death had appeared natural—the woman was lying on her bed with no sign of violence done to her—but the next-door neighbor who'd called 911 in the first place claimed the old woman had taken in a young, mentally disturbed woman a few days prior to the neighbor's last contact with her. Sidearms in one hand, flashlights in the other, the smell of rot in their nostrils, August and his fellow officers had cleared the condo's surprisingly large first floor and basement. Although he feigned nonchalance later, when the residence had been found empty, during the actual process of opening doors to rooms and closets, he had been certain he could feel the madwoman in the house with them, waiting like a cliché from a horror film to leap out at them, butcher knife in hand. The air had seemed to vibrate around him, the way it does the instant after a loud noise.

Intense as it had been, the fear that had made the beam of his flashlight tremble had been generated from within, the sight of the old woman's cadaver merging with his memories of one too many slasher films. What halted his advance up the tower stairs was the polar opposite, a sensation that assaulted him entirely from without, as if this portion of the tower were subject to its own weather of the emotions. It was forty below and terrifying. He wanted to move in the worst way, to lift his foot onto the next step, but he was filled with dread that, were he to raise his leg, it would shake so badly that, when he tried to set it down, he would fall on his face, unable to rise, defenseless against whatever used these stairs, against the vampire.

"August."

He raised his eyes. Tony had stopped five steps ahead of him. "August," he said, "come on."

August tried to speak, to say he couldn't, he was too afraid, but his teeth chattered too much for him to say anything.

"Mundt," Tony said. "Your body is reacting to him."

August nodded, his head jerking as he did.

"It's a natural response," Tony said. "He's completely antithetical to everything in you. I'm sorry; I should have thought of this. If you can focus on something else, it helps. Do you know what I do? I remember all the poems I know, all those fusty Victorians I used to teach. Would you like me to recite one for you?"

Why the hell not? He nodded.

"*My first thought,*" Tony said, "*was, he lied in every word / That hoary cripple, with malicious eye / Askance to watching the working of his lie / On mine, and mouth scarce able to afford / Suppression of the glee, that purs'd and scor'd / Its edge, at one more victim gain'd thereby.*'"

The poem was longer than August had anticipated. Much of its beginning, he struggled to follow, the fear continually snapping his attention. From the way his father's voice rose and fell, flowed and ebbed, he had the sense he was overhearing someone talking to himself. As the poem progressed, so did his focus, until with a jolt, he heard Tony describe "*the round, squat turret, blind as the fool's heart, / Built of brown stone, without a counterpart / In the whole world.*'" For the remaining lines, all of his concentration was on his father's words. When the old man finished speaking, August said, "That's it?"

"That's it."

"But—"

"Can you move?"

He could, if poorly, his leg shuddering madly as he pushed up onto the next step. "Can you recite it again?"

"Of course. Let's try to keep climbing."

"*My first thought,*'" Tony began, and August raised his left leg. The speaker of the poem—some kind of knight, from what August could tell—left the road he'd been traveling to cross a gray field, bare of everything but weeds and scrub grass. On the stairway's surface, the images of the maze shimmered, as if full of black water. The knight encountered a starved horse, forded "*a sudden little river*" that was "*unexpected as a serpent.*" Above and beyond Tony, a doorway was visible. The knight came upon ground churned muddy by a savage fight, beheld an "*engine,*" a "*wheel, / Or brake, not wheel,*" a "*harrow fit to reel / Men's bodies out like silk.*" Faint light flickered within the doorway. At last, the knight arrived at the object of his quest, the "*round, squat turret.*" Two steps down from the doorway, Tony paused. He looked back at August.

"That's a terrible ending," August said.

"You aren't the first person to say so. How are you doing?"

"I'm managing. Thanks."

Tony pointed at the door. "Things are about to get worse."

"Great."

"I'd like to ask if you're ready, but there isn't much choice."

"It's okay."

"The door should be across from where we emerge. As I've said, though, the geography of this structure can be rather fluid, so if you don't see it where it's supposed to be, look around. Remember: it'll be the doorway with the black frame."

"What about Mundt?"

"Let me worry about him."

"You're going to take on a vampire."

"Remind me of your experience with the subject."

"What happened to all that overwhelming terror?"

"It hasn't gone anywhere, don't worry. But seeing you . . . I'd really like to see your stepmother and little brother again."

"A knife's going to be enough?"

"It's what they use to dispatch Dracula."

"I never read that book."

"Neither has Mundt. Don't worry—I picked up a couple of tidbits from the books in Mundt's library that should prove useful. Let's go."

The room into which they stepped was big as a banquet hall. A scattering of torches set shoulder high cast orange light over plain brick walls, leaving the vaulted ceiling in shadow. Opposite Tony and August, a door with a thick black border opened to a patch of green grass and sunlight, the meadow at the bottom of the back hill. Hope and relief surged through August. Despite his protests to the contrary, he had understood that Tony might not make it out of here with him. August had been trying to work out how he would get his father home should Edon Mundt appear, but the only solution that presented itself—shove the old man through and stay to deal with the monster himself—was not particularly inviting. Now, though, it appeared no such sacrifice would be necessary for either Tony or him. If only his legs would move faster, he would be on the other side of this chamber and out of this nightmare in no time.

They were less than halfway to the door when the voice breathed his father's name: *"Anthony."* It rustled around the room, a breeze rattling dead leaves, somewhere beneath the screaming. *"What have you brought me?"*

"Don't stop," Tony said.

"Don't worry."

"Is that little Augustus?" the voice continued. *"Your son? Your firstborn? You've brought him here to me?"*

The doorway was farther away than it had appeared. Or had the room grown larger? In the wavering torchlight, it was difficult to tell. One moment, the space was vast as a cathedral; the next, it contracted to the size of a large hall. It was as if he and Tony were inside a great heart made of brick and shadow. Each time the chamber expanded, August had the momentary impression he glimpsed something out of the corners of his eyes, something awful, but when he glanced in either direction, the room shrank, and all he saw was bare brick.

"The door," Tony said. "Keep your eyes on the door."

"*Of course,*" the voice said, "*you never really wanted him, did you? His mother's decision: wasn't that what you said? You couldn't stand that, could you? Couldn't accept the* unfairness *of it all, of her having so much control over you. So much power. You've never been able to forgive little Augustus for the way his mother used him against you, have you? Never been able to love him all the way, unconditionally. The way a father should. Not like his brother—Forster, isn't it? You wanted that child. Oh yes you did. And now you've brought me this one as what? Payment for your exit from my company?*"

"Mundt," Tony said, "shut the fuck up."

"Hey," August said, "what happened to 'language'?"

"You don't argue with the devil; he always wins."

"The two of you have spoken, though."

"I've been in here a long time. So has Mundt. Over the years, he proposed a number of . . . truces, I suppose you could call them. He'd had his fill of blood and was interested in other pursuits, in conversation. It was a while before I accepted his offer. Even then, I was fairly certain I was heading to my death."

"Why go, then?"

"Curiosity. A change from the monotony of worrying about evading capture by him and running into the mirror's children. The chance to learn something about my captor that might help me get the better of him."

"Uh-huh. So what's it like having dinner with a vampire?"

"Like sitting at the table with a cobra. I think I was even more afraid than I was when I first arrived here, when I watched him slash open my double's throat. Every time we met, I was aware that I was in the presence of a creature utterly lethal. He wears death like a waistcoat."

"Which didn't stop you from telling him all about me."

Tony paused. They had drawn nearer the doorway, though exactly how close they were was difficult to ascertain, as the distance kept telescoping out and in with the shifting light. "August," he said.

"It's fine," August said, pushing past him. "None of it's exactly a surprise."

"None of it's exactly true, either."

"*But true enough!*" the vampire said. "*And that's too true for comfort, isn't it, Augustus?*"

"Fuck off," August said.

The strip of grass visible through the doorway was fading. "What's happening?" August said.

"The tower's shifting," Tony said. "We don't have that far. Run."

Although his legs were not fully recovered from their paralysis on the stairs, August lurched forward. As he did, the air filled with the sound of flapping, as if a great flock of birds were taking wing. From all over the room, pieces of blackness loosened themselves from the surrounding shadow and darted to a point to his and Tony's left. They spiraled into a whirlwind that reached to the ceiling, then shrank and condensed into the form of a man. Dressed in black robes that eddied about him, Edon Mundt wore a mask shaped to resemble the head of an ebony bird with a long, cruel beak. Without hesitation, he strode toward August and Tony, his robes catching on shadows as he came. The torches flickered, dimmed.

"Almost there," Tony said.

The light flared, and August saw that the floor was crowded with corpses, with dozens of bodies torn asunder. August had the sense that they had always been there, he had simply been unable to see that he could see them. All of them were Tony. Here was his father with his throat torn out. Here was his father with belly opened, his intestines strewn about him. Here was his father with the top of his skull gone and its contents removed. Here was Tony's right arm.

Here was his blue eye staring. Here was a scattering of his fingers. Here was his father's mouth open again and again, as if the true source of the screaming that rang the air.

"August!" Tony shouted. "Keep moving."

August was almost at the door when Mundt slid in front of him with a sinuous motion that, yes, called to mind an enormous snake. August staggered to a halt, almost tipping forward into the vampire. "Augustus," Mundt said, as if they were old friends who had run into one another unexpectedly. This close, Mundt was unbelievably tall. His robes were bedecked with long feathers or scales that clacked and clashed as he moved; his mask was sewn of a leathery material that appeared to grow out of the exposed flesh of his cheeks and jaw. His teeth were not visible, but his breath was foul, as if his gums and tongue were diseased, rotten. His presence flooded August with despair immediate and total. How had he thought—how had he *dreamed* he could escape this creature? His father had compared Mundt to a cobra; August suddenly knew what a mouse must feel, watching the hood open, the jaws part, the tongue flick out, tasting the fear in the air.

"Go!" Tony shoved him to the right, away from Mundt. He could see the doorway in which the rectangle of sunlit grass had not faded completely from view. Tony uttered something he didn't understand, and white light burst in the room. Mundt shrieked, a pair of knives scraping together. His eyes dazzled, August stumbled in the direction of the exit.

"That will not save you," Mundt said.

"It wasn't supposed to," Tony said.

August stretched out his hand and touched the smooth wood of the door frame. *Concentrate on where you want to go*, Tony had said. He pictured the meadow, the hill sloping up from it, the yellow cape visible beyond the crest. "All right," he called, "I'm here. Dad! Come on!"

Tony repeated the strange syllable, and brightness scorched the air. "Go!" he shouted. "Go on! I'm right behind you!"

August stepped through the door, glancing back as he did. In the instant before he passed through the fall of black water, he watched his father drive his knife into the center of Mundt's form, twisting his body to give the blow all of his strength. At the same moment, Mundt's head surged forward, joining with and absorbing his mask, becoming a black scythe that he drove into the base of Tony's throat. Tony's blood hissed over Mundt's flesh.

August's cry accompanied him out the doorway's other side, into the meadow on whose grass he collapsed. He had not moved when the pair of sheriff's deputies charged down the hill a minute later. While one surveyed the meadow, the trees beyond, the other knelt beside August. "You're August?" the deputy said. "Your father— where's your father?"

He could no longer hear the tower. If he looked, he knew, he would not see it. "He isn't here," August said. "He's gone. My dad is gone."

—*For Fiona*

MOTHER

JOE McKINNEY

The cruiser fell in behind him as soon as he crossed the DeWitt County line.

Ed Drinker glanced at the cop car in his rearview mirror, then at the white envelope on the passenger seat, and prayed he wasn't about to make the worst mistake of his life.

He was passing through desolate country, thousands of acres of flat farmland stretching off to the horizon in every direction. They grew sweet potatoes down here, and the leaves were just taking on their color, carpeting the endless fields in green. He was alone out here with the cop. If he played this wrong, he was toast. The surrounding countryside was so huge, so vast and empty, nobody would ever hear a gunshot.

He continued on several miles until he saw an abandoned gas station up on the right. It was the first structure he'd seen in a long while.

Behind him, the police car's emergency lights came on.

The deputy blipped the siren.

Ed put on his blinker and pulled into the lot, driving around to the back.

The deputy who climbed out of the patrol car was tall and lanky and red as a boiled crawdad from the South Texas sun. Like every other small-town cop Ed had ever met, the man looked arrogant and imperious behind his sunglasses.

Ed rolled down the window as the man approached.

"I've got the money."

Deputy William Kohler didn't speak—just stood there watching him. Not knowing what else to do, Ed reached over to the passenger seat, retrieved the thick white envelope, and stuck it out the window for Kohler to take. Kohler opened it and fanned through the bills. Ed watched him count, the deputy's mouth moving silently as the numbers got bigger, and tried not to feel too bitter about the payoff. He'd scraped most of that money together after a recent visit to a used bookstore, during which Ed had offloaded nearly all of his reference library.

Twenty-five years of work.

"There's only twelve hundred here," Kohler said.

"That's all the money I could come up with." It wasn't a lie. Selling his library had only gotten him so much. The rest he'd taken out of the three-hundred-dollar travel budget the Patterson Cryptozoological Institute had given him.

And even that hadn't been enough.

Still, it'd be worth it if Kohler came through for him.

Ed held his breath.

"How soon will you have the rest?"

Ed allowed himself a glimmer of hope. They were negotiating, at least. "I get paid again on the first of the month."

"That's eight days away."

"That's the best I can do," Ed said. "Please."

Kohler put the money back in the envelope and tapped it on the magazine pouch on the front of his gun belt, evidently thinking it over.

Then he went back to his patrol car without another word.

Ed watched him in the rearview mirror. "Please, please," he muttered.

A moment later, Kohler came back carrying a thick accordion folder.

"Yes!" Ed said.

Kohler held out the accordion folder but pulled it back when Ed reached for it. "You better be good for the rest."

"I am," Ed said.

Kohler nodded, then turned to study the surrounding fields. "You know, what you need to do is get a TV show, like Marsh has. He came in here two days ago buying drinks for everybody at the Holiday Inn, promising to put everybody in his show. People love being on the TV."

"Tell me about it," Ed said under his breath.

"He's got everybody all fired up. I haven't seen folks this excited about the *chupacabra* since the last time you were in town."

"I bet."

"It's the cameras that does it, you ask me. Everybody thinks a little better of you if you been on the TV."

"I've been in documentaries," Ed said, all the while telling himself to please, please hold it together, don't draw this out more than necessary. But the slope got slippery pretty fast whenever he talked about Charles Marsh, and he couldn't help that.

"Yeah, but you ain't famous like Marsh is. He's the real deal. He's got his own TV show. You ever thought of doing that?"

There'd been a time, years ago, when the idea of buying off local cops would have turned Ed's stomach. But what other choice did he have, really? Charles Marsh, who had the financial backing of the Science Network, had used his clout to get a federal circuit judge to clamp a gag order on the local cops. That was his way. Once Marsh smelled blood in the water, he moved in and muscled everybody else out. It was a strategy that served him well. There was no way to fight an opponent like that, and as much as Ed hated to admit it, he was close to being beaten.

But he wasn't down for the count. Not yet anyway.

After all, they had five dead kids down here in DeWitt County, and if that wasn't a story tailor-made for the bestseller lists, he didn't know what was.

"I'm just calling it like I see it," Kohler said. "You get yourself on TV, like Marsh, and you could write your own ticket."

Ed glanced over at him, surprised that he'd let himself wander. It was the heat, he thought. It made him miserable. "Thanks for the tip," he said sullenly.

"No problem." Kohler handed him the case file. "Listen, I'll do you one better."

"Yeah?" Ed said. "How's that?" He steeled himself for the insult that was surely about to come.

"You know we got a lot of wetbacks down in the southern part of the county, right?"

Ed hadn't expected that. Insults to his professionalism were old hat these days. When you worked with cryptids, one learned to live with the occasional sneer from one's colleagues. But Ed's mother was Hispanic, Indio actually, and even though he'd inherited many of her features, like her short stature and her dark skin and her round, plump cheeks, racism wasn't something he'd had to deal with since he was a teenager. "Excuse me?" he said.

"Just what I said. Nobody ever talks to the wetbacks. You guys didn't talk to them the last time you was here, and I know Marsh ain't talked to them yet this time around neither. It's *their* kids getting murdered, is all I'm saying. Seems to me, if you really wanted to know what was going on, that'd be the place to start."

Despite his indignation, Ed was suddenly interested. "Are you sure Marsh hasn't talked to any of them yet?"

"Positive. Something to think about, if you ask me."

"Yeah," Ed said. "Yeah, I guess so."

Ed knelt down next to the bed in his motel room and pulled out the contents of the accordion file Deputy Kohler had sold him. Research had always been Ed's thing, what he did best, and combing through old books and autopsy reports and microfiche facsimiles of long-dead newspapers was like putting on a comfortable pair of shoes.

But twenty-five years of fieldwork had taught him that the best evidence came from the encounter itself, and in cases like this, that meant going to the crime scene photos.

So he pulled those out, thinking he'd make his own judgments first, before reading the opinions of detectives and pathologists, and immediately realized he'd been screwed.

There were only about sixty photographs in the file.

Any decent police investigation into the murder of a child, not to mention *five* children, should have included thousands of photographs.

Marsh, he thought. *Goddamn Charles Marsh.*

With that man, no amount of trickery was off the table. He'd probably paid the deputy to keep the really important pictures out of the file.

Except that that wouldn't be Marsh's style, would it?

Maybe Marsh had paid to make sure Ed saw only this specific information. It wouldn't be the first time he'd taken advantage of Ed's knowledge for his own ends. In fact, that had pretty much defined their relationship these past fifteen years, dating all the way back to the publication of Ed's first *New York Times* bestseller, *American Nightmares*, back in July 1996.

Marsh came out with his own debut bestseller two months later, *Vampires of America*, and as they were both publishing with Simon & Schuster, Ed thought nothing of it when Marsh came to him for help on a new book he was writing. The idea, Marsh explained, was to show how real-life professionals would handle a confirmed sighting of a cryptid—in the case of Marsh's next book, a lake monster.

Intrigued, Ed had answered all of Marsh's questions, the result totaling some eighty pages, almost twenty thousand words. Marsh had gushed with thanks and promised Ed would be properly and prominently recognized for his contribution.

And then the book came out.

Operation American Nessie got starred reviews from all the trade journals. It was an instant *New York Times* bestseller. Several actors and other celebrities, many of whom contributed little more than a two-sentence comment or a modest sidebar about their involvement in some ridiculous horror movie, were billed as featured contributors. Bestselling author Ed Drinker, meanwhile, whose total contribution came to about one-fourth of the book, was barely given credit. There were several ads that named a bunch of celebrities and then somewhere down near the bottom a single line that read, "and many other noted experts." That, and a mention in the acknowledgments section at the front of the book, was all the recognition Ed received for his trouble.

He was furious, and over the next year, at several conventions, Ed voiced his contempt for Charles Marsh. Never in public, of course, because that wasn't his style; just up in the con suite, where most of the attendees were drunk and supposedly off-duty. A friendly word of warning to colleagues here and there.

Still, word got back to Marsh.

A bitter and (if Ed was absolutely and ruthlessly honest with himself) one-sided feud developed between the men. Ed's books got more scholarly and less popular, while Charles Marsh, who could talk the shine off a new penny, got one lucrative publishing deal after another. Soon the man even made the jump to TV, and his show,

American Monsters, became one of the most popular reality adventures on cable.

The thing was, and this was what really galled Ed, Charles Marsh wasn't a two-bit hack. If he'd really been nothing more than a talking head, Ed might have been able to dismiss him, and maybe even gotten over the *Operation American Nessie* incident. But Charles Marsh could actually do some really solid work when he put his mind to it, and that royally pissed Ed off, because the man rarely did his own thinking anymore. He made his living off the research of others.

Still, Ed had these sixty photographs, and he'd paid dearly for them. They were a foot in the door, if nothing else, and that was all he'd ever needed. Charles Marsh be damned. He could make his own way from here.

He opened a beer and started flipping through the images.

The first series was of a young girl named Amanda Valdez, age eight, who was found in the weeds next to Farm-to-Market Road 474 with her skirt bunched up around her waist. She was on her back, her head obscured by some tall weeds. Looking at her skirt, Ed's first thought was that the girl had been sexually assaulted, and a sickening knot formed in his gut. But thankfully there was no mention of that in the autopsy report, and if he needed any more reassurance, the little girl's underwear was still on. That made looking at her autopsy photos a little easier, but not much. He took a deep breath, steadied himself, and went back to studying the scaly white skin on the girl's hips and thighs. A few of the close-ups made her skin look like the surface of a head of cauliflower.

There was identical patterning around the front of her neck.

The pictures of Amanda's six-year-old brother, Hector, who was found eighty feet away, facedown in two inches of ditch water, showed the same scaly patterning on the back of his neck and on his right wrist.

Ed had become something of an expert on sarcoptic mange the last time he was in Cuero, and the patterning on the kids looked an awful lot like the skin he'd seen on the alleged *chupacabra* specimen they'd shown him.

But this was not the same thing.

The mite that caused sarcoptic mange did so by burrowing under the skin and laying its eggs to hatch. They could be seen with the naked eye, so the fact that there was no mention of them in the autopsy report made it highly unlikely they were the culprits here.

Plus, it usually took weeks for that scaling to show up, and neither child had a history of scabies, the human version of mange.

The pathologist who had performed the autopsy wasn't able to explain the skin condition. She couldn't link it to cause of death, which was listed as cardiac arrest due to extreme dehydration, even though she indicated that such a connection was "extremely likely," as much of the fluid loss appeared to have traveled through the affected areas.

Ed put the photos down and drained the rest of his beer as he thought about the implications of that last part. Conspiracy theorists would have a field day with that. Proof, they'd say, of vampirism. The *chupacabra* was real!

Ed scoffed aloud at that and then forced himself to change gears. Suppose Marsh was responsible for limiting the contents of the police report. Suppose Marsh was allowing him to see only the parts of which he couldn't make sense. Ed could certainly see why his rival was stumped. Something usually popped out during these investigations, something obvious. The last time around, it had been the animal itself. Witnesses claimed it was a classic *chupacabra*, with short forelegs and long, lanky hind legs. What Ed had seen on the video, though, was a marginally misshapen animal that ran very much like every other dog he'd ever seen. And when he actually sat down to examine the half-rotted remains of the specimen a local rancher had shot three days before his arrival, he saw the obvious features of a coydog, the offspring of a male coyote and a female domestic dog. Such hybrids were rare, but they did happen, and when the scourge of sarcoptic mange was thrown into the mix, one got a creature very much like the legendary *chupacabra*.

And that was fine, within the original context.

Prior to his first visit to Cuero, local ranchers had reported several instances of slaughtered goats, all of which showed signs of a canid attack. That was the *chupacabra* MO. Attack goats, suck them dry. That was how they got their name, after all.

But not this time around. None of the five murdered children appeared to have been killed by anything like a dog. They had no open, tattered wounds, no bite marks, no obvious injuries like you'd expect from a dog attack.

Instead, they had cauliflower skin and massive fluid loss. The latter certainly offered a suggestion of vampirism, and the skin condition was scaly enough to call to mind the reptilian flesh of the *chupacabra*. Plus, all five children had been killed in the same general area where the poor mangy creature was spotted last time around.

Which, to Ed's mind, was more than enough to suggest an affirmative link between the dead children and the mythical *chupacabra*.

That's what Ed wanted to believe, anyway.

He was still thinking of the *chupacabra* when one of Amanda Valdez's autopsy pictures slid from the bed to the floor.

Ed reached down to retrieve it, and froze.

It showed the little girl's face, her eyes open and vacant and dead, and yet haunted with more pain than any eight-year-old should know. Her cheeks were sunken, her lips puckered and wrinkled and dark, like dried fruit. Ed swallowed hard and sat up, the picture staring at him from the floor. Something Deputy Kohler said came back to him.

Nobody ever talks to the wetbacks . . . It's their *kids getting murdered.*

Maybe, he thought, it was time he changed that.

Ed got in his Suburban early the next morning and headed down to the southern part of DeWitt County.

The last time he'd been down this way was in 2010. The people of Cuero had decorated every shop and pickup truck with cartoon drawings of something that looked like it had escaped from the set of a fifties-era creature feature. They had visions of the *chupacabra* doing for their town what the little green men and their spaceships had done for Roswell, New Mexico, and the whole county, it seemed, had turned out to hunt the thing down. Pickup trucks had lined the shoulders of the little dirt road for miles. Parking was impossible. Squads of men with shotguns and orange hunting vests turned out for the hunt, some from as far away as Tulsa, chewing tobacco and hurling curses like marine drill instructors; yet there was an air of fun to the gathering, everybody laughing and joking about what they were going to do when they finally caught the goatsucker. They even had news crews to cover the spectacle. It had been like a day at the fair.

But there was none of that spectacle now. There were no pickups, no cartoons, no news crews. Just a lot of flat, open ranch land and sweet potato crops stretching as far as the eye could see, the view broken only by a series of crosses next to the road.

Five of them, strung out over about a quarter of a mile.

He pulled over.

The first cross he came to was made of fence planks that had been painted white and fastened together with a great deal of care. A bouquet of black-eyed Susans and Indian paintbrushes rested at its base with a jumble of sweet potatoes and corn and a cooked rabbit carcass, perhaps three hours old. The ants hadn't even gotten to it yet. Colored plastic beads were strung over the bar. Nailed to the center of the cross was a picture of a little girl in a blue dress, maybe four years old. He hadn't seen her picture in the case file.

He glanced down the road, toward the old abandoned church that stood at the intersection of Farm-to-Market Roads 474 and 3008. In between, there were four more of the little crosses, each similarly decorated.

Five little lives cut savagely short.

When he'd headed out that morning he'd been so excited, so ready to make scientific history. But now, he felt uncomfortably sober. This wasn't a joyride he was on. This was bigger than his career. Bigger than his feud with Marsh. Bigger even than the quest for the truth that had propelled him for so many years. It was all about this little white cross, this one little life that had no voice. Maybe he could change that.

He got back in his Suburban, drove down to the intersection, and parked behind the old abandoned church. The tarpaper shacks where the five dead children had lived were across the road. He saw smoke rising from cooking fires and a few figures moving in between the houses, but more goats than people.

Ed crossed Farm-to-Market Road 3008, another dirt track that passed for a highway in these parts, and entered the little village of the murdered children.

He saw a girl of seven or eight, sitting on a black rock, surrounded by goats. She wore an ochre-colored blouse and a white skirt, and though she didn't smile when she saw Ed approach, he could see a jumble of white teeth, big as pebbles in her mouth. Ed tried to say hello, but before the girl could answer, an old woman darted out of a nearby shack and pulled her inside.

Alarmed by the sudden appearance of the woman, Ed stopped and looked around. There were many children standing there, watching him, but within seconds, cautious mothers and grandmothers were hustling them inside.

"Hey, asshole," a man said from behind him.

Ed turned.

A group of men were standing there, some of them armed with metal pipes, others with knives.

"What the fuck you want, man?" one of the men said. He was about twenty-five, dressed in jeans and a long-sleeved white T-shirt. His black hair was a thick mess, and the mustache on his face had yet to fill in, but he carried himself like the village tough guy. He pointed a knife at Ed. "What the fuck you want?"

Ed put his hands up. "My name is Ed Drinker," he said in Spanish. He patted the air between them. "Easy, please. Easy. I'm with the Patterson Cryptozoological Institute. I'm here to help you."

"You want to help, huh?"

"Yes. Please, I just want to ask you some ques—"

Before he could get the words out, somebody hit him in the back with something hard. Ed collapsed to the ground, dizzy, disoriented, and rolled over onto his side. A young woman was standing over him with a shovel.

"No, wait!" Ed said.

The woman raised the shovel over her head and slammed it back down, aiming for his head. At the last second, Ed shifted to his right, the shovel slapping the dirt where his face had just been. The ground was wavering beneath Ed's feet, but he still managed to stand. The men were closing in on him, and he felt rough hands grabbing his shirt, trying to throw him back to the ground.

"Get off me!" he shouted.

He twisted and turned, slapped at the hands groping about his face, and somehow found himself running toward the road, an angry crowd gathering behind him.

They closed on him just as he reached his Suburban.

He ran to the driver's side of the vehicle and stopped short. The back tire had been slashed and the Suburban looked to be kneeling in the dirt at the feet of the old church. He wheeled on the angry crowd, spit flying off his lips, his lungs burning, hands raised to defend himself. They circled around him, pipes and knives waving in the air, their faces twisted with rage and something deeper that Ed could recognize but not understand.

He had nothing left and he had come very close to begging for his life, when suddenly the crowd cowered and backed away.

Ed let go of the breath he'd been holding.

The villagers were retreating, but their attention wasn't on Ed anymore. Rather, they were focused on the train of three black Cadillac Escalades closing in on their position. The Escalades skidded to a stop and a horde of cameramen poured out. With the cameras pointed in their faces, the villagers shrank back, with only a few hazarding an angry glance backward as they retreated.

Ed, who had collapsed to his knees from exhaustion, found cameras crowding around him. He tried to shield his eyes from the blinding white lights, but it did little good. He saw a heavyset man in a blue guayabera shirt and white linen slacks step out of one of the Escalades and he knew Charles Marsh had set him up.

Marsh pushed his way through the cameramen and knelt at Ed's side. It was all very dramatic, all very obviously staged. Despite the heat of the morning, the fat man smelled of cologne.

"Goddamn lucky we came along when we did," he said, and of course the cameras were right there to capture the whole exchange. "Are you all right, Dr. Drinker?"

Ed looked up at him.

"They almost had you, didn't they?"

Ed just stared at him.

Marsh rose to his feet, turned, and addressed the cameras. "Well, that's the risk field investigators face. This could have gone really bad, but luckily we were here."

He turned back to Ed.

"Dr. Drinker, it looks like somebody has disabled your vehicle. If you want, we can give you a ride back to town."

Ed glanced back at his Suburban, and that was enough to clear his head. He had a spare in the back. He could make it out of here by himself, even if replacing the tire would cost more than he had to spend.

Which was exactly what Marsh wanted, wasn't it?

"You son of a bitch," Ed said.

Marsh shrugged. "Cut!" he said. He made several hand gestures to the cameramen surrounding him, motions that to Ed looked an awful lot like instructions to keep filming, and said: "Ed, seriously? Come on, man, this is good stuff. Think about it. All the dangers a field investigator has to go through, all the risks. It's solid gold."

"Fuck you, Charles," Ed said. "You did this, didn't you? You cut my tires."

"What? No, you're crazy. How could I have done that? We just showed up."

"You did! Goddamn you."

Marsh made a slicing gesture across his throat, and instantly the cameramen backed off.

"Ed, what are you doing?" Marsh said in a low voice. "This is good stuff here. Think of the publicity. Think of what this could do for your career."

"What? As the stooge you rescued? You set this up, you bastard."

Marsh backed away, not frightened, but looking sad, shaking his head as though in pity. It made Ed furious.

"I'm sorry," Marsh said. "I really am. But none of that's true. I'm sorry you're so upset, but I haven't done anything to hurt you. I'm trying to help you, if you let me."

Ed was so mad he couldn't even speak. He stared at the cameras ringed around him and he wanted to break something. Starting with Charles Marsh.

But he didn't dare. That would ruin him for sure.

Instead, he glanced down at his fists and forced them to open. It took a long time for the color to flood back into his white knuckles.

"I don't need your help," he said at last.

Marsh nodded, turned to his film crew, and motioned for them to return to their vehicles. "Load it up, boys! We're moving out." Then, when the cameras were gone, Marsh closed on Ed again. "So tell me," he said. "Why did you come here? What did you hope to learn from these people?"

"The truth," Ed said.

"What truth? What does that mean to you?"

For Ed, that was the tipping point, the one bit of proof he needed to bring everything into focus. Charles Marsh was lost. For all his money and connections, he had absolutely nothing to go on. Even now, with everything going his way and Ed's professional ruin in his hands, Charles Marsh was begging for Ed to give up the clue that had eluded him.

"It means you'll have to do your own work for once, Charles. I'm not giving you shit. Not ever again."

Marsh's expression turned cold. He glanced over his shoulder at his film crew packing up their vehicles. Then he turned back to Ed. "You're gonna regret this, Ed."

"We'll see."

And with that, Ed went to the back of his Suburban and pulled out the spare tire. He wedged the jack under the vehicle. It started to rain hard as he cranked the tire iron. He bent his head, his rage turning to frustration, but refused to let his frustration give way to sobbing. If some of Marsh's crew were still filming him—and it would be unlike them to miss an opportunity such as this—and they caught him wallowing in his own misery, he would never be able to hold his head up at a convention again.

Once the tire was changed, he closed the back door to his Suburban and thought for sure he was done here. He was in the process of climbing back into his Suburban when an old woman staggered out of the rain, a bucket in her hand. He put a hand over his eyes yet still had to squint against the downpour to see her. She made no attempt to shield her eyes though.

"You're wrong," she said in Spanish.

"About what?"

"About the children. About what happened to them."

Ed dropped his hand from his face. The water was running into his eyes, but he didn't notice. "What do you mean?"

"There is no *chupacabra*," she said. "There never was."

"I know that." He had to shout to hear his own voice over the pounding rain. "So who did kill those children?"

The woman put her bucket down and pointed up the road.

Ed glanced that way, but he couldn't see a thing through the heavy rain. "What am I supposed to be looking at?"

"You're the one who told them it wasn't a *chupacabra* the last time." It wasn't a question.

"That's right."

"Do you think that is the work of the *chupacabra*?"

"What?"

"Those crosses. Did a *chupacabra* do that?"

Ed shook his head. "No."

She nodded. "There's a woman that lives in the house down the road, that way. The dog you found last time was hers."

"Okay," he said. He had no idea what she was driving at. "Do you think she's responsible?"

The woman didn't answer. She picked up her bucket and made like she was going to walk off.

"Wait!" he said. "Please, wait."

He took a step toward her but slipped on the muddy ground.

"Please, wait," he said again. "Why are you telling me all this?"

She pointed down the road again. "Because you were the only one who stopped to look at the crosses."

And with that she was gone.

Ed remembered seeing a ranch house down the road from the old church, near the banks of Atascosa Creek. Nobody made mention of the house the last time he was down in this area several years ago, which didn't really surprise him. The townsfolk had been in high spirits back then, and despite all his claims to scientific integrity and the completeness of his investigations, he too had been so caught up in the excitement of possibly getting to study a real-life *chupacabra* that he'd failed to learn anything about the geography of the county. His attention had centered on dash-cam videos and interviewing ranchers and looking at rotting canine carcasses.

But he remembered that the rancher they'd brought Ed to see at the time had also lived along Atascosa Creek. A little farther north from where he was now, but still in the same area. Maybe the specimen that rancher had killed really did belong to the woman down the road. A loose dog, even one afflicted with mange, would have had no trouble straying a couple of miles. And the mange was known to dehydrate its victims, which would explain why the dog would stay close to the water. Ed didn't see how that connected the dog's owner to the five children who had been killed, but it was a better lead than anything else he had to go on.

He pulled out of the church parking lot and headed back up Farm-to-Market Road 474, toward the creek. The rain was still coming down pretty hard, but he could see the house well enough, and it was immense, even by the ranch-home standards of South Texas. It looked tumbledown though, almost like it was abandoned. There were no lights in the windows. The roof sagged at one corner, and parts of the porch railing that had once ringed the entire front of the massive one-story house were warped and broken. Others were missing altogether.

He was tempted to get out and explore but didn't relish the idea of slogging through knee-deep mud. Plus, this was Texas, and people in these parts hung signs in their yards that said things like THE SECOND AMENDMENT MAKES ALL THE OTHERS POSSIBLE and YOU CAN CALL 9-1-1, I'LL CALL .357.

The idea of getting a gun muzzle jammed into his ear appealed to Ed even less than wading through the mud, so he decided to head back to his motel. It'd give him a chance to clean up and unwind with a beer while he did some research online.

On the way, it looked for a time like the black pickup that had fallen in behind him on County Road 17 was following him, but it turned off as he entered town and Ed dismissed it as nerves.

And after the day he'd had, who could blame him?

His room was on the second floor of the Cuero Motor Lodge, all the way at the end of the parking lot.

The rain had slacked off a little, but it was still coming down, and so Ed walked to his room with his eyes on the ground as he fiddled with his keys, his mind still on the old woman he'd met in the churchyard.

He didn't notice his door was open until he reached it.

He froze. Somebody was rummaging around in there, and through the crack in the door he could see his room had been trashed.

"Hey!" he said, and pushed the door open.

His stuff was all over the floor. A man in a green T-shirt was standing by the bathroom door, his back to Ed. As he stepped into the room, Ed had just enough time to realize the man was wearing pressed jeans when a second person he hadn't seen blindsided him.

His attacker drove his shoulder into Ed's rib cage and smashed him into the wall, knocking the wind from him. Ed slumped to the floor, his vision a swirling mess, and came close to losing consciousness.

"Let's go!" the second man said. "Grab the computer and the file and let's go!"

The one who'd roughed him up was already out the door. Ed never got a look at him. But he recovered quickly enough to see the guy in the green shirt and pressed jeans scoop his laptop and the accordion file from the bed. As the man ran for the door, Ed lunged at him, throwing his arms around the thief's knees.

They both went down on the wet walkway outside the door. The man in the green shirt managed to hold on to the file, but Ed's laptop hit the ground with a nasty crack. The man kicked again and again, trying to plant his heel on Ed's chin. He missed Ed's face but managed to hit the nerve at the base of his neck, and once again Ed felt the fight drain out of him.

With his last bit of strength, Ed dropped a feeble hand on the top of the broken laptop and pulled it toward him. The man in the green shirt tried to wrest it away from him, but Ed started to yell for help, and the two assailants finally gave up and ran down the walkway toward the stairs.

With a groan, Ed pulled the laptop out of the rain and crawled back inside his room.

Ed pushed the clothes and bags of chips and newspapers off the bed and put his laptop there. It was gritty with mud. He wiped that away with part of the bedsheets and studied the computer. The left-side hinge was busted so that the monitor and keyboard wouldn't close correctly. He opened it as carefully as he could, but the plastic casing was broken, and he had to prop the monitor up against a pillow to keep it in place. The screen was spiderwebbed with cracks, and the space bar had popped out. He tried to snap it back into place, but it wouldn't fit. Ed tried typing a few words on the keyboard, but every time he hit the space bar it popped out of the housing.

Frustrated, he threw the long key across the room.

His side ached where the thief had kicked him, but the sudden sense of defeat and malaise that washed over him was worse.

He'd written eleven books on this machine.

Eleven fucking books.

Marsh, he thought. *You miserable goddamned bastard.*

Ed's whole professional life was in this laptop. He had nearly everything backed up to Dropbox, and he had duplicates on memory sticks scattered all over his office and his apartment and in the glove box of his Suburban, but the laptop itself was his life. He'd put more miles than he could count on that keyboard, and now it was just a piece of junk.

Ed leaned forward and took the laptop's cracked display in both hands.

His feelings of defeat and bootless frustration vanished. What was left of him, his recalcitrant pride, caught fire and turned to anger. *Marsh*, he thought, *you will not beat me. I won't let you.*

A peal of thunder shook Ed from his thoughts.

He turned toward the door. Marsh's goons had shattered the frame, and it wouldn't close right. Every time the wind blew, it yawned open. Ed stood up, careful of his aching ribs. It was getting dark outside, and at some point while he'd been lost in the Internet, the rain had stopped and a second wave had come in, threatening to roll over the little town of Cuero.

He went to the door and stood there, thinking about what he'd learned. The air smelled of wet asphalt and grass. He looked across the parking lot to the crumbling two-lane road that ran through the middle of town. Steam was rising from the roadway, even as a glowering sky the color of a fresh bruise rolled in from the south.

A flash of lightning made him jump.

He closed the door and faced his wrecked room.

Marsh, he thought. The bastard had tried so hard to break him. He'd put a gag order on the cops, and when that failed to keep information out of Ed's hands, he'd sabotaged his vehicle, robbed him, and even sent his goons to beat him up. But he hadn't won.

Not yet.

Ed took out his phone and dialed Deputy Kohler's number. He was pretty sure the deputy was in Marsh's pocket, but Ed required information he couldn't get anywhere else. He needed a local, and Kohler was the only one he could possibly turn to.

"You got a lot of nerve, calling me at work," Kohler said in a low whisper.

"I want to know everything you can tell me about Anna Aguillar de Medrano," Ed said.

"What?"

"You heard me. The woman who lives in the ranch house down by the crossroads. What's her story?"

"What makes you think I'm gonna tell you anything?"

"Two reasons," Ed said. "One, Charles Marsh has you bought and paid for—"

"Excuse me?" the deputy said, clearly angry. But that was okay. That was what Ed wanted.

"You heard me. Either Charles Marsh owns you, in which case you'll run to him with everything we're about to talk about—"

"Or?"

"Or, you're an honest cop who wants to know who killed those five little kids, in which case you'll tell me all you know about Anna Aguillar de Medrano."

There was a long pause before the deputy spoke. "What is it you want to know?"

That was a good question, because Ed didn't really know. He'd spent most of the day trying to work on his mangled laptop. He'd learned that the ruined ranch house he'd seen down on FM 474, and the three thousand acres of prime South Texas grassland that it sat on, was worth a mere eight hundred thousand dollars. Hardly the true value of a prime piece of real estate in the heart of ranching country.

The owner was listed as Pedro Medrano, who, according to an obituary Ed had found from September 2009, had been one of the leading advocates for Texas cattlemen up until his untimely death from a heart attack at the age of forty. He'd left everything—his house, his land, and his numerous business affairs—to his thirty-eight-year-old wife, Anna Aguillar de Medrano, whom Pedro had brought to Texas from Mexico, and who apparently knew absolutely nothing about running a ranch.

Within two years, Mrs. Medrano had sold off nearly five thousand head of prize-winning cattle, allowed her once-glorious home to descend into a tumbledown wreck, and all but resigned from society. If she was still alive—and Ed had no proof of that beyond what the old woman from the migrant worker village had told him—she had become a shut-in.

"Tell me what happened to her house," said Ed. "I checked the county tax assessor's website and it looks like it's only worth a fraction of what it should be."

"You've seen the place. It's a trash heap."

"Yeah, but even so, with that much land, it should be worth a fortune."

"It used to be," Kohler said. "Before her husband died."

"Heart attack. I read about that, too."

"That's right. You get that from the obituary?"

"Yeah."

"It left out the part about her being pregnant when he died, didn't it?"

That caught Ed by surprise. "She was pregnant?"

"Doña Anna has had it pretty rough these last few years."

"Doña Anna?"

"It's what we call her around here. It's a sign of respect. A woman like her, who's had the bad breaks she has, deserves a little consideration."

"What kind of bad breaks?"

"Health issues, mainly. She got sick after her husband died. Started losing weight, wasting away. You know how people can get when they're heartsick."

"Yeah," Ed said. "What about the baby?"

"Oh, well. She, uh, she lost the baby. It's buried on the property."

"What's that supposed to mean?"

"Just what I said. She lost the baby."

"No," Ed said. "The other part. You sounded like there was more to that story. What aren't you telling me?"

"Nothing but local gossip and superstition."

"That's where I live," said Ed. "Tell me."

"It's the wetbacks over in that little village down the road from her property, mainly. They're the ones who say it. Respectable people don't believe it, of course."

"Believe what?"

"Well, like I said, it's those wetbacks, mainly. But they say she carried that baby for four years before it finally came out stillborn."

"Four years? That's impossible."

"That's what I'm trying to tell you," Kohler said. "It's just ignorant people talking about stuff that ain't their business."

"But . . . how does a rumor like that get started? How come I didn't hear about it when I was here last year?"

"'Cuz it only happened about six months ago."

"You're joking."

"I told you. Nobody believes it. Nobody respectable anyway."

"But what's the story?" Ed asked.

"About six months ago, one of them wetbacks from the village come into town in one of Doña Anna's pickups and bought a headstone. Paid cash. He didn't make no secret it was for Doña Anna's dead baby. Said she'd delivered her baby stillborn and wanted to bury it on her land."

"I didn't see any reference to that. If she had a stillborn child, there should be records, right? A death certificate?"

"Well," Kohler said, and Ed could almost picture the man shrugging his shoulders, "nobody really bothers Doña Anna. We did pay her a visit, shortly after that, but she didn't answer when we knocked on the door and we didn't push it."

Ed let that sit for a moment, trying to take it all in.

"What about her dogs?" Ed finally asked.

"She used to raise champion Weimaraners. Back in the day."

"Does she still?"

"I don't think so." Kohler paused for a long moment. "Why do you want to know about Doña Anna anyway? 'Round here, we just leave her alone."

"I think it was one of her dogs I dissected last time I was here."

"No," Kohler said. "No, that ain't possible."

"I think it was."

"I thought you said it was some kind of dog-and-coyote hybrid with mange."

"It was. But the dog part of it . . . I think it was one of *her* dogs."

Kohler didn't say anything, and Ed could almost hear the wheels turning in the man's mind, like he was trying to figure out what to do with the information he'd just learned.

Ed didn't feel like waiting for him to come around.

"I'm going out there," he said. "Tonight."

"What for?"

"Answers," Ed said. "And you can tell that to whoever wants to know."

Ed didn't see anybody following him while driving out to the ranch, but that didn't surprise him. This was the big reveal. Ed could sense that. Whatever the answer to this riddle was, he was close. And Marsh knew it, too. He'd be careful. Hang back. Wait for Ed to do the dirty work before swooping in to claim the credit and the glory.

So Ed took his time.

He stopped in front of the Medrano home and waited for night-fall. Storms rolled in from the south, and soon it was raining hard again, but that didn't bother him. It would work against Marsh and his crew, and that was good for Ed.

What he wanted—what he needed—was some kind of link that connected Doña Anna to the murdered children. As it was, he had the word of an old woman whose name he didn't know, some local gossip, a dead dog-and-coyote hybrid with mange, and a lonely, heartbroken, middle-aged woman, but no real proof of anything. He couldn't even say the five dead children had been murdered. Ed required something tangible, some sort of affirmative link that tied it all together.

A through line.

Ed grabbed his flashlight and walked around the house, taking in its faded glory and slow collapse as he made his way to the back-yard.

Ed stopped when he saw the gravestone.

It was a white marble cross under a sprawling live oak. There were other crosses too, lashed together from oak twigs, huddled around the marble one.

The rain was beating down, but Ed didn't hurry. He walked to the white marble cross, knelt in front of it, and wiped the mud from it with his thumb. The inscription read:

Baby Girl
February 21, 2014

So that part was true, he thought.

Ed rose from the grave and studied the other crosses. Fresh earth. No grass on the mounds. None of the graves were marked, but from the sizes of the various mounds, he knew what they contained.

The poor woman had buried her dogs out here, next to her baby.

Some people treat their animals like humans. But this was the first time he'd ever seen them buried alongside a child. Crazy.

Then, from the house behind him, he heard the sound of a screen door slamming.

Ed backed under the live oak and watched the house. In the dark and through the rain, it was hard to make anything out. He could sense movement somewhere, but little else.

Then he saw her, Doña Anna, standing bare-ass naked at her back door. In a flash of lightning, he saw that she was almost bald. What little hair remained was hanging in clumps from her diseased scalp. There was something wrong with her arms. From the elbows down to her fingertips, they looked white and swollen, her hands thick like the meaty end of a baseball bat. Her breasts looked darker than the rest of her, and in the blue glow from another flash of lightning, he saw why. She'd drawn a ghastly, skeletal-looking face on each sagging breast. And as she walked out her back door and around the side of her house, her grotesquely swollen belly rocked from side to side. Ed watched her trek across the yard and gain the road. Even with the rain slashing at her face and naked body, she paused and scanned one way and then the other. Then she turned toward the crossroads, toward the little tarpaper village, and started walking into the night.

Ed followed after her.

Somebody, years ago, had tried to board up the church. There were still a few slats nailed across the windows, and there was one rotten two-by-four still holding on above the front door, but over time, teenagers and varmints and thieves had done their work. Ed had no trouble ducking through the doorway, and when the lightning flashed, he saw the nude woman kneeling at the altar at the far side of the abandoned church.

It was so dark he figured there was no way he could shoot video, but he didn't have any other choice. He took out his phone and started shooting, careful to stay in the shadows at the back of the church.

A familiar voice spoke behind him.

"You know what you're looking at, don't you?" Charles Marsh said.

Ed lowered his phone and turned around.

Marsh walked past him, a few feet into the darkened church, and stopped. He turned and smiled at Ed. "You know what she is, right?"

Ed shook his head.

"*Civatateo*. The mother of vampires."

"What?"

Ed's first thought was that Marsh had lost his mind. He was about to say as much when Marsh waved away his objection.

"Watch this," Marsh said, and gestured toward an unseen crewman somewhere in the dark. Instantly the whole church flooded with a glare from spotlights mounted on metal racks against the walls.

"Excuse me," Marsh announced. He cleared his throat and advanced on the kneeling woman. "Mrs. Medrano, my name is Charles Marsh. I host a television show called *American Monsters*. I'd like to ask you some questions, please."

Doña Anna shrank from the glare, one white, badly deformed hand coming up to shield her eyes.

"Why are you naked, Mrs. Medrano?"

She hissed at Marsh, her hand still covering her face.

"What can you tell me about the children who were killed out on the road?" Marsh went on. He walked as far as the first pew and stopped. His two cameramen kept moving into the space at the foot of the altar, flanking her. "Did you have anything to do with their deaths?"

"Leave me alone!"

"Not gonna happen, Mrs. Medrano. I want answers. What happened to those children?"

Then one of the cameramen got too close. He knelt down for a better angle, no doubt trying to make her look bigger than the stooped, scabby woman that she was. Doña Anna lunged for him, easily knocking him over. He fell on his back and the camera hit the floor.

"Hey!" Marsh yelled. "Careful there. That's expensive equipment."

But Doña Anna ignored him. She climbed on top of the fallen cameraman, straddling him like a lover, and wrapped her hands around his throat.

The man tried to push her away, but before he could, his head was wrapped in a moving, buzzing haze. He made a startled sound somewhere between shock and pain. He began to buck and writhe, trying to get out from under the woman, but couldn't dismount her.

Ed lowered his phone. The light from the camera was hitting the pair as they wrestled on the floor. In the blue-white glare of the spotlight, the haze that had enveloped the man's head took shape.

Ed was frozen in disgust and horror. He stood there, his phone at his side, forgotten but still recording, as tens of thousands of specks floated around the man's face. A memory from his time in the army rose up, unbidden. He'd seen a few men sleeping in their bunks once, swarmed by a similar haze.

Those are mites, he thought. *Oh Jesus, she's got scabies.*

The man's torture seemed to go on forever, but eventually Doña Anna's victim stopped struggling. In a grotesque moment of defeat and acceptance, his hands fell away from her wrists. His legs twitched like those of a man dangling from the end of a rope and then went still.

Ed had just enough time to realize the man was wearing pressed jeans when Marsh let out a yell. "Help him!" he roared to the other cameraman. "Do something!"

The crewman looked like he couldn't figure out what to do. Finally he put his camera down and ran over to Doña Anna, grabbing her by the shoulders.

Without getting up from her first kill, she half turned and threw an arm around the second crewman's right shoulder. The haze of mites enveloped the man so quickly he barely had time to yell out.

Within seconds he dropped to his knees, his expression twisted with shock and pain. Then he fell over on his side and began to convulse, just as his partner had done.

"Stop it!" Marsh yelled.

Doña Anna turned in Marsh's direction, then slowly rose to her feet. The haze of mites that had enveloped the two fallen men seemed to shrink back into her hands, and she walked toward Marsh, her hands coming up, groping at the air for his throat.

"No," Marsh said. "You get away from me."

He backed up, stepped on a pile of loose debris, staggered, and nearly fell.

"Stay back!"

Marsh glanced over his shoulder at Ed, and in that moment, Ed saw unadulterated fear in his old rival's face.

Doña Anna let out a scream and sprinted for Marsh. He turned to run, but his foot caught on something on the floor and he went sprawling facedown in the center aisle. She fell on Marsh, straddling his back just as she had done to the cameraman's stomach, and locked her hands around the back of his throat.

"Help me!" Marsh screamed. "Drinker, please, help me!"

Ed didn't move. He stood there in the shadows, watching the mites float around Marsh's head. The man's hair dropped off, and as Ed watched, Marsh's skin turned white and knobby and puckered.

Inspiration came to Ed at that moment. The little girls who had fallen victim to Doña Anna had the same chalky white skin around their groins and around their necks, and now Ed understood why. When Doña Anna fell on them, straddled them the way she'd done with Marsh's cameramen, her legs must have pushed their dresses up around their hips. The mites would have swarmed wherever there was skin-to-skin contact, which would explain the chalky rings around the neck as well. It would also explain why the only little boy to fall victim to Doña Anna didn't have that chalky skin around his groin. His jeans would have protected him from that.

But even as his mind worked through the mechanics of her kills, he thought of what Marsh had said.

Civatateo. The mother of vampires.

The Aztecs, Ed remembered, bestowed warrior status on pregnant women. There was no higher honor for a woman in Aztec culture. But it was a double-edged sword, for with the glory of warrior status came the crucible of death. The women who died in childbirth were said to come back as servants of the goddess Tlazolteotl, the filth eater, goddess of the moon and of human sexuality. Those servants, those *civatateo*, were said to haunt the crossroads. They preyed upon children, perhaps to replace the ones they'd lost, and could use their power to seduce men and lead them to their doom.

Ed had seen pictures of hieroglyphs from Aztec temples, and he'd seen the fanciful renditions of modern artists, but it had never occurred to him that such a thing could really be. For as much as he wanted to believe, his fate in life had become that of the professional debunker, and that change had hardened him to the faith that had once sustained him. He had stopped believing.

Ed's gaze wandered across the floor, settling at last upon the death mask of fear and pain still lingering on the face of Charles Marsh's corpse.

Marsh had seen the truth first, Ed realized. For all the man's many sins, for all his arrogance and thievery, he'd gotten to the right answer long before Ed had. And it was Marsh, his old rival, who had been the one to pull back the curtain and show him the truth. Ed didn't know how to process that.

A rotten board made a muffled crack somewhere across the room.

Ed looked up sharply and saw Anna Medrano coming for him.

All his strength left him in that moment. Her tattooed breasts rocked on her enormous, swollen gut. Her hands, swarming with mites, clutched at the air between them. It hadn't seemed real until that very moment, but looking into her black eyes, Ed realized he wasn't seeing Anna Medrano. He was looking at the *civatateo*, the mother of vampires.

He felt stricken, powerless to move. It was like his feet were rooted to the floor.

I'm about to die, he thought.

He didn't dare look at her face. He stayed perfectly still, certain that if he did try to run, he would be dead for sure.

"Drop your phone on the floor," Doña Anna said.

Ed closed his eyes. He could hear the air between them crackling like waxed paper. The hairs on his arms stood up as he imagined thousands of mites crawling over his skin, burrowing beneath the surface, draining him.

"Drop your phone," she said again.

Ed tossed it to the ground at her feet.

"There's a piece of brick on that pew next to you. Smash the phone."

In a numb daze, Ed picked up the brick fragment, knelt at Doña Anna's feet, and smashed the smartphone. He didn't get up. He thought of swinging the brick at her head. One swift lunge would do it. But he knew even as the thought went through his head that to do so would be suicide. All she needed was a moment. Any contact at all would be enough for the mites to do their work on him, to drain him dry. And if she was truly a *civatateo*, she would have no trouble catching him.

Off in the distance, a police siren wailed.

Ed glanced over at Doña Anna's feet. They were caked with mud. Her toenails had to be four inches long, curled and gnarled. She took a few steps toward the altar, leaving a trail of footprints, and knelt down next to one of the cameras. She examined the many buttons and knobs, then in one swift motion hurled it against the altar. The camera shattered into a thousand pieces.

Outside, the siren grew closer, and Ed realized with a strange sort of detached objectivity that it must have stopped raining. He could no longer hear it pounding on the church's roof.

Then the muddy feet were standing next to him again. He didn't look up.

"Don't come looking for me again," she said.

The sirens were piercing now, right outside. Ed heard car doors open and slam, and the sound of men yelling at each other.

Doña Anna walked toward the altar. The breath hitched in Ed's throat as he finally found the strength to lift his gaze.

The woman was gone.

He crawled on his hands and knees toward the facedown corpse of Charles Marsh. He grabbed the body by the shoulder and rolled him over onto his back.

Nearly two decades, he thought. *I've chased this man for nearly two decades. And now it's come to this.*

From somewhere behind him, voices shouted into the church, calling Marsh's name.

Over the years, Ed had filled his heart with jealousy and hatred for this man. Now Ed had finally won. He had no proof, of course. All of that was gone, erased from the cameras or smashed to bits on the floor. But he had this brief moment of victory.

And yet it held no flavor for him. It only filled him with emptiness.

From somewhere behind him, Deputy Kohler shouted Charles Marsh's name.

"He's over here," Ed said.

He heard boots pounding on the floor and men fanning out around him. He glanced up and winced at the flashlight beams in his face. Everywhere he looked, there was a gun pointed in his direction.

"I've got two down over here," somebody said.

Somebody grabbed Ed and threw him facedown on the ground. They pulled his arms behind his back and he felt the cuffs bite into his wrists.

"What did you do?!" Kohler screamed at him. "What the hell did you do?!"

But Ed didn't answer. He'd turned his head toward Charles Marsh's body and found himself staring into the dead man's still-open eyes. Little Amanda Valdez's face had looked much the same in her autopsy pictures, her eyes just as empty, her cheeks just as sunken and puckered.

It was funny how things had a way of coming full circle. Ed had searched for answers, for fame, and yet when it came right down to it, he'd been unable to look above the *civatateo*'s muddy feet. He thought about her cracked nails and her cauliflowered skin and wondered if he'd ever be able to drive that image from his mind.

Somehow, he didn't think so.

BLOOD

ROBERT SHEARMAN

In the morning, Donald and Chrissie would go down to the breakfast room, and there they'd have croissants. Donald would have his croissants with *confiture* and with *beurre*. He liked saying *confiture* and *beurre*, he liked exaggerating the accent, he especially liked rolling the Rs in the *beurre*. Chrissie told him that if he wanted to look French he should eat his croissants plain, that was the proper way to do it, and Donald noticed how disapproving the waitress was when he hacked away at his croissants touristlike with his knife fair bleeding jam. But then, as Donald thought privately, maybe you could get away with eating *good* croissants plain, but these croissants weren't very good. The hotel itself wasn't very good. It was small, and it was discreet, and that was enough.

There'd be cold meats too, threadbare slices of ham and salami, and Donald would eat these as well. Chrissie stuck to her croissants; she was a vegetarian. She said she didn't mind Donald's eating meat, and that was one of the reasons he liked her—she was so sweet and forgave him all his flaws. So long as he brushed his teeth before he kissed her, just in case any scraps of dead animal were sticking to them.

And after breakfast, the happy couple would set out and explore

Paris. They had done all the popular tourist sites, and there was nothing wrong with that; no doubt they were popular for a reason. They went up the Eiffel Tower. They walked down the Champs-Élysées. At Montmartre, Donald paid twenty euros so that an artist could draw a sketch of Chrissie, and Chrissie was delighted, and flung her arms around Donald nice and tight, and she told him that she loved him very much.

She told him she loved him quite often, and he was always pleased to hear it, but he sometimes thought the words came out a little too easily. Still, it was probably nothing to worry about.

Of an evening, they would stroll hand in hand by the bank of the Seine, no matter that it was quite a hike from their hotel, no matter that it was usually raining. They looked up in the sky, right up at the moon, and pretended it was a different moon from the one they had back at home.

"I love the Paris moon," said Chrissie.

"Me too," he said.

He told her he loved her quite often as well, and each time he said it he felt a little giddy, and he had to force it out, as if it were a confession.

Chrissie was the one who said they shouldn't go back to England. She said it on the fourth morning, just before they went downstairs for the croissants. They'd just stay here, together, forever. And Donald had already had the same idea. He'd had it a week ago. He'd had it when he'd locked the front door to his flat in Chiswick, when he'd got the taxi to the airport—he'd kept on expecting that someone might stop him—he'd kept expecting he would stop *himself*—he'd thought, *Everything's going to change, I may never be able to go home again*. He hadn't told Chrissie because he hadn't wanted to scare her. He never wanted her to be scared, he just wanted to protect her, always, always. Through the entire flight he'd been shaking and he'd had to pretend it was excitement.

"Do you mean it?" said Donald. "Do you really want to stay here?" And Chrissie said yes, didn't she? As if it were the simplest thing. She asked whether he had enough money to support them, and he told her not to worry, but the same thought had been nagging away at him ever since they'd arrived in Paris. They wouldn't be able to afford to stay in a hotel for long, not even a budget hotel like this. They could get a cottage somewhere, maybe in the countryside, that would be cheap—he'd have to get a job, and so would she—maybe they could be farmers!—maybe they could keep chickens and grow their own food and things!—maybe they wouldn't need money! Maybe, maybe.

And yet that day they'd flown off together, he'd doubted she'd even be at the airport waiting for him. But no, there she was, looking so very happy, and so very different without her uniform, and she was happy because of *him*, and she was waving her passport, she was running right up to him and giving him a big kiss. "Not until we're in France," said Donald, really rather sternly, and Chrissie had said sorry—then she'd beamed at him, "Do you like my new suitcase? I bought it specially!" and she showed him some pretty little pink thing on wheels.

In Paris she had blossomed. She was the one who did most of the talking. She was the one, after all, who was studying French. She'd order for them in restaurants and wine bars, she'd be the one who'd make pleasantries with the locals. She gave him helpful phrases he could try out for himself, and he'd practice them at museums and souvenir shops, and she'd laugh. "I'm the teacher now!" she'd say. "I like being the teacher." She said it rather a lot, and it hadn't stopped being charming yet.

Charming, too, was the way she kept on using their false names. "Come on, Monsieur MacAllister," she'd say, and take his hand to pull him along the Paris streets, or, "I'm hungry, Monsieur MacAllister," when she wanted to stop for lunch, or, "Are you happy, Monsieur MacAllister?" when she caught him looking a bit too thoughtful. They'd given their false names to the receptionist when they'd checked into the hotel; Donald had wondered whether they should have chosen something more French sounding, but Chrissie didn't think he could pull that off. She was Mademoiselle MacAllister, just mademoiselle—Donald had been prepared to call her madame, but the receptionist had automatically assumed she was his daughter, and perhaps it was better left like that. They ordered a double bed. The receptionist didn't care.

Donald slept on the left, because he liked sleeping on the left. Chrissie slept on the right, and didn't mind. And they lay side by side, and they held hands, and they kissed. They didn't have sex. Donald said he didn't think they should have sex until she was sixteen, then everything would be proper and aboveboard. She said that was fine. She had looked a little disappointed—or maybe she hadn't, it was hard for him to tell, and he wasn't sure whether he wanted her to be disappointed; he supposed he wanted her to be disappointed just a bit. Getting the sex issue cleared up was a weight off his mind; he felt guiltless, as light as air, what they were doing was perfectly innocent. When she kissed him she flicked her tongue across his teeth, and he liked that, he liked the courage she showed too—he wanted to say, Don't you know I could just bite it off?—but he didn't, she might think it odd. They both got undressed separately in the bathroom with the door shut, so he hadn't seen her naked yet, but he could feel that nakedness so close in the dark, it was all lurking just beneath her pajamas. He wore pajamas too. His pajamas were the pale blue ones he'd worn for years, they were nice nondescript pajamas. Chrissie's pajamas were covered with pictures of Disney characters, and that made Donald feel uncomfortable, and each night he vowed he'd buy her a new pair the next day, and he never did.

So, no sex, but the kisses were good, and Donald thought in time he might get better at them, maybe once he relaxed a little. Sometimes they'd kiss a bit in the morning when they awoke, and Donald would say they could just stay in bed and carry on kissing all morning and not bother with breakfast after all. But then Chrissie would say she needed a coffee and up they'd get.

Chrissie drank a lot of coffee, and smoked a few cigarettes, and said she didn't do much of either in England but it was all right now she was on holiday. All the girls in France drank coffee and smoked, she was just fitting in. She would laugh and ask what was he going to do, put her in detention? Donald supposed he ought to mind, but it made her look a little older and gave more flavor to the kisses.

"Let's just stay here," she said. "Let's never go back to England!" And it sounded like a joke, the sort of thing people on holiday always say to each other, but he took her at her word.

That evening it was the first time it didn't rain, and they walked farther along the Seine than they'd managed before, and Donald got quite caught in the emotion of it, and they kissed in public for the first time. On the way back to the hotel he looked in the kiosk for the British newspapers, and there still weren't pictures of him on the front pages.

They went back to bed, and cuddled, and Donald worried that his erection was poking Chrissie too hard in the back, but she didn't say anything, and maybe she hadn't even noticed.

He woke up, and she was gone. And he knew she was gone for good, and it was properly this time, not like on Tuesday when she'd popped down to the lobby for a cigarette. There was no note, not a thing, and he wasn't ever going to see her again—not unless, he supposed, he saw her in court, because that's where she'd gone, she'd gone to the police, she was with them right now, but would he even see her in court, maybe they'd protect her from the whole court experience because she was a minor? Yes, he was pretty sure her statement would be enough. And he knew that if he opened the wardrobe, he could see whether her clothes were still there, as well as that little pink suitcase—or look in the bedside drawer, he wouldn't even need to get out of bed, just roll over and open the drawer and find out if she'd taken her passport. No. No. He didn't want to look. He didn't have to look. Not yet. He didn't want to spoil the moment. Because there was a part of him that was pleased she was gone. That it was all over. That it was over at last, because it had to end at some point, why not now, and if now it meant the suspense was over, good, he could be happy. He was happy. He was happy. He stretched out wide beneath the sheets; the bed was all his.

"Where have you been? Where have you bloody been?" He was embarrassed to realize he was shouting at her, and that he was crying too, and she just stood there in the doorway, that little mouth an O of childish surprise. She came to him. She tried to give him a hug. He pushed her away sulkily, though a hug was what he wanted most in the world.

"Please," she said. "It's all right. It's a treat. I got us breakfast. Breakfast in bed, it's a treat." He was still crying, but he wasn't angry anymore, and she giggled, she dared to giggle. She kissed away a couple of his tears, she pressed her lips to his face and sucked the tears in. "It's all right. Hey, now. Baby. I went to the market. There's a market out there, selling fresh fruit!"

Dressed as she was, she climbed under the covers beside him. She opened her shopping bag, let all the fruit spill out on the bed over them.

"*Ananas*," she said. "*Framboise. Pamplemousse*." She said the words slowly, as if to an infant; he repeated them back, and she was pleased. They cut their grapefruit in half with plastic spoons from the tea service; it was quite an effort, but they were game, and laughing, and the juice squirted everywhere. They sprinkled the grapefruit halves with crushed-up sugar cubes.

"What do you want to do today?" he said to her. "I'm sorry. I'm sorry. I'll be better. Where do you want to go? Your choice."

"Well," she said. "I do have somewhere in mind."

Donald knew that the moral responsibility of what they were doing rested solely upon his shoulders—that was how the authorities would see it, and his family, and his friends, and everyone he'd ever held dear. He accepted that. And indeed, he felt there was something almost heroic in that acceptance. When at night in his Chiswick flat he thought of Chrissie it was only of how he wanted to shield her from the world and all the ugly accusations it would throw at them. He would take full blame. He wanted to ensure that her life was never tainted by scandal, that when she left him (and one day she would, he knew she would, and even that gave him some thrill of self-sacrificial nobility), she could enjoy the rest of her life free from any recrimination.

But in his heart of hearts he couldn't have let the relationship continue unless he'd believed that she was as *emotionally* culpable as he was. After all, she was the one who had started it.

And that was the irony; before she had seduced him, he'd never given her even the slightest thought. If there had been a girl in his fifth-form class he *might* have fancied (and he hadn't, naturally not), it would have been Sheila Bennett, who was blond and curvy and good at essays on film theory. It wasn't that there was anything wrong with Chrissie, but there hadn't been anything especially right about her either—at least, nothing so right that it could have tempted him. Chrissie sat at the back of the class, mostly, and didn't say much, and the not much she did say wasn't very interesting.

After class one day, Chrissie asked if she could speak with him privately. He said yes.

"There's a teacher who fancies me," she said. "And I don't know what to do about it."

Donald was duly shocked, of course, and asked who the teacher was.

"I don't want to get him into any trouble."

Donald said that she mustn't worry about that, and that she should report the incident. And then he supposed that was exactly what she was doing, and he wondered why she wanted to report it to *him*. He asked what the teacher had done. What he had said to her.

Chrissie bit her lip. "Well, it's not what he's actually *done*," she said. "Or what he's, you know. *Said.*"

Donald was studiously patient. He nodded.

"But it feels weird, sir. Knowing there's someone out there who desires you. Don't you think?"

Later on, it was that *desires* that haunted Donald. It seemed such an adult word somehow. "I don't know," he said. "I suppose it must be."

A few days later she came to see him again. "It's you," she said. "You're the teacher. I'm in love with you."

He thought it was a bad joke, that behind the door there was a gaggle of schoolgirls spying on them and sniggering, that this was a prank, a dare. But he looked at Chrissie, properly, and really for the first time, and her eyes were so big and earnest, and she was being so very brave, look at her, she was shaking, how brave was that? "Hey," he said, "hey," and he asked her to sit down, and she shook her head, and he said, "It's going to be all right," and "There's nothing to be ashamed of." And all he really wanted to say was, *Why? Why do you love me? Why?*

She said it again.

"You don't love me," he said, and he tried to sound sympathetic, and he felt he was being such a good teacher and such a good adult. "You think you do, but you have all these hormones, and they're whooshing about, and you're confused."

"I'm not confused."

"It's perfectly normal to have a crush. I had a crush when I was at school." And he tried to think of one, and actually he couldn't.

"I've tried not to love you," she said. "Because it'll be so very hard for you, won't it?"

"Why?"

"When you start loving me back."

He manfully resisted falling in love with her, and he was successful for very nearly three whole weeks.

Some days she wouldn't talk to him after class at all, and those were the good days, and those were the bad days too. One day she cornered him beneath the blackboard and said she was so much in love that she was desperate, that she was frightened it was something she'd never be able to control, that she couldn't live without him. She desired him. Beyond all measure.

He told her they couldn't discuss her feelings at school. Well, where then? He'd give her a lift home in his car. But don't meet him in the staff car park, he'd pick her up from a side road, somewhere nice and private. He knew he was being stupid, but he really did believe still he was just protecting her, he would do his best to talk her out of it.

They sat at the far end of a Sainsbury's supermarket car park, which offered free parking to customers. She kissed him first and he kissed right back. Then they had to go inside the supermarket to buy some groceries so he could get a token for the exit barrier.

They agreed to go on a date. No, not a date, Donald said—it was just a meeting, they were meeting up. That Saturday, they went to the cinema. Donald had wanted to see the new Scorsese but then realized that his new girlfriend was beneath the appropriate age, and they'd settled for some rom-com instead. A cinema was good, to be out in public—it meant that they wouldn't make a mistake like last time. They both sat there in the darkness, and they didn't kiss, didn't even touch, they were both well behaved. They were so well behaved that Donald relaxed completely and wondered what on earth the problem was—so they were just friends, and what was the harm in having friends?

Afterward he took her to an Italian restaurant half an hour's drive away so they wouldn't be recognized. The conversation was easy. She was such a mature girl, he had had no idea, and she knew quite a bit about current affairs and politics and art—and her opinions were so clearly her own, she wasn't just parroting her parents' views, she was fiercely forthright on a couple of points where she disagreed with them and he found that ferocity enchanting. She was witty, and he was on good form too, he made a few wry comments that made her laugh. He bought her wine, and she stroked his leg underneath the tablecloth with her foot, and then, later, she stroked his hand.

He made her understand the need for discretion.

"Because they wouldn't understand, would they?"

"They wouldn't understand," he agreed. "But it's nicer like that, isn't it? Because what we've got, it's *ours*. It's ours, and nobody else's, and it's pure. Don't tell anyone, not even Maureen Slater, Maureen Slater's your best friend, isn't she? Is she? Or is it one of the other girls?"

Chrissie agreed not to breathe a word to Maureen Slater. She was very good at the whole discretion thing, and in class sometimes she barely looked at him, and if she did, it was with such bored indifference that her entire face seemed to change. He admired how she could do that. It hurt him.

They broke up three times—always, as she'd say with a laugh afterward, because he'd been "thinking too much."

Chrissie had suggested they go to Paris together. Her parents wouldn't mind, she said, she'd just say she was going on holiday with a friend. Donald couldn't believe he'd agreed. He couldn't believe they had actually gone. He couldn't believe how happy having her all to himself made him.

That morning when she went out to get fruit from the market they had their very first argument.

"I'm sorry," he said. "I'll be better. Where do you want to go? Your choice."

She didn't even have to think about it—she had her answer right away, and that surprised him.

Fine, he said. Of course they could do that! If she had a certain restaurant in mind, then of course they should go there. (Was it expensive?)

She said she didn't know. She didn't think it was expensive. No, it wasn't expensive.

Fine, he said. It didn't matter anyway. Not even if it was expensive! They could afford to splash out on a decent meal! What sort of restaurant was it?

She didn't know.

He said, fine, that was all fine.

She said it was supposed to be very romantic, and she gave him a wink that he didn't much like, it felt a little too self-conscious. The place had been recommended to her by a friend. The friend had been certain they would enjoy it.

She went to the wardrobe, and to her little pink suitcase, and from a side pocket took out a sheet of paper. On it her friend had written down the restaurant's address, even drawn a fairly detailed map to help them find it.

She said it was a bit of a distance, and she tilted her head in some sort of apology.

He said, "Who's the friend?" And at that she tilted her head to the other side, shrugged.

He said, "I thought we'd agreed. We wouldn't tell anyone we were going to Paris. What we were doing. Who's this friend, who's giving you restaurant tips? Is it a girl from school?"

She said it was no one from school. Did he think she was that stupid? She wasn't stupid. She wouldn't tell a *kid*. No, this was a grown-up. The word *grown-up* made her sound so childish.

And he hated this, that their second argument was so hot on the heels of their first, but he had to know, he couldn't let it drop. "A friend of your parents?"

No, a friend of *hers*. She had her own friends. God, did he think he was the only grown-up friend she had?

He wanted to hit her, and he'd never felt that way before, not about anybody.

She said, "I'm so tired of you thinking what we're doing is *bad*. It isn't bad. And you're not a bad person. I don't think you're a bad person."

The rage went out of him, and he felt so tired, and he sat down hard upon the bed.

She said, "You're not a bad person, baby."

He said that he knew he wasn't.

She said, "We have to go to the restaurant. I promised my friend. And he went to so much effort. I don't want to let him down."

He gave a nod, just a little nod, but it was enough, it was agreed.

And in spite of that, they managed to have a good day. They went to the Louvre. Chrissie saw some paintings she liked, Donald saw some he liked too, and they stood in the queue for the *Mona Lisa* and were surprised how small it was. David told Chrissie that one of the men pictured in Géricault's *The Raft of the Medusa* looked like Mr. Turner the PE teacher, and Chrissie thought that was very funny, and she found a portrait that looked just a little like Miss Bull. Everything was going so well, and Donald thought the upset of the morning might be forgotten—and then he offered to buy her a pastry at a *boulangerie* and she smiled and said she wouldn't, she didn't want to spoil her appetite for later.

They went back to the hotel, Chrissie wanted to get changed. She wheeled her little pink suitcase into the bathroom; she was there for the best part of an hour. While she was busy, Donald looked through the guidebook to see whether Paris had anything to offer they hadn't done yet; it hadn't.

At last Chrissie emerged. She was wearing a pink dress, very nearly a ball gown—she'd spent the week in her sweater and jeans, and now she was a movie star. She was wearing makeup too, and her face seemed heavy beneath the weight of it all; nail varnish, pink like her dress, and Donald was no expert but even he could see she hadn't put it on right, he saw the uneven patches, he saw the streaks bleeding onto the fingers. She looked beautiful. She also looked like a little girl who'd raided her mother's wardrobe.

Donald wished he'd packed something smart too, but the only jackets he had were the ones he wore to school, and he didn't want to be seen in those.

"You look nice," he said.

Chrissie smiled widely, and that made her face crack. "*Merci bien*," she said. She walked over to Donald, and he got up from the bed, stood to attention. She took his arm. "Shall we go, Monsieur MacAllister? *J'ai faim!*"

They reached an obscure metro stop in the eighteenth arrondissement. It was deserted. Donald was surprised—when they had left the hotel, it had still been quite light; somehow while they'd been underground night had fallen hard. There were a few stars out. There were streetlamps too, though many of them weren't working, were they broken? A few shops and houses, all had their curtains tightly drawn. It had been raining.

"Is it far?" Donald asked, and Chrissie didn't exactly answer. She got out the map her friend had drawn, studied it for a moment, and then set off confidently.

She turned them down a narrow side street, and Donald supposed that meant they must be nearly there, but the side street ran into another side street, and that one into another narrower still. They walked arm in arm, and that was a little romantic, but it also forced them to walk slowly, and the pools of light cast by the streetlamps seemed to be getting farther and farther apart. But he held on to her tightly regardless; the rain had made the cobbled streets look slippery, at every footfall he expected them to slip him over. Best not to look at the cobbles at all. Yes, that was sensible.

"What's this restaurant called?"

"All I've got is an address."

There were high stone walls flanking them on either side, and it seemed to Donald they were getting taller and thicker; they looked as if they'd been built to withstand some medieval siege. "This friend of yours wasn't having you on?" he asked. "Got a sense of humor, has he?"

"Stop," she said, and so they stopped, and she pulled him out of the lamplight and into the darkness. She kissed him hard on the lips.

"Yes, that's very nice," he said.

"We're in Paris."

"I know."

"This is an adventure. Enjoy it!"

"I am enjoying it," he said. "I know I'm in Paris. I'm enjoying the whole thing."

She flung away his arm, and he wasn't sure whether that was out of irritation or some new urgency in their search for food. His stomach growled at him, and it was only the latest part of his body to ask what the hell he thought he was doing.

"I think," said Donald, "you know what I think? I think we should just stop at the first restaurant we come to. I mean, this is farther out than we imagined, isn't it? And we're getting hungry. You must be hungry, you haven't eaten since breakfast! What do you say we just stop at the next restaurant?" And it was such a good plan, except they hadn't passed a single building for at least ten minutes. Chrissie was striding on so fast now, maybe she couldn't hear him. At last he tried again. "We should turn back. Yes? Chrissie? Do you agree?"

"This is it," she said suddenly, and he shut up.

There was a door set into the stonework of the wall. It was made of thick, black wood. There was no handle to open it, no knocker, nothing as frivolous as a bell. It was ridiculous that it was there, with no hint of a building behind it—worse, it was wrong, it felt wrong.

He expected Chrissie to be disappointed, and he was about to re- assure her, tell her it didn't matter; they'd retrace their steps, go back into the city, find a McDonald's if nothing else was open—but she was beaming, she was so excited. "We found it!" she said. "At last!"

"Darling, if there ever was a restaurant here, it's long gone. Your friend, this friend of yours"—and he didn't like the way his voice became so sarcastic whenever he mentioned him—"this Parisian expert friend, you know, he must have been here years ago."

"I'll knock," she said cheerfully. And he was about to stop her— there was no point in knocking—and don't touch it, don't touch the door—but it was too late, she was thumping upon it with her fist. But the wood was so thick she barely made a sound.

"You tried," he said. "Let's go." He offered her his hand.

The door opened.

For all its weight, for all its *age*, the hinges were silent. Maybe that was what horrified him, that it could just swing open so stealth- ily, like a beast that had only been pretending to sleep—and the blackness of the door was replaced by an altogether thicker black- ness pouring out from within. Donald stepped back instinctively. And out of the blackness, his head shining in the little light of the alley, emerged a man, an old man, Donald couldn't see him well but he knew he was *old*, and the man stood firm on the threshold and stared out at them. Donald stared back, he had no choice. The man seemed to be dressed in a smart black suit, and that only meant the light fell into him and was smothered. He cleared his throat. He looked at them quizzically.

Chrissie spoke in French. The old man inclined his head and stepped backward to let them in.

"Don't," said Donald.

"*Merci*," said Chrissie, and she went through the door, and Donald followed.

Down a long corridor, and at last, into the light. And Donald realized that the man wasn't merely old, he was ancient—and not just with age, that was the oddness of it, he was *sick*, and you could see the bones beneath the skin, he was wasting away in that waiter outfit hanging around him so loosely. Hardly a good advertisement for a restaurant, Donald thought, and he wanted to nudge Chrissie, make a joke, share a laugh—and he actually made to do that, but in an instant he felt such a wave of revulsion, he didn't want this man touching food, he didn't want him anywhere near food, touching anything they might want to put into their mouths—and yet here he was, he was touching *them*, he was taking the coats from off their backs and they were surrendering them to him, willingly! It wasn't a quizzical expression he had on his face, the eyebrows had just set that way.

And then into the restaurant itself. More a cavern than a room, the stone floor studded here and there with tables and chairs. No real order to it, some clustered close together, some out on the fringes like little islands. There was light, yes, but it was a heavy light, Donald thought it was slightly green—and he couldn't see where it came from, there weren't any lamps, the light seemed to leak from the bricks and the rocks and the earth.

It was empty. Of course it was empty. Who would come here—? No, in the distance, on one of those islands bobbing about, there sat a man on his own, fork in hand, tucking into something Donald couldn't make out in the gloom, reading a book. He looked up briefly at the newcomers and without apparent interest, and Donald saw he had one of those silly pencil-thin mustaches only suave sophisticates from France are able to get away with.

"Are they open?" Donald asked Chrissie. "Ask them if they're open. I don't think they're open." But their coats had been taken, hadn't they? The waiter had now draped them over his arm and seemed to be clinging on to them hard, he wasn't going to give them up easily. The waiter led them to a table. It wobbled on the uneven floor. He pulled out a chair so that Chrissie could sit down, but he didn't have the strength to accomplish the task with any grace; the coats he was carrying hardly made the operation any easier. Chrissie thanked him nicely. Donald sat down without help.

Chrissie took out a cigarette. Donald began to tell her he didn't think she could smoke here, but the waiter didn't seem to mind, and with his free hand, he took out a lighter for her. With the same flame, he lit a blunt candle squatting unhappily in the middle of the table—the little light it gave off was quickly quenched by the greenish glow of the room.

Then the waiter strode away without even looking back at them, and Donald wondered whether they would ever see their coats again.

"Jesus Christ," he said.

Chrissie puffed and grinned. "Isn't it wonderful?" she said.

"Is it?"

"You don't think it's romantic?"

"Are you sure they're open? You should ask if they're open."

Then the elderly waiter was back, sloping to them across the floor with renewed energy and confidence. He carried a bottle of red wine and two glasses. He set the bottle down upon the table.

"We haven't ordered that," said Donald.

Chrissie said, "But we do want wine, don't we?"

"Yes, but we haven't ordered."

The waiter fixed Donald with his not-quite-quizzical look, then set to work on the cork. It released from the bottle with a subdued pop. The waiter picked up the bottle with both hands and aimed its contents somewhere toward Chrissie's glass.

"*Parfait, merci*," she said, and sipped.

The waiter nodded, poured Donald a glass. Donald sniffed it. It smelled good.

Chrissie drank deeper, and the waiter stood beside her and watched, as if needing further confirmation that she enjoyed it. She turned to him, smiled, nodded. He nodded in return. And then he reached out that skeletal hand of his toward her neck, and he brushed away a few stray hairs from her shoulder.

"Hey," said Donald.

And then he left.

"Hey. Did you see that?"

"What?"

They both worked on their wine. Chrissie worked on her cigarette too, taking shallow puffs and turning her head away to exhale the smoke. Donald tried to think of something to say. He wondered why it was so hard. With all the many other problems they'd had to face, right since that first date cuddled together in the car park, conversation had never been a difficulty.

Maybe it was because there was no music. Every restaurant played music; without it, the pauses seemed longer and burdened with meaning. "I love you," he said.

"I love you too."

"I'm hungry."

"I'm hungry too."

She finished her cigarette, but there was nowhere for her to stub it out, so she set it down upon the table, standing it upright on its filter. The table wobbled. The stub refused to fall over.

"We should call the waiter," Donald said at last. And he suddenly thought, *Perhaps he's died*, and that made him laugh, just a single bark that sounded too loud and too rude. "I can call the waiter. What's the French for *menu*?" But on cue the waiter appeared, and in both hands he was carrying a single dinner plate, and, in his breast pocket, a knife and fork. It was only when he set the plate down in front of Chrissie that the couple could see what the meal was.

"*Non, non, non*," said Donald. He pointed at Chrissie. "Vegetarian. *Veg-e-tari-en*. Um. *Legumes*."

Because there in front of her, proud, unabashed, was a hunk of steak. There was nothing to disguise it, or to distract from its obvious meatiness; there were no greens around, no scattering of *pommes frites*. It was rare, it was pink. "It's all right," said Chrissie. "Just this once. I'm on holiday, aren't I?"

"But we didn't order it. Tell him we didn't order it. Tell him we want the menu."

Chrissie said something brief in French, the waiter said back something briefer, Chrissie nodded, smiled. The waiter walked away.

"Well?"

"They don't do menus here," she said.

"Well, how does that work?"

"Do you mind if I start?" she asked.

And he watched her as she sliced off strips of her steak, as she speared them with her fork, as she lifted them to her mouth. "Is it really all right?" he asked.

"Mmm, juicy," she said, and she spoke with her mouth full, and he could see a fat ball of meat roll around her tongue wetly, and she grinned at him. Then her attention was back to the dead animal on her plate, she tore into it so eagerly, and the farther into the carcass she ventured, the pinker it got. Bright pink, but not quite as pink as her chipped fingernails, nor as pink as the pink of her stupid pink suitcase sitting in the hotel wardrobe.

He watched her, unhappily, hungrily.

And without any music all he could hear was that chewing.

"I love you," he said.

She nodded, chewed on.

"I thought we could stay here in France and be farmers. What do you think?"

At last the waiter reappeared, and this time he was carrying Donald's dinner, and he swooped it down in front of Donald with a flourish that was almost elegant.

Donald looked down at his steak. It quite brazenly stared back up at him.

"*Non*," he said. "I want it well-done. What's the French for *well-done*?"

"*Bien cuit.*"

"I want this *bien cuit, oui*?"

And the waiter shrugged, and Chrissie shrugged, and Donald said, "I can't eat this."

The steak was thicker than Chrissie's piece had been—it looked not so much like meat, more something newly hacked off a living animal and dropped straight onto the dinner plate. It wasn't even pink; it was blue. It lay there, dead, or dying, and dribbled blood.

"You could at least try it," said his vegetarian girlfriend. So Donald prodded it with his fork, he tamped it down with the flattened underside of the prongs, and the steak felt spongy and soaking wet, and an almost acrid smell like copper came off it.

He turned it over. He thought it might look better if he turned it over. He prized it from the plate; it pulled free from its moorings with a low reluctant squelch, and then he let it splash back down onto its belly. He looked at the underside. He wished he hadn't turned it over. He wished he'd left it as it was.

He looked around to see whether the other diner in the restaurant had been given raw meat, whether he cared, whether he was shoveling it in under his pencil mustache quite cheerfully. But the other diner had gone.

Back down at the steak.

There, across the whole breadth of it, ran a single vein. The vein was raised off the flesh, like a tapeworm, Donald thought, or an elongated leech—it didn't look as if it had grown out of the meat at all, he could have grasped it between thumb and forefinger and peeled the worm off—it was thick, and rubbery, and gorged with blood.

He looked back up at Chrissie. For some sort of help, any help—but she wasn't even watching him, she was fully occupied by her own dinner. And there was a rhythm to the way she ate her steak now, the slicing, the forking, the ceaseless grinding of her teeth as she tipped a new gobbet of flesh past her lips and into the machine—and the swallowing, oh, the utter remorselessness of that swallowing.

She pushed the plate aside; at last she was done. She smiled. There was blood on her teeth.

"Aren't you going to eat?" she asked.

"Please," he said. "Please."

"You should eat." She continued to smile. "Come on, Monsieur *MacAllisteurrr.*" She elongated the accent; it made him sound like such a silly man.

So he picked up the fork once more. He put the merest pressure onto the meat. At contact, the vein began to bulge. He watched it; a small bubble began to swell from it. It was round and thick like a balloon, and it was a perfect dark red, shiny with blood. He took the fork away. The bubble stayed firm, bobbing up at him. He approached with the fork again. A different angle this time, he'd be careful. He'd attack it more stealthily from the side. The first bubble deflated, yes, he watched the blood drain away from it, he couldn't help but sigh with relief—and then, there it was, another bubble, closer by, rising out of the vein loud and proud, bigger and juicier than the last. And he knew, he knew if he pressed down any harder that the balloon would burst.

Chrissie frowned, sighed. She picked up her cigarettes. And in an instant the waiter was back by her side with a lighter. She exhaled smoke away from Donald, but not so carefully this time. "Come on," she said. "I enjoyed my meat. Why can't you?"

"We could be farmers."

"Yes, yes."

They were both watching him now, his girlfriend and the waiter. And the waiter somehow contrived to contort that quizzical look he had, he strained his forehead and bent the eyebrows into something more angular, something more mocking.

The waiter idly picked a few more hairs off Chrissie's shoulder, and this time he let his hand stay there, and those bony old fingers began to play at the nape of her neck.

"Just one bite, baby," said Chrissie, "just one bite for me," and she smiled, and she made her voice light and encouraging, but Donald thought he could hear the anger behind it. And she looked older than her fifteen years, all made up, smoking like a grown-up, her own eyebrows arched into an expression of oh-so-mature disappointment.

Donald plunged his fork into the dead animal, and it was too much for the vein to take, the bubble burst, it sprayed blood across his hand and a little on his face—mostly red, a dark red, but also some blue, and also something that seemed white and speckled.

"One bite," she said, and she nodded, and the waiter nodded too, and they were both leaning forward now in anticipation, the waiter was biting down hard upon his bottom lip and he was making it bleed—and so Donald did it, Donald raised a forkful of raw flesh to his mouth, and for a moment it wasn't in his mouth and in the next moment it was, and he was chewing frantically, and he did it, he did it, he did all the chewing and all the swallowing too, it was out of his mouth and down his throat and that chunk of meat was gone for good, he would never have to see it again.

He sat back, panting. He looked at her, and he winked, and he half expected a round of applause.

Chrissie stubbed out her cigarette on her plate; there was a quick fizz as the lighted end touched the wet blood. She said something to the waiter in French—it must have been French, surely, but the words seemed so hard and clipped. The waiter's eyes still burned, he hadn't yet recovered from the excitement of watching Donald eat— now he calmed down, he wrenched his face back into a more professional, more skeletal pose. He nodded, he licked his lips, he wiped the blood from his mouth with the back of his hand, he wiped the blood on his suit, he went to fetch their coats.

It was only after they were outside into the dark and the rain that Donald realized they hadn't paid for the meal. Chrissie told him it had all been taken care of.

They didn't talk much on the way back to the hotel. No, that's not true—they talked about lots of things, Donald hoped that the weather would be better for tomorrow, and Chrissie translated all the advertisements on the metro—but they didn't talk about anything important.

"I'll use the bathroom first," said Donald, quite cheerfully really. He locked the door behind him.

He got undressed and changed into his pale blue pajamas. He brushed his teeth and then brushed them again, hard, very hard. He studied his face in the mirror, and it didn't look any different than it had before. Then he sat down upon the toilet lid and began to draft a letter.

I've made a terrible mistake, he wrote. *I'm sorry.* He couldn't get beyond that *sorry*—it was meant to be the floodgate for everything he needed to tell her, so why on the page did it look like an ending?

He started when Chrissie knocked upon the door: "Are you going to be much longer?"

While she undressed, Donald got into bed. He'd pretend to be asleep. He might even fall asleep if he were lucky, and then he wouldn't even have to pretend. He closed his eyes and stared at the blackness in his head. When the bathroom door opened, he couldn't help it—he looked at her. The pink dress was gone, the lipstick, nail varnish, all gone. She was wearing her Disney pajamas again, and she seemed so sweet, and so young, and so easy to understand. She smiled. He smiled back. He watched Tigger bounce gently in the gap between her breasts.

She climbed into bed beside him.

"Well, good night," she said.

"Good night," he agreed.

She turned out the light.

He closed his eyes once more, once more pretended he could sleep, that he even knew what sleep was or how it could ever be reached again.

He wondered if she still might say anything about what had happened in the restaurant, and his body tensed in the expectation of it. But minutes went by, and then he heard her breathing regularly, and he relaxed, he'd got away with it.

He didn't even sense her moving closer until he felt her hand around his penis.

At first he wasn't even sure that it was her—at first, stupidly, he wondered whether it was one of his own hands creeping between his legs unawares—at first, stupidly, his impulse was to lift up the sheets and check. He didn't lift the sheets. He lay there, rigid.

The hand didn't flex. Now that it had found the penis, its mission seemed accomplished. It held on to its prize firmly, through his pajama trousers. Not so firmly that it demanded anything from it, firmly enough that it couldn't escape.

The slightest extra pressure of the fingers—the very slightest squeeze—and that would have been different, that would have been something Donald would have needed to address. Donald would have had to turn on the lights and sternly remind Chrissie of the boundaries he'd set up for their mutual protection. So he diligently waited for it, waited for that little pressure, for the slightest flex—he lay there focused, intent only upon his penis and her hand and any change of relationship vis-à-vis the two of them.

His penis swelled a little, the blood rushed to it in blameless curiosity, and the fist opened out slightly to accommodate it.

He felt himself breathe faster.

He turned to look at Chrissie. Tried to make out her face in the dim light. Her eyes were still closed. He thought she was asleep. And then—and then maybe the clouds parted a bit, because the Paris moon stretched across the bed and in the light of it her eyes opened at last, and they looked straight into him and straight through him. The rest of the face was still an impassive mask, utterly cold, utterly without expression, and looking so adult once more. But the eyes, was there a challenge in them? He thought there was.

He held his breath. He licked his lips. He didn't say anything.

Nor did she.

And then her eyes closed again.

The grip of her hand didn't relax, not even now. The blood drained out of his penis. It started to wilt.

He waited ten minutes, maybe more, not daring to breathe properly, not daring to stir her again. Until he was sure she must be asleep, and then he edged away from her, very gently, and as he pulled his body into the cold outer fringes of the bed, he pulled his penis away with him. By now it was just a stump, there was nothing left for the hand to grip on to. He felt the hand clasp and unclasp uselessly for it, then slow, then stop.

A little later, he carefully got out of bed. He wanted to go back to the bathroom. To brush his teeth, wash his face, finish the note, whatever.

He felt his way slowly through the darkness, and he was making good progress—and then his foot collided hard with something firm and round, and it hurt, and he couldn't stop himself, he cried out in surprise if not in pain, and the grapefruit he'd kicked rolled across the carpet and bounced against the wall. *Pamplemousse*, he thought to himself involuntarily.

"What are you doing?" Chrissie asked, drowsy, irritated.

"Nothing."

"Come back to bed."

"I'll come back to bed."

He got back under the sheets, and didn't dare move again, and at some point he must have fallen asleep.

When they woke the next morning, she gave him a kiss, and it seemed perfectly well intentioned and well executed.

At breakfast, he decided not to spread *confiture* or *beurre* upon his croissants. "Look," he told her, "I'm having them plain, just as you suggested! Are you proud of me?" She smiled, and congratulated him, and told him he was being a proper Frenchman. Even the waitress looked pleased, she hardly glared at him at all.

In the morning, they went to look at some church or another, and in the afternoon, they went to some museum or another. They found a fountain. Donald said he'd read that if you tossed a coin into a fountain it meant you'd come back to Paris, but he wasn't sure it was this fountain—and Chrissie laughed, and said he'd got it wrong, that was Rome—and Donald said, why would tossing a coin into a fountain in Paris mean you'd come back to Rome—and Chrissie said he was a silly darling man, and hugged him. And it was all very nearly normal. It was all very nearly loving. And they both tossed coins into the fountain anyway, and Donald knew it meant they were leaving Paris after all, they were going home, it was decided.

They ate at little bistros, and Chrissie ate only vegetarian food, and Donald ate meat, but the meat seemed to him so dull and so flavorless.

They spent three more nights in Paris.

The cab to the airport took a particularly circuitous route, but Chrissie didn't seem to mind, she stared out of the window and pointed out all the parts of Paris they hadn't done yet, Paris had more to offer after all. And Donald sat, and held her hand, and mused, and realized what he really wanted to say to her in that still-unfinished letter.

The airport was very busy. Everyone was trying to escape Paris. "I'm sorry, sir," said the woman at check-in, "the flight is very full, I don't think you and your daughter can sit together." Donald got very forceful, and said that his daughter was a very bad flyer, and if she wasn't able to sit with him, she'd scream the plane down. They got their double seats, and Donald was quite proud of himself.

As the plane took off, Donald listlessly leafed through the in-flight magazine, and Chrissie looked at some revision notes for her GCSE exams.

At around ten thousand feet, and somewhere over the English Channel, Donald proposed to her.

"What?" said Chrissie.

"You said I wasn't a bad man. I'm not a bad man, am I?"

"You're fine," said Chrissie.

"Marry me," said Donald. "I'll make you very happy. I'll give you whatever you like."

"Can we live in Paris?"

"Yes."

"Or somewhere else?"

"Whatever you like."

Chrissie thought about it. "All right," she said.

"We can't get married *now*," said Donald. "We'll have to wait until you're older. But it's a commitment, isn't it?"

"Of course," said Chrissie. "For when we're both older."

"I love you," said Donald, and Chrissie said she loved him too, and Donald felt relieved, she hadn't said it in ages.

After the stewardess announced they were coming in to land, Donald once more interrupted Chrissie's schoolwork.

"This is a big mistake," he said. "We shouldn't leave France."

Chrissie laughed. "Silly! We're on the plane!"

He said, "Then we can get straight onto another plane, can't we, and fly back? We can get our suitcases, and then we'll buy some tickets for the very next flight to Paris. We don't even need our suitcases, I can buy you a new suitcase, brand-new. Please," he said, and he squeezed her arm, "Please." He squeezed hard until at last she put down her work and gave him her full attention. "If we go back to England, I'll lose you."

She looked at him with such innocent eyes. "But we have to go back to England," she said. "I've a friend meeting us at the airport."

"What do you mean?"

"I don't want to disappoint my friend."

Donald had thought there might be policemen waiting for him as soon as he put foot on British soil. There weren't. Instead, a man holding up a placard for M AND MME MACALLISTER. Chrissie squealed when she saw it, and ran straight into the waiting man's arms, and for a moment that wasn't what made Donald jealous at all, what made him jealous was that the assumed names they had thought up together, that had been *theirs*, had been stolen. He wondered how the man had found out what they were.

"Well, well!" said the man. "And did you have a good holiday?"

"I did!" said Chrissie. "Paris is as beautiful as ever. Oh, and this is Donald, he's my friend."

"Is he coming with us?"

"We can give him a lift, can't we?"

The man nodded. "As far as he wants to go, as far as he wants to go!" The man was probably older than Donald but still looked better—he was tall and slim, he was confident, he had the sort of pencil mustache that only pure Englishmen of a certain background can get away with.

Donald said, "I'm not just her friend. I'm her fiancé."

"Indeed?" said the man. "Indeed! Well, I'm sure some sort of congratulations must be in order. The car's waiting, so come along, Monsieur MacAllister!"

They set off for the car, Chrissie and the man linking arms, Donald wheeling the little pink suitcase behind.

When they reached the car, Donald got into the backseat. He assumed Chrissie would join him there. She didn't.

"*On y va!* Now, where oh where shall I take you both?" And the man laughed, as if he'd made the funniest joke in the world, and Chrissie laughed too. The engine roared, the car started, and Chrissie was full of stories of her adventures in Paris, how tall was the Eiffel Tower, how small was the *Mona Lisa*, how wet the Seine—and it was odd, but none of the stories ever seemed to include Donald, but Donald couldn't be sure—to hear her he had to lean forward uncomfortably, and to join in the conversation he had to shout. But no one was listening to him, and his head was hurting, so he soon just sat back and was silent. If he stared ahead he could see how animated Chrissie was, and he didn't want to see that—and he could also see how her friend had stretched out his hand and was brushing the hair off her shoulders and was stroking the nape of her neck. He didn't want to see that either, not any of that—and so instead he looked out of the windows at the English countryside, and he didn't recognize any of it, not a bit of it, and he wondered where they were taking him.

THE YELLOW DEATH

LUCY A. SNYDER

"Lady . . . ," I whispered.

My sister stood there in the doorway of the Freebirds' clubhouse, the fall wind blowing dead leaves in a dervish around her sandaled feet, ruffling the hem of her dandelion-bright sundress, and suddenly the laughing and roughhousing stopped. All the bikers and their sunburned old ladies just stared at the girl.

The silence probably only lasted twenty seconds, but in my mind it stretched out to an agonizing hour. I didn't know whether to trust my own eyes. She didn't look like the sister I remembered, but she'd only been twelve when I ran away from home. And that was eight years ago. A lot can happen to a girl in nearly a decade. Adolescence, for instance. And also the apocalypse.

The young woman in the doorway was tall, nearly as tall as me, but slender and elegant as any of the ballet dancers we used to admire as they walked home from the theater. Her dark hair looked impossibly clean and cascaded down past her shoulders. The bikers called me Beauty to mock my scars, but they'd call her that because they hadn't the words for anything better. Any old French poet would spend sleepless nights trying to capture this strange girl's pulchritude in serifed letters. But she had the same cornflower eyes and she gave me that dreamy smile I remembered so well. I didn't wonder how she'd tracked me down. She'd always been the one to locate the missing book behind the couch, our mother's lost earring in the drain, forgotten song lyrics in a notebook in her bag.

"Hey, Louise." The years had turned her voice seductive, husky. Pure aural sex. I could practically smell the men's sudden desire, a musky pheromone note cutting through the stink of beer, motor oil, and tobacco. And I could feel their old ladies' anxiety and jealousy build alongside it, like the charge in the air before a lightning strike.

"Found you," she said, and made a languid motion as if she were tweaking my nose.

My brain teetered between joy and terror. Because if that wasn't Lady? We were probably all fucked five ways to Sunday. I craned my neck to try to see past her, see if the prospects on guard duty were still up on the wall or if their guts were scattered across the concertina wire. I saw nothing but the glaring floodlights and darkness beyond.

The problem with vampires is that before they get inside your veins, they crawl inside your mind. You think that you've opened the door to your neighbor or your aunt Heather, but in reality you've just let in a pallid, toothy monstrosity that's about to rip your jugular out and drain you like a juice box. If you're lucky. If you're not so lucky, the local hive needs more hunters and it's just there to nip you, grab a quick drink, and flap away, leaving you to your slow, torturous metamorphosis.

I knew what that looked like better than most living people. My fiancé, Joe, got bitten in the first wave, right before anyone outside the CDC had any inkling there was a problem. He'd carried the trash out to the alley in the dark. Something hiding in the ivy covering the low cinder-block wall attacked him. He never got a good look at it, or even a sense of its size, so we figured it was a rat. We washed the bite with peroxide and got him to the doctor the next day. Antibiotics and rabies shots cleared out what was left in our bank account, but we imagined he'd be fine after that.

He ran a low-grade fever—the doctor's office said the rabies vaccine could cause that—and his mood went straight to hell. Joe was normally pretty *hakuna matata* about money, even when we were flat broke, but suddenly he wanted to count every miserable cent coming in or going out. It was almost enough to make me call home and beg forgiveness just so we'd have access to the trust fund I'd given up years before. Almost. I accidentally spilled some Tylenol down the drain one day and he made me wait while he counted and re-counted the rest in the bottle so he'd know exactly how many we had to replace. It didn't matter to him that we still had plenty. He was losing his mind right in front of me and at the time I figured he was just cranky.

When his eyes turned yellow from jaundice, it seemed like a side effect of the antibiotics. He refused to go to urgent care, because that would be fifty bucks we couldn't afford. It was only four more days until his next doctor's appointment for another rabies shot anyhow. I was worried, but I let it ride.

That night, he woke me up around four a.m. when he started going berserk in the living room. Joe was yanking books and movies off the shelves and throwing them around. He'd smashed the big blue sunfish lamp he made in ceramics class and the floor was covered in jagged shards. The bottoms of his feet were in tatters, but somehow he wasn't bleeding. He picked up my special-edition Blu-ray of *Sorcerer* and made a motion as if he was going to snap it in two.

I tried to grab it away from him. He slugged me in the mouth and I dropped like a sack of potatoes; I didn't know how to take a punch back then. The sight—or maybe the smell—of the blood from the gash on my lip then sent him into a whole new orbit of madness.

He grabbed me by my hair, dragged me screaming to the radiator, gagged me with a dirty handkerchief, and lashed my hands to the pipe with the cord from the busted lamp.

Joe stared down at me for a long time, not saying anything, his expression shifting between rage and confusion. He paced back and forth, asking me who I was and if I'd seen the sign. I was on my back, my head and neck pressed against the radiator and my hands tied high to the top pipe. Stuck. There was no way to pull myself up to reach the rag in my mouth to try to yank it out to talk to him, so I just lay there, waiting. A dog started yapping a few houses down. So then I thought, well, we'd both made a whole lot of noise after he hit me. Surely someone had heard him and called the cops.

I felt a surge of hope when I heard a police siren, but it passed us by. And then I realized that what I'd thought was a dog was really a woman barking, "*Fuck you!*" over and over.

Joe abruptly stopped interrogating me and flopped down on the couch. He turned on the TV—the one thing in the room he hadn't tried to wreck—and just started flipping through channels as if nothing had happened. The local station was showing a live feed of a female reporter standing near a police car in some other neighborhood. I started trying to work the stiff cords off my wrists, as quietly as I could.

"*We're here at the site of a hostage situation on Grant Street,*" the reporter said. "*This is the tenth such situation that local police have been called out to in the past three hours. News Ten is sending teams to the other locations. We will update you as we get more information. It's not clear if this is some terrible, violent coincidence or if it represents coordinated terrorist activity. Police are asking that people stay in their homes—*"

My boyfriend switched off the TV and stared at me. The madness was wearing a new face, and he seemed to recognize me again.

"They'll kill you," he whispered. His eyes had turned so yellow they looked like they'd been carved from brimstone. "You're not of the body. You're not in His image."

Joe went into the kitchen and came out with a sharp boning knife. "If they don't see the sign, they'll kill you."

I started struggling in earnest then, desperate to get loose, but he dodged my kicking legs and sat on my chest, pinning me to the scarred hardwood floor. He grabbed my hair with one hand and slashed the left side of my face with the other. The pain of the blade razoring through my flesh was bright, intense. The second slash nearly made me vomit. The third made me pass out. I came to a little while later. Joe was licking the tarry pool of my blood off the dirty floor. When had his tongue gotten so long?

"I saved you." He grinned, pleased, his teeth red with gore. "I'm your savior."

I passed out again.

The next week or so is still pretty hazy; I can't sort out what was a hallucination, reality, or nightmare. I heard voices and screaming. When I was finally fully conscious, my head was baking with fever and the slashes on my face were a throbbing agony. My left eye was swollen shut, and for a while I was scared he'd cut it out.

Joe came in and out of the room, sometimes just staring at me, sometimes pacing and rambling about cosmic signs. The words coming out of his mouth sounded like English, but they just didn't make any sense.

Joe must have realized my mutilated face was horrifically infected because he started feeding me his antibiotics along with water and occasionally a piece of bread. But he didn't seem to understand the part where I needed to go to the bathroom, or the part where the antibiotics would give me diarrhea. I was lying in terrible filth; I could feel my skin blistering and ulcerating under my clothes. I prayed for death.

I was a disgusting wreck, and so was the house. But Joe looked clean and healthy, his hair combed, wearing his good khakis and best button-down shirt. He appeared that way as long as I was looking at him straight on, that is. When I glimpsed him from the corner of my eye . . . I couldn't quite make out what I was seeing, but the shambling, tattered-looking thing wasn't the Joe I knew.

I finally awoke one morning and my fever had broken. I was weak as hell, but at last I had the focus to grasp a fragment of broken lamp between my toes, and flip it up toward my hands. I finally realized that after six flips I wasn't going to catch any shards, and even if I did, my fingers were too numb and clumsy to do anything. So I concentrated on trying to stretch the cords again. After what seemed like fifteen years, I was finally able to slip off one of the loops. The others were easy to shake off after that.

I climbed painfully to my feet, back and sides aching, and dropped my ruined pajama bottoms and panties. Joe kept his grandfather's shotgun in the back of the coat closet. He'd shown me how to handle it once. I found the weapon in its tan canvas case and the shells under a pile of winter hats on the upper shelf. It took me a couple of tries to get them down, each sending sharp pains through my strained, stiff shoulders. Once I got my hands working well enough to load the old double-barrel, I crept through the house with it, dreading what I would find. I remembered the corner glimpses of something terrible and I knew Joe wasn't simply insane. Something much worse had happened. My hands ached and the weapon seemed impossibly heavy in my weak, shaking arms.

Upstairs was empty of any life but a few scuttling cockroaches and spiders. I took a deep breath, held it. My aching guts told me he was still in the house, but he had to be down in the basement. The very last place I wanted to be.

Once I got my hands to quit shaking, I ducked into the bathroom to wipe off the worst of the filth, slipped on a pair of his boxer shorts and some old sneakers, and slowly went downstairs.

The stench of spoiled meat hit me the moment I pushed open the basement door. I wanted to puke, but there wasn't anything in my stomach.

Three pale, bloodless corpses lay on the concrete basement floor. Two were neighborhood kids; one was the old lady who'd lived next door. Their throats had been torn open, their exposed flesh pale as raw chicken meat. Not a drop wasted. They were still wearing all their clothes. Perversion paled in comparison to murder, but it was nice to know that Joe's madness had its limits.

I hadn't thought of the word *vampire* until then, but with all that evidence spread before me, nothing else made sense. In my mind, I could picture Joe reaching out to them, trying to bring them to the house to protect them like the good guy he was. But once they came inside, he saw me tied to the radiator and realized that if he saved them, he'd have to drain me. Because a guy has to eat, right?

My heart beating so hard I was light-headed, I stepped over the corpses and opened the utility room door. The creature my boyfriend had become was curled up in the corner by the washer, asleep in a nest of soiled clothes and pages torn from old books. The sight of it should have made me want to run screaming, but that demanded energy I just didn't have. Its hairless skin was a dark yellow, and its body was practically skeletal. I remembered that birds have hollow bones so they can fly. His spindly arms hadn't quite transformed into batlike wings yet. There was a little of Joe left in the thing's distorted face, enough to make me sure it was him, but not enough to make me pause before I blew its head off.

The recoil from the shotgun knocked me flat on my blistered ass. After I got myself up, I found a bottle of Drano on a shelf and poured the gel all over the creature's still-twitching body. The caustic goop made its flesh sizzle like bacon in a pan. The stink was incredible, and made my eyes water and nose run, but I wanted to be damned sure the thing was dead. I'd have set it on fire, but I knew I was too weak to abandon the house. I shut the utility room door, blocked it with an old trunk, then went upstairs and locked the basement door behind me.

We still had electricity. I found my cell phone in the bedroom but the battery was dead; I plugged it in and tried 911. Got a busy signal. I tried my friends' numbers; they all went to voice mail.

I stared down at the phone, feeling sick again. I left it charging on the middle of the bed and went to get cleaned up and examine my wounds. The bathroom looked about the same as I'd left it; I guessed vampires weren't much for hygiene. I killed the cockroach I found in the tub, flushed it, and took a hot, soapy shower to get the filth off my skin. My crotch, ass, and thighs were covered in a constellation of sores and pustules. Some broke at my touch, and I soaped up again and tried to clean out the wounds as best I could. At least the antibiotics Joe had given me had seemingly prevented the worst infection. After I dried off, I found a tube of diaper-rash cream left over from when we'd babysat Joe's infant niece and slathered myself up.

Then it was time to check the real damage. I wiped the steam off the mirror and took a look at my face. The left side was still puffy under a scab the size of a saucer. It itched something fierce, but I didn't want to touch it to risk reopening anything. I didn't know if Joe had bitten or licked me while I was unconscious. But neither my skin nor my eyes looked yellowed. I hoped for the best.

I got dressed in a pair of loose palazzo pants and a T-shirt and raided the fridge. Half the food was fuzzy with mold, but the tortillas and lunch meat still looked edible, as did a couple of tangelos. You wouldn't think you'd be able to eat knowing you were standing just twelve feet above three dumped murder victims and a dissolving vampire, but you might surprise yourself. Hunger is a powerful drive. I made myself eat and drink slowly so I wouldn't get sick. I knew I couldn't afford to waste food.

My adrenaline finally ebbed after my belly was full, and suddenly I felt as though I were wearing a lead bodysuit. It was all I could do to drag myself upstairs and brush my teeth before I passed out on the bed. I had exactly the kind of nightmares you'd figure I'd have, but I slept for over eighteen hours anyhow.

When I woke, I ate again, washed again, and tried to figure out what I should do next. My eyes and skin still weren't yellow. The TV stations were all static, so either the cable was out or something far worse was going on. I tried my friends' numbers again and left messages.

I almost wet myself with joy when 911 answered. A pleasant-sounding young woman took down my details—I told her my boyfriend had killed some people but didn't detail the bit about his becoming a vampire because I still cared about whether people thought I was crazy or not. She said she'd dispatch an officer to my house.

Sure enough, fifteen minutes later there was a knock at my front door. I answered it, and a nice-looking, red-haired uniformed policeman stood on the porch.

"I'm Officer Curtis," he said, polite and pleasant as a Boy Scout selling candy bars. "May I come inside?"

"Sure." I turned to set aside my shotgun—

—and got a glimpse of the thing at my door from the corner of my eye.

When the smoke and haze of blood in the air cleared, I realized I'd blown a hole in the screen door and had blasted the vampire's head clean off its spindly yellow shoulders. The rest of the bat-winged body that lay sprawled and jerking on the concrete steps was practically a clone of what Joe had turned into.

I shivered. It wasn't even wearing any clothes; nothing about the vampire actually looked like the cop I'd seen. I glanced up at the sky. It was early morning and overcast to boot . . . but it certainly wasn't dark, either. These things could stand daylight, or at least some of it.

As I got more experience killing vampires, I learned that they went blind in bright light. The sun would never make them burst into flames, but fifteen minutes was enough to give a vampire a blistering burn and after that, the light made their bodies sprout grotesque tumors. Their mutability always made me uneasy about leaving one staked out to die in the noontime glare, lest it turn into some day-stalking monstrosity. Their wiry strength was formidable and they were plenty tough, but they weren't immortals that could be slain only with a stake through the heart or decapitation. A couple of solid body shots with hollow-point bullets would settle any flapper's hash, as would a dozen crushing blows with a Louisville Slugger.

Their biggest weapon was their psychic camouflage. And even after three years, I still had a hard time seeing through their glamour. But I knew full well that a clever vampire could wreak diabolic chaos in a room full of people by making everyone see something different.

So, as my sister, Lady, stood there in the bikers' clubhouse looking nearly as improbable as the angel Gabriel bearing two large supreme pizzas from Donato's . . . I was doing all manner of eyeball calisthenics to try to glimpse her sidewise. No matter how I gazed upon her, she still looked the same.

Lady finally broke the silence that had fallen on the room.

"Aren't you going to say hello?" She stepped toward me and reached out to touch my cheek.

I flinched away from her, wishing I hadn't left my pistol back in my bunk. I had my KA-BAR strapped to my belt and a throwing dagger hidden in the top of each of my tall boots, but you don't take a knife to a vampire fight if you can help it. She didn't seem to notice my discomfort.

"You've got the sign," she whispered, gazing in awe at my scars.

I reflexively covered my cheek with my hand. "What?"

"The sign." She held up her wrist. Just below her delicate blue veins was an ornate tattoo, a beautiful version of the weird symbol Joe had carved into my flesh. Seeing her ink was like being hit with a Taser. Until that moment, I hadn't seriously thought that the marks on my cheek meant anything outside the confines of my boyfriend's fevered mind. Some people had claimed it looked like part of a misshapen Chinese character for *fate* or *death* or whatever, and one old man claimed it was a stylized Arabic curse, but I'd figured it was just a living Rorschach blot.

"What does it mean?" My voice shook.

"It's a sign to the minions of the King." She gazed at me earnestly. "It tells them that although you are not of His body, you are not to be touched."

She leaned in close and whispered, "Someone must have loved you very much to mark you so."

I remembered the agony of steel cutting skin and muscle, the torment of lying bound and bleeding in my own filth. That didn't feel like love. If that was supposed to be genuine love, I wanted no part of it.

"This fucking thing is supposed to protect me?" I couldn't keep the anguish out of my voice. It made me feel naked in front of everyone, frail in front of people who already mocked me for my supposed weaknesses, and I hated her a little for it. If my face hadn't been all fucked up, they probably would have called me Brownie Scout instead. "I've had plenty of creeps come after me."

"The King allows his servants to defend themselves and their hives. And once a servant joins the body, some measure of free will remains." Her cool gaze moved across the men and women in the room, all of whom had earned at least one felony conviction apiece before the vampires showed up. "Not all choose to obey the laws."

Bear, the Freebirds' sergeant at arms, snorted and slid off his bar stool. His booted feet clomped loudly on the wooden floor.

"What's all this yammer about vampires an' laws?" His voice was belligerent and slurred by beer. "Ev'r'body knows them things is just giant bloodsucking bugs. Mansquitoes." He laughed at his own pun.

Lady just watched him warily as he swaggered over.

"Ain't you a pretty little thing, though." He reached out to paw her breast, but I pushed his meaty hand away from her. He scowled at me. "Don't step twixt a dog and his meat, *Beauty*."

"She's not your meat. She's my sister. You need to step back, please." I held his stare in mine. Everybody else was silent; if tension were electricity, you could have lit a skyscraper with what was in that room.

I knew it was dangerous to challenge him, but I also knew what the men did to women and girls they saw as pretty enough to be proper bike decorations. And Lady was far more beautiful than any of the strippers, runaways, and drug addicts the Freebirds normally attracted. When the club members found me on the road, exhausted and half-dead after four months of trying to survive on my own, I was deemed too ugly to fuck and therefore probably useless, but the club president took a shine to me anyhow. They assigned me the same scut work they gave the prospects: cleaning toilets, disposing of bodies, cleaning up puke, and degreasing engines. Because I was female, I'd never earn my way to a patch and club colors, but most of the time I thought I'd at least earned their respect, especially considering how good I was at killing vampires. I'd been able to stop rapes and abuse before. So I figured there would be a little staring contest and Bear would back off and get back to his drinking.

But I guess he could see how much Lady meant to me, and he was enough of a sadist to want to hurt me that day. Or maybe his unspeakable grief needed an outlet, and I was a handy target. His old lady had just lost their baby; the stillborn infant would have been his son and the first new child any of us had seen since the horror began. The army had put something in the air and water to try to kill off the vampires, but the only thing it definitely did was fuck up women's hormones and make us all infertile. It seemed a mercy, really; this was no longer a world fit for children. But Mama Bear's pregnancy was a great joy for the men and women of the club, and it seemed nothing short of a miracle while it lasted.

Nobody minded when he cried over the tiny body the night she went into premature labor, but after that, the rest of the club expected him to man up and get over it. We saw death every day. But how can a man get over something like that? So Bear had to swallow down his misery, pretend it wasn't there. I wasn't surprised that it had grown into something terrible there in the shadow of his soul, and I really did feel sorry for the guy, but I wasn't about to let him molest my sister. Not for fun or spite or out of despair or anything else.

"I don't take orders from ugly cunts." Bear spat on my boots.

"It isn't an order, friend, but I'm here to protect family," I said, just loud enough that I was sure the whole room could hear me. "I was there when she was born, and if you or anyone else tries to hurt her, I will stop it by any means necessary."

His gaze turned hard and distant. I can't be sure he was suicidal, but I can't say that he wasn't, either. He never struck me as the smartest guy in the club, but he'd have to have been an idiot to ignore what I was capable of.

"Fuck you, gash face." Bear gave me a hard shove and grabbed Lady.

I'd braced myself and he didn't knock me over. What happened next took less than a second. I drew my KA-BAR and swung the knife at him as hard as I could . . . and I swear to this day I meant to hit him upside his thick head with the flat hammer pommel. I just wanted to knock him out. But he let go of my sister and dropped, and when he lay there sprawled on the floor, I saw I'd sunk my blade into his temple, nearly all the way to the hilt. His staring eyes were empty lights.

"Oh no," whispered Lady.

I heard the click of a Ruger Redhawk being cocked right behind my head.

"Hands up, Beauty."

I raised my arms and slowly turned around. Eric "Gun" Gunnarson, the club president, was pointing the huge revolver right between my eyes.

"I didn't want that to happen," I said, trying to keep my voice steady. "I'm sorry."

"I figured." Gun's expression was hard, and his pistol hand didn't waver.

I looked him right in the eyes, and it was like he didn't recognize me. What I saw in his stare reminded me of Joe the night he carved my face up. I'm sure no bystander would ever guess that just two weeks before, Gun had kissed me on my forehead and confessed that he loved me. Just like they never would have guessed that he'd wept alongside Bear over the body of his tiny nephew.

He pressed the revolver up under my chin and moved in close.

"I get that she's your sister." Gun whispered in my ear, too quietly for anyone but maybe Lady to hear. "But Bear was my brother and a club officer. If you were *anyone* else, I'd have killed both of you by now. Fact is, you're too damned useful to kill. So that means you get to live this time. But there's a price to pay."

He called two guys over to haul Bear out to the dead shed, where his son still lay wrapped in his baby blanket, waiting for the weekly cremation out in the field.

"Clear off that pool table and put my chair over there," he ordered. "Rentboy! Rentboy, get your skinny ass over here!"

A young, model-handsome prospect ducked out from behind the bar, hurried over, and stood at attention in front of Bear. I could see the hard-on in his Levi's; it was impressive even to men raised on a steady diet of hard-core porn. He looked completely terrified.

That's why he was a joke to all the guys: fear made him pop massive wood, every time, unless he was close to passing out from booze. On one of my many nights of insomnia, I found him drinking at the bar by himself. He started weeping and told me his aunt did something awful to him when he was little. But that was as much as I ever knew; I didn't press for more details, and I kept it to myself. He probably wouldn't talk about it even to a sympathetic counselor—boys don't get raped by women, right? They just get lucky—and so there was no way in hell he'd confide in any of the Freebirds. He pretended like it was a fun thing, a party trick, and so scaring him into an erection was an unending source of hilarity around the club.

"We need us a show, Rentboy!" Gun pointed at the cleared-off pool table. "Take the lovely lady over there and show us what you can do."

Rentboy's eyes bugged out of his head and he stammered, "But . . . but I don't think she wants to."

"I don't care what she wants." Gun was impassive, immovable.

"Please, sir, don't make me." Rentboy looked like he might start crying.

At that, Gun turned his revolver on Rentboy, and in the back of my mind I knew I could grab the weapon, but I was still the center of attention in a room full of armed men. I'd die, and so would my sister. I had to wait for a better opportunity and pray that one actually came along.

"Do you want to get patched, son?" Gun demanded harshly. "Or do you want to get carried out to the shed?"

"Please don't do this," I whispered. I'd spent enough time around Gun to know he was capable of awful things, but until that day I'd seen him commit his crimes only out of need. I couldn't think of him as a monster. Not yet. But I knew the pressure we were all living under was burning away his decent parts bit by bit. Maybe monstrosity would be all that was left of us, whether we ever got bitten by vampires or not.

He turned the revolver back on me. "Did you say something, you ugly whore?"

His question was loud and clear. No respect offered me in front of the club. No admission of the feelings he'd declared to me in private, not even a simple nod to all the blood and sweat I'd poured into the club's common good. I didn't even rate the consideration the other females got because I wasn't anyone's old lady.

Sure, Gun could have stepped up and told everyone Bear got what he had coming to him. Gun could have told everyone that I was *his* lady, had been for over a year, and he could have made me the new sergeant at arms, because I'd be a fuck of a lot more competent at the job than his brother had ever been.

Gun could have done all that. And monkeys could have come flying out of my ass, too.

"Did you say something, whore?" he asked again.

I shook my head, my mouth clamped shut, rage firing through every synapse in my body. The train had left the station, and there was no easy way of stopping it now. Gun was acting how he thought a boss should, and what he was doing made sense by a certain sociopathic logic.

Problem: a strange, beautiful woman shows up, and you know your men are going to fight over her because they don't see her as anything more than some kind of trophy to be won.

Solution: tarnish her shine and break her, then hand her off to a lieutenant like a toy you're tired of.

Problem: the woman you love just killed your brother in defense of said beautiful stranger and challenged the club's power structure.

Solution: humiliate her in front of the club and break her, too. A boss has to make personal sacrifices sometimes. Besides, you can always find another gun hand and another woman to declare your secret passion to.

"Good," Gun replied. "Keep your whore mouth shut until it's time for you to open it."

He waved the Redhawk toward the pool table. "Get over there and kneel in front of my chair."

At least I knew where I stood, right? My whole body shook with the anger I couldn't express, but I did what I was told.

He settled himself in the worn leather recliner, unzipped his fly, and pulled his cock out. Rapped me on top of my head with the barrel of the revolver like I was a misbehaving dog. "Do what you're good at."

Goddamn it, I thought. *Goddamn him and this whole place all to hell.*

Meanwhile, Rentboy hadn't taken a single step toward my sister. He stood there, his eyes closed as if through sheer force of will he could make himself teleport to someplace far away.

"Boy, what did I tell you?" Gun barked.

"Yessir!" Rentboy hurried over to Lady and took her by the hand.

"No." Lady tried to pull away, but the kid held her fast.

"It'll be okay," I heard him plead, his voice low. "There's no choice—let's just do it and it'll be over soon."

"It's over when I say it's over," Gun replied loudly, lord of all he surveyed. "Someone bring me a TV table and a beer."

Two prospects hurried to obey him. He rapped me on the top of my head again, harder. "And what did I tell *you*?"

So I started doing the thing I'd done a hundred times before, always in the dark in Gun's room, always under the illusion that I was doing it for a man who cared about me. A man who wasn't a complete and utter fucking bastard. I focused on Gun's hardening tool, tried to block out the sound of my sister's and Rentboy's misery on the pool table behind me.

I chanced a glance around; almost nobody was looking at me. A few horrified or titillated gazes were aimed at the table; most everyone else I could see was staring at the floor, unfocused, sending their minds someplace else.

You guys could stop this, I thought to them all, wishing I were a vampire so I could project the idea into their heads. But they should have gotten that idea all on their own.

Someone stop this.

Nobody did anything but watch.

After that, I let my faster hand trail down to the cuff of my boot, where a dagger rested, and kept track of the Redhawk out of the corner of my eye. I prayed to every god I could remember for some kind of a chance.

I heard my sister choke, then the sound of her vomiting. Puke splattered on the floor behind me. Gun's cock went soft.

"Goddamn it!" He slammed the Redhawk down on the wooden TV table in frustration.

I remember what happened next in quick strobe flashes. I drew the dagger and rammed it up through his balls and into his bladder. Then the Redhawk was in my hand and I was blasting away at all the people who'd just stood and watched my betrayal and my sister's violation. Something inside my head disconnected for a few seconds, and when I came back to myself, I had another pistol in my hand—a svelte little .38 semiautomatic—and my naked sister was standing between me and Rentboy, her hands up, pleading. Thin vomit dripped down her chin and her face was very white. He was curled up in a ball under the pool table, sobbing and wailing like the world had come to an end.

"Louise, Louise, stop, please stop," Lady begged. "You did it. They're all gone. Just stop. The boy didn't want to."

Dazed, I looked around. I'd murdered everyone in the clubhouse. Patched members, officers, old ladies, prospects . . . everyone.

Faces and chests were blown apart. I'd slit a prospect's throat with my other knife, and try as I might, I couldn't bring up even a hazy memory of doing so. But my blood-covered hands and shirt told the tale. I couldn't find any wounds on myself except for a couple of scrapes and a bloody nose.

"Are there any other biker guys?" Lady asked. Her voice and expression were supernaturally calm. I wondered if this was what PTSD looked like on her.

I counted, realized we were seven short, and remembered that the vice president had taken his favorites to search for food in a nearby abandoned town. They'd be back at dawn. His old lady lay among the bodies; I'd put a round through her pretty left eye.

"Yeah. We better get the hell out of here."

While Lady put herself back together, I washed the blood off at the bar sink and then quickly gathered supplies—weapons, ammo, food, a medical pack, and jerry cans of gasoline, plus my rucksack of clothes and what little personal stuff I'd kept—and got my battered Yamaha V Star ready. Lady had arrived on her own bike, a shiny Honda NC700X. Meanwhile, Rentboy wouldn't stop crying and didn't want to come with us, and frankly I didn't want him along anyhow.

"Are you okay?" I asked her as we walked out of the clubhouse to load the bikes.

"I'm fine." Her face was a pale mask.

For the first time, I noticed she was wearing an antique gold signet ring and was twisting it round and round her index finger.

I knew all about trauma, but I sucked at knowing what to say to help people through it. I guess if I had any talent for it, I'd have majored in counseling instead of English. "If you need to talk—"

"I don't. Honest." She flashed me a quick, unconvincing smile. "What's done is done, and once we've left this awful place, I can put it all behind me."

"Okay," I replied gently. "Where do you want to go?"

"Our father wants you to come home," she replied. "He wants our family back together."

I stopped in my tracks. My first thought was, *No fucking way.* The second was, *That old bastard's still alive?*

"Seriously? This is for real?" I asked her aloud.

"Of course," she said. "Father wants you home."

"He didn't exactly beg me to come back after I left," I said. "In fact, when I called Mom to let her know I wasn't dead in a ditch, she said he'd disowned me."

Lady shrugged. "I know he wasn't very nice to you back then. I was there for most of it, remember? I know how hard he was to live with."

I let out a short, bitter laugh. "But he liked *you*. You were his little princess. I was just a tomboy who never liked what he liked and never did as he ordered."

"I promise you, he's had a change of heart. The world is different, and so is he."

I thought back on all his narcissistic rages and Napoleonic mood swings, and my stomach twisted in dread. But I also remembered his hugging me and telling me he was proud of me, once. Maybe that could happen again. "Really?"

She nodded, smiling brightly, and drew an X over her chest. "Cross my heart."

We hit the road and put three hundred miles between ourselves and the massacre before we stopped to rest at an abandoned gas station along I-10. I did two searches of the property to check for vampires before we set up camp in the part that used to be a convenience store. The shelves still held stale candy bars and boxes of crackers under a thick layer of grime blown in from the road through the broken glass doors.

"Did you know our family's royalty?" she asked as I set up my camp stove to warm some water for tea. She was fiddling with her gold ring.

I laughed. "All you need to be royalty in this country is money, and Father always had plenty of that."

Our father got his money the old-fashioned way: he inherited it. And despite his talent for waste and alienating other people, he did have a certain knack for playing the stock market, and he started out life with enough capital to keep the cash flowing in.

"No, I mean we're *actual* royalty," Lady insisted. "Father showed me the documents. We're the most direct descendants of Duke Louis de Calvados Castaigne. You're even named after him. Alfonso the Third promised he would rule over New Spain once it was reclaimed in the name of the King."

She pulled off her ring and showed it to me. "See? Our father inherited this. It bears the sign of the King."

I paused, not sure how to respond. "But that whole reclaiming thing never happened, did it?"

"Look around," she said. "Who rules the land now?"

I shivered.

After a sleepless night in which I thought way too much about Gun and Bear and the stillborn baby, we rode on for my parents' house in Mill Valley. The morning sky was a flat, gray-yellow expanse, and the air smelled of sulfur. Xinantecatl was blowing ash down in Mexico. The new eruptions of the long-dormant volcano started a few months before the first vampire attacks were recorded, and so some people claimed that the mountain had released the ancient, parasitic race from hibernation deep in the rocks. I didn't know if the tale was true or not, but the coincidence was compelling. People told all kinds of stories about the vampires. Some folks claimed NASA brought them back from Mars. Ultimately, their natural history didn't matter. Staying alive did.

The highways were holding up pretty well considering they hadn't had any maintenance in two years. Everything seemed pretty well deserted, even the parts of Los Angeles we traveled past. I'd braced myself to have to flee from roving paramilitary or urban gangs, but the city was a ghostly expanse of silent concrete, decaying buildings, and weed-eaten blacktop. San Francisco was nearly as desolate, although I glimpsed a few figures hurrying to duck into buildings or behind vehicles when we approached.

It occurred to me that I might have single-handedly wiped out a double-digit portion of the remaining human population in Arizona, and I didn't feel very good about that.

We got to the house shortly before sunset. The roads leading up to it were choked with vines and ferns, but everything inside the tall iron gate was pretty much as I remembered it. The rolling expanse of lawn was weed-free and freshly mowed. I could even see the lights of the dining room chandelier.

"I've kept the place up," Lady said as she punched in her security code. The gate creaked open. "Me and a couple of the servants, anyhow."

Servants. That used to be a normal thing for me: living in a house with a butler, a couple of maids, and a gardener. Some of the people I related my story to shook their heads and told me that I was crazy for walking away from so much money and privilege and choosing to live in a world where spilled Tylenol mattered, but I was miserable in Mill Valley. I could remember happiness in my life: it was with Joe, before something bit him in the dark.

She saw me gazing at the chandelier. "The solar panels cost six figures, but they were an excellent investment; we were off the grid well before the King awoke his minions."

"That's good," I said absently. My sister's talk of the King was starting to get on my nerves. She'd always been a little strange, but now I was starting to wonder if she was delusional. Still, her eyes were clear of jaundice, and the house looked fine. I knew to stay on my guard—I was *always* on my guard—but I was pretty curious about what my family had been up to since I'd been gone.

We rode up the long driveway and parked our bikes in the circle around the bubbling marble fountain; Father had it imported from somewhere in France.

Lady eyed my gun belt and the machete I wore in a leather sheath strapped across my back. "You don't need those in the house."

"I'd feel naked without them."

She shrugged, smiled dreamily, and knocked on the front door. Our old butler Mr. Yates answered and escorted us inside. He didn't look much different than he did back when I still lived there. The inside of the house was bigger than I remembered, and all the marble and mahogany and brass fixtures were burnished to glossy shines.

"This way, gentle ladies," Yates said. "The rest of the family is gathered in the parlor."

We followed him back, and he pushed open the double doors. My father sat in his favorite easy chair. My mother stood behind him, and my aunt Hilda and her grown children Constance and Archer sat on the sofa nearby, drinking tea from bone-china cups.

My heart soared, and I forgot my old hatred of my father. The whole family had survived? It was nothing short of a miracle.

"Welcome home, Louise," my father said.

But then Yates moved off to the left . . . and I caught a glimpse of him from the corner of my eye.

Instinct took over before I had a chance to think. I drew my machete and swung at the elderly butler. My blade met its mark and the vampire scrambled back, shrieking and hissing, clutching its severed wing.

"No!" shrieked Lady, cowering away from me.

At that point I'd glimpsed the rest of the family sidewise, and what was still human in me wept while I drew the .38 and started pumping hollow-points into everything that moved.

A huge vampire flapped toward me, its wings yellow tatters, the gunshot wound in its leg dripping ichor like amber sap. "Explain yourself!" it boomed in my father's regal voice.

I danced aside like a matador, met it with the machete, and took its head raggedly off.

And when it died, the house around me changed. The light sconces glowed not with electricity but guttering oil lamps made from old cans; I recognized the smell of burning human fat. The brass was green with corrosion, the windows shattered. The fine couches were torn and stained with blood from a hundred victims. What I had taken for plush, clean carpet was a matted pile scattered with human remains, and in the dimness beyond, I saw the gleaming eyes of dozens of vampires huddled against the walls.

And I realized I could hear them whispering, *The princess is dead . . . long live the Queen . . . the Queen . . . the Queen.*

Lady was on her knees, weeping. She still looked human enough, but her yellow dress was ragged, her hair thin and tangled, her eyes dull and uninteresting. The only thing upon her that retained its previous luster was the golden signet ring.

I pointed at her with my ichor-stained machete. "Why? Why did you do this?"

"You were the firstborn," she sobbed bitterly. "I couldn't be Queen while you lived. I *couldn't*."

I almost asked "Queen of *what*?" but I saw the clustered vampires and could hear their whispers all over the house. They *feared* me. More than that, they respected me. I had a power I'd never asked for and surely didn't want. But it might come in handy anyhow.

I stared down at her. "And you brought me here . . . to die? So you could be Queen?"

She nodded. "Yes. I only ever wanted to serve the King and now I can't."

"But you saw what I did at the clubhouse." I shook my head, still not able to wrap my mind around what she'd tried to do. "You *saw* what I'm capable of. You could have made me leave my weapons outside but you didn't."

"They were just *people*." Her tone was supremely dismissive; she was her father's little princess, all right. "I didn't think you could hurt the family."

"Why do they need a human queen?"

"To lead them to new prey."

I almost said, "I'll never do that," but I suddenly realized my will had nothing to do with it. I could hear their whispers because my brain was connected to the hive-mind now. The vampires could see through my eyes, hear through my ears. The moment I found survivors, friendly or not, the hive would know exactly where they were.

And if I closed my eyes, I could feel the King watching me from someplace far away, a land lit by dark stars, a world the ancients called Carcosa.

"What happens when they run out of prey?" I asked, already fearing the answer.

She shrugged. "The servants will starve. And the world will be silent but for the wind in the trees and the waves crashing upon the empty shores, just as the King wishes it to be."

Neither of us said anything for a long time.

"I can't ever trust you again," I finally told her. "I take betrayal *very* badly."

"I know." She sniffled, wiped her eyes, pulled off the ring, and set it on the stained carpet. "That's yours now. I just ask that you make it qui—"

I brought the machete down on the back of her neck before she could finish her sentence. Her head rolled away into darkness. The vampires chittered and gazed at me, waiting. I was useful to them, and so I could live. For now. For a price.

If I'd been a better person, I would have reloaded my pistol, put it to my head, and ended things right then and there. Done my bit to save humanity. But . . . I couldn't do it. It wasn't just that I'd been raised to think of suicide as a sin. I had struggled so long to stay alive, and I'd once sworn to myself I wouldn't die in my father's house.

I rescued the ring from being drowned in the spreading pool of my sister's blood and shoved it onto my finger. It felt as though it had been made just for me.

Two days later, I was back at the Freebirds' clubhouse. I found Rentboy all alone, dragging bodies out of the shed to pile them in the field. It was cremation day. His pretty face and bare chest were covered in bruises.

"They beat the hell out of me when they got back," he said, only looking at me from the corner of his eye. "But they let me live. And then they left. Said they couldn't stay here no more and I couldn't come with them."

He heaved a dead woman onto the pile and turned to face me. Then just stood there, squinting, puzzled. "Beauty? Is . . . is that really you? You look . . . different. Where'd your scars go?"

I twisted the ring on my finger. "I'm a bona fide queen, did you know that?"

Rentboy was staring at me, mesmerized by my new glamour. What was that I saw in his eyes? Was it fear? Was it hatred? No. It was utter adoration. It should have made me feel uncomfortable, but I took it as my due.

I held out my hand bearing the ring, and he fell to his knees and kissed it.

"Do you pledge allegiance to your queen?"

"Yes, ma'am."

"Do you swear your life to me?"

"Yes, I do."

"Good." I made him get up. "Pack up the supplies. We're going into the desert where nobody lives, and we're never coming back."

THE LAST SUPPER

BRIAN KEENE

A few minutes before he heard the sound, Carter became convinced that the trees were following him.

He'd been walking from the Edgefield Hotel toward the town of Troutdale, just past the point where Halsey Street turned into historic Highway 30. The moon shone overhead, three-quarters full in a cloudless sky, providing enough light to see—not that he needed the illumination. Carter saw clearly even on the darkest of nights, and his hearing and sense of smell were equally hyperattuned.

A vast mountain range spanned the horizon to his left. He thought that the peaks might be related to Mount Hood, but he couldn't be sure, and there was no one to ask. Nor could he pull out his phone and find out via the Internet, because both had stopped working months ago. He walked on, once again certain that the trees were following him. He heard them behind him, shuffling forward, tiptoeing on their roots. Every time he stopped and turned to glare at them, the trees stopped, too.

"I'm crazy."

His voice sounded funny to him, and his throat was sore. How long had it been since he'd spoken aloud? He couldn't remember.

"I'm crazy," he repeated. "That's all. And I'd have to be, wouldn't I? Living alone like this? It's enough to drive anyone crazy."

He walked on, trying his best to ignore the trees. To his right was a field lined with rows of grapes. The unattended crop had grown wild. Vines, heavy with fruit, sprawled out into the road and snaked up trees and telephone poles.

The rustling sounds started again. He was sure they were real this time. He spun around.

"Stop following me!"

The trees didn't answer.

Carter turned, stumbled over a pothole in the road, and winced as a jolt of pain ran through his leg. He'd broken it two weeks before, which was why he'd holed up at the Edgefield Hotel for so long. Before the epidemic, such an injury would have healed more quickly, but food had been in scarce supply, and thus, it had taken longer. Before the Edgefield, he'd last eaten in Seattle, and that had only been a starving, rail-thin feral dog—barely enough blood to sustain him and certainly lacking in the vitamins and nutrients he needed to effectively heal.

He'd spent a few days in Seattle, scrounging, before ultimately moving on, but the dog had been his only encounter. Seattle, like everywhere else in the world, had been emptied by the plague, its population reduced to nothing but bags of rotten meat filled with congealed, sludgelike blood. The stench wafting out of the city had been noticeable from miles away, and Carter had been certain that it would have been even to someone without his heightened sense of smell.

Unfortunately, there had been no one else left to smell it.

He'd made his way on foot from Seattle down into Oregon. Driving had been out of the question. The roads were choked with abandoned cars, wreckage, downed trees, and bodies. They'd cleared a bit in Oregon, but he'd continued walking anyway, because it made it easier to hunt. He'd reached Troutdale and broken into the Edgefield, intent on sleeping through the day and then continuing on toward Portland that night, when a stray beam of sunlight had altered those plans. He'd been climbing a stairwell, listening to his footfalls echo through the deserted building, sniffing around and sifting through the thick miasma of dust, mildew, long-spoiled food, even longer-spoiled corpses, when the first light of the rising sun had drifted through a window and struck him on the arm. Flinching, Carter had recoiled. The next thing he knew, he'd lost his balance and tumbled down the stairs. He heard his leg break before the pain set in. Then, he'd lost consciousness.

When he awoke, daylight had begun to stream through the empty halls. Panicked, Carter crawled into an alcove behind the stairwell and huddled in the darkness, shivering with agony and shock. He'd remained there until nightfall, when at last, feverish and half-delirious with pain, he crawled out again and managed to find a hotel room with a door ajar. He'd dragged himself inside and shut the door. With great difficulty, he'd draped a moldy bedspread over the room's lone window before collapsing with exhaustion. Then he'd slept.

On his second night in the Edgefield, he'd heard a faint skittering from out in the hall. Alert, he'd sat up in bed, sniffing the air. Slowly, he crawled to the door and opened it. Then he lay there, still as death. He waited a full hour before the rat investigated, and it took another twenty minutes of motionlessness before the animal was brave enough to come close to him and take an experimental nibble, at which point Carter reached out and grabbed it, seizing the creature with both hands. After he'd eaten, he rested again, allowing his leg to heal.

And now, here he was, intent upon exploring Troutdale before sunrise. If his efforts were unsuccessful, he'd move on to Portland tomorrow night. He doubted that Portland would offer anything more than Seattle had, but it was something to do. And, in truth, it wasn't just food he was looking for. It was companionship.

Carter was lonely.

The irony wasn't lost on him. He was, as far as he knew, the last living human on the planet, except that he wasn't alive and he wasn't human. He hadn't been either for a long time.

The breeze shifted and Carter caught a whiff of the grapes. It had been decades since he'd tasted grapes—or jelly or wine or anything else made from them. Decades since he'd tasted food of any sort—pasta, beef, ice cream, vegetables. Chocolate.

Carter sighed. He'd loved chocolate as a boy. Sometimes, he tried to remember what it had really tasted like, but the memory was fleeting. A ghost—a gossamer phantasm as insubstantial and romanticized as the memory of a first kiss. Over the years, he'd grown accustomed to being a vampire, but Carter had never quite gotten used to not being able to have chocolate. He'd tried several times—once right after his transformation, and a few times since. On each occasion, the chocolate had acted as a toxin in his system. All foods had the same effect. He wasn't lactose or gluten intolerant. He suffered from a food allergy, and it encompassed all foods. All except blood.

Carter died on June 17, 1967, at the Monterey International Pop Festival, during the beginning of the Summer of Love. A still mostly unknown Jimi Hendrix had just begun the opening chords of "Wild Thing" when Carter, high as a kite and feeling happy, had gone outside the fairgrounds hand in hand with a beautiful brunette who had never given him her name but had looked a little bit like Grace Slick. They'd begun to make love in a dark area behind a porta-potty, except that the love turned to terror very quickly, as the girl's soft, eager kisses on his throat had turned frenzied and then sharp. And then . . .

. . . nothing.

He'd been lost in a dream haze, not unlike an acid trip. To this day his memories were sketchy at best. Someone, perhaps a fellow concertgoer or one of the outnumbered security guards, had interrupted them. They must have, because she'd never had the opportunity to drink him dry. If she had, he wouldn't be here today. Carter had a vague memory of being loaded into an ambulance, and another of a paramedic leaning over him, aghast, and muttering, "Jesus, look at his fucking throat! It's like a wild animal got at him or something." Then, much later, he'd regained consciousness inside a morgue. His first thought, upon waking, was that he'd missed the rest of Hendrix's set but had certainly experienced his very own wild thing.

Carter had figured out fairly quickly what he was. That was the easy part. Discovering which portions of the vampire legends were true, and which were bullshit, had taken a little longer. He was vulnerable to sunlight and garlic, but things like crosses and other religious trappings had no effect on him. He saw himself in the mirror just fine, albeit his reflection didn't age the way others did. He was perpetually twenty-two. He didn't know if a stake through the heart could kill him or not, but gunshots, a stabbing, and being hit by a tractor-trailer one time in the eighties hadn't. He'd recovered from those injuries as easily as he'd reknit his broken leg. He'd also recovered from a spinal fracture suffered shortly after his transformation, when he'd jumped off a building in an attempt to turn into a bat. That last part of the vampire legend, as it turned out, was also just myth, as were the supposed abilities to control animals such as rats or influence and hypnotize people.

He'd never again seen the vampire who'd turned him. Indeed, in the years that followed, Carter had known only two others like him. One had been a girl he himself had turned in the early seventies—a redheaded flower child named Lindsey. They'd met at a Grateful Dead concert, and Carter had fallen in love almost immediately. For months, he kept his secret from her, until one night, when Lindsey was high and fantasizing out loud about what a cool trip it would be to live forever, and Carter had told her that he could make that possible.

And then he had.

Lindsey hadn't accepted it well, and a few days later, when the hunger for blood had become overwhelming, she'd opted to commit suicide by watching the sunrise, rather than feeding on another human. Sometimes, when he slept, Carter still smelled her burning and heard her accusatory screams.

The other one like him had been Nick, a witty, fast-talking Greek who claimed to be over two hundred years old. Nick also claimed that he had helped to invent socialism. They'd met in Berkeley in 1986. Carter had been feeding in an alley behind a bookstore, after attending a poetry reading. When he'd finished, he'd become aware of the other vampire's presence. Nick had stood watching, a bemused expression on his face. Carter had been astonished to meet another like himself, and Nick became a mentor of sorts. He'd told Carter their kind were few and far between. Pop-culture depictions of vampire hierarchies and councils were bullshit. The only community Nick had known about was in the backwoods of West Virginia, and they were foul, savage creatures, more akin to a feral dog pack than civilized beings such as Carter and himself.

Nick had gone to North Korea shortly after Bush succeeded Reagan. Carter hadn't heard from him since. He often wondered what had happened to his friend, especially since the plague.

He was so lonely.

Nick had sometimes teased Carter about his friendships with humans, asking him if the butcher made friends with the cows before he slaughtered them.

Carter thought of that now, as Troutdale grew closer. And yes, he thought, yes, the butcher would befriend the cows, because he'd be so happy just to have someone to talk to again.

He walked into town, passing under a wrought-iron arch with a fish statue on either side. A sign proclaimed WELCOME TO TROUT-DALE—THE WESTERN GATEWAY. A gateway to what? Carter wondered. Another world? How wonderful would that be, to slip from one dimension to the next, and travel to a reality where the plague had never happened and he wasn't starving and there were people to talk to and laugh with. If only it were that easy.

Carter passed an outlet mall. Most of the storefront windows were broken, and a tree had fallen through the roof of the bookstore, allowing the elements to get inside. He paused for a moment, listening and sniffing the air, but as far as he could tell, the mall was deserted. If he got closer, it might be possible to discern a rat or squirrel living among the ruins, but that would have involved an arduous climb down a steep embankment. Carter instead decided to try his luck deeper into town.

The main drag was lined with small shops—a tattoo parlor, several attorneys' offices, a chiropractor, a dentist, a hair salon, and a spa were mixed in among numerous bars and restaurants. All of them were deserted, their occupants long gone. He paused in front of an antiques store. A faded, yellowed newspaper cartoon had been taped inside the window. Its edges were brown and curling. In it, a young boy and his pet tiger were snuggled together in bed. The caption read, *Things are never quite as scary when you've got a best friend*. Carter supposed this was true, because he was fucking terrified. His nights were spent in constant fear. Mostly, he was scared of being alone.

The other side of Troutdale butted up against the Sandy River. There, in a wooded area behind the Depot Rail Museum, he found the remains of a homeless encampment. A blue plastic tarp had been stretched out between four tree trunks and tied fast, forming a makeshift roof. Beneath it was a stone fire pit, filled with charred sticks. Judging by the mud inside the circle of rocks, it had been quite some time since a fire had burned there.

"Hello," he called. Rather than echoing, his voice seemed to fall flat, as if the forest itself had swallowed it. It faded all too quickly, replaced again by silence. Carter longed for the drone of an airplane overhead, or the rumbling of a train or a bus passing by, but there was nothing. Even the birds and animals had gone silent, no doubt as a result of his presence.

Sighing, Carter turned back to town, intent on finding something to eat. Out of the corner of his eye, the trees seemed to turn with him. He wheeled to face them.

"I told you to stop following me! Leave me alone."

And that was when he heard the sound. It started as a distant whoosh of air, with a low, mechanical hum beneath it. He recognized the noise right away. It was the faraway sound of a car on the highway, coming closer. Carter glanced around frantically, trying to determine its origin. Then, as it drew nearer, he ran back down the street. While flying or transforming into a bat might have been the stuff of fanciful legend, Carter was indeed equipped with unnatural speed and strength, both of which he relied upon now, dashing the entire length of Troutdale in just under thirty seconds. But the exertion left him winded, and he was still weak from hunger, and he had to stop again beneath the fish archway, panting.

He had to be imagining it. Deep down inside, he knew this to be true. There couldn't be a car. It was a mirage. A hallucination. Just like the trees.

But what if it wasn't?

The hum of the engine and tires grew ever closer. He limped quickly to the overpass and gazed out at the highway below. There, on the horizon, he saw headlights. It was real! Carter had no idea how the driver had managed to navigate around the assorted wreckage choking the highways, but at that moment, he didn't care. His pulse hammered in his throat as the car drew nearer. Human beings! One, at the very least. His excitement gave way to panic. What if they were . . . bad? Carter had seen enough postapocalyptic movies and read enough dystopian fiction that visions of leather-clad punk-rock marauders filled his head. But, no. Given just how much of humanity had died off, the driver and any possible occupants couldn't be bad. He couldn't justify this assurance with any sound logic, but that didn't stop him from clinging to the emotion. They had to be decent, and surely they'd be grateful to see him, as well.

"Hello," Carter shouted from the overpass. "Up here!"

He realized they'd never see him from atop the overpass. While the car wasn't speeding, it was nighttime, and the driver was probably focused on the road ahead, alert for any wreckage or obstructions in the dark. He hurried down the embankment, heading toward the road. The occupant of the car must be driving with the window down, he decided, because now he could smell them. The scent was faint but undeniable. A woman, unless he was mistaken. Although he couldn't be sure, he suspected she was alone.

He slid down the hillside and dashed out into the roadway. Headlights speared him. Carter raised his arms over his head and waved them enthusiastically.

"Hello," he called. "Stop the car! Please stop."

Tires squealed as the driver locked the brakes. He smelled rubber burning and caught a glimpse of the frightened woman's face through the windshield as the car swerved to one side and spun out of control. Then, as if in slow motion, the car flipped over and slid on its roof. Metal shrieked, and so did the driver. Sparks danced in the darkness like fireflies. There was a deafening crash as the upside-down vehicle slammed into the concrete support beneath the overpass and then folded in on itself like aluminum foil.

Carter's heart beat once. Twice.

The driver had stopped screaming.

"No!" He ran toward the car, broken glass crunching beneath his feet. The stench of burned rubber and scorched metal was thick in the air, but even thicker was the smell of blood. The odor simultane-ously filled him with excitement and dread, and Carter hated him-self for feeling both.

He reached the wreck, got down on his hands and knees, and peered inside. Remarkably, the driver was conscious. She was pretty, African-American, and in her mid-to-late twenties. Carter couldn't determine much else about her because she was covered in blood. The smell of it seemed to assail him, and he reeled back, weeping.

"Didn't . . ." Blood trickled from her mouth as she spoke. "You . . . surprised me."

"I'm sorry," he choked. "I'm so sorry. Are you okay?"

It was a stupid question, he knew. Judging by the lacerations on her body and the position of several limbs, the young woman was anything but okay. But after all that time spent talking to inanimate objects and himself, Carter was having trouble focusing on how to talk to another person. He took a deep breath, smelled the blood, and tried again, shivering as he did.

"My name is Carter. What's yours?"

"A . . . Ashley. Are you . . . really alive?"

He nodded, unable to form enough words to lie.

"It's . . . nice to . . . meet you, Carter. I . . . thought I was . . ."

"Alone," Carter finished for her, and smiled.

She returned the gesture and tried to nod. When she did, her ex-pression changed to one of anguish.

Carter's choked laughter changed to a sob. "Don't try to move. Just stay still. You're going to be okay."

"I'm cold," she whispered. "Will you . . . stay with me?"

It was Carter's turn to nod. "Of course I will. I wouldn't leave you for anything. It's just . . . I just . . . I thought I'd never talk to anyone ever again."

"Me too." More blood trickled from Ashley's mouth.

"I thought you were like the trees."

Ashley frowned in confusion. "W-what?"

"Never mind. It's not important."

Carter studied the wreckage. He could free her easily enough. A fire-and-rescue team's Jaws of Life had nothing on him, but if he did, she'd probably die within seconds. Mashed and mangled as she was, the twisted steel pressed so tightly against her was the only thing still keeping Ashley alive. Despite that, she probably only had minutes.

Carter began to cry.

"I'm sorry," he moaned. "I didn't mean to . . ."

"It's okay," Ashley reassured him. "Tell me . . . about yourself. Talk to me . . . until . . ."

So he did. As tears ran down his perpetually young cheeks, Carter spoke through muffled sobs. He shook with emotion while she trembled with shock. He held her hand, and it was soft and warm. They talked for a while, and then her hand turned cold, and she was gone.

Carter was still weeping as he began to feed.

SEPARATOR

RIO YOUERS

The loss was evident even ten months after the storm. Palla's streets were cramped and stifling, thronged with restructure, with people, traffic, and noise. A note of emptiness remained, however. It resonated in the cracked walls and boarded-up windows. In the sorrowful movement of trees. Mostly, it occupied the expressions of those who called Palla home. They mustered hope in tiny increments, but the light had been drawn from their eyes. The storm had taken something from them all.

More than three thousand confirmed fatalities across the region. Damage in excess of two billion US dollars. News footage showed Alayna moving into the Leyte Gulf, gathering strength—a Category 5 super typhoon by the time it made landfall on Samar Island. Wind speeds reached 180 miles per hour. Buildings were dismantled, blown away like handfuls of straw. Trees were uprooted, vehicles flipped. There was no safe harbor. No shelter. Aftermath footage showed miles of devastation beneath a mocking blue sky. Survivors stood amid the ruin, outnumbered by the dead. Images of loss and faithlessness. Mass graves and temporary morgues. An endless, apocalyptic landscape. World news showed the desperation, the lack of food and water, the rescue centers set up by NGOs. American networks focused on the droves of corpses; the weeping, orphaned children; and the relief efforts of the US military.

For most, it was hell on earth. For others—the looters, scaremongers, hate groups, and businessmen—it was an opportunity.

The music was part techno, part rock—a frenzied, metallic barrage. The walls trembled and the lights stuttered, as if the entire room were a rapidly blinking eye. The club was called Snakebite. A concrete-and-steel structure raised out of the ruins. An effort to shove Palla back on its feet, or at least its knees. Dancers pirouetted on tables or twisted their lithe bodies around poles, disrobing for pesos. Shooter girls dressed as nurses sold "antidotes" in three-ounce hypos. A huge reptile cage had been built into one wall, where the clientele took selfies with a king cobra—frantic in the cacophony, spreading its hood, banging its head against the glass.

David Payne downed his *lambanog* in a single, head-swirling hit. Slammed his glass on the bar. Clutched the underside of his stool. He closed his eyes as the club revolved, feeling as if he had been thrown into some rolling barrel of sound. Equilibrium returned, though not completely. He swayed, flipped open his wallet, enticed one of the dancers with a five-hundred-peso note. She stepped toward him on knifepoint heels. Beautiful skin, green contact lenses, a shimmering blue wig. She threw one leg over him, ground her hips into his.

"What can I get for this?" David tucked the note into her satin thong. She grinned and rolled her tongue over his lips. It felt warm, full, and sweet. He shook another note from his wallet and raised his eyebrows. The dancer unclipped her bandeau and it fell between them. She grabbed a bottle of *lambanog* from the bar, splashed it over her small breasts, and invited David to drink. He did, tasting alcohol and coconut and a dry perfume. He pulled her left nipple into his mouth, chewing lightly, feeling it swell against his tongue. She slipped from his lap, trailing long fingernails gently across his cheek, snatching the five-hundred-peso note from his hand and tucking it with the other.

"Thank you, Mr. America."

"I'm Canadian."

She smiled and whirled away. David slouched against the bar. The club revolved again. Smeared faces, flickering lights, the cobra hammering angrily against the glass. David took a deep breath and held on. Beside him, Crisanto—his business associate—grinned and tipped the rim of his glass.

"Welcome to the Philippines."

Beneath the blue wig, her hair was short enough that—when he ran his fingers through it—he could feel her scalp sweating. She kept her contact lenses in, at his request, and her eyes flashed wildly in the room's single light. David looked into them as he hooked the backs of her ankles onto his shoulders and eased himself into her, and the assertiveness—the confidence—she had shown at Snakebite momentarily dissipated. She whimpered and arched her back. Her shoulders trembled. Then she curled herself around him. Rolled her hips evenly. Used her body like she had used her tongue at the club. Warm, full, and sweet.

He pulled out, removed the condom, and came into the shallow of her stomach. Smeared it over her thighs and breasts, watched it dry and harden. She got out of bed, perhaps to shower, perhaps to leave, but he pulled her back and told her to stay. They lay for a while, neither touching nor speaking. Eventually, they slept. David woke a short time later, surprised to find her still there. She slept on her stomach, one arm looped beneath the pillow. Her contact lenses were on the nightstand, thin as fish scales. The sight of her slender body, the dip of her spine, her boyish haircut, got him hard again. He rolled another condom on and woke her. It was rough and quick.

Morning light broke through a gap in the drapes. David pulled on his jeans and stepped out onto the balcony. The partially rebuilt city stretched below him, the streets quiet now, but the stall owners would soon trundle their wares to the roadside, the stores would open, the trucks and motorcycles and jeepneys would appear. Another day in Palla. Another day with Alayna in the rearview, and that emptiness slowly being filled. To the south, San Pedro and San Pablo Bay shimmered coolly, reflecting a membrane of pink light that fanned across Samar Island. The view from the other side of the hotel—looking north—was less appealing: the buckled outskirts of the city, like cracked shells, and a riot of vegetation, given space and light to flourish in. It consumed debris, plantations, probably bodies. Beyond this, like a giant patchwork stitched into the land, Tent City. Alayna had mustered formidable power in the Leyte Gulf, advancing from storm warning signal number two to number four within hours. Ninety-five percent of the city had evacuated. Most had returned to find everything gone. Tent City was the solution: temporary shelter for the tens of thousands still without homes, waiting for the government to build the bunkhouses they'd promised.

This was where David came in. More particularly, his employers. New Reality Land Development had purchased—and begun to raze—forty hectares of tropical rain forest to the north of Palla and would construct apartment complexes, hotels, and a number of lucrative attractions. David's role as consultant was to ensure the project ran smoothly, dealing with regulatory agencies, designers, engineers, outraged locals, eco-warriors. He would iron out the wrinkles as they appeared—something he was good at. The next three years of his life would be spent between Toronto and Palla, expanding both his résumé and his bank account. Indeed, David expected to have his own land development company by the time he turned forty-five.

Professional and driven, he always got what he wanted.

Almost always.

A bead of light winked off his wedding ring, drawing his gaze from the quiet streets below. He wondered what Angie was doing. Twelve hours behind—still *yesterday* in Toronto—she'd be settling down for dinner, perhaps, or napping on the sofa after a long day at work. *I don't know how long we can keep trying*, she'd said before he left. *We need to make a decision.* Their kiss had been honest and intimate, and for a long moment they'd held each other. Her fractured expression had occupied his mind the entire seventeen-hour flight to Manila.

David wiped his eyes, looked through the balcony doors to where the dancer slept in his bed. Guilt was like the cobra at Snakebite: flexing, banging its head furiously against the glass, unable to strike.

The city woke. The pink light on the bay turned gold.

Crisanto sat on the hood of his car, fresh-eyed and smiling. He wore a light suit. No tie. His shoes were polished, but there was mud on the heels.

"How's your head?"

"Been better," David replied. His breakfast of apple juice and Advil had set a buzz behind his eyes, but the ache remained, like a stone wrapped in cloth. "Let's get this done so I can go back to bed."

After ten, warm already, a closeness to the air that felt, to David, like the air in a crowded streetcar. They trickled north, bunched in traffic. Aromas of ginger, *pandan*, and fish flowed through the vents. As did the sounds: horns and hawkers blaring, vehicles rumbling, original Pinoy music thumping from various speakers and radios. The traffic thinned as they headed out of the city, passing through neighborhoods where restoration work had barely begun. There were roofless buildings, drifts of debris, notice boards littered with photographs of missing loved ones. Fewer people lined the streets and nobody sold anything. David saw an elderly lady sitting beside a pile of rubble that, presumably, used to be her home. Nearby, a pack of lank dogs nosed for scraps.

"You know," Crisanto said, "I can take you to someone who'll cure that hangover in seconds."

"A witch doctor?"

"Something like that," Crisanto said. "*Albularyo* . . . a healer."

"I'll pass; I don't believe in any of that shit." David plucked Advil from the inside pocket of his jacket. Popped three into his mouth and swallowed them dry. "I'll stick to my tried and tested pharmaceuticals."

"North American witchcraft."

"We call it *science*."

Out of Palla. To the west, gulfs of open land where coconut and rice plantations once prospered. To the east, Tent City, reaching for miles, like a great white flag of surrender. The conditions were third-world, with children dressed in rags and thin fires burning. NGO vehicles twined between shelters, distributing aid.

David looked away, first at the road ahead, then at his hands. He spun his wedding band and thought again of Angie, who'd be settling into their downy bed, encased in pillows, perhaps with a book or the TV remote.

I want this, he'd said to her. *I'm not giving up.*

His head throbbed. He pulled a clipboard from between the center console and the passenger seat, flipped pages.

"Tell me about the woman."

"Dalisay Magana." Crisanto steered around a carabao laden with firewood. "Fifty-seven years old. So the paperwork says. What's the English word for a woman who doesn't marry?"

"*Spinster.*"

"Yes, a spinster. She's lived in the forest all her life. Speaks no English, only Waray."

"That's fine," David said. "You can translate."

Crisanto nodded. His gaze flicked from the road to the sky. He set both hands on the wheel and exhaled slowly.

"Why the change of heart?"

"She thought she was going to be rehoused elsewhere in the forest." Crisanto's eyes flickered with uncertainty, and David detected the slightest tremor to his voice. "She refuses to live in a hotel, even temporarily. She says the trees give her protection."

"They won't protect her from a bulldozer," David said with a dry smile. He looked at the document he'd flipped to, ran his finger along her signature. "A signed contract trumps a change of heart."

The asphalt gave way to a dirt road that snaked into the rain forest. Grit rattled off the chassis and doors, and now the perfumes coming through the vents were damp and green. Within a mile they came to the build zone, marked by security fencing, a billboard displaying the New Reality logo, and another depicting the architects' vision for the site: a sprawl of modern buildings, with a grinning Caucasian family in the foreground. Crisanto parked beside the field office—a gleaming site trailer—where they signed in and donned their high-visibility vests and hard hats.

"We walk from here," Crisanto said.

They moved west through the forest, away from the mechanical shriek of the harvesters. David saw their powerful yellow bodies through the trees, thinning and stripping, with forwarders collecting the trunks, like death carts gathering corpses. If there was any wildlife in this part of the forest, David neither saw nor heard it. As they moved farther from the machinery, though, the air came to life with fat bugs that tapped at his skin and buzzed. Farther still, he saw cockatoos bristling between branches, and long-tailed macaques, some foraging, others playing.

"We're nearly there," Crisanto said.

David saw the shack moments later. An assemblage of odd boards nailed together. A warped, sloping roof. There were several glassless windows screened with dirty fabric—perhaps to keep the critters out, David thought, although they'd have no problem squeezing through the gaps in the boards. Clothes were hung to dry outside, stiff and stained, and there was a basin of dirty water in which insects had drowned belly-up.

"She doesn't want to move from *here*?" David sneered, and shook his head. "It's a goddamn dump."

Crisanto had fallen behind as they approached, appearing hesitant. David looked at him over one shoulder.

"Mr. Translator," he said. "I'm going to need you."

At twenty-eight, Crisanto was ten years David's junior but notably more masculine, with a pronounced brow and rugged jaw. At that moment, however, he appeared to have regressed many years, adopting the cowed demeanor of an uncertain child. *Timid* was the word that came to David's mind.

"What is it?" David asked.

"Nothing."

"Nothing?"

"Filipino superstition. You wouldn't understand." Crisanto took a deep breath, then squared his shoulders, strode forward. "Let's get this over with."

She stepped outside as they approached the door, and David glimpsed inside the shack. A gloomy, small space, with things—indeterminate—strung from the ceiling. He caught a whiff of boiling meat and fat, or something similar. A bird fluttered within, probably trapped.

"Tell her to take off the shawl," David said.

"She won't," Crisanto said.

"Tell her."

Crisanto spoke in Waray, the tremor from earlier still evident in his voice. The exotic language could not disguise it. The woman—Dalisay Magana—shrugged or shook her head. She snapped a single word—"*Diri*"—that, coupled with her body language, needed no translation.

David crouched and stepped toward her, hoping to see her eyes; it was difficult to be charming—persuasive—without the benefit of eye contact. The shawl covered her face, dropped to her waist. The same gray fabric that blanked the windows. She was hunched, slightly twisted. Some spinal malady, David thought. She wore a long black skirt beneath the shawl. Her feet were bare, dusted with dirt.

"Ms. Magana, my name is David Payne. I'm a consultant at New Reality Land Development. I'd like to talk to you about—"

"*Putang ina mo,*" she cut across him, and something flashed behind the fabric. Her eyes, perhaps, but David couldn't be sure.

Crisanto had backed to the edge of the woman's property, appearing yet more childlike with the trees towering behind him. He looked at David and shook his head. In the distance, the harvesters ripped and buzzed.

"We'll cut to the chase, shall we?" David met Crisanto's uncertain gaze. "Please assure Ms. Magana that New Reality is sensitive to her position, but that our work is a lifeline for the community. Many jobs will be created. There'll be an increase in tourism and a boost to the economy. With this project, we're putting Palla back on its feet."

Crisanto nodded. He spoke quietly, his head low.

The woman's hands appeared from beneath the shawl. They were almost elegant. Pale skin and long fingers.

"Remind her that she signed a contract." David held up the clipboard. "In so doing, she signed her land and everything on it over to New Reality and, as of June twenty-third, has been trespassing on property she no longer owns."

Crisanto told her. Sweat dripped from the brim of his hard hat. The woman responded, her voice thin and strange. The angle of her body suggested she was looking at David as she spoke.

"She says she didn't know what she was signing," Crisanto translated. "The language was confusing. Written by idiots."

"Tell her those same idiots have deposited a generous sum of money into an account in her name." David smiled. He crouched again, trying to catch the flash of her eyes. "And she will be rehoused in a comfortable hotel until we can find something to her satisfaction."

A brief exchange in Waray.

"She says she's already satisfied," Crisanto said. "And that she doesn't want your money."

"She has ten days."

A mosquito latched on to David's neck and drew blood. He slapped at it, looked at his palm, wiped the crushed insect across his pants leg with a grunt of both satisfaction and disgust. Another bug had landed in the basin of dirty water. David watched it drown, listening to the distant machinery and to the bird trapped inside the shack.

"Ten days," David repeated, "then we're coming through here, whether she's in that shitty little shack or not. Make sure she understands."

Crisanto spoke hesitantly, looking at his shoes.

No response from the woman. She drew away from him, her elegant hands snapping open and closed.

David wiped sweat from his brow. This meeting had not played out the way he had hoped. Still, she was one woman, virtually crippled, and if he had to drag her out of the shack kicking and screaming, he would.

"Thank you for your time, Ms. Magana."

"*Birat ka nim iroy.*"

Crisanto offered no translation. From the venom in her voice, David assumed she wasn't bidding him a good day. She muttered something else, then disappeared into her gloomy home.

"Let's go," Crisanto said. "Please."

David sneered. "I expected better from you."

Crisanto walked away without replying. David watched the back of his high-visibility vest moving swiftly between the trees. He shook his head and followed.

"You want to tell me what that was all about?"

Palla loomed in the windshield like a boxful of broken things strewn across the ground. Palm trees rattled their fronds and twisted. Dust clouded the road.

"Sorry," Crisanto offered.

"We have to be on the same page," David said. "The moment you show these people any hesitation—any weakness—they seize it. Next thing you know, we're involved in a drawn-out battle, losing money. And one thing I don't like is losing money."

They had driven from the site in silence. David had popped more Advil and tried to catch a ten-minute nap, but Crisanto's odd behavior had irked him. He wanted an explanation.

"So?"

"Like I said before," Crisanto said, running a trembling hand across the back of his neck. "You wouldn't understand."

"Try me," David said. "If I have to drag that old bitch out by the hair ten days from now, I'd at least like to know why you were so scared."

Another silence. Tent City sprawled to the east, like some campground gone to hell. David saw people waiting in line for food boxes distributed from the back of an NGO truck. A few bony children played with a deflated soccer ball. Another child—maybe five years old—sat alone at the roadside, her brown body mottled with the exhaust from passing cars.

Crisanto applied the brake and pulled over, the rear tires raking through the grit and gravel. He dug through the detritus cluttering the center console and retrieved an open packet of dried mangoes.

"Come on."

He stepped out of the car. David followed. They crossed the road and approached the child. Crisanto greeted her with a smile and said something in Waray. The little girl nodded. He handed her the dried mangoes. Her lips trembled.

"What do you think she's most afraid of?" Crisanto asked David. "Hunger, perhaps? Or another typhoon?"

David shrugged. He had no idea where this was going. He shielded his eyes against the swirling grit. The heat—the stench—was terrible.

The girl devoured one of the mango pieces. Crisanto smiled, crouched beside her. "Let's find out," he said, and asked her.

She responded by lowering her eyes and curling her shoulders. Her mouth glistened through strands of dirty hair. Crisanto touched her arm gently, whispered in Waray. The girl nodded, then pointed in the direction of the rain forest.

"*Aswang,*" she said. Her eyes were wide, frightened.

Crisanto stroked her hair and said something that made her smile. She went back to her mangoes, holding them protectively to her chest so they couldn't be taken away. Crisanto stood and looked at David.

"Every Filipino child grows up afraid of the *aswang,*" he said, and David detected the quaver in his voice, even now. "It's part of our folklore. Our culture. The equivalent, I suppose, of your 'monster in the closet.'"

"Okay," David said. "But that doesn't explain your behavior."

"It has various forms across the islands," Crisanto continued. "Werewolf. Ghoul. Shape-shifter. Many people in Palla, and the surrounding villages, believe the woman in the forest is an *aswang*—a *manananggal*, specifically."

They crossed the road, heading back to the car. David palmed sweat from his throat. His eyes were bloodshot and sore. Partly because of the alcohol from the night before. Mostly because of the swirling grit and acrid air. He was tired and irritable, and in no mood for fairy tales.

"*Mah-nah-nan-gal*," Crisanto said, sounding the word out clearly. "There's no direct translation to English. 'To separate' would be close—or a thing *that* separates. According to myth, the *manananggal* is a female vampire that grows wings and detaches herself at the torso. She leaves her lower half standing, while her upper half flies around in search of prey."

David opened the passenger door and slumped into the seat. He lowered his face into his hands and shook his head. He wanted desperately to be home. Drinking Sleeman Cream Ale on his deck. Barbecuing Alberta livestock. Flopping into his recliner and watching the shows he had lined up on the DVR.

"They're ravenous, bloodthirsty creatures," Crisanto added, sliding behind the wheel. "They'll eat anything with a heartbeat, although they have a preference for children and pregnant women."

"I've heard enough," David mumbled.

"They have extremely long tongues that they use to root fetuses from the womb."

"And you believe this shit?" David snapped. "You're a grown man. Highly educated. You speak four languages and write a regular column for the *Philippine Daily Inquirer*. Yet you believe the woman in the forest is some kind of . . . of *vampire*?"

Crisanto drove toward Palla. The cracked road vibrated through the seats.

"I don't know what to believe," he said. "But that childhood fear runs deep, and I saw enough today to unsettle me."

Here was the broken edge of the city, like the frayed hem of something long-worn. He saw a woman in tears. A dead goat. The shattered hull of a fishing boat that had been lifted from the harbor a mile away. David didn't believe in monsters, but the ghosts here were impossible to refute.

He closed his eyes and wondered what Angie was doing.

Her hair was tucked behind her ears and corn-colored, and she had that look in her eyes—that *look,* unique to her, to *them*—that felt like she was staring into both the past and the future. She unbuttoned her blouse. Unhooked her bra. David watched her, tilting the screen to minimize glare, praying the hotel's Internet connection would hold out. Angie cupped her breasts and plucked at her nipples, occasionally flicking her eyes to the webcam. David showed her how hard he was and she grinned, slipped out of her jeans. "I miss you, baby," she said, and David's lips moved but he didn't reply. "I miss you *so* much." She rubbed her clitoris with patient, circular motions and her labia drooped heavily and she whimpered in a way that David knew. She spoke his name. Twisted her body. Lifted her hips. David masturbated with trembling legs, chest drumming. The room's air conditioner hummed but his skin still shimmered with sweat. He came hard on his chest and showed her and played with it. Angie sighed and her eyes danced. She hooked her legs over the arms of the chair and came, too. Her orgasms were always short but powerful, as if someone had tightened every string inside her and then cut them at once.

He cleaned himself with a damp towel left on the bed. Poured three fingers of a Filipino whiskey called Calibre 69. Dropped ice into the glass and listened to it pop and settle. Angie had vacated her chair. David looked at the living room of his Toronto home, over eight thousand miles away. He saw the lamp they'd bought at IKEA just after they married, the edge of his recliner, most of their *Danaë with Eros* replica. He sipped his drink and thumbed sweat from the pockets beneath his eyes. Angie returned wearing a Maple Leafs sweatshirt. She fairly bounced into her chair and grinned.

"Did I tell you how much I miss you?"

"You did."

"Feels like you've been gone forever."

There was a notable sound delay that—even more than the look in her eyes—made him painfully homesick. It exposed the distance between them. She was to him, then, what the painting of Danaë was when sitting in his living room: a corn-haired girl who could be seen but not touched.

"I'll be home soon," he said.

"Soon?"

"I have some issues with a resident." Another sip of whiskey. His heart still drummed but it felt good. "Hope to have them resolved within a few days."

The clock on the nightstand ticked deeper into the night. Outside his hotel window, the street sounds faded to thin traffic. They talked about their neighbor's dog, their gifted niece, upgrading their smartphones. David poured and sipped. Three fingers became six. Became nine. The screen softened at the edges. Thunder rippled in the distance.

"You look tired," Angie said. "You should go to bed."

"Yes."

"We can Skype again Saturday."

"We will."

"I'm home all day."

He drank the last of his whiskey and set his tumbler down. The room started to roll, then righted itself, as if it were counterbalanced. David touched the screen. He said, "How we left it . . ."

"No," she said. "Let's not discuss it now."

"I've been giving it some thought—"

"Baby—"

"And I think we should keep trying."

Angie smiled. "We'll talk about it when you get home." She touched the screen, too. "I promise."

Thunder again. Nearer. More a thump than a ripple. Rain knocked on the window, stealing David's attention. When he looked back at the screen, Angie's image had frozen. Her smile was locked in place. Her left hand was extended, reaching for him across the miles.

"I love you," he said, but she didn't hear. The connection was lost.

Crisanto quit the following day. David asked for two weeks' notice but he refused. He'd been offered a full-time position at the *Inquirer*, he said, and had to leave for Makati City immediately. David asked if his decision had anything to do with the woman in the forest. Crisanto shook his head, but the truth was in his eyes. That childhood fear really *did* run deep.

Torrential rain delayed clearing by three days, with several heavy-equipment operators also quitting as the work neared Dalisay Magana's troublesome little shack. This bought her more time as David sought replacements for the workers he'd lost, which proved challenging—incomprehensibly so, in a region crippled with unemployment.

Word had gotten out that Dalisay Magana had refused to vacate, and it appeared nobody wanted to make her do so.

David gave her a final warning—a brief, simple notice that he pinned to her front door, with the date, *HULYO 21*, circled in red.

His irritation stemmed not from having to iron out wrinkles—that was the job—but from their ridiculous nature, and from having to delay his return to Canada. His mood escalated to rage when, on the morning of July twenty-first, he arrived at the site to find it abandoned. The machinery was parked in a cold yellow row, hulking and silent. Nothing in the field office but empty desks. David e-mailed his supervisor to inform him of this development and to assure him it was under control. He clicked send and then flipped over one of the desks and threw an electric fan against the wall. It was ten a.m. and he desperately wanted a drink—a serious head-fuck of a drink, more like a gunshot—but first, he had business to attend.

She had seen his final notice. It was screwed into a ball, floating beside the insects in the basin of dirty water. He called her name and thumped on her door. No reply. He waited, then thumped again. Still nothing. *Bitch has gone*, he thought. *Vacated after all. Or maybe out sucking babies from wombs.*

Dull fabric flapped in the nearest window and David snatched at it, tearing it free. He looked inside the shack, hoping to find it empty of possessions—a sure sign that the woman had acceded. The meat smell was nauseating and he covered his nose and mouth. In the gloom, he saw a table and chair and a wood-burning stove with a few ashes glowing. There were several dead macaques strung from the ceiling by their tails. He saw a bucket with a hole in it. A straw mattress. A pair of legs upright in the corner with nothing above the waist.

David recoiled, inhaling suddenly. His lungs flooded with foul air and he turned away, spluttering. He went back to the window, looked again, saw long shadows in the corner and nothing more. One of the macaques twisted on its tail and it had no eyes but still stared at him. Something bristled across the ceiling, then a large bird—perhaps the one that had been trapped when he and Crisanto came here—broke for daylight and rose into the clear sky.

He spat in the dirt and backed away.

"Nobody home," he said.

Good enough.

The keys to the heavy-duty machinery were in a lockbox in the field office. David selected one of the medium-size 'dozers and plowed a route through the forest. He didn't hesitate when he reached the shack that once belonged to Dalisay Magana. It toppled in a cloud of dust and stink, ground into the dirt beneath the dozer's continuous tracks. He scraped the trash up with the blade and rumbled over it again, feeling it pop and crack, like standing on a carton of eggs. His eyes were manic, delighted circles.

He gathered the debris again and looked at it—everything reduced to unrecognizable pieces. Half a truckload, no more. He nodded, satisfied. This particular wrinkle had been well and truly ironed out. Dalisay Magana was no longer an obstruction. Now, perhaps, the workers would return.

David turned the bulldozer around and rumbled away, and he heard, even above the engine's snarl, a long, hurt sound from the treetops. Some rain-forest creature. Something that screamed.

He knew her as Illusion. Her real name, she said, was Maria.

Rain against the window, too wild to be soothing, and a wind that bullied more than blew. They matched the storm for passion, for energy. David with his body ceaseless, Maria rising into him with the power and delicacy of warm air. She wrapped her legs around him, ankles crossed at the small of his back. He spoke her name— Illusion, not Maria—and her tongue glazed his throat. They finished breathless. She took her contact lenses out.

They sat afterward at the window, in the same chair, the same sheet wrapped around them. They watched the storm. In the last hour, PAGASA had advanced the warning signal from number two to number three. It wasn't Alayna, but people were understandably scared. Many had packed what they could and left their homes, intent on reaching points farther inland. The storm was named Diwata, meaning "goddess"—mostly benevolent, but known to evoke wrath if not afforded sufficient respect.

David stood and walked naked to the table. The laptop he'd used to Skype with Angie was shut down, lid closed. Next to it, a fresh bottle of Calibre 69 and a glass. He unscrewed the cap, poured generously.

"You want some?"

"No."

"I have another glass."

"I'm okay."

He nodded, sipped. Maria gathered the sheet to her body and he shook his head. She removed it completely.

"Open your legs."

She did.

He stood for a moment and looked at her, sipping his whiskey. She smiled, then gestured toward the window.

"Aren't you scared?"

"I don't scare easily," he said.

His flight to Manila had been canceled. Consequently, he would miss his connection to Hong Kong, and then Toronto. This trip had proved demanding, and all he wanted was to go home. A visit to Snakebite—with its unbridled sound and strong alcohol—had numbed his exasperation. Maria was there, as Illusion, with her blue hair and green eyes. The banknotes in David's wallet led like bread crumbs to his hotel room. That was when the storm rolled in, wilder than forecast.

He sat with her again. She curled herself around him. He kissed her hand and she kissed his—his left hand, close to his wedding ring.

"How long have you been married?" she asked.

"Eight years."

"You have children?"

"No," he replied after a pause. He drew his hand from hers. "I'm not comfortable talking about this."

"Okay."

"She's a better wife than I am a husband." He finished his whiskey. "That's all you need to know."

She sighed and kissed his shoulder. He felt the quick tick of her heart against his back. The wind roared and something wet slapped against the balcony door. Maria jumped and clutched him, but it was only a palm frond. It tapped plaintively against the glass before being whipped away.

"What about your family?" David asked. "What do they think about what you do?"

"My father and two brothers were killed by Alayna. Too proud to evacuate. My mother lives with a family she barely knows in Tent City. It's cramped and uncomfortable. She has no privacy, no respect. I dance—I do what I do—so that I can buy her clean clothes and warm blankets, so that she doesn't have to eat out of a box. I'm also saving for a place for us both to live. Away from Palla. I want to put all this behind me and start again."

"You're ashamed of yourself?"

"I was raised an honest Catholic girl. This is why I wear the blue hair and green eyes. It's a mask. It would break my father's heart if he could see me . . . but I do what needs to be done."

"Where's your mother tonight?"

Tent City had been dismantled, packed into boxes, to be reassembled when the storm had passed. The residents of this makeshift town were bused elsewhere. It was no way to live.

"Somewhere safe," she said. "I hope."

The lights fluttered, then went out, along with the glowing green digits of the clock on the nightstand, and the air conditioner. Power outages were frequent, even on calm days. Neither David nor Maria flinched. She curled closer in the darkness. A few seconds later, the generator kicked in. The lamp came back on, not quite as bright. The air conditioner pulsed more than flowed.

"Let's go back to bed," David said.

They never made it.

The drapes on both the window and balcony doors were open; David wanted to see—and feel closer to—the storm. Privacy wasn't a concern; they were on the top floor, sixty feet above street level. Nobody could see in. David, therefore, assumed the woman swirling on the other side of the balcony doors was Maria's partial reflection. At least to begin with. Then he realized it couldn't be; Maria was facing the wrong way, and as she stepped toward the bed—away from the doors—the "reflection" loomed nearer.

David's mind struggled to explicate the impossible. Other details filtered through, confusing him further. The reflection had yellow eyes that pierced the rain, the darkness, like tiny headlights. She had nothing below the waist but a tied rope of intestine that thrashed in the wind. She had wings.

"No," David said. A single syllable—a roadblock—between his eyes and brain.

Even when Maria turned, saw the creature, and screamed, he still refused to believe it was real. It was an ornate kite or elaborate prop. Something thrown up by the wind. Soon it would clatter harmlessly against the building and be carried away. He wiped his tired eyes. Looked again. The woman outside—the *half* woman— angled her muscular wings to combat the storm. Her long hair whipped and snapped.

Maria had stumbled backward, tripped over the sheet she had recently thrown from her body, and dropped to her knees. Urine squirted from between her legs. She scratched her eyes, as if she could claw what she had seen from them.

"*Manananggal*," she said, and then screamed it: "*MANANANG-GAL!*"

David blinked, and in that millisecond he saw a dirty child pointing toward the thing she feared most of all. He saw a pair of legs with nothing above them standing in the shadows, and a decrepit shack folding beneath the blade of a Komatsu bulldozer.

"No," he said again.

The *manananggal* grasped the balcony rail in bony hands, like a bird clutching its perch. She howled even above the storm. A long tongue unfurled from her mouth, rippled in the wind like a scarf. The balcony door trembled—the glass cracked—as she slammed her forehead against it. David thought of the cobra at Snakebite, always furious, always banging. He'd linked it to his guilt and that felt right.

She struck the glass a second time. And a third. The crack lengthened. A gust of wind filled her wings and she battled it, grasping the rail with one hand. She lowered her shoulders and threw her forehead against the glass once again. It shattered. The storm blew inward. The creature, too.

Rain and broken glass whipped around the room. It lacerated David's face and chest. He curled into a ball and screamed. The *manananggal* clawed across the floor with her entrails bumping along behind, then unfolded her wings and lifted herself into the air, shrieking. David saw teeth unevenly spaced, brownish yellow, sharp as fishhooks. Rainwater sprayed from her wings as she worked them.

Maria reacted first—not surprising, given David's state of disbelief. She grabbed his laptop from the table and threw it at the creature. It thumped between her sagging breasts and dropped to the floor. Maria followed with the whiskey bottle, then the glass, then the lamp. Each projectile found its target, but the *manananggal* barely flinched. Maria shook her head. She spread her naked arms and wept. The creature attacked.

Brutal power. Maria was whipped from her feet and thrown against the wall. Her pelvis shattered. Her skull cracked. She moaned and rolled in broken glass and tried getting to her feet, but there was no way. The *manananggal* flexed her wings and attacked again. Her ribbon tongue coiled around Maria's throat and squeezed until blood leaked from her eyes. She let go and bit Maria's face three times, tearing her lips and nose away and chewing them. Maria's screams were weak and choked with blood. The *manananggal* flipped her onto her stomach. Tore chunks out of her lower back. Uncovered the base of her spine, grabbed it in one tight fist, and pulled. There was a tearing—almost a *purring*—sound as the vertebrae detached from the rib cage. Maria's limbs jerked and flopped and she died with her throat bulging. The *manananggal* ate her stomach through the hole in her back. Her tongue slithered deep into Maria's chest, grasped her heart, and plucked it free. She held it for David to see and then swallowed it completely. Her wings slapped at the swirling air. She grabbed Maria's dangling spine in both hands, lifting her upper body from the floor, and with a savage twist—a revolting crack—she separated Maria's head from her shoulders. It swung at the end of the vertebral column, like a watch on a chain, reminding David of the monkeys strung by their tails in the old woman's shack. He blinked stupidly, his hold on reality weakening with every ragged breath, every drop of blood and rain. He watched the *manananggal* swing Maria's head against the wall, leaving red prints the size of footballs, until it popped loose from the spine and rolled toward him. The creature scooped it up and smashed it repeatedly against the corner of the table, like a bird cracking a snail against a stone, until the skull first crumbled, then opened. She ate the brain quickly, noisily, then pushed her fingers into Maria's mouth and split her jaw open. She ate Maria's tongue and crunched the thin bone of her hard palate. Shell-like remains spilled through her fingers. Another shriek—still hungry—and she turned her glowing eyes on David. He screamed again and ran for the door. The *manananggal* grabbed the back of his neck, lifted him from the floor. She twisted her half body and threw him effortlessly across the room, out the window, into the storm.

He plummeted forty feet screaming. Rain stung his eyes, but he saw the sidewalk rushing toward him. In the second before impact, a hand fastened to his ankle and lifted. He first slowed, then reversed direction. The *manananggal* worked her wings and carried him away.

Over rooftops and furiously swaying trees. His body whipped in the storm and turned gray-cold. He couldn't breathe. His arms hung like wet sleeves. The *manananggal* screeched and either lost her grip or let him go. He caught the wind like a sheet and was blown sideways, landing in a palm tree, tumbling then onto a steel roof that clattered beneath him. He bled from so many wounds. His right leg was broken and twisted beneath him. The wind rolled him across the roof and he fell twelve feet to the street below. Floodwater broke his fall. He floated belly-up and was reminded of dead insects in a certain basin filled with dirty water.

Nobody on the street. Abandoned vehicles cluttered the road. Rain fell into his open eyes and bounced off his chest. He sank beneath the surface and emerged a second later, blinking and gasping. The flowing water carried him between vehicles and he wondered if he could use one of them to hide in. He saw the creature through flashes of rain. She looped in the sky.

"Please," David said. He rolled onto his front and grabbed the door handle of a small car turned sideways in the road, driver's window open. He pulled himself inside, screaming as his broken leg was bumped and pulled. Water flooded the car, but he was protected somewhat from the wind and rain. He could breathe, at least. More importantly, he was—hopefully—hidden from the creature. He crawled onto the backseat and wept.

She'll find you, he thought, teeth clenched, shivering. *Just like she found you at the hotel. Tracked you like a bloodhound. She knows your scent.*

"Please . . ."

Do you believe now? Or are you still in denial . . . the way you deny your actions, your sins?

He buried his face in his hands and screamed.

Are you sorry?

"Yes . . . *yes!*"

A now-familiar screech that was not the storm, but equally real, and more feared. David lowered his hands. He looked through the open window and saw the *manananggal* land on the roof of a jeepney, maybe thirty feet away. She folded her wings and peered through the darkness, the swirling rain. Her yellow eyes tracked left to right, looking for him.

David moaned and lowered himself into the water behind the driver and passenger seats. Only his face broke the surface, like a floating mask. His heart hammered so hard that he imagined the water trembling, ripples forming. His blue lips moved silently.

Please . . .

She screeched again, the sound cutting through the storm. A palm tree fell nearby and the force of it nudged the car through the water. It caught the current, and David cried out—couldn't help himself—as it edged toward the jeepney. He raised his head and braved a look. The *manananggal* tasted the air with her long tongue. Her eyes searched brightly. The car bumped another vehicle, turned a slow circle, but kept moving toward her.

She extended her wings and hovered, arms hanging.

David held his breath and slipped beneath the water. He bled and trembled. But for this storm—this act of God—he would be on a plane back home. But for this creature—decidedly ungodly—he would be in his hotel room, blissfully sinning.

He heard his heartbeat, felt his guilt, banging . . . banging.

I'm sorry.

He imagined safety, happiness, comfort. Not his Toronto home with its luxury furnishings, but his wife. She gave him these things, and so much more. The only thing she couldn't give him—and what he desperately wanted—was a child. But it didn't matter. Angie was, in every other way, everything he needed.

I'm so sorry.

The little car struck the heavier jeepney and stopped. David came up for air. He wiped his eyes. The windshield was blurred with rain, but he saw her terrible wings clearly.

She pulled him through the open window and he was too limp to fight. High into the sky, the storm ebbing now, still ferocious. Her tongue lashed over his open wounds and came away red. She bit off three of his fingers and dropped him. He landed on a concrete wall, back broken. The *manananggal* circled and swooped and plucked him—dead from the chest down—into her strong arms and carried him to the outskirts of Palla.

The rain forest here had been partially cleared, not by the storm, but by harvesters, forest mowers, and forwarders. There *was* storm damage, though: two glaring billboards had been blown to the ground. One depicted the site's shimmering future. The other brandished the land developer's name and logo. The *manananggal* dropped David on this latter billboard. He landed faceup, his body buckled. The final precious beats of his life were spent watching the creature tear him apart. She chewed off his withered penis and swallowed it, grinning. She gobbled his testicles, then thrust her hands

into the wound between his legs and tore upward, unzipping him to
the sternum. His guts flopped out and steamed. She fed on them and
he felt nothing but the pain inside—the pain of loss, fear, and understanding. He blinked rain from his eyes and died.

The *manananggal* licked her lips, spread her wings.

Blood covered most of the billboard. It pooled across the company logo and part of the name.

Above David Payne's separated corpse, in a font designed to
catch the eye, the word REALITY.

She landed in Manila on time, but her connection to Palla was delayed. She knew it would be; the city was on its knees after the latest
storm. Damage was estimated at one hundred million US dollars.
Sixty-three dead. Reporters the world over said the same thing: a
tragedy indeed, but nothing—a mere breeze—compared to Alayna.

Angie sat on a hard chair at Manila's airport, head down, locked
in her grief. She waited six hours and finally boarded her flight. It
was late evening by the time she arrived in Palla. She'd arranged
transportation from the airport—had been told not to trust taxi
drivers in foreign countries. A woman traveling on her own should
take few chances. A *pregnant* woman should take none.

They had been trying for six years. David—who claimed to
always get what he wanted—insisted they *keep* trying. *I want this*,
he'd said to her. *I'm not giving up.* She'd had surgery to open her fal-
lopian tubes. Two failed IVFs. Doctors told her she had only a 2 percent chance of natural conception. She felt unworthy. Unwomanly. It
broke her heart.

David had been in the Philippines for only a few days when she
found out. She had woken that morning feeling different. Nothing
she could put her finger on. Just . . . *different.* She went immediately
to the bathroom cabinet and took out one of the pregnancy tests she
kept on hand. Peed on it without expectation. Fell trembling to her

knees and cried tears of disbelief when two blue lines appeared in the little window.

Angie came close to calling him right away—didn't care what time it was in the Philippines or what he might be doing. After some thought, she decided to wait for his return home. She wanted to *feel* his reaction, not just hear it. She'd bought a pacifier and had the due date printed on it. The plan was to pop it into his mouth when he closed in for that first kiss.

The storm—Diwata—had raged eight thousand miles away but still managed to turn her world upside down. Instead of giving David the child he so desperately wanted, she was flying to the Philippines to identify and bring back his body.

The driver was waiting for her at the airport in Palla, holding up a misspelled sign—PAIN—written in blue ink. He spoke English but chose not to. They drove into the city in silence, passing countless scenes of devastation and loss. Angie clutched her belly instinctively. The setting sun drew orange shades across the sky.

The buildings leaned into one another, as if huddled, as if afraid.

WHAT KEPT YOU SO LONG?

JOHN AJVIDE LINDQVIST

Translated by Marlaine Delargy

The woman standing by the side of the road wasn't a typical hitchhiker. Most are young men, then there are a few young women, plus a small number of older men. The woman who had carefully positioned herself some twenty yards before the rest area with her thumb outstretched belonged to the almost nonexistent category of older women.

My ability to see in the dark has improved significantly since I became infected, so in spite of the November twilight, and the fact that the woman was standing outside the beam of my headlights, I could see that she had medium-length gray hair, and blue eyes with an alert expression, which is unusual in hitchhikers.

Her only luggage was a scruffy rectangular rucksack, yet she was wearing an expensive quilted jacket suitable for use in the mountains, and designer boots. She would have looked more at home on some exclusive Alpine trek rather than by the roadside somewhere between Härnösand and Sundsvall.

It was this discrepancy in her appearance and my curiosity rather than the thirst for blood that made me slow down; the air brake hissed as I maneuvered the truck into the rest area where I had slept through a short winter's day just two weeks earlier.

I flashed the brake lights a couple of times to indicate that I really had stopped to pick her up. I could see her in the wing mirror, jogging alongside the forty-foot trailer. I leaned across the passenger seat and opened the door. A couple of seconds later, her face appeared above the seat.

"Hi there," I said. "Where are you heading?"

"South."

I smiled and nodded in the direction of the highway. "That's pretty obvious, but where exactly?"

"Does it matter?" Before I had time to reply, she asked another question. "What's your destination?"

"Trelleborg."

She glanced back at the trailer. "The docks, I guess?"

"Correct."

"Excellent."

She swung herself up onto the step with surprising agility, the rucksack slung over her shoulder; she settled down on the seat and pulled the door shut. Our brief conversation hadn't exactly told me a great deal about her.

If she meant mainland Europe when she said "south," then my offer of a ride all the way to Trelleborg should at least have made her pretty happy, if not ecstatic. After all, we were talking about a distance of some six hundred miles that she was going to be able to cover in one fell swoop, and yet she had accepted the information as self-evident, just one fact among many others.

As I put the truck in gear and drove out of the rest area with half an eye on the trailer, I decided that for the time being I would assume that "south" meant "away." That she didn't have any particular destination in mind but just wanted to get away from the place where she happened to be at the moment.

The irregular roar of the old V-8 engine became a steady hum as I changed up to cruising speed and zoomed along the highway into the night.

Perhaps I would drink her, perhaps not. I had many hours ahead of me in which to reach that decision.

Last year, I clocked up twenty-five years as a truck driver, trucker, slave to the highway. I did my first trip with a provisional category-C license burning a hole in my pocket when I was twenty-two. Pet food from Värtahamnen in Stockholm to a wholesaler in Västberga. Only a year or so later, I gained my CE license and was able to start driving articulated trucks. Since then I've acquired my ADR certificate, which allows me to transport hazardous material, and taken a couple of courses on how to handle goods and livestock. To put it briefly, I can drive anything at all from point A to point B, and I can also load and unload the truck by myself if necessary.

It's a profession that is full of contradictions; maybe that's why I like it. On the one hand you're free, your own master, yet on the other, you're totally ruled by driving regulations and timetables. Everything is highly technological, with GPS and computerized tachographs, yet at the same time it is utterly primitive. Pick this up and move it to there. You're kind of omnipotent out there on the road with forty tons behind you, but you're also the most vulnerable when it comes to ice and snow, accidents and holdups.

But I have spent twenty-five years in the industry without being involved in anything more serious than the odd dent and scrape, and a few pallets that came off because they hadn't been properly secured. Of course I've had a few close shaves, and admittedly I've run into or over just about every breed of wildlife in this long, narrow country of ours (because it certainly *is* long and narrow, I can confirm that), but nothing more. I'm a good driver, that's all there is to it.

Bearing in mind what I've just told you, I ought to be forty-seven years old. It's true that I have lived for forty-seven years, but I am no longer quite so sure about this age thing. I'm almost starting to believe that I could carry on driving up and down these roads forever and ever. I've been wondering whether to switch to another haulage firm to avoid arousing suspicion.

Only the day before yesterday, Lena in the office said: "Jesus, Tompa, you look younger with every passing day!" She meant it as a compliment, but it took a real effort for me to smile and say: "Have you forgotten to put your contact lenses in?"

I don't think I'm getting younger, but I do believe I'm not getting any older. I stopped at forty-three. Which means that to those who are aging normally, like Lena, it can look as if I'm getting younger. People might admire that for a few years, but only up to a certain point. I have to be careful.

"What are you driving?"

We had just passed Sundsvall when my passenger broke the silence. I dragged myself back from the landscape of diffuse images that constituted my brain's daily diet while I was on the road.

"You mean the truck? She's a Scania—"

"No, what are you carrying?"

"Some kind of steel. Fixings for rolling mills, among other things. They're being shipped overseas."

"Where to?"

"Haven't a clue."

"Aren't you interested?"

"Why should I be?"

The woman shrugged and looked out through the front windshield, where the Kronan Bar and Restaurant was gliding toward us like a cube of light through the darkness. I used to enjoy their meatball sandwiches with beetroot salad, back in the days when I still thought food tasted of something.

"What about you?" I asked.

"What about me?"

"Are you being shipped overseas?"

She gave a snort of laughter at the way I had put it and seemed to be on the point of answering, but then she folded her arms and slid down in her seat as she let out a sigh. When she hadn't said anything for a minute or so, I went back to my thoughts and that meatball sandwich. It did nothing at all for me these days.

The memory from a lost world of tastes and flavors gave me a hollow feeling in my chest, and my thoughts drifted to the first time I succumbed.

It was just over a year after I had been infected. I was falling apart. My body was plagued by a constant nagging, gnawing hunger. Food tasted of nothing, but I ate anyway just to keep going. And yet it wasn't enough, somehow. My doctor had given me food supplements and vitamins, but nothing helped because I still hadn't accepted what was within me.

Everything changed over the course of a couple of days in 2009 outside the MoDo terminal in Örnsköldsvik. Ten thousand gallons of ethanol were to be transported to Helsingborg, and I had driven an empty tanker up from Stockholm. I was standing on the snow-covered loading area with my hands in my pockets; I nodded to the guy who was paying out the hose and was just about to go inside to have a cup of coffee and get warm while the tanker was being filled up when I heard him swear.

I don't know exactly what had happened, but presumably the guy had dropped the heavy hose valve and trapped his fingers. Anyway, he was standing there staring at his hand as the blood dripped down onto the snow. After a few seconds he pulled himself together, tucked his hand under his armpit, and lumbered off toward the terminal and the first-aid box.

I stood there staring at the dark red stain on the snow. I took a step forward, and then another, until the stain was right in front of my feet. My mouth was watering in a way that it hadn't done since I got back from Barcelona a year ago.

And yet still I hesitated, for two reasons. The first is obvious: because it was madness. The second is that when I say "snow," you might imagine something soft and fluffy and reminiscent of "White Christmas." In which case you've never been in the loading bay outside a chemical factory, where the snow is slushy and gray from diesel exhaust fumes and God knows what kind of spillages. In spite of that, I had to swallow several times to prevent the saliva from trickling out of the corners of my mouth.

I really didn't want to do it, but it was as if something else seized the upper hand. After a quick glance around I squatted down, scooped up a fistful of the blood-soaked snow, and without further ado, stuffed the slushy mass into my mouth.

At first I was aware of only cold, water, and indefinable chemical tastes. But then . . . it was indescribable, but I'll try. Think of the best thing you've ever drunk, along with the best thing you've ever eaten. Then add the sensation of your first kiss. Put all that together, and it still isn't enough. My knees almost gave way from sheer bliss.

I swallowed and swallowed, running my tongue around my mouth until there wasn't a trace of that glorious deliciousness left. I was panting and leaning against the tanker for support when another guy came along to take over from the one who'd hurt his hand.

"What the fuck's the matter with you, Tompa? You look like shit."

It was Allan; I'd sat with him over a cup of coffee several times. Apart from a certain fixation with illness and disease, he was one of the good guys. He seemed to be wearing at least two Helly Hansen fleeces underneath his protective jacket in order to keep out the cold, and yet the only thing I could see was a warm, pulsating body filled with *pints and pints* of . . . I ran a hand over my eyes, straightened up, and said: "I'm fine. Just a bit dizzy, that's all."

He picked up the hose and screwed the valve in place, then gave me a skeptical look. "Are you sure? If you come off the road carrying this there'll be one hell of a fucking bang . . ."

"I know," I said, unnecessarily aggressive. "I said I'm fine."

Allan made a face and shrugged before heading back to switch on the pump. Soon I could hear the 90 percent spirit gushing into the tanker. I felt like an empty vessel into which someone had poured just a few drops of liquid, making it echo even more emptily. What had so far been terrible and difficult to bear had now become too terrible and utterly impossible to bear.

Something had to be done, and soon.

The woman had produced a bar of chocolate from her rucksack and was now munching away with an expression of indifference, not unlike the way I probably looked when I ate normal food. We were just passing a Statoil gas station, and I glanced across at her in the brightness of its floodlights.

She was about my age, or a few years older. She was neither beautiful nor ugly; her appearance was pretty unremarkable, apart from her hair, which was entirely gray, and a certain hardness in the lines of her face. She didn't look like the kind of person who could be lured to some isolated spot on a pretext. If I was going to drink her, then an element of cunning would be required. Or speed.

"We all do what we have to do, don't we?" I said, hoping to open a conversation that would give me some clue as to what kind of person I was dealing with.

To my surprise, she responded with a certain amount of enthusiasm. "Absolutely. You're right. I've thought the same thing many times. It's a kind of consolation."

There you go. At a stroke, the tone between us had changed completely, so I carried on along the same track. "The problem lies in accepting it. But once you've done that, there's kind of no turning back."

She nodded. "It can take years. And yet you're still not sure."

She was confiding in me. Excellent. That gave me the opportunity to probe further. I needed to know whether other people knew she'd been planning to hitch. I needed to know whether she had a cell phone that could be traced. Among other things.

You can't just go around killing people. Once, maybe, provided you don't have any kind of relationship with the victim. But if you intend to do it again, it takes planning and thought so that you don't leave clues that could be put together to form a pattern.

My hands were shaking and my body was a screaming, empty hole when I drove away that day in 2009 from the MoDo terminal with my highly explosive load and six hundred miles ahead of me. I was an accident waiting to happen, an accident big enough to destroy a small community.

Twilight was falling, and it seemed to me that the E4, which is as straight as an arrow, was slowly undulating first to the left and then to the right, like a gigantic water snake. I was drawn to the side of the road, and when I tried to correct it, I almost skidded as the heavy load pushed me forward. When I spotted the compact outline of the Docksta Bar up ahead, I decided I had no choice but to pull off the road and park in order to catch my breath and come to my senses.

I switched off the engine, folded my arms on the steering wheel, rested my head against them, and closed my eyes. It was no longer possible to pretend, to ignore what had happened to me that night in Barcelona a year ago. With the help of logic and reason, I had managed to keep it at bay because it was an impossibility, but now my body had spoken.

The hooker had infected me; the infection was a slow poison, and now it had started to work in earnest.

The dock area in Barcelona could accommodate a small kingdom in its vast expanse. This was in 2008—I had traveled down with a load of office furniture from Kinnarps and had decided to spend the night in the truck's cab. Sometimes I rented a cheap room down there or even up in the city, but that particular night I was so tired that I couldn't even bring myself to walk the necessary five hundred yards. It was easier to crawl into the compartment behind the driver's seat and get a few hours' sleep before it was time to pick up a load of Moroccan clementines, nectarines, satsumas, whatever the hell they were called, and then set off for home again.

I had closed the curtains and started to get undressed when there was a gentle tap on the door. I peered out and saw a woman standing in the darkness by the truck. She made a gesture to clarify her intentions, and I thought it over. A whore. A truckers' hooker. Presumably there was also a name for them in Spanish, but I didn't know what it was.

I had availed myself of their services a couple of times in Germany, and I recalled the smell of perfume that had remained in the cab for an unexpectedly long time, a lingering sense of regret. Although it would be nice, a little relief on this miserable January night, and after all, I'd saved money by not renting a room, so I opened the door and asked: "*Cuánto?*"

"*Francés?*"

"No, *sueco*." I shook my head as I remembered. She hadn't been inquiring about my nationality, but about what I wanted her to do, so I corrected myself and said: "Ah, no. *Sí. Francés.*"

"*Treinta.*"

Thirty euros. Three hundred kronor. I wasn't exactly an experienced client, but the price seemed reasonable, so I shifted over to the passenger seat and waved her inside, then I switched off the light and pulled down my pants. When she closed the door behind her it was dark in the cab, and I could see nothing but the faint silhouette of her head. I felt her long hair caressing my left thigh as she bent down and got to work.

I was hard in no time, and she was good at her job. Only then did it occur to me that the price was pretty low, and that I hadn't really seen her face. She could easily be a transvestite; there was no shortage of those in Barcelona.

Whatever.

The service she or possibly he was providing was very enjoyable in any case, and the transaction could be completed without my needing to know one way or the other, so I leaned back in my seat as best I could and allowed the simple pleasure to surge through my scrotum with each movement of the hooker's lips and tongue.

I was getting close to shooting my load when I caught sight of a bright light out of the corner of my eye; I heard the sound of an engine, and the next moment three things happened more or less simultaneously. I heard a loud bang, the cab shook, and the hooker sank her teeth into my cock just before she was thrown to the floor.

"Fucking hell!"

The part of my body that had just been a source of enjoyment was now a burning rod, sending jabs of pain all the way up into my gut. Instinctively I switched on the light in the cab to check out the damage and discovered to my relief that the involuntary bite had only punctured the skin, and a single drop of blood was oozing out.

I could hear shouting outside the truck in some Eastern European language as the hooker scrambled up into the driver's seat. She looked fucking terrible, to be honest, and I don't think I'd have been able to get it up if I'd seen her face before she started.

She might have been around fifty years old and had black, badly colored hair. Her face was wrinkled and sunken, and so thickly plastered with heavy makeup that I couldn't tell if it really was a man or a woman, even in the bright light. One side of her neck was covered in a bloodstained dressing the size of the palm of a hand.

Fucking disgusting.

As I pulled up my pants, I asked in broken Spanish what had happened. She let loose a tirade of which I understood less than half; I was able to pick up only odd words—*anoche, pareja, viejos, locos,* and *suecos.* Some crazy old Swedish couple, last night. Then she held out her hand, demanding her money, just as someone knocked on the passenger door.

I couldn't have her hanging around while I sorted out the accident, so I paid up. Three hundred kronor to get bitten on the cock. Bargain. The hooker slid out through the driver's door as I opened up on my side with some difficulty, then spent a couple of hours on paperwork, telephone calls, and general chat with two Romanians who had a problem with their hydraulic braking system.

As the hitchhiker tucked her legs underneath her and rested her head against the side window, I glanced at her rucksack. There is usually a connection between how much baggage a person has and how far they are traveling, but the woman's small rucksack didn't even look full. Okay, so she exuded an air of integrity, but after all, I had done her a favor in picking her up, so I ventured a question in a casual tone: "Are you on the run?"

She sighed. "No, I wouldn't say that."

"So what's going on, then?"

"I'm a . . . traveler."

"So am I, but there's a purpose to my traveling."

"Mine, too."

"Do you mind if I ask what that purpose is?"

"I do mind, yes."

I turned to look at her, and her eyes met mine. There was something in them, a kind of inner light. As if she could see in the dark.

Over the years I have never met anyone else who is . . . it goes against the grain to use the word, but . . . a vampire. It carries a number of associations: on the one hand, gloomy, forbidding castles, and on the other, extremely good-looking young people with super-powers, when in fact it is nothing more than an infection, a disease.

But that was what I had to accept that day in the parking lot outside the Docksta Bar. I had been infected with the need to drink blood, and now that I had tasted it, there was no going back. I sat there with my eyes closed, my head resting on the steering wheel as that word went around and around in my head: *Vampire. Vampire. Vampire.*

"Hey there, Tompa—are you sleeping on the job?"

I vaguely recognized the voice outside, and when I looked up, I saw Gunnar Gravel standing in front of the cab with his hands by his sides. He once tipped a whole load of gravel in the wrong yard. That wouldn't have been enough to give him his nickname, but the family's dachshund ended up underneath the pile. Since then, he was always known as either Gunnar Gravel or Splat. He was a wiry little man of about sixty who smoked and took snuff, often both at the same time.

I lowered the window and stuck my head out. Gunnar came around the side and stared at me. "Jesus, Tompa, you don't look too good. Long trip?"

"No, it's just—"

Gunnar interrupted me. "I get it. MoDo, and you already look fucking worn out. Come and have a beer."

"That's a great idea—drinking and driving."

Gunnar waved a hand in the direction of the building where you could rent a basic room; I'd spent the night there myself once or twice. "Ah, just a low-alcohol beer. I've driven up from Travemünde and I thought I'd crash here overnight."

I looked at Gunnar. At the deserted parking lot. At the motel, which was in total darkness. Then I opened the door, jumped down, and followed him as he babbled on cheerfully about some strap that had come loose and slapped a German customs official right in the face. I found it difficult to comment because my mouth had gone so dry that I could hardly move my tongue.

When we reached his little room, he opened the refrigerator in the tiny kitchen area and took out a six-pack of Falcon Bayerskt. "Help yourself. I just need to pee. Gotta make some room."

He left the bathroom door open, and I could hear the urine splashing against the porcelain as he carried on talking. I opened the top drawer and saw a serrated bread knife with a plastic handle among the few simple utensils. I tucked it along my right forearm, grabbed a beer, then sat down on the only chair in the room as Gunnar continued his monologue.

". . . and when I was ready to clear customs, the bastard had gone on his lunch break, so I had to run around like a scalded cat because the refrigeration unit had switched itself off. It's always the same when you're transporting fresh goods . . ."

Gunnar emerged from the bathroom zipping up his pants; he picked up a beer and sat down on the bed. The room was so small that our knees were almost touching. Gunnar took a long drink, then wiped his mouth. "And smoking's bad for you too. I've started on those goddamn e-cigarettes. Bought them in Poland, have you tried them?"

My jaws were clamped together; my body was so rigid that I could only just manage to shake my head.

Can I do this? Can I?

Fortunately Gunnar was the kind of man who thought there was a conversation going on just as long as he was allowed to continue his monologue; he didn't appear to notice the strain I was under, but he reached down to pick up a box from the floor next to the bed. The back of his neck glowed white just inches away from me.

At the time I didn't really know what was happening. Since then, I've come to understand it a little better. I stared at the back of Gunnar's neck, still weighing up the pros and cons, but before I had time to make a decision, it was as if someone or something seized my right arm, sweeping it forward and upward so that the blade of the knife slashed Gunnar's flesh as he began to straighten up.

He sat up. In one hand, he was holding something that looked like a cigarette with a glowing red tip that went out as soon as he dropped it. He was staring at me with his mouth wide open. Then came the blood. Oh my God, so much blood.

The serrated knife had opened up a deep gash in his neck, and great gouts of blood came spurting out. Gunnar twisted around and my face was splashed with it. I licked my lips, the taste filled my mouth, and I was consumed by madness.

One flap of Gunnar's overalls fell down over his shoulder as he curled up, then flung his arms wide in despair. To me it was an open invitation. I got up from my chair and fell on him, pressing my mouth to the wound and drinking, drinking while Gunnar's sinewy hands struck impotently at my head.

Afterward, I slid down onto the floor. I felt totally satisfied, full up and alive. Crazy, too. And remorseful, pointlessly remorseful. I picked up the e-cigarette, pressed the button that turned on the red light, and took a drag, exhaled steam. It tasted of nothing. Gunnar's body lay sprawled on the bed like a bundle of rags. There was blood all over the walls, the bed, the floor.

I did this.

I, Tomas Larsson, forty-four-year-old trucker, husband of Angelica and father of a seventeen-year-old daughter, once a pretty good table tennis player, had killed another human being and drunk his blood. Something like that changes things. Something like that changes a great deal. For example, at that very moment I realized that I could never see my daughter, Moa, again. The movement of the knife had been involuntary. Other things could happen the same way.

There was a rush within my body. A gushing, vibrating, wonderful rush that temporarily washed away my regrets. I fetched a dishcloth from the kitchen area and wiped the e-cigarette, the knife, the beer can, and everything else I thought I might have touched. As I left the room, I wiped the door handle. Not that the police already had my fingerprints on record.

But I might do this again.

"**D**o you have family?"

The woman's question followed a silence that had gone on for miles and miles of the uneventful E4, where my thoughts had returned to my victims, as they so often did. After Gunnar, I had taken more care. A long period of time and a considerable distance between incidents. Four so far. One in Uppland, one in Skåne, one in the Netherlands, and one in Germany. All buried, by me, none found, as far as I knew.

Family.

"A daughter," I said. If the woman had asked a follow-up question, I probably wouldn't have wanted to answer, but she said nothing. In the silence, I could see Moa standing in front of me, and after a while she forced me to add: "Moa. She's twenty-one. Training to be a teacher."

"Are you close?"

"No, I can't say we are. I haven't seen her for three years."

The woman straightened up in her seat, clearly interested. Before she had time to ask anything else, come tiptoeing even farther into my pain zone, I returned the question: "How about you?"

Her shoulders dropped a fraction as she nodded and said, "Two sons. Both working in health care. As far as I know."

Now it was my turn to be interested. The woman's final words suggested that her situation was similar to mine. The faint suspicion or hope I was harboring grew a little stronger. The hooker in Barcelona had been infected by someone, and they in turn had been infected by someone else, and so on and so on. There had to be more of us out there.

It was a long shot and it was highly unlikely, but I still wanted to probe a little farther, so I asked: "Why don't you know?"

"Because I walked out on my family. About a year ago."

"Because it was . . . necessary?"

"Yes. It was necessary."

"But it's painful?"

"Yes. Extremely painful."

I took a deep breath, then exhaled slowly. My heart, which these days beat only a few times per minute, sped up to almost the normal rate.

It has no doubt become clear by now that there is nothing romantic about my infection, but in fact it's worse than that. It is more or less a constant torment. First of all, the hunger, which grows and grows until I can no longer bear it and am compelled to do what I have to do. Then the feelings of guilt over what I have done, which as the weeks and months go by gradually turn into hunger once more, and the cycle begins again. It is terrible. And on top of all that, the hunger returns after a shorter interval each time.

And the positives? You don't usually ask about the positive aspects of a disease. So you have lung cancer and you've lost your hair due to radiotherapy? Oh well, at least you don't have to go to the hairdresser.

The advantages I have are slightly greater, I must admit. I can see in the dark. I have grown stronger. And recently I have also begun to develop a certain ability to . . . change. If I think hard enough about altering a certain part of my body, a metamorphosis takes place. My nails grow longer, my teeth acquire sharp points. In conjunction with this my thirst for blood has increased, as I said, and I have become more and more sensitive to light. I realize what is happening to me. The disease is spreading.

Then there's the fact that I have stopped aging, but I don't regard that as an advantage. To be perfectly honest, I detest my very existence, and the thought that the way out via old age and death appears to be closed fills me with despair.

Is there any alternative? No, there is no alternative. I am *meant* to travel these roads like an Ahasuerus with four hundred horsepower until I am no longer meant to do so. That was something else I realized that day, between Örnsköldsvik and Helsingborg.

It was somewhere around Gävle that what I had done really caught up with me. The image of little Gunnar Gravel, lying there limp and lifeless on that shabby bed. Never again would he go home to his wife, Birgit, and their cats; four grandchildren had lost their grandfather so that I could slake my thirst.

And the knife. The knife. It haunted me. As soon as I closed my eyes, it was there, seared on my retinas like a brightly lit exhibit in a museum. The faded, rough handle and the pliant blade. There was something so *undignified* about killing someone with a knife like that, and I just didn't understand how I could have been capable of such an act.

Anything would have been better. A cutthroat razor, a hunting knife, a hammer, a chain saw. I hardly knew myself what I actually meant, but the fact that I had done the deed with that cheap bread knife seemed to me to be the worst thing of all, and it haunted me the entire night.

I don't want to make out that I'm any better than I really am, paint a picture of a deeply repentant murderer. Behind these images and this remorse lay the *strength* the blood had given me. The life.

Physically I felt much better than I had for a long time, and if it hadn't been for my guilty conscience weighing me down, I would have cheered, laughed, and sung along to the upbeat song playing on the radio. Instead I switched it off and sank deeper into brooding blackness as the miles went by.

I passed Stockholm, Södertälje, and Norrköping as a new form of madness grew within me. Under normal circumstances I would have needed a break at that stage, but instead I was wide awake and more alert than ever. I was in top form and the depths of despair at the same time, and I felt as if the tension between the two would make my brain explode at any moment.

I was driving way too fast, particularly in view of the load I was carrying. Part of me wanted to be stopped by the police, even arrested. Another part just wanted the speed and the rushing, singing, vibrant life. But no one pulled me over, and my insane journey continued past Linköping and down toward Lake Vättern. I was doing almost ninety, and sometimes the rig listed slightly with a warning sucking, lapping sound from the tanker behind me.

Something snapped as I reached Brahehus. I was approaching the long, steep hill known as Huskvarnabacken, and I could see the lights of Jönköping glittering in the darkness down below on the southern shore of Lake Vättern. As I reached the summit and began the descent, I instinctively lowered my speed.

No. No. NO!

I was halfway down the hill, and on the right-hand side there was only the barrier between me and the drop to the lake. Me and my load. Ten thousand gallons of ethanol. If I careered off the road the whole thing would probably explode with such ferocity that it would take a DPF to find anything that was left of me. It was an appealing thought, to say the least. It was the *right* thing. Obliterated from the surface of the earth, without a trace.

I put my foot down and began to turn the wheel to the right; in the wing mirror, I could see the tanker swerving behind me. I held my breath and . . . that's when it happened.

In the same way as the bread knife was drawn across Gunnar's neck by some external force, it was as if two hands were laid on top of mine and . . . no, that's wrong. It was as if two hands slipped *inside* mine like a pair of gloves, and without taking any notice of the gloves' feeble protests, they turned the wheel to the left and corrected the movement of the tanker until I was once again safely positioned in the middle of the highway. My speed had dropped too.

With hands that still didn't feel as if they belonged to me, I maneuvered my way down the hill and pulled into the Eurostop outside Jönköping, where I sat motionless in the cab for a long time, studying my palms as if I might find an answer in the lines etched upon them.

How should I interpret what had just happened? One option was that I had gone completely crazy and was no longer in control of myself; I might even start hearing voices telling me to do things, terrible things, more terrible things.

The other option . . . I didn't know if it was better or worse, but it was more difficult to grasp because it carried the message that I was *meant* to carry on, that I had no chance of ending this of my own volition. And who or what was behind this intention? Something within the very structure of existence. A balance, a purpose. I didn't know.

But regardless of which option was correct, one thing was clear to me. With a right hand that once again belonged to me, I got out my cell phone and called home. When Angelica answered, I told her I wanted a divorce. She thought I was joking, but when she realized I was serious, the tears came, the questions. Was it anything to do with the fact that I had been so strange recently? Had I met someone else, had I . . . and so on.

I talked. I answered. I lied. Once more it was as if a different voice was speaking behind my own, but unlike the experience coming down Huskvarnabacken, this felt like a normal psychological mechanism. I couldn't process the fact that I was saying the things I said, and therefore it seemed as if someone else was saying them. Presumably. Presumably.

I ended the call, then went into the café and bought a cup of coffee. I drank it standing outside in the windy parking lot. It tasted of nothing.

"Sometimes I feel as if I'm completely alone. As if I'm the only one of my kind. Do you feel that way?"

"Yes," the woman said. "I know what you mean."

During the hundred and twenty miles or so we had covered, she hadn't once taken out her cell phone to check or send a message, make a call, or just generally mess around with it the way most people do these days. I assumed she didn't have one, but it no longer mattered. I was on a different track now, but I had to proceed with caution.

"Did you start to feel this way at . . . any particular time?" I asked in a further attempt to sound out the terrain.

We were just passing Gnarp, and as on so many occasions in the past, it felt like a knife thrusting into my warped, infected heart when I saw the lights shining in the windows of the houses, the flickering glow of TV screens, and the silhouettes of people living their ordinary, cozy lives together. I usually sleep in the cab these days. Sleep during the day. Drive during the night.

"Something happened to me," the woman said. "At first I didn't understand what it was. I had no one to ask."

I had to make a real effort to prevent my voice from trembling when I asked: "Did it feel as if you had been given . . . a task to fulfill?"

"Yes," she replied. "You could put it like that."

That's what I can't understand. Since I accepted what has happened to me, what I have become, I have been unable to escape the sense of a kind of *purpose* running through all the repulsiveness, as if this is what I *have* to do.

My first one after Gunnar was just under a year later. A hooker at a rest stop outside Aachen. A transaction that was concluded in a mixture of English and German, after which she led me into the forest, where I slit her throat with a Japanese chef's knife specially acquired for the occasion; it was as sharp as a razor blade. As she was dying, as I drank her, as I dragged her farther into the forest and buried her, it all felt just as natural as loading up my truck, driving, and unloading at exactly the agreed time. Doing the right thing.

The remorse and anguish came later, the fear of being found out, but every time while it was actually happening it felt as if I was simply fulfilling the task I had been given. As if the slaking of my thirst was part of a bigger picture, and I was doing my bit.

That feeling has not grown weaker—quite the reverse. My latest victim was a young guy, a hitchhiker I picked up outside Ljungby. After a few miles, I said the suspension was making a funny noise and asked him to help me check it out. As we squatted down and peered under the trailer, I did *that* for the first time. Used my mind to make my teeth sharper, turn my nails into claws. Then I grabbed hold of him, pierced the skin over the carotid artery.

It was euphoric, a sensation of being in total contact with the universe as my hands grasped his head, covering his mouth while I sank my teeth deeper and deeper into his flesh so that the blood poured into my own mouth. I was a wolf hunting down its prey, a squirrel leaping through the air, I was a creature doing exactly what it should be doing. Then I dragged him away and buried him, all with the same deep feeling of meaningfulness.

And so it grows, it is consolidated. It is a road I am destined to travel, I will travel along it for all eternity, and I am not allowed to deviate in any way. It is appalling.

I flicked on the right-turn signal, slowed down, and pulled into a rest stop just outside Hudiksvall. A couple of toilets, a few picnic tables. No people. This was where I had vaguely planned to drink the woman if the signs were favorable. I switched off the engine; it fell silent with a weary sigh from the hydraulics, then I simply sat there, my hands folded in my lap.

"What are you doing?" the woman asked. "Why have you stopped?" There was no fear in her voice, only neutral curiosity.

"I feel as if we have a great deal in common," I said.

Perhaps that wasn't the best thing to say. Some women might take it as the prelude to an approach, maybe even rape. But I didn't think she would do that, because we understood each other on a different level. At least I hoped we did, and her next words confirmed it. "I feel the same way."

"I'm going to ask you straight out," I said. "This task you've been given. Does it have something to do with . . . blood?"

For the first time since she climbed into the cab, there was genuine emotion in the woman's voice as she replied in a trembling exhalation: "Yes . . ."

I turned my head and looked her straight in the eye as I whispered: "Are you the same as me?"

For a long time we sat there with our eyes locked together, not even blinking as something indescribable flowed back and forth between us. Then she said: "Close your eyes . . ."

I leaned back and did as she said, trying to make sense of this unexpected development. What did it mean? What was going to happen next? What were we going to do? Was I at long last going to get some of the answers I had yearned for? Out of the darkness behind my eyelids, I heard the woman say:

"It was just after New Year's in 2009. That's when it happened. I was in the laundry, I was just putting some sheets into the washing machine when I had an . . . attack. My head was filled with images. A port somewhere, a truck. A woman with black hair and a blood-stained dressing on her neck. It was so powerful that my nose started to bleed. It dripped all over the sheets."

As the woman was speaking, I heard the rustle of nylon fabric as she took something out of her rucksack. What she was saying was not at all what I had expected, and I wanted to open my eyes, but suddenly my eyelids felt so heavy, my body so uncooperative that I remained sitting exactly as I was while she went on:

"It took me a long time to realize that it was a calling. Several years. I thought I was going crazy. Maybe I am crazy. Maybe we're both crazy. But a year ago, I set out. Out on the road. Because that was all I knew. That the person I was looking for was out on the road somewhere."

When I felt the pressure over my heart, I finally opened my eyes. In her left hand, the woman was holding what looked like a billiard cue that had been broken off and sharpened to a point, which was pressing against my chest. In her right hand was a small hammer, ready to strike.

"Because it *is* you, isn't it?" she asked.

I nodded and her face contorted in what might have been pain as she raised the hammer another inch or two.

"I don't understand," she said. "But I'm just doing what I have to do, exactly like you. Isn't that right?"

I pushed my infected heart harder against the sharp point, closed my eyes, and said: "What kept you so long?"

BLUE HELL

DAVID WELLINGTON

They bathed her and perfumed her body, perfecting her for the god.

Then she could hear it, the sound of a drum.

They cut her toenails with copper shears and pierced her ears with gold.

And in the distance, the sound of a drum.

Slaves painted her skin, dark bands across eyes and mouth, blue everywhere else.

Coming closer, the sound of a drum.

Blue for water, blue for Chaac. Blue for sacrifice.

And before her, the sound of a drum.

They placed the peaked headdress atop her lacquered hair.

And now, beside her, the sound of a drum.

They walked her across the dry stone, the withered grass, holding her hands.

Behind her now, the sound of a drum.

To the edge of the cenote, its waters shrunken by the drought.

And faster now, the sound of a drum.

Prayers were uttered, prayers for rain. Prayers for mercy.

Thundering in her ears, the sound of a drum.

Her head swam with visions and the hopes of her people.

And now the drumming stopped—

And they cast her in.

Blue for sacrifice. The water below was blue. Her fall seemed to take forever, as if some god were playing a trick on her, stretching out the day like thread between a weaver's hands. She put her arms out to her sides as the wind rose up around her.

The cenote was a natural well, round as the moon, fifty arms across and twenty deep. Ferns and long vines hung down over the abrupt lip of the well. Sheer walls fell away to perfect blue water at the bottom. The same blue they'd painted her skin. Over the years, so many sacrifices had made it that way.

She braced herself for the cool of the water, the way it would feel between her toes. She promised herself that when she sliced through the blue depth she would not struggle, would not try to swim. She would let herself sink. Down into Chaac's domain, where she would be put upon a smooth, carved bench and be brought the food of the water realm. Where servants would plait her hair and sing her underwater songs.

She would not try to swim. This was paramount: if she resisted, if she fought the water and tried to keep it out of her mouth, Chaac would know the sacrifice was made with only half her heart, and he would not bring back the rain. She must open herself to the blue, let it fill her. Let it consume her.

One life, her little life, for the rain. The rain that would bring back the corn. One little life to save so many others. She was a hero, like the great twins. She would be remembered forever, and given a place of honor in the underwater hall.

She would not struggle. The wind around her face made tears fill up her eyes, and she could not see. She would not resist.

She would not.

Please, she begged, *let me not resist.*

Time had not slowed down, not truly. That was all the time for thinking she had. Before she could even get her knees up, she was at the bottom of the cenote.

But the gods did play cruel tricks. As her foot split the blue water, instead of the depths of the cenote, instead of the cool blue water of Chaac, her toes found hard stone. A ledge, hidden just below the surface.

Underneath her, the bones of one leg bent like a bow strung by a strong warrior. Bent, and then snapped. Shattered.

The pain was brighter than the sun.

She knew she screamed.

She remembered very little else.

There had been no sleep, no darkness inside her head. The sunlight that bounced off the sheer walls of the cenote burned behind her eyes, still, as it had without break, without interruption.

Yet she was sure that time had passed, time she had not reckoned.

The pain had been so large, so hard to compass, that it had stripped away thoughts and passions and even language from her brain. Slowly things came back to her. Her name. The faces of her family. Why she was here.

The knowledge, certain and deadly, that she had failed.

She had screamed when her leg snapped. And that was inexcusable. By crying out, she had likely ruined everything. Chaac would be offended because she did not offer herself willingly—her scream had prolonged the drought. She had ensured more of her people would die of hunger and want.

That hurt nearly as much as the pain in her leg.

For a long while, she could do nothing but weep. She was barely aware of where she was, only that she had wasted her death. She could do nothing but stare through her tears, stare at unfocused sunlight, stare and take great jagged breaths that hurt her chest and made her shake on her watery ledge.

Eventually though, she wiped at her eyes, smearing the band of dark paint there. She looked up, thinking to see her people staring down at her in shame.

But up at the lip of the cenote, so far above her head, there was no one. Ferns and flowers swayed their heads in the breeze. Long lianas fell straight down toward her, spills of green against the gray stone walls of the cenote. Above, only blue sky. A paler blue than the water below. This was a sacred place. No one would come here until they were ready to perform another sacrifice. That could be many days from now. As far as her people knew, she was dead—they would not come to look for her.

Having wasted her death, she now began to think about life, and how it could be preserved.

The cenote was almost perfectly round, and the water was still, so it looked like a king's mirror. Its walls were sheer and smooth. No one could climb down to bring her out, even if she dared to hope someone might try.

The liana vines hung down straight and sturdy like natural ropes. She was a strong girl and she knew how to climb. If she could have reached one of them, jumped up and grabbed its curling end, maybe she could have gotten out on her own. There was one on the far side of the cenote that maybe she could have reached, if she could jump for it. But her leg was never going to let her jump again.

The ledge she was on was a finger's depth below the water, invisible from above, but under her hands she could feel its rough surface, find its limits. It was about twice as long as her body but very narrow. If she was not careful she might roll off, into the much deeper water. She would drown there—something she had wished for so recently but now seemed a terrible death.

She knew why the water was so blue. Every sacrifice ever made in the cenote had worn the same paint that covered her skin from her forehead to the soles of her feet. It was good paint, very durable—permanent, even, which was why it was saved for rituals of the gods. The water in the cenote had been clear once but now it was the color of all the people who had been thrown into its depths.

Blue.

If she fell into the water now and drowned, the water that filled her belly would be stained by human skin and rotting flesh. The pain in her leg had already made her nauseous. The idea of dying like that certainly didn't help.

But what was her option? To die of hunger on the ledge? She could try to take her own life, but how? She had no knife with her, no weapon of any kind. Even her peaked headdress had fallen off when she struck the ledge and was presumably at the bottom of the cenote. She wore nothing but a thin shift. She could tear it into strips, make a rope with which to hang herself. But what would she attach it to?

She could, she supposed, spend the rest of the time she had left begging Chaac for forgiveness. Apologizing to him for how she had ruined his sacrifice. She knew the prayers—she had been raised to be a priestess, which was why she had been chosen for this job when the rains failed to come and the maize didn't grow. Maybe if she begged him enough, if she made the prayers sound sincere, he would understand that she had not ruined the sacrifice by choice. That she was blameless.

For a while she tried. She mumbled her way through the words she'd memorized, repeating the same lines over and over.

But the pain in her leg was just too much. It clouded her mind, made it impossible to concentrate. The words got tangled in her mouth, like the quipu strings the tax collectors used. She felt herself growing weak, tired. She slept again.

Her dreams were not good.

When she woke, darkness had fallen. At first she did not understand why she had awoken. Then she realized she was not alone in the cenote.

She did not cry out this time, though even as she opened her eyes she was gripped by terrible fear. Some base instinct kept her quiet as she watched the water of the cenote ripple in spreading circles.

It was just a fish, she thought. At worst, an eel with snaggled teeth, twisting its way through the blue water. She forced herself to calm down.

It moved again and she heard it this time, the little splash as it cut through the water. If it had been a fish it would have darted about, she thought. If it were an eel, it would have twisted. But as she heard another splash, saw a pale shape crest the blue water a third time, she was gripped by the certainty this was no creature of the watery realm. That it was not swimming but walking through the water.

A delusion, surely. An imagining brought on by the pain that surrounded her every thought, crushed out all logic.

Above, the night sky was bound by the round rim of the cenote, like a colossal eye full of stars looking down at her.

She chided herself for being such a little girl. For letting fear and emotion get in the way of proper thinking. She had been trained to be better than this. As a priestess she would have had to watch the world, observe it dispassionately. Search the clouds and the streams in the forest for signs and tokens of what the gods wanted. She would have

worked out careful formulae for how to appease them for the better-
ment of the city. Such work required a clear head and a strong heart
for making hard decisions. If she had been a simple child, jumping at
every story of the lords of Xibalba and their demons, she would never
have been chosen to die for Chaac's pleasure. The priests would not
have trusted her to die without struggling.

Of course, that hadn't worked out so well.

For a long time the water of the cenote was still. The ripples she'd
seen reached the walls and reflected back but in time they died out
and the stars appeared on the dark face of the water once more, un-
broken.

She rolled her eyes and sighed deeply, putting a little cynicism
into the gesture. It sounded affected to her ears but it helped a little.
She settled herself down on her ledge, getting as comfortable as her
broken leg would allow, and closed her eyes. She would sleep until
the morning. Perhaps then someone would come and look down
and see her, and get a good rope, and bring her out of this place. She
knew how unlikely that was, but imagining the possibility soothed
her. Took her mind off the fact that she was starting to get very
hungry, and—

She heard another little splash. And more. A croaking, clicking
sound, like something trying to talk.

Instantly her eyes opened and she pulled herself up to a sitting
posture. Pulled her legs away from the end of the ledge, though
every movement was agony.

She stared out into the darkened cenote, searching the water for
the source of the noise. At first she could see nothing but then—
there? Perhaps . . . a round shape, a little paler than the water around
it. About the size of a little basket turned upside down. It did not
move but it lay at the center of the ripples. She watched it with fasci-
nation, with horror. Feelings that only increased as the thing started
to grow.

No, not grow. It was simply rising from the water, showing more of itself. It became rounder and fuller, pale in the starlight. A dome, a hemisphere that dripped with the dark water. She could make out only a few details of its surface, two dark pits on its front. And then, suddenly, she understood.

She was watching a skull emerge from the water. Those pits were eye sockets. And deep in those dark hollows burned two tiny fires, just sparks of light. Blue light.

She screamed for the second time, then.

But whatever the thing wanted, this skull-thing, it came no closer.

She shouted at it. Splashed water at it to try to make it go away. Prayed to Chaac for help she knew she did not deserve.

Nothing seemed to faze the creature. But eventually, after watching her for a long time, it sank back into the water and left her alone.

It became very hard to keep herself awake.

The fear worked, for a while. The terror she'd felt when she saw the monstrous shape in the water. But fear is like a little fire—if made without enough kindling, if you do not constantly blow on it, it gutters out. The pain in her leg made it difficult to think in chains of logic and she had to remind herself over and over that she was in danger, that the skull thing was still out there.

She knew it had been no hallucination. She had seen those eyes burning clear as daylight, seen the blue sparks the same color as the water of the cenote. But whatever the thing was, it did not return. And she was so hungry . . .

The next time she woke, the sun had come back and was burning her face. She struggled to pull herself away from the heat and light and a new stab of pain made her pass out again for a while.

She felt so weak, so fragile. When she looked down at her leg, she saw it had swollen, the joint of her knee like a mamey fruit ready to burst. The skin of her calf, where the bone had shattered, was purple and shiny and she didn't dare touch it.

Thirst tugged at her. She didn't like to drink the blue water, knowing what it contained, but she could not help herself. She cupped her hand and brought a little of it to her lips. Despite her squeamishness, it tasted wonderful. She drank deep, then lay back and just tried to breathe normally for a while. Even that took effort.

What had she really seen? What had it been?

She had been taught what the gods looked like, of course, had even seen the secret carvings inside the pyramid at the center of the city. She knew there were gods who looked like human skeletons with rolling eyes and grabbing hands. Cizin, the lord of the underworld, was one like that, one of many. But the thing she'd seen out in the water had no human eyes to flash and stare. And what would any god be doing submerged in the water of a cenote? The gods were haughty, tricksome beings who spoke like thunder. They didn't croak like frogs.

That sound—it haunted her more than anything. She had been sure the creature wanted to talk to her. That it was trying to make itself understood. But the sound had been nothing like human speech. It had been like—

Like jaws clicking together, like teeth clacking. Like the sound a fleshless mouth might make, if it tried to speak.

The heat of the day could not stop her from shivering.

She was still thirsty, so she scooped up more water, and then more. She worried she would give herself stomach cramps, but the water helped with the pain, a little. It made her feel less desperate, something she very much needed. She reached down again to lift up some more water and then she screamed.

Because her fingers had found something she hadn't expected. A bone, long and thin. She scuttled away from the edge of her perch, convinced that the creature with the glowing eyes had come back for her, that it was lying in wait just below the water's surface.

The water didn't move, though. After a time, she convinced her-self she'd been mistaken. She even forced herself to move back over to the water. To reach in with one darting hand and see what it was she'd touched.

She grabbed it and pulled it up out of the blue water. And saw she'd been right—it was a bone. A thigh bone, she thought.

But it was connected to nothing. It wasn't from the creature she'd seen. It had to have been from one of the previous sacrifices in the cenote. One, she could only assume, who hadn't struggled. Who had died properly.

She dropped the bone back in the water, feeling like she had profaned a sacred thing. Then she lay back on the wet ledge and wept a little.

The creature did not return during the day.

No. It waited until night fell.

It was summer and the nights were not cold, not truly, but lying in a little water like that sucked the heat out of her body and she was shivering, passing fluidly back and forth in and out of conscious-ness, feeling feverish, feeling so hungry, feeling fear and pain and not much else. Feeling like she barely knew where she was, who she was. Feeling like she was floating in the sky. Feeling like she was buried in the ground.

When the fingers came over the ledge and pressed down, pushing the creature up out of the water, for a moment she thought she was dreaming. She stared at the bony fingers in sheer curiosity, with de-tached interest. What she had thought would be just bare bones, skeletal fingers, were something more. There was skin over them, stretched as taut as the hide on the top of a drum. She could see narrow tendons moving under that skin, make out individual pores in it.

Slowly, because this was a dream and in dreams one was never really in control of oneself, she followed with her eyes the shapes of the bones, back to the wrist, the forearm like a pair of twigs rolled in a leaf. Up to where the shoulder blade pressed out against the skin of the creature's back. Its round head was the fattest thing about it, the most fleshy part. The head, the skull, was bent over her, bobbing up and down. She wished she could see more of its face, which would make it less terrifying, somehow. She pushed herself up a little—something was trying to hold her down, but she struggled up a bit, lifted herself, and saw that its face was buried in the swollen flesh of her broken leg.

She reached down, still certain this was a dream, her head still reeling with fever. She reached down and pushed at the side of the thing's skull.

She was too weak to scream. Too tired. Even when she felt her own skin tear. Felt its teeth rip free of where they'd fastened on her swollen leg.

Blood and yellow pus oozed from the creature's mouth. Her own body's fluids. Its blue eyes burned brighter than ever.

It slapped her hand away and lowered its face back onto her leg. She did not feel so feverish now—terror had anchored her in her body, dragged her senses back from her febrile dreams. She cursed it with words so small they barely made it out of her mouth. Called out for help, shouted out prayers. Tried to push at the creature, force it away from her, but she was still so weak.

She could feel her heart pounding in her chest and knew it was stealing her blood, sucking it right out of her veins. If she didn't stop the thing, it would drink all of her, suck her life out of her, and she would die there, lying in the water. The thought was more horrible to her than anything.

That gave her some strength. She grabbed the thing with both hands and shoved it off of her, thrust it out into the dark, rippling water. Its teeth clicked together madly—it was chattering out a complaint, a protest.

"No," she managed to say, pushing the word out on a huge breath. "No!"

Its skull head crested the water, just like the first time she'd seen it. It climbed up onto the ledge with her and she saw the skin pulled so tight over its sunken chest, wrapping its rib cage and its angular pelvis. She saw its chest throbbing. Pulsing, its heart beating with her stolen blood.

It took a step closer.

"No," she said, a whimper. She hauled herself back, away from it, pushed her back up hard against the wall of the cenote.

It took another step. It moved so slowly. As if it were nearly as weak as she was. But it wanted her blood—she could feel its need like a haze of heat around the thing. See it in the blue eyes, the way they burned.

It opened its mouth and croaked out words she could not quite understand.

Until—until suddenly she could. She could make out one word it had used.

Please.

It was begging for her blood.

And that just made everything worse. She thrust her hand out, down into the water. Groped around until she found the thigh bone she'd touched before. It was sacrilege to touch such a thing, but she needed a weapon.

When the skeletal creature came close enough, she smashed it across the face with the bone, as if it were a war club.

The creature was weak. Even with the little force she could manage, she knocked it backward into the water.

It kept trying to rise and come for her, throughout the night.

Each time, she was ready.

But she could not keep this up.

It would win in the end, she knew. She had overpowered it in the night, but eventually she would weaken to the point where she couldn't fight anymore. When daylight stained the top of the cenote's walls, she knew she could relax a bit—the sun was too much for the thing, depleted as it was—but she also knew this was going to be the hardest day of her life.

She needed to get out of the cenote, or the thing would kill her. She did not know if she had even one more night's worth of strength left in her body.

She could not afford to sleep. She let herself rest, but every time she started to drift away, she would strike the most swollen part of her calf with the thigh bone. New, fresh pain would waken her. She conserved her energy as much as she could. But eventually, she needed to move.

All thoughts of sacrifice, of how she had offended Chaac and let down her people, were gone from her mind. That day, she thought of nothing but escape.

There was one chance for her. A liana that hung down farther than the others. It still looked too high for her to reach, but she had to try. The problem, of course, was that it was on the far side of the cenote from her. She did not know if there was a submerged ledge over there, or anything for her to stand on while she jumped to try to grab the lowest end of the vine. If it was just deep water there beneath the liana, she was certainly doomed. The only way to know for sure was to go over and check.

She could not have walked, even if there had been solid ground all the way over to the liana. She was not sure she could even get to her feet now. Her broken leg moved in a sickening way when she lifted it, like a fishing net full of gravel. She would never stand on that leg again, she knew.

She closed her eyes and forced herself to think of the goal ahead. This problem—this escape—could not be solved all at once. If she kept thinking about how hard it was going to be, she would never get away.

She half pushed, half rolled herself into the water.

The thing, the skeletal blood-drinking thing, was down there, sleeping on the bottom. It could reach up at any moment and grab her ankle, pull her down into its embrace—*please*, it had said *please*—

No, she would not think such things. She struggled to keep herself from slipping down farther into the water, using her arms to thrash and her one good leg to kick, twisting her head around to keep her eyes above the deep blue. She could feel the strength flow out of her as surely as the blood the thing had stolen, feel it drain from her limbs as they grew heavier, as they moved more slowly. She could feel herself slipping down into the water and knew she would never come back up once it closed over her plaited hair.

Kick—thrash—she swung her arms and it was hopeless, she would never get anywhere like this, she was making no progress at all, she had killed herself, and then—and then her fingers touched stone and she grabbed at it, but it was sheer, the smooth wall of the cenote, there was nothing to grab on to, she waved her arm wildly about, her fingers stretched as far as they could go and there—yes, there! She felt a rock just below the water, felt the bottom, another ledge, a ledge like the one she'd abandoned. She grabbed and hauled and heaved herself up onto it.

It was no more than an arm long, and half that wide, but it was a place to rest, to stop and just breathe, to recover some of her strength. She forced herself not to move, to lie as still and limp as she could without falling off this new ledge.

Eventually she opened her eyes and looked, to see what she had accomplished.

She had crossed perhaps five arm lengths of the way around the side of the cenote. The distance she normally could have walked in two seconds.

She wept a bit then, but bit down hard on her tongue and stopped herself. Even weeping was going to kill her. It took away energy she needed.

She made herself think, think about what she had learned. She could swim, barely. She could move a little at a time. And there was more than just the one ledge below the water. Maybe there were plenty of them. Maybe there were ledges all around the circumference of the cenote. Maybe one below the low-hanging vine.

There had to be.

She forced herself to rest again.

Eventually, she made herself swim again. Rolling off the ledge into the blue water was a good incentive, to struggle a little more.

She found more ledges. Not as many as she'd hoped, and none as big as the one that had been her original place of refuge. But they were there.

Sometimes she would look down into the deep blue mirror of the cenote. When the ripples had gone, she could see her own face. See the blue paint on her cheeks, see the dark bands painted across her eyes and mouth.

She could not see the thing, the blood drinker. It slept deep.

She tried not to think about it down there, on its bed of the bones of all the sacrifices who had come here to please Chaac. Girls like herself, who had been willing to give away everything for the rain. It was obscene how the blood drinker profaned this, their resting place. Made it unclean.

How long had it been down there? How long had it been preying on the sacrifices, the ones who came before? It subsisted, she was certain, on the blood of those like her. On the blood of the dead girls who thought they were pleasing the god, who had no idea what thing they truly died to propitiate.

She would not let it have her, too.

She would not.

It took hours to make her way around the cenote. For every few thrashing seconds in the water, she would spend long minutes unable to do anything but lie there and breathe.

But she did not stop. She did not give up.

The liana hung down only three arms from the surface of the water. Its end was furry and loose, tufted like the end of a braid of hair. It was as thick as her wrist and woody in texture. She did not know if it would hold her weight.

It would have to. There was no other way for her to climb up and out of the sheer-walled cenote.

She spent a while fantasizing about what she would do once she reached the top. She could call for help and people would come with a litter, carry her back to the temple. They would want to know why she had struggled, why she had defied Chaac. But surely once she told them about the blood drinker, they would understand. They would forgive her, and welcome her home, and her mother would brush out her hair and scrub the blue paint from her skin. And warriors would come down on ropes and find the blood drinker and smash its bones with war clubs.

And someone else would be cast into the resanctified cenote, and the rain would come. Or maybe they would never do such a thing again. Perhaps the king of the city would outlaw such observances. The cenote would be abandoned, and in time, its water would run clear again.

She never wanted to see anything blue, ever again.

She could tell them. She could convince them. But first—

First she had to climb this liana.

And she was running out of time.

Already a shadow was crawling down the wall of the cenote. The sun was sinking in the west and when it was gone, when darkness fell, the blood drinker would come back. It would come for her, and this time she did not have her thigh-bone club with which to fight it off. She had less than an hour left, she thought. She would have to use that time well.

She had found a ledge that was not too far from where the liana hung down. It was out there above the water, too far to reach, even if she could have jumped. But she was so close. There had to be a way.

Maybe—maybe she could make it swing toward her. She reached down into the water and felt around for a stone. What she came up with almost made her shriek, but she had learned in the last few days how not to scream. It was a human skull she'd picked up. Somehow she did not throw it away from her. The skull in her hand was just a dead thing, just bone bleached by water and sun until it was a bluish-white stone, that was all. Even when a little worm came wriggling out of the eye socket, she did not let herself drop the skull.

She lined up her throw very carefully. She thought of the players in the ball courts and how hard it was to make a goal through the stone hoop. It could take them days to score. She needed to strike the first time. She waited until her arm had stopped shaking, and then she threw.

The skull hit the liana a glancing blow. Enough to send it swinging, to make it veer back and forth, away from her, now closer, away—closer—

It was still too high for her to reach. Not from a sitting position.

The next part of her plan was the hardest. It was the one she'd forbidden herself from thinking about until now. How to stand up.

Her broken leg was useless, but her other one was still whole. It should be possible. Just moving was pain, but familiar to her now. It was not something that could be ignored, yet like a boorish houseguest who had overstayed their welcome, it could be worked around.

She pushed herself back against the cenote wall. Her wet shift stuck to the rock. On her back, she could feel a little warmth that the wall had soaked up during the day, but she could also feel it growing cool now as the shadows lengthened in the cenote. As darkness probed its long fingers toward the blue water.

It had to be done now.

She pushed herself up against the wall, grabbing at the warm stone with both palms, grinding her shoulder into the rock. She could hear herself grunting and sobbing in exertion, though she had no desire to waste energy on making sounds. She forced herself up onto her good foot. Instantly she felt waves of exhaustion ripple through her muscles. It was unbearable. The urge to shift her weight to her other foot—as stupid as such an idea was—could barely be suppressed.

Still the liana swung toward her, now away. And it was slowing in its pendulum swing, getting farther away each time before it swung away from her again. She kept one shoulder against the wall and reached out for it with the other and knew it would not be enough.

She let some tears explode from the corners of her eyes. Gave vent to a cry of frustration. She couldn't do it. She could not escape, not even after all this effort, all the wrenching, excruciating work. She couldn't reach.

The far side of the cenote was already in shadow. Darkness was seeping into the water. She was certain she could see the pale dome of the blood drinker's head cresting the surface over there. She knew it was only waiting. It was weak, but not as weak as her.

She could see it moving. Edging closer, sticking to the shadow. Waiting. Only waiting.

"No," she said.

And then she threw herself away from the wall, pushed hard, and launched herself out over the water, her hands stretching out instantly to grab, to pull at the liana. Her left hand felt the woody length of it, and her fingers clamped shut. Her right hand reached up, found purchase. And then the liana swung away, swung hard, and she struck the far wall.

Her bad, broken leg was pinned against the stone, all of her weight, all of her momentum, crushing it.

She had thought she understood pain, that she had become a scholar of hurt. In that second white light lanced through her, exactly like lightning. Spears were driven through her chest, impaling her, keeping her from breathing. Her sense of hearing increased a dozenfold, so that she could hear the skin tear open as the sharp fragments of bone inside her calf cut their way out.

But somehow she did not let go.

Somehow she clung to the liana, and somehow, somehow, it did not break under her weight, and somehow, somehow, she was still alive.

She opened her eyes. Saw the walls of the cenote swing crazily past in scything rhythm.

She could feel blood trickling down her leg. Feel it dripping from her swollen toes. Wetting the liana. Dripping into the blue, blue water.

And when she looked down she saw—

—them—

There were dozens of them.

The one she'd seen, the one she'd fought, was just one of them. The fleshiest, the least decayed. Some of the others had only one eye burning in their skull heads. Some were missing limbs.

They were all dripping blue water. They were all so very, very hungry. They craned their heads upward, stretched their jaws wide to catch the little tiny drops of blood that fell from her leg.

Dozens—so many—crouched there in the dark. And she saw something for the first time that made her let go of the vine.

Some of them weren't just blue from the water. Some were painted that way. Some of them had bands of black painted across their eyes and their toothy mouths.

Just as she had.

Blue. Blue paint, paint so good, so durable, it was saved for the gods.

Blue for sacrifice.

Blue for eternity.

The tour guide mopped sweat from his forehead with a red hand-kerchief. "As late as five hundred years ago," he said, and some of the tourists listened, and some just took pictures, the way it always was, "this was a holy place for my ancestors. A place of sacrifice. We'll never know how many young people were thrown down here." He leaned a hand on the wooden guardrail. "You've got to imagine what it was like, before we put these stairs in. A lot harder getting back up without them, hey?"

Some of them laughed. He didn't care anymore if they liked his patter or not, except when they did he got bigger tips. He'd told the same joke every day for nearly six years.

"It was drought that ended the Mayan empire, you know? Not the Spaniards. Not aliens from space. They lived in these cities, all crowded like Mexico City is today, and they relied on the cornfields for food. When the rain didn't come, they starved. They didn't know why, of course. They thought their rain god was angry with them. So they threw their children down here. Divers have gone down in that water and they found at least forty-seven sets of bones. What's that?"

One of the tourists had asked a question. "Did it work?"

They all laughed, this time.

"Well, if it had, we'd still be doing it, yeah?" Another laugh. The tour guide turned and started up again. Way too many steps. "Come on, let's let them sleep in peace, okay? No, I can't let anybody go swimming down here. You see that blue? It would stain your clothes, that's why. Our next stop is the famous pyramid. Yes, yes, you can take all the pictures you like."

One by one they filed out, up the long wooden stairway to the surface. It was the last tour group of the day. Already shadows were stretching down the cenote's wall, moving toward the blue water.

And when that darkness filled the cenote, the little sparks showed. The little sparks at the bottom of eye sockets long since eaten clean by fish. Little sparks of blue.

Please, she croaked.

Please.

ACKNOWLEDGMENTS

Enormous thanks to each of the contributors to this volume for bringing me their sharpest edges and darkest corners. Thanks to the entire Gallery Books team, especially to our maestro, Ed Schlesinger, and to my excellent agent, Howard Morhaim. Finally, nothing good is possible without the support of my wife, Connie, who doesn't love the monsters herself, but who loves me . . . and that's enough.

—*Christopher Golden*

ABOUT THE AUTHORS

JOHN AJVIDE LINDQVIST is the author of *Let the Right One In, Handling the Undead*, and *Little Star. Let the Right One In* has been made into two critically acclaimed films. The Swedish film won top honors at sixteen film festivals around the globe. The American remake of the Swedish movie, titled *Let Me In,* received rave reviews. Stephen King called the film "a genre-busting triumph. Not just a horror film, but the best American horror film in the last twenty years."

KELLEY ARMSTRONG is the author of the *Cainsville* modern gothic series and the *Age of Legends* YA fantasy trilogy. Past works include the *Otherworld* urban fantasy series, the *Darkest Powers* & *Darkness Rising* teen paranormal trilogies, and the Nadia Stafford crime trilogy. She also co-writes the *Blackwell Pages* middle-grade fantasy trilogy as K. L. Armstrong with M. A. Marr. Armstrong lives in southwestern Ontario with her family.

LAIRD BARRON is the author of several books, including *The Croning, Occultation,* and *The Beautiful Thing That Awaits Us All.* His work has also appeared in many magazines and anthologies. An expatriate Alaskan, Barron currently resides in upstate New York.

LYNDA BARRY has worked as a painter, cartoonist, writer, illustrator, playwright, editor, commentator, and teacher. She is the creator behind *Ernie Pook's Comeek,* the seminal comic strip that was syndicated across North America in alternative weeklies for two decades. She is the author of more than twenty books, including *The Freddie Stories, One! Hundred! Demons!, Cruddy: An Illustrated Novel,* and *The Good Times Are Killing Me,* which was adapted as an off-Broadway play. Her graphic novel *What It Is* won the comics industry's 2009 Eisner Award for Best Reality-Based Work. She lives in Wisconsin, where she teaches at the University of Wisconsin, Madison.

GARY A. BRAUNBECK is a seven-time Bram Stoker Award–winning author who writes mysteries, thrillers, science fiction, fantasy, horror, and mainstream literature. He is the author of twenty-four books, and his fiction has been translated into Japanese, French, Italian, Russian, and German. Nearly 250 of his short stories have appeared in various professional publications. His fiction has received numerous awards, including multiple Bram Stoker Awards, a Black Quill Award, three Shocklines "Shocker" Awards, and the International Horror Guild Award, and has also been nominated for the World Fantasy Award.

DANA CAMERON can't help mixing in a little history into her fiction. Drawing from her expertise in archaeology, Dana's work (including traditional mystery, noir, urban fantasy, historical fiction, and thrillers) has won multiple Agatha, Anthony, and Macavity Awards and earned an Edgar Award nomination. Her third Fangborn novel, *Hellbender,* will be published in March 2015 by 47North. Her most recent Fangborn short story is a Sherlockian pastiche,

"The Curious Case of Miss Amelia Vernet." Her story "The Sun, the Moon, and the Stars," featuring Pam Ravenscroft from Charlaine Harris's acclaimed Sookie Stackhouse mysteries, appears in *Dead But Not Forgotten: Stories from the World of Sookie Stackhouse*. Visit her at www.danacameron.com.

DAN CHAON's most recent book is the short story collection *Stay Awake* (2012), a finalist for the Story Prize. Other works include the national bestseller *Await Your Reply* and *Among the Missing*, a finalist for the National Book Award. Chaon's fiction has appeared in *Best American Short Stories*, *The Pushcart Prize Anthologies*, and *The O. Henry Prize Stories*. He has been a finalist for the National Magazine Award in Fiction, as well as the Shirley Jackson Award, and he was the recipient of an Academy Award in Literature from the American Academy of Arts and Letters. Chaon lives in Ohio and teaches at Oberlin College.

CHARLAINE HARRIS, a native of the Mississippi Delta, has lived her whole life in various Southern states. Her first book, a mystery, was published in 1981. After that promising debut, her career meandered along until the success of the Sookie Stackhouse novels. Now all her books are in print, and she is a very happy camper. She is married and has three children.

BRIAN KEENE is the author of more than forty books, mostly in the horror, crime, and dark fantasy genres. His 2003 novel, *The Rising*, is often credited (along with Robert Kirkman's *The Walking Dead* comic and Danny Boyle's *28 Days Later* film) with inspiring pop culture's current interest in zombies. Keene's novels have been translated into German, Spanish, Polish, Italian, French, Taiwanese, and many more languages. Several of Keene's novels have been developed for film, including *Ghoul*, *The Ties That Bind*, and *Fast Zombies Suck*.

SHERRILYN KENYON is a *New York Times* and international bestselling author, and a regular at the #1 spot. Since 2004, she had placed more than seventy novels on the *New York Times* bestseller list in all formats, including manga and graphic novels. Her current series are *Dark-Hunter, Chronicles of Nick,* and *The League,* and her books are available in over one hundred countries. Her *Chronicles of Nick* and *Dark-Hunter* series are soon to be major motion pictures, while *Dark-Hunter* is also being developed as a television series.

MICHAEL KORYTA is the *New York Times* bestselling author of ten suspense novels. His work has been praised by such writers as Stephen King, Dean Koontz, and Dennis Lehane, among many others, and has been translated into more than twenty languages. His books have won or been nominated for prizes such as the *Los Angeles Times* Book Prize, Edgar Award, Shamus Award, Barry Award, Quill Award, International Thriller Writers Award, and the Golden Dagger.

JOHN LANGAN is the author of two collections, *The Wide, Carnivorous Sky and Other Monstrous Geographies* (Hippocampus; 2013) and *Mr. Gaunt and Other Uneasy Encounters* (Prime; 2008), and a novel, *House of Windows* (Night Shade; 2009). With Paul Tremblay, he co-edited *Creatures: Thirty Years of Monsters* (Prime; 2011). His next collection, *Sefira and Other Betrayals,* is forthcoming in 2015. He lives in upstate New York with his wife and younger son.

TIM LEBBON is a *New York Times* bestselling writer with more than thirty novels published to date, as well as dozens of novellas and hundreds of short stories. Recent releases include *The Silence, Coldbrook, Into the Void: Dawn of the Jedi (Star Wars), Reaper's Legacy,* and *Alien: Out of the Shadows.* Forthcoming novels include the thriller *The Hunt* from Avon, and Titan will be publishing *The*

Rage War trilogy and also the *Relics* trilogy over the next few years. He has won four British Fantasy Awards, a Bram Stoker Award, and a Scribe Award, and been shortlisted for World Fantasy and Shirley Jackson Awards. A movie of his story *Pay the Ghost*, starring Nicolas Cage, will be released soon, and other projects in development include *My Haunted House*, *Playtime* (with Stephen Volk), and *Exorcising Angels* (with Simon Clark). Find out more at www.timlebbon.net.

SEANAN McGUIRE is the author of more than a dozen novels, under both her own name and the pseudonym Mira Grant. She won the 2010 John W. Campbell Award for Best New Writer, and can generally be found either skulking around cornfields or heading for the nearest Disney Park. Seanan lives in California with her collection of Maine Coon cats and creepy dolls; keep up with her at www.seananmcguire.com.

JOE McKINNEY has been a patrol officer for the San Antonio Police Department, a homicide detective, a disaster mitigation specialist, a patrol commander, and a successful novelist. His books include the four-part *Dead World* series, *Quarantined*, *Inheritance*, *The Savage Dead*, *St. Rage*, *Crooked House*, and *Dodging Bullets*. His short fiction has been collected in *The Red Empire and Other Stories*, *Speculations*, and *Dead World Resurrection: The Complete Zombie Short Stories of Joe McKinney*. His latest works include the YA werewolf thriller *Dog Days*, set in the summer of 1983, and *Plague of the Undead: Book One in the Deadlands Saga*. McKinney's novels have twice been honored with the Bram Stoker Award. For more information, go to joemckinney.wordpress.com.

LEIGH PERRY is Toni L.P. in disguise, or perhaps vice versa. As Leigh, she writes the Family Skeleton mysteries. *The Skeleton Haunts a*

House, the third, is due out in Fall 2015. As Toni, she is the author of three *Where Are They Now?* mysteries and eight novels in the Laura Fleming series; an Agatha Award winner and multiple award nominee for short fiction; and the co-editor of urban fantasy anthologies with Charlaine Harris. Leigh and/or Toni lives just north of Boston with her husband, fellow author Stephen P. Kelner, their two daughters, two guinea pigs, and many, many books.

ROBERT SHEARMAN has written five short story collections, and collectively they have won the World Fantasy Award, the Shirley Jackson Award, the Edge Hill Readers' Prize, and three British Fantasy Awards. He began his career in theater, both as a playwright and director, and his work has won the *Sunday Times* Playwriting Award, the Sophie Winter Memorial Trust Award, and the Guinness Award for Ingenuity in association with the Royal National Theatre. His interactive series for BBC Radio Four, *The Chain Gang,* ran for three seasons and won two Sony Awards. However, he may be best known as a writer for *Doctor Who,* reintroducing the Daleks for its BAFTA-winning first series in an episode nominated for a Hugo Award.

SCOTT SMITH is the author of two novels, *A Simple Plan* and *The Ruins.*

LUCY A. SNYDER is the Bram Stoker Award–winning author of the novels *Spellbent, Shotgun Sorceress, Switchblade Goddess*, and the collections *Orchid Carousals, Sparks and Shadows, Chimeric Machines*, and *Installing Linux on a Dead Badger.* Her latest books are *Shooting Yourself in the Head for Fun and Profit: A Writer's Survival Guide* and *Soft Apocalypses.* Her writing has been translated into French, Russian, and Japanese editions and has appeared in publications such as *Apex Magazine, Nightmare Magazine, Jamais Vu, Pseudopod, Strange Horizons, Weird Tales, Steampunk World, In the Court of the Yellow*

King, Qualia Nous, Chiral Mad 2, and *Best Horror of the Year, Vol. 5*. She lives in Columbus, Ohio, with her husband and occasional co-author, Gary A. Braunbeck, and is a mentor in Seton Hill University's MFA program in Writing Popular Fiction. You can learn more about her at www.lucysnyder.com and you can follow her on Twitter: @LucyASnyder.

DAVID WELLINGTON is the author of seventeen novels, which have appeared around the world in eight languages. His horror series include *Monster Island*, *13 Bullets*, and *Frostbite*. His thriller series starring Afghanistan war veteran Jim Chapel includes *Chimera* and *The Hydra Protocol*. In 2015, he will publish *Positive*, a zombie epic about rebuilding the world after an apocalypse. He lives and works in Brooklyn, New York.

RIO YOUERS is the British Fantasy Award–nominated author of *End Times* and *Old Man Scratch*. His short fiction has appeared in many notable anthologies, and his previous novel, *Westlake Soul*, was nominated for Canada's prestigious Sunburst Award. Rio lives in southwestern Ontario with his wife, Emily, and their children, Lily and Charlie.

ABOUT THE EDITOR

CHRISTOPHER GOLDEN is the #1 *New York Times* bestselling and Bram Stoker Award–winning author of such novels as *Snowblind, Tin Men, Of Saints and Shadows*, and *The Boys Are Back in Town*. His novel with Mike Mignola, *Baltimore; or, The Steadfast Tin Soldier and the Vampire*, was the launching pad for the Eisner Award–nominated comic book series *Baltimore*. As an editor, he has compiled the short story anthologies *The New Dead, The Monster's Corner*, and *Dark Duets*, among others, and has also written and co-written numerous comic books, video games, and screenplays. Golden was born and raised in Massachusetts, where he still lives with his family. His original novels have been published in more than fourteen languages in countries around the world. Please visit him at www.christophergolden.com.